EVELYN ARVEY ◦ NANCY BONNINGTON
SUSAN WHITING KEMP

we grew tales

Evelyn P. Arvey
Susan Kemp
Nancy Bonnington

Treble House Publishing
Seattle

Publication History
"Happening with the Gods" by Nancy Bonnington, Texas A&M BigTex[t] 2006.
"Evolution, Accelerated" by Susan Whiting Kemp, Blue Lake Review, 2011.
"Celebrating Sydney" by Evelyn Arvey, Stealing Time Magazine, 2013.
"Quicksand" by Evelyn Arvey, Pentimento Magazine, 2016.
"Eat This" by Susan Whiting Kemp, Hobart Magazine, 2018.

Acknowledgements

We would like to acknowledge the support of our wonderful families for their enduring interest and feedback for this project: Evelyn's husband Richard for his encouragement throughout the writing process and who has read every word she's ever written; Susan's husband Bill and her children Alissa and Daniel, for always being there when she needs them most; and Nancy's siblings, Tom Bonnington, Ann Louden and Jim Bonnington, for enthusiastically reading and critiquing earlier story versions.

Also a special thanks to our editor, Tiffany Yates Martin, FoxPrint Editorial, whose astute edits and comments helped us to fine-tune all of the stories in *We Grew Tales.*

About the Authors

Evelyn Arvey's fingers are never still. Whether she's weaving silver wire into graceful chains, knitting with yarn that she's spun herself, playing the classical guitar, or working on her newest piece of writing - she simply cannot imagine a life of not being creative. Evelyn holds a BFA in oil painting from the University of Washington, and has been published by *Ellora's Cave, Stealing Time Magazine, Pedestal Magazine,* and *Pentimento Magazine*. Her website can be found at EvelynArvey.com

Nancy Bonnington has a BA in Creative Writing from the University of Washington and works as a software development engineer at Fred Hutchinson Cancer Research Center. Her short stories have appeared in *Arnazella, Paradigm Vol. 1, The Adirondack Review*, and *BigTex[t]* literary magazines. "Do the Right Thing" was a semi-finalist in *Carve Magazine's* 2013 Raymond Carver Short Story contest. Her first literary novel, *Executing Darcy*, is in progress. In addition to writing, she studied music at Cornish College of the Arts and the University of Washington, and performs in the Seattle area on classical guitar.

Susan Whiting Kemp has a BA in drama from the University of Washington and has taken graduate and extension courses in marketing and social media. She studied French at the Sorbonne and Alliance Française, and theater at École Étienne Decroux and Studio Magenia in Paris. Her theatrical performances include one-woman shows and comedy improvisation. Susan has been published in *Hobart, HowlRound, The Blue Lake Review, The Writer's Workshop Review*, and *Marketing Magazine*. As the marketing manager for an environmental and geotechnical engineering company, she is responsible for writing and editing news articles, blog posts, marketing materials, and social media posts. Her blog at SusanWKemp.com features short fiction and writing-related articles.

Introduction

In *We Grew Tales*, three Pacific Northwest writers present a collection of stories as varied as their artistic backgrounds (literature, theater, music, and art) and shaped by their collaboration in a selective writing group.

This is a book for adventurous readers, writers, and those curious about the creative process.

Presented in two sections, the book encompasses stories written over many years, some previously published in literary and popular magazines, as well as more recent works created for the group's regular critique sessions at a local coffee shop.

In the first half of *We Grew Tales,* the authors cultivated their material from a variety of inspirations—both personal and imaginative.

The second half of *We Grew Tales* presents short stories that were created from monthly writing prompts. The prompt (shown in this book along with each story title) was usually a cryptic phrase such as "Saturday at 6:25 p.m." Each author took a turn suggesting a prompt, pulling it out of thin air or basing it on a line of poetry. One prompt involved eavesdropping on a random public conversation.

Overall, each tale in this book established its final structure and narrative through the group's interaction. The result is a wide variety of intriguing short stories—humorous, speculative, literary, and contemporary.

Contents

Stories Based on Writing Prompts

Celebrating Sydney

By Evelyn Arvey

This morning Sydney, my almost thirteen-year-old daughter, padded into my room, her slippers making *shush-shush* sounds on the hardwood floor. Like every Saturday morning since Sydney was a toddler, I scooted to the middle of the mattress right next to Jeffrey, my husband, so she could sit beside me. But instead of sitting and launching into long-winded dramatizations of last night's dreams, she stood by the bed and jiggled.

Sydney doesn't jiggle. Sydney twirls. Sydney scoots. Sydney bounds and leaps and dawdles and hovers—but *jiggling*? Never.

I sat up, clutching the covers to my chest, eyeing her.

She looked at her still-asleep dad; she studied my bedside lamp; she stared at the mirror above my dresser; then she fingered the fringe on the edge of my bedspread. "Mom," she said, her voice hushed and serious, "there's *blood* on my sheets."

"Sydney!" I pulled her arm until she plopped onto the bed beside me; then I hugged her, hard. "You got your period. That's *wonderful*!"

Leaning into me, still playing with the fringe, she smiled. She'd stopped jiggling. "I guess so."

I took her hand with its chipped and sparkling purple nail polish. "It is! Believe me. Do you feel okay? Any cramps?"

"Maybe? Like something twisting my guts from the inside, kind of?"

"Yes. That's a perfect description if I ever heard one. Yes."

"Then I've got cramps."

She glanced at me, then twisted her lips and jutted out her chin and crossed her eyes (which I can't do because, dang it, that *hurts*); I closed one eye and let my mouth hang open and flared my nostrils. We do this, sometimes, when the mood strikes. A handsome pair of women, the two of us.

Two women.

I hugged her again.

"Tell me if they get worse; I'll give you something." I held her at arm's length. "Oh, Sydney. This day is special. You're growing up!"

"Are you *crying*, Mom?"

"You remember our talks?" I asked, ignoring the question. "How to take care of yourself? Where I keep the pads? All that?"

"I'm not an *idiot*, Mom."

"Good. Do you remember what else I told you?"

Her eyes met mine. "Something about a surprise…?"

I clapped my hands. "Yes! That's right. We're going to celebrate—we're taking you out to dinner tonight. Jeffrey!" I leaned over and touched his shoulder. He lay there pretending to sleep. I would have fallen for it but for the smile playing at the edges of his lips. "Our little girl is becoming a woman. She just got her period!"

"Mom!"

And that's how Sydney's special day began, with me embarrassing her. Even eight-year-old Joel, who wandered into the bedroom, curious, got a watered-down version of what the excitement was all about.

After breakfast, Sydney sat on the swivel bar stool by the refrigerator, listening to every word on the speaker as I called Grandma Grace and Grandma Louise, then Aunt Sally in Illinois and Aunt Rhoda in Vermont with the news. Sydney listened, not saying anything, spinning in slow circles, her lips pursed in a half smile behind a cascade of long brown hair.

"It's not that big a deal," she said.

As soon as I hung up the phone she grabbed it and called her fifteen-year-old cousin, Jen. Sydney sat hunched on the bar stool, her back to me, twirling a lock of hair around her finger. Her voice was hushed. I had to stop washing dishes and swab pancake syrup off the table instead, so I could hear her.

"Hey, Jen." Sydney's feet kicked at the stool's lower rung. "What do *you* take for cramps? I've got them bad."

The girl has style.

I gave up pretending to clean anything. I sat down at the table and sipped my tea.

Sydney soaked up Jen's words of wisdom. She nodded. She murmured. Nodded again. Then she spun the stool around to face me. "Yes!" she said, her voice rising, "They *are* taking me out! We're going to the Spaghetti Factory."

"That's right!" I said. "Tonight."

"It's a family tradition? You went out too?"

"I did," I said. "Grandma and Grandpa took me to Opal's Steak House…" And then I saw the look on Sydney's face—*get a life, Mom*—and realized that she hadn't asked *me*.

Sidelined, I went back to scrubbing the table.

Maybe at dinner I'd tell Sydney our family history. I'd tell her how my own grandmother, a nurse, had started the tradition back when most families hid their menstruating daughters in the toolshed. Back when girls had to pin sanitary napkins the size of bath towels into their underwear. When boys would hold their noses and say, "Whew! What's that stink?" to their female classmates. And I'd tell her how lucky we are—how most families, even today, do nothing at all to celebrate their daughter's first periods.

Sometime after lunch Sydney disappeared into her room. She came out later wearing the dress we'd bought her for her best friend's bat mitzvah: a knee-length, simple yet elegant sheath of velvety fabric so deeply purple it looked almost black.

Sydney hates wearing dresses.

"Well, look at you," said Jeffrey. "Very pretty."

Sydney shifted from foot to foot. She didn't know what to do with her hands, clutching them in front of her stomach, then touching her hair, then letting them drop to her sides. She'd redone her nails in a lovely pinkish-red shade. "Can we go now?"

"It's Saturday at four forty-five," said Jeffrey, shaking his head, slipping on his shoes. "But sure. It's your day. Let's go."

Sydney always picks the Spaghetti Factory whenever we ask her where she wants to go.

As the hostess seated us, Sydney hip-checked Joel so she could sit to the left of her dad—*her* place, no matter what table we're sitting at.

"I'm going to order the mizithra cheese," she said, biting her lip.

"Order whatever you want to," said Jeffrey, tapping the

menu with his salad fork. "You should get one of those Italian sodas you drooled over last time."

"I want one too!" Joel said. "A strawberry one!"

Sydney shook her head. "You can't. It's *my* dinner."

I leaned toward them. "Honey, we're all celebrating. We'll all have Italian sodas! How about that?"

"Fine," she said. "I want chocolate raspberry."

World War III averted, I pretended to study the menu. But really I was studying Sydney. She was alternating between being excited and withdrawn; going from chatting with the waiter about our new kitten, Charles, to rolling the corner of her place mat into a tight cigar, then unrolling it to study the factoids printed on it. One moment I saw the girl who still loved to run through the sprinkler on a hot day, and in the next the light would catch her in a certain way and suddenly that girl was gone and in her place was a young woman with almond-shaped eyes and a long, slender neck.

Sydney's bashful pride flooded me with memories of when my parents celebrated *my* first period all those years ago. I knew that Sydney was proud of her fledgling status as a brand-new woman, but at the same time she was embarrassed by the attention we were showering upon her and the fact that everyone, even the waiter, knew she got her period.

Joel told him.

Which is fine—we already broadcast it to female family members all over the United States—but *still.*

We ordered. I requested mizithra, same as Sydney. She grinned; she adores it when people copy her.

She liked me that day. Which was nice, because she doesn't always. The day before, too, I was in Sydney's good graces. I am an artist, with a ceramics studio in the basement of our home, and on that particular day I'd set up an art project for us to do together—a real doozy. A *doozy*, according to my daughter, is a project so brilliant it earns a coveted space at the top of her very own Art Project Hierarchy.

A *doozy* is followed by, in descending order, a *spinner*, a *geek*, and a *turnip*.

Yes, a *turnip*.

We were in the basement, where I'd dragged a box of my own ceramic failures into the far corner. "Watch!" I said, picking up an overfired teacup. I held it high over my head, and with a theatrical flourish I hurled it—*crash!*—right onto the concrete floor, where it smashed into a hundred pieces as Sydney watched, open-mouthed with delighted surprise. They flew around our ankles, green and blue and lavender and white, spinning shapes of pure color, none alike. I motioned for Sydney to help me pick up the best shards and lay them pretty side up into a box. Sydney bounced on her heels, waiting for her turn to smash and destroy; in what world would Sydney *not* love this? Soon we'd reduced my supply of chipped plates and botched bowls and ugly flowerpots to a thousand brilliant pieces.

"Breaking stuff," Sydney proclaimed. "Sweet. This project is now a spinner!"

We trooped upstairs and plunked the box of ceramic shards onto the kitchen table. The project earned its doozy status when we began to glue those pretty little chips to a board.

"A mosaic!" Sydney said, clapping her hands.

"Yep," I said.

For two and a half hours Sydney and I leaned over the table, happy in our creative togetherness, chatting, laughing, revisiting favorite moments from our shared history: *That was so funny when Joel was a baby and we put him in a dress! He was so* cute *in a dress. Hey, remember when we made blueberry muffins and the blueberries flew out of the bowl?*

And softly spoken questions: *Did you ever cry in school? Were you ever so scared you peed your pants? Do you suppose we come back as ghosts after we die? Do you think Grandpa Elliot is a ghost now?*

All the while we carefully glued ceramic shards to the board, making a thousand small decisions as we worked. We made winding trails of brilliant red chips and hot spots of spinning, gyrating spirals. We filled in the background with cerulean-blue pieces and made a border of hunter green. Together we slowly created a glorious, wild mosaic that didn't represent anything at all. When it was finished, I set it upright on a kitchen counter. Sydney and I stood on the other side of the room, admiring its abstract energy. The mosaic was longer than it was wide, and heavy. I turned it on its side.

"Nope," Sydney said, and turned it back again.

My daughter knows what she likes.

❖ ❖ ❖

It was only five fifteen, but the Spaghetti Factory smelled of tomato sauce and garlic and other wonderful things, and we were famished. We all sat up straighter when the waiter set small plates of salad in front of each of us and plunked a steaming loaf of sourdough bread in the center of the table. Jeffrey reached for the bread and began to saw at it with a knife so dull he could probably do the same thing to my arm and not leave a mark.

Sydney was gazing at the waiter.

I looked at him too, really looked. His name badge said *Hi, my name is Derek.* I tried to see him through her eyes and admit that he might be considered cute by an almost thirteen-year-old. His bangs hung over his eyes just a little too far. His lips curled in a charming smile. His Adam's apple bounced up and down as he chatted with her.

Lord.

My daughter was *seeing a boy.*

The waiter moved off. I took the slice of bread Jeffrey held out to me, smeared it with garlic butter, sprinkled a good amount of Parmesan cheese on it, then passed the cheese shaker to Joel. Sydney, flushed, started spearing chunks of lettuce with her fork.

"Did you think he was cute?" I asked.

"Mom!"

"Because he was, sort of."

She scowled at me.

"His name is Derek."

Jeffrey lowered his chin, cleared his throat, and glared at me through bunched-up eyebrows. His *stop it, Erica* signal.

I sighed. I sound just like my mother sometimes.

I supposed Sydney would be mad at me now. My intrusive meddling probably tipped the balance—but I couldn't help myself. Yesterday, when we were talking, she wouldn't have minded the question at all.

I stole a look at her as I sipped my iced tea. She was mad, all right. She'd pointedly turned her head away from me and was giving me, almost literally, the cold shoulder. Sometimes she gets so furious it takes my breath away. Once in a while she even seems to hate me.

Sydney isn't the only one who can rank things. I have my own ranking system for her.

The lowest rank of the my-daughter-is-being-a-brat hierarchy is *hot sauce.* A hot sauce episode is not terribly painful and is over quickly—a glorified case of the grumps. A hot sauce happens when, say, I wake her up when she's fallen asleep in the car. I can handle a hot sauce.

An episode with a bit more energy I call the *riot.* This is the grumps with an extra boost, such as Sydney being woken up *and* being hungry. I have a harder time dealing with a riot.

Then there's the dreaded *train wreck*, which leaves everyone in the family, even Joel, feeling exhausted and misused. The last train wreck happened three weeks ago, when Sydney hid dirty dishes under the sink.

Last is the *Sydney cyclone,* which sucks the air from the house and spits it right back out in a firestorm of twelve-year-old fury—one happened just last night, in fact. She freaked out after my fourth request to set the table, snarling and screeching and throwing her homework all over the floor. If I'd known dinner was going to be a Sydney cyclone (and honestly, who would have guessed after our delightful doozy only a few hours before) I would have ordered pizza for dinner to avoid having to ask her to set the table.

Bad parenting, I know. You can't order pizza every time your kid acts up.

But wouldn't it be nice?

❋ ❋ ❋

At our little table in the Spaghetti Factory, under a purple-fringed lamp shade, eating enormous plates of spaghetti, I was glad for small things. I was glad that Sydney cyclone goes away quickly after her meltdowns are over. I was glad art projects plaster the walls of our home, the turnips as well as the doozies. They tell stories well beyond what they depict, like a new form of archeology.

Art Project Archeology: the study of how things are connected. The way our mosaic will forever in my mind be linked to Sydney's first period.

Sydney was smiling again. "I *love* this place."

I was forgiven.

"Me too," said Joel, slurping the last noodle from his plate.

Derek the waiter came to our table again.

"Finished?" he asked, but he was just being polite. He was already stacking red-smeared plates on his arm. "I'll be back in a moment with ice cream."

Sydney smiled up at him.

As soon as Derek was gone Jeffrey set a small box wrapped in shiny silver paper on the table in front of Sydney.

Her mouth dropped open and her lips formed the same half-heart shape they had when she was a toddler. "For me?"

"For you," Jeffrey said.

Joel bounced in his seat, leaning toward Sydney so he could see better. Sydney, still grinning, looking like a very young, excited twelve-year-old, drew him onto her lap. "Help me pull off the ribbon, little bro?"

Together they worked the bow and the ribbon carefully from the box and set them on the table. Then they unstuck three bits of Scotch tape and removed the wrapping paper. Joel smoothed it as best he could.

"Ready?" she asked.

He nodded.

She opened the box. Inside was the pair of tiny ruby earrings Jeffrey and I had picked out for her in anticipation of this day, earrings meant for a young woman, not for a girl. Earrings that were clearly post earrings, the type that will go only into pierced ears—but Sydney didn't have pierced ears.

Yet.

"Oh, my God!" she squealed. "*Thank* you! Thank you, Dad! Thank you, Mom! I *love* them!"

Heads turned from the table next to us. A chubby-faced little girl stood up, took a step toward Sydney, and tried to see the gift. Sydney took the box and held it out for the child to examine. "Beautiful, aren't they?"

The child nodded, struck dumb.

I regarded the two of them, Sydney and this little girl only a few years younger. My eyes filled with tears as I snapped their picture with my cell phone; it wasn't so long ago that Sydney was this child.

"I can't wait until I get my period so I get a present too," said Joel.

Oops. I guess my explanation was a bit too watered-down.

"Honey," I said, "only girls get periods."

Sydney took over. "Joel. Remember when Bonnie was pregnant with her kittens?"

He nodded. "Bonnie is Charles's mother. I know that."

"That's right. Girls—and girl cats—have periods so that we can have babies!" Sydney looked at me for confirmation. "Isn't that right, Mom?"

"Yes. That's right."

Derek the waiter came back with ice cream. He served us Spumoni—and then, with a flourish, he presented Sydney with a single red rose.

"For your special day," he said. He was blushing almost as much as Sydney was.

"Thanks," she whispered, accepting it.

Derek smiled at her. "I have sisters," he said, then he turned and walked away.

I took another picture, then another—of Sydney, of all of them—finding it difficult since, for some reason, my eyes were blurry and wet.

Sydney sat tall and proud, delicately spooning her spumoni.

I took another picture.

Jeffrey reached across the table and squeezed my hand.

"I know," he said. "I *know*."

Do the Right Thing

By Nancy Bonnington

Zee screwed the top off an Oreo cookie and handed the bottom half, with all the cream, over to me. "Little sugar for my sweetie-pie," she said, dipping her part in a glass of bourbon. I hated the term *sweetie-pie*, or any other name that sounded edible, but I loved Zee. She was actually Maggie Zylstra, and she was my father's girlfriend the summer my parents slept in separate bedrooms. Zee was my father's big secret, and my own introduction at nine years old to the complex world of adult lies. "Don't you ever tell anybody," my father commanded. Sometimes my complicity came easily, but sometimes I would take bribes—candy, a movie, trips to the beach, or even dinner at a restaurant that had tablecloths.

"I never saw you so pretty," Zee told me as she sipped her bourbon, snuggled tight up to my father on the couch. My father winced and avoided my glare. He had forced me to wear a dress just to please Zee, and I didn't take well to dresses. I looked like a devil child, with bright red satin and white taffeta frills and a mean grimace across my face. I had pouted the whole way from our house to Zee's trailer. She lived near 99, the intercity highway with drive-in food, car lots, and a strip club that screamed XXX on its towering sign. I knew all about the strip club because Zee had told me she worked there during community college and had no trouble being topless, "'Cause my body's no temple, honey."

My mother was working that summer. She had just acquired her real estate license and embarked on a career that she later told me was meant to make her independent from my father, although it failed miserably. Whenever my mother was working, my father, who was in between jobs, was supposed to look after me.

He was a pushover, and he hated disciplining me. On the rare occasions that my mother would insist I had earned a spanking, my father would come into my bedroom, shoulders stooped—as if he were carrying ten of me up there—his hands dangling at his sides. "I don't have to do this, do I?" he would always say. And I would always say, "No." And he would always say, "Tell your mother you got what was coming to you…and remember, from now on, *do the right thing*." And then after a while of examining my toys and touching my stuffed bears and fiddling with my curtains, he would turn, still burdened beyond repair, and saunter out of my room. It was actually as good as a spanking, because I hated putting him through the charade.

"Whadd'ya wan' for your birthday?" Zee asked me. She had chocolate crumbs on her lower lip and slurred her words as she always did on her second or third drink. I didn't mind. The more Zee slurred, the more generous she became toward me. (One time, when she drank herself into a stupor and my father and I tiptoed out of her trailer, I got my very first watch the next day—a silver Timex with a royal-blue band just my size.

"Zee felt bad we had to leave so suddenly," my father told me. "But if your mother asks, say it was from me.")

"Her birthday's not for months," my father told Zee. He reached over and took her bourbon glass, which caused a small tug-of-war before Zee gave it up. He smiled at her, but I'd seen that wan smile before when my father thought something was askew, like if a dog had messed on our porch and he didn't have the energy to clean it up.

"So? I'm just asking," Zee said. "Is that a crime, honey?"

"Janie," my father said, "You wait here a bit and watch TV. Zee and I are going into the other room to talk."

With Zee's hand rubbing my father's leg, and my father red around the collar and wanting to get up so quickly off the couch, I knew they did more than talk. But I never once let myself think about it. I switched on the TV as my father walked behind Zee, his hand in the small of her back, guiding her to the bedroom. He was always gentler with Zee than I'd ever seen him be with my mother.

For a while I heard muffled sounds coming from the back room, but then I focused on an episode of *Superman*. Once in a while I could hear sirens blaring down 99, and once the neighbor came home on his Harley, which shook the windowpanes and drowned out *Superman* until he finally shut it off.

Then there was a moment of silence, and a commercial on TV, and I was just getting bored when an argument erupted in the bedroom.

"I do *not* drink too much!" Zee yelled. "You don't have the right to tell me how to live my life!"

"I'm telling you for your own good!" my father shouted. His voice was cautiously angry, almost a whine.

"Do you think you're perfect?" Zee yelled. "Do you? Huh?"

"Calm down," my father said; then their voices were lowered just enough to vibrate through the walls without articulation.

After a minute or so Zee came pouncing out of the room, my father behind her, and scooped up her purse and jacket. She turned to my father and said, "Let's take Janie to the zoo."

My father nodded and grabbed Zee and pulled her to him. Then they kissed in front of me, which I thought was rude and I couldn't watch.

"Okay," my father said. "Let's get some air." He held out a hand to Zee, who clutched her keys close to her body and squinted her eyes at him. "Don't you dare even say it. I'm fine to drive and you know it."

Whenever the three of us went somewhere, Zee always drove her Buick, because the back of my father's car was about as cramped for me as a pickle jar. My father shrugged. I had heard Zee tell my father once how she liked driving almost better than sex.

"You up for the zoo, Janie?" my father asked.

I nodded and switched off the TV. I was getting too old for *Superman*, but never too old for the zoo.

We headed south on 99. Traffic was moving at a good clip, because it was Sunday afternoon. Zee had her left elbow resting out the rolled-down window, and I felt the breeze hit me in the face every time she rotated her arm to turn the wheel.

"You like the baby animals?" Zee shouted at me.

"Sure," I said.

"We'll start at the petting zoo then—see if they have any babies. I heard there's a new monkey...."

My father was quiet until we came to a stoplight and Zee turned on her blinker.

"Where are you going?" he asked her.

"Stop for a pack of cigarettes," she said.

"I thought you quit."

"You thought wrong."

"You told me you quit." My father looked at her like she was the first person to ever slip up.

"I did," Zee said, "back when I told you I did."

"How long did that last?"

"Jesus. Whatever."

The light turned green and Zee hit the gas and turned the car to the right and we sped down a side street.

"Why don't you try to quit again? Like today. Right now. We'll get something to eat at the zoo...."

"For Christ's sake, are you going to start acting like we're married?" Zee shot a hateful look at my father, then glanced in the rearview mirror at me. "You okay back there, sugar plum?"

I nodded.

"Don't get upset when we argue a little. Grown-ups do like to argue, but it doesn't mean a thing."

"Duh," I said, surprised that Zee was treating me like a baby.

Then my father screamed, and we all felt a big bump and heard a thud. I had no idea what had happed.

"What the hell?" Zee pulled the car over to the curb and stared at my father with wide eyes.

"You went through a stop sign!" he yelled. "You hit somebody!"

"There was nobody there!" Frantic, Zee yelled back in a shrill pitch.

"He was crossing, Zee! He was just starting across the street! Oh my God!" My father stared over his shoulder past me. I felt my stomach plunge as I realized what had happened. My father grabbed for his seat belt and jostled it off his shoulder, then struggled to undo it for a moment, like a man in a plane wreck, until it gave. Then he shouted, "Jesus, Zee," and bolted out the passenger door.

Zee looked at me in the mirror, her face pale like a china plate. "I swear to God, honey," she said, "there was nobody there."

I swung around in my seat and spied a figure almost a block away, lying in a heap on the ground. It could have been a sack of garbage. My eyes swelled with fright.

In only a minute my father came charging up to Zee's window just as Zee was getting out. "Don't!" he ordered her. "Stay in the car."

He came around and got in on the passenger side. He was shaking and there was a small bloodstain on the left side of his chin the color of my dress.

Zee stared at my father, who shook his head. Finally he whispered, "He's dead."

"What?"

"He's dead," my father told her, probably forgetting that I was in the car.

I stared down at my sweaty palms, as though I'd done the deed myself, and I felt that my lungs weren't breathing on autopilot anymore. I struggled to get air.

"Are you sure?" Zee asked.

"I know dead. He's dead." My father turned white. His whole body had mild tremors. Zee sucked in a great gulp, like it was her last breath, then began to cry.

"Stop it," my father ordered. He got out of the car again, and this time came around to Zee's side and told her to move over.

"Oh, God. God help me," Zee whispered.

"Nobody saw." My father sidled into the driver's seat. Then

he turned into a repetitive machine—: "Nobody saw, goddamn it.... Nobody saw...."

I wanted to throw up, but I knew to hold it together and not disturb anyone. My father drove the car down the block, turned a few corners, and came out again at Highway 99. I figured he was looking for a cop. But then he drove back to Zee's trailer, all the while muttering, "We gotta think now. Just be quiet and think."

We examined the front bumper of the Buick. It was dented, as if we had hit a telephone pole. Then we went into Zee's trailer and they got out the bourbon. This time my father didn't complain about her drinking. They both drank and paced the room. Finally my father forced Zee to sit down beside him on the couch. I squatted on the floor by the TV. The fright that hung in the air was new to me.

They were breathing heavily and crying and swearing and shaking, and I was the one who finally said, "Shouldn't we call somebody?"

My father looked at me. The room grew quiet as death. He held me with his eyes like a thing he suddenly loathed, and I felt coldness cut through me like an icicle.

"Don't you...*ever*...tell anybody about this," he said.

* * *

Days went by. Each day water came down from the sky like an ocean unleashed. It tore down the roof, got choked in the clogged spouts, and overflowed the gutters. Through my bedroom window I watched a waterfall cascade off the eaves, as if I was stuck in a car wash. When the heat kicked on it fogged my window, where I drew pictures of houses and stick figures and a dog attacking a mailman. I tried not to think about that horrible day.

My father and I didn't speak about it. I cried into my pillow at night. My mother, seeing my eyes red and swollen, asked me what was wrong. I told her I had allergies, and she frowned but let it go.

I had a best friend. Her name was Ellie and she used to come over all the time to ask me to ride bikes. I started saying no every time she asked. I was used to being honest with Ellie; I knew I couldn't see her without spilling my guts. Besides, Ellie was a chatterbox and couldn't keep a secret.

My fourth-grade school year began—the sky still a torrential downpour—and I couldn't go. I was ill. I told my mother I had the flu. In reality I didn't know what was wrong with me. I suffered in a deep funk, like every fiber of my body wanted to give up on me. My father had started working at a cement factory; my mother was looking for a *real* job, as she hadn't sold any real estate. I heard my mother's worries about money as she listed the bills to my father each night after dinner. I heard my mother's claims that we might lose the house. But that was nothing, I thought. A man was dead!

I can't say why I didn't tell my mother, except that I was scared. I had grown to trust my father's infidelity as something justified, but a dead man was way out of my league. Time passed as I tried to push it out of my head.

One Saturday the sky finally cleared. I was draped over the bed on my stomach, pretending to be an orphan—my mother was out, my father nowhere to be seen—and I heard birds chirping in the evergreens. I went to the kitchen to forage for snacks and couldn't help gazing out the window at the mist rising from a soaked landscape, slowly drying the sun's rays. I had an idea, and for the first time since the accident I felt some relief.

I sat down and began composing an anonymous letter to the police department. *Dear sirs, if you're wondering who hit that man who got killed near 99...*

The phone rang. I picked it up and heard Zee's stilted voice on the other end, like a stranger. "Is your father home?" she asked. She didn't call me honey or sweetie or sugar plum. She was all business. "I want to talk to him," she demanded.

I went down to the basement, where I found my father whittling a handmade pipe. He nodded at me and picked up the phone when I told him it was Zee.

Back upstairs I almost hung up the extension, but I put it up to my ear instead.

"...heard on the news," my father was saying.

"I think we should talk," Zee said.

"There's nothing to talk about." My father paused, then added that the man was nineteen and left behind a pregnant girlfriend.

"I know that." Zee's voice was unmoved. I had never heard her talk so steely before. "What about your daughter?"

"I told you, that's not a problem. And I don't ever want you calling this house again."

"It doesn't have to end here," Zee said.

"It sure as hell does," my father replied. "It's over, Zee. For the rest of my life I don't ever want to hear a word from you, or a word about...it. It's over."

He hung up the phone and then I hung up the phone.

I went downstairs and stared at my father whittling the pipe. I stared at him until he acknowledged me and asked what was up.

"Why aren't we telling the police?" I asked him. "It wasn't your fault. *She* was driving."

"Because I love her," my father said. He stopped whittling and looked at his thumb, where an indentation from the blunt end of the blade was turning red. "Someday you'll understand. Besides, it's too late. I'm complicit now."

"What's that mean?"

"It means you must never tell anybody." He set down his knife and held out his arms. "Come here."

I went to my father, knowing he was wrong, knowing that if he was complicit, so was I. I went to him and allowed him to hug me. He held me for a long while, his arms uncomfortably tight around my back. He smelled like pipe tobacco and whiskey, and I noticed a store-bought pipe lying on its side on the coffee table.

"Sometimes doing the right thing is complicated," he told me. "One life was lost. There doesn't need to be any others ruined."

I tried that on for size as my father let me go. I hadn't thought of that. If he went to prison, my mother would lose the house. And we would have no money. And that would ruin more than just Zee's life.

On the other hand, that pregnant lady was always going to wonder who killed her baby's father.

"How come you're smoking?" I asked him. "I thought you hated it when Zee smoked. You always said smoking's bad for you...."

My father brushed some shavings off his lap onto the floor, then he looked right at me. His eyes were watery and he seemed to struggle for words. Just then, I could see exactly how he had been as a child.

"This is a pipe," he finally said. "There's a difference between pipes and cigarettes."

Back upstairs I tore my letter to the police into little bits. I tossed each bit into the garbage one by one, watching them fall like snowflakes. Then I took the garbage out to the trash can at the end of the driveway, just as Ellie was pulling up on her bicycle. "You wanna ride?" she asked.

I nodded and pulled my own bike out from beside the woodpile.

"Where have you been?" Ellie asked. "You been sick?"

I shrugged and swung one leg over the bike seat. I took out a piece of Juicy Fruit and offered one to her. Then I looked my best friend right in her sky-blue eyes: "You promise not to tell anyone, Ellie? Cross your heart and hope to die?"

We Grew Tails

By Susan Whiting Kemp

We began to grow tails. At first none of us knew that everybody else had hard knobs above their buttocks, so we hid our shame under our skirts and pants. We must have known somehow that it wasn't treatable, so we didn't see our doctors.

As the knobs grew thicker and slightly more extended, we stopped frequenting swimming pools, beaches, and gyms. Husbands and wives hid their tail stumps from each other, convinced that the new appendage would chase their spouse into the arms of a tail-free lover. Parents hid the tail stumps from their children, who had none and were blissfully unaware of the new adult trauma. Employees hid the tail stumps from their bosses and coworkers by sleight of hand, focusing their attention instead on bar charts and graphs, and thick new strategic plans.

When the tails grew as long as a foot or two or three, we tamed them with girdles, ACE bandages, and packing tape. The strapping down was uncomfortable, like restricting an arm, only worse, because our emotions now abandoned our faces and lived in our tails instead. Our tails wagged with happiness, slashed with annoyance, or curled under in fear, in spite of our attempts to still them.

Inevitably we became aware of the bulging, shifting behinds of others, and suspected the truth. We were not alone in our shame. Close friends and family members finally told one another of their traumatic development. All at once, everybody knew.

The most daring of us released our tails and let them swing free. Then the rest of us. It was immediately apparent that no two tails were alike. One was thick as a sapling, scaled like a rat's tail; another was wide, furry, and gray-toned like a squirrel's, another straight and black, like a Labrador's.

Race, personality, and sex had no effect on tail assignment. An old person could sprout a Saint Bernard tail, while a young person might grow only a deer puff. A white person could grow a brown tail; a black person's could be beige.

A brisk business grew around tail adornment and maintenance. Tail wigs, extensions, clip-ons, jewelry. Butt scarves were especially popular, as it was difficult for most to show an anus to one and all. Furniture and toilets now came in bold new shapes to accommodate the tails. Flea powders and tail shampoos came in a myriad of pleasing scents.

Some considered the tail the work of the devil. Some thought it God's work. Some blamed aliens from outer space, others environmental pollution. There was an explosion of thought regarding the theory of latent DNA, which had been like a time bomb hidden in our bodies' codes.

There was above all a rush to advocate that a certain type of tail made one person superior to another. Bushy versus smooth. Long versus short. Prehensile versus canine. Circular wag versus linear. There was a great confusion of interviews, advertisements, proofs, disputations, and scientific inquiries. Tails varied widely within a family, so those who advocated tail superiority alienated friends and family, or pitted friend against friend.

Society reshuffled itself around the theories of various scientists, charlatans, and seers. Some of them told us it was the beginning of the end: We would now all revert to our inner animal selves. We watched for signs of other animal features developing on our bodies: snouts, body hair, the tendency to drop to all fours. We remained human, to the relief of some and the disappointment of others.

Although we didn't immediately transform further after growing tails, most people saw it as progress. The next step in evolution, a step toward a new state of mind, a step forward. That's why we were all so shocked when the tails began to go away. It traumatized each of us much the same as growing them in the first place, but instead of hiding our fear, we wailed and cradled our limp tails like dying children.

The loss took several months. When our tails were gone—fur shed, flesh melted—we searched for the meaning of the transformation, but couldn't come to any consensus. Like many events over the course of a lifetime, we knew we might never understand the purpose, but that didn't stop the debating, the mulling, the rehashing.

After many years we grew old and tired, and our conversations and expressions dulled, until someone or another would mention the year of the tails. Then we would light up, even if briefly, remembering the drama, the color, the wonder, the passion.

At night sometimes, between dreams of flying and dreams of being chased, we dreamed we were wagging our tails once more.

Quicksand

By Evelyn Arvey

S*eattle*— Few things are worse than telling your seventeen-year-old daughter and fourteen-year-old son that their father is in the clutches of a disease. I prepared as best I could for the Big Reveal: The Tuesday after William's diagnosis, trying not to notice my shaking hands, I made spaghetti and French bread, everyone's favorite dinner. I served pasta on my wooden platter, a souvenir from last year's trip to the Peruvian jungle, a hand-carved, fanciful thing with toucans and monkeys on the rim. I was finishing my special meatballs with fresh herbs when a mud-slung Nick burst into the kitchen after soccer practice, lifted the lid from the frying pan, snatched the smallest meatball, popped it into his mouth, then turned his grinning face to me, still chewing. "What's the big occasion, Ma?"

Blinking, I turned away to drain the spaghetti noodles.

At the table, William placed a manila envelope beside his plate. I knew its contents all too well: a printed MRI showing lesions on his neck and spine, four cloudy blobs that looked to me like miniature time bombs. The kids would have questions, so three days ago William and I had gone to the bookstore, where he chose two books about multiple sclerosis and I tried not to look at a young woman making her painful way down the aisle while clinging white-knuckled to her walker. It was red, a red walker with sparkles embedded in the glossy enamel.

William read the books the next day, filling a page with notes. Getting ready.

"Damn, Emily," he said. His eyes said, *This isn't me.*

"Oh, honey," I said, putting my hand over his. I was in the middle of the second book. "I'm so sorry." My eyes also held a message: *I am with you.*

And now here we were. Tuesday. Dinner. Time for the Big Reveal. Laura slid into the seat next to her father, then reached for a piece of French bread and the butter dish. William didn't tease her about having a little bread with her butter, and Laura didn't come right back with a zinger about his habit of having a little steak with his salt.

No. He just watched her.

Laura didn't notice her father's quiet new fragility, but I sure did. After only one week I was developing a new sense of William, a new gathering of threads that went from him to me, pulling me toward him, keeping me aware of his every movement and facial expression and inflection of voice. Was this normal, this exquisite tuning-in to an ill spouse?

"Kids. We need to talk," William said. He cleared his throat. "Ever heard of MS?"

"Multiple sclerosis," I added.

"Naw, I don't know anything about it," said Nick after a moment.

"That's, like, what Jane's mother has, I think." Laura set

down her bread, then picked it up again. "Yeah. I'm pretty sure that's what she has. Why?"

"Well, I have it," William said.

The kids stared at him.

"MS?" said Laura, her voice thin. "You have MS?"

William nodded. "I was just diagnosed last week." He picked up the MRI file. "You guys are the first to know, other than Mom and me."

Nick glanced sideways at his father. "Dad. That totally sucks."

"Yeah," said Laura. "Really sucks."

The three of them bent over the MRI images. William explained that the myelin lining of his spinal cord was eroding in several spots, which would eventually—*might* eventually, I silently added—lead to damage of the nerves within the cord, which in turn *might* lead to an unknown level of impairment.

"I've been diagnosed with primary progressive MS," he told them. "It's the most aggressive kind. There's no cure. The only treatments are for the other kind of MS." He took a deep breath. "I won the lottery, guys. Men like me in their late fifties aren't supposed to get MS. It's usually a young woman's disease."

Right, I thought, but it happened anyway.

I pushed my plate away. How was it the kids seemed so calm? I leaned back in my chair, picking at a tomato-sauce spot on my jeans as William explained how balance was one of the first things to be compromised, told the kids there was a slightly higher chance they might develop MS because they had a parent with it. I held my breath, looking from William to Laura, to Nick, then back again. The kids had to have known something. You couldn't live in the same house with him and not notice things: the strange hitch in his gait, how he tired too quickly during outdoor activities, how he fell apart in higher temperatures, the way he gripped the back of a chair when standing up. All symptoms of MS, although we hadn't known. Had the kids thought their father was accident-prone all this time?

And there was Peru. We'd all known something was going on in Peru.

Four days later I heard low voices wafting from our bedroom. I peeked in to find Laura sprawled long-legged on the day chair. She'd dragged it across the room to where William still lay in bed. Their heads were close, their voices solemn. "Daddy, does it hurt?" I heard her ask as I crept downstairs to the kitchen, leaving them be.

Later that afternoon, after Nick's soccer practice I heard William's car drive up and park in front of our house. When they didn't come in I pulled aside the front curtain. There they were, still sitting in the fogged-up car. All I could see of them were the dark blobs of their heads and occasional flashes of Nick's blue jersey. They stayed there, in a cocoon of their own making, for over an hour.

That evening William set aside in the corner of our bedroom his prized possession from our trip to the Amazon jungle—a walking stick with an anaconda head carved on the handle. Sighing, he went on the *other* Amazon and ordered his first official mobility device: a folding walking cane with a specialized hand grip.

* * *

Amazon Jungle, Peru— William was tired and out of sorts, which was a shame because this was the last day of our Amazon jungle adventure. He was exhausted. We'd been in this no-electricity, no-running-water research lodge on a tributary of the

Amazon River for almost a week and we'd barely had a chance to rest.

Everyone agreed it had been stunning. We'd gone on crack-of-dawn trips in wooden canoes to look for birds with our guide, Ruben, a charming young man with a gap between his front teeth. He'd taken us through the jungle in search of monkeys, poison dart frogs, and medicinal plants. Nick and Laura had even played *fútbol* with young men from a local village. *Local* meaning half an hour down the river in a canoe; *village* meaning ten palm-thatched stilted huts loosely arranged around a grassy field.

William managed to pull himself together for one last excursion.

"This walk, it is not difficult," Ruben insisted as we gathered on the split-plank deck. "We will visit a beautiful, how do you say? *Cascada?* Fall of water? You will like it very much, I promise you."

"Waterfall, dude," said Nick.

"I want to see a waterfall," said Laura.

I swatted a mosquito. Already it was make-me-into-a-dripping-mess hot out, and we'd only just finished breakfast. "How far, Ruben?"

"Not far, Mrs. Emily." Ruben held up his hand, showed me his thumb and finger an inch apart. He thrust a pair of rubber jungle boots at me after tipping them upside down to dislodge creepy-crawlies. "We will swim, and there maybe will be river dolphins." Ruben grinned, handing Laura another pair of mud-flecked boots. "You have swim clothes on?"

She nodded. We all wore swimsuits under our clothes, adding an additional layer of sweaty itchiness to our heat-and-mosquito-tender skin.

"My boots are too loose," said William, stomping on the deck, making sloppy *clump-clump* sounds. "These are way too big for me, Ruben. Can you find the ones I wore yesterday?"

"I'm sorry, no." Ruben explained that another guest had taken them. "Don't worry. These will be okay. See? My boots, they are big also." He grinned. "Okay? We will leave now?"

"They're too *big*," William muttered.

I wiggled my toes in my own generously sized boots, my eyes following flickers of brilliant yellow in the trees: Was it a parakeet that darted, flitted, and chattered just out of sight? Or was it a golden-tailed, black-bodied oropendola? Birds were my favorite part of the jungle.

Ruben led us to a waiting boat, a metal one this time, shining and sun-hot. The four of us were uncharacteristically quiet as Ruben steered the boat into ever-shallower tributaries with a small outboard motor. I gazed at a dazzling land, violently green: layers of viridian and teal, lime, emerald and chartreuse, hues I hadn't known existed. Ruben killed the motor every ten minutes and we held our collective breath, waiting as jungle sounds rose around us—whistles, rustles, and mysterious splashes. An hour up the river, Ruben tied the boat to a low branch. He jumped out and hacked at vines with his machete. "Here it is! The trail to the *cascada*."

"I'm not sure I can make it up there in these boots." William frowned at the steep if not very high slope.

Ruben helped him up the muddy bank. There was an overgrown path leading into the jungle. Ruben slashed invading greenery with his machete, and we followed behind, single file. William walked at the end, picking his way carefully through slippery, muddy ground, over roots and fallen vines. He looked like he wanted to grab the occasional branch as we passed, but he didn't. William grabbed onto me instead.

"I can't keep my balance," he said. "*How* far is it, Ruben?"

"Not far. First we will cross a little river."

"Cool," said Nick. "We're going to ford a river!"

"A river?" I gasped. "On foot? In flood season?"

"A small river," Ruben insisted. "It is so little it has no name. No problem. You will see."

❊ ❊ ❊

Seattle— William's one cane became two canes. His daily naps became fatigue-driven slumbers lasting an hour and a half. He found it harder to dress himself, to bathe, to read the thousand-page biographies he adored, to keep more than two things in his head at once. He no longer coached Nick's soccer team; instead he and I took walks around the block. He'd loved going to University of Washington football games; now he watched his Huskies on TV.

"What *else*?" he said to me after a particularly sluggish walk. "What else will this disease take from me, Emily?"

I didn't know. I just didn't know.

William was on a mission to do everything and anything that might help: He met regularly with his neurologist and went to physical therapy once a week. He injected himself daily with a drug meant for the other kind of MS. He tried a cleansing diet prescribed by a naturopath. Nothing helped. William was getting worse.

Some nights I cried myself to sleep, lying next to him in rigid self-imposed silence so as not to disturb him, wishing I could *vanquish* this thing!

I was still in denial. Or perhaps I'd moved on to anger. This wasn't supposed to happen to *my husband*! William was twelve years older than me, and retired—but he was still young. We had plans. We were going to see the world, and Peru was supposed to have been only the beginning. We were going to take dance classes. We were going to hike the mountain trails that surrounded Seattle. We were going to take extension classes at the University of Washington. We were going to *enjoy* ourselves.

After our walk, we settled into our recliners. On the far wall was a framed print of the four of us mugging for the camera, crossing a no-name river in matching teal-colored jungle hats.

For the first time I thought he looked old. We both did. My life was slowly slipping into his because someone had to be with him, fragile now, all the time. What did the future look like for us? Was I going to be his caregiver one day? I didn't want to be a caregiver. I wanted to be a *wife*.

Beside me, William muted the TV. He turned to me. "Emily."

I raised my eyebrows.

"Thank you," he said softly.

When the box from Amazon arrived he opened it, lifted out the plastic-wrapped parts, then threw them back in. "Idiots! They sent the wrong one! Who would want a red walker with *sparkles*!"

❊ ❊ ❊

Amazon Jungle, Peru— Ruben and the kids were waiting for us at the river, wide but slow-moving, dark with forest tannins, and swampy. I imagined it harbored piranhas, electric eels, and anacondas, or at the very least leeches, but Ruben assured us, "It is shallow in this place. In and out. We've never lost a guest yet."

Someone had fixed a synthetic green rope from a tree to a jutting stone on the other side. The cord dipped in the center, falling below the waterline.

Nick and Laura were already ankle-deep in the water.

"Hold the rope and follow me," Ruben said, "Mr. William? Do you wish to rest?"

"Now is fine," said William, watching the kids, frowning slightly. "I guess."

I waded in after Nick, clutching the rope. The water was refreshingly cool, the silty riverbed firm and easy to walk on. Water rose past my calves, my knees, up to midthigh, stopping at my waist.

"Take our picture, William," I said over my shoulder. "Can you do that?"

"Already did," he said. "I'll pass the camera forward and ask Ruben to take one of all of us. Here it comes!" William sounded better.

The best was yet to come. Ruben's waterfall was at the center of a sun-dappled clearing rimmed with jungle. The waterfall leaped over a craggy stone cliff and splashed into a pool, sending spray all the way to where we stood at the end of the trail.

"What did I tell you?" said Ruben, grinning. "It is worth it, no?"

Nick had already shed his clothes down to his swimming trunks and had his toes in the water. "Can we go in, Ruben? Can we?"

"Only if you wish to have fun!" Ruben shrugged off his T-shirt, tore off his boots, and took three bounding steps into the pool.

"Dude!" said Nick, following him.

"I'm going to sit down." William sighed. "Go ahead and swim with the kids if you want, Emily. I'll take pictures. I'm... so...hot." Rivulets of sweat carved trails down his temples.

"Dad!" called Laura. "C'mon!"

I didn't like the exhausted grayness of William's face. I lowered my voice, put my hand lightly on his shoulder. "You'll feel better if you go swimming. Just hang out and enjoy the cool water with me. Please?"

A slow smile lit up his face. "Ever kissed under a waterfall?"

❊ ❊ ❊

Seattle— My fun-loving husband made a brief appearance in the Great Wheelchair Race. William challenged Jessica, a fellow MS patient with a sporty yellow wheelchair, to a competition in a rarely used hallway in the physical therapy clinic, but I found out about it only after the fact when I picked him up from his appointment.

"I blew her *away*." William's face showed more color than it had in weeks as he executed a slick transfer from his wheelchair to the driver's seat. He still drove our car using the hand controls we had installed. "You would have loved seeing us fly down that hallway, Emily. We started out even...then Jessica pulled ahead."

"Oh, no."

"But she started laughing so hard she lost momentum and I raced past her. She didn't stand a chance."

"You won?"

"I won."

"I wish I'd been there," I said, laughing. "You always pull through at the last moment. Remember Peru?"

He lifted his legs into the car, using his hands. He didn't answer.

❁ ❁ ❁

Amazon Jungle, Peru— Too soon it was time to leave our private paradise. The five of us dried off, tugged clothes onto our still slightly damp bodies, then left forever that lovely clearing with the waterfall and its sweet memories of spray-blasted kisses.

William picked his way along the trail, heavy step after heavy step, me lending a shoulder or an arm. I kept a worried eye on him, hoping he hadn't caught some horrible illness on our last day in the Amazon. After a while the kids asked if they might go on ahead with Ruben.

"Fine." William sighed. "Go ahead. I'm slowing everyone down."

As soon as they disappeared from view, I wished we'd asked them to wait. Instead, William and I picked our way alone along the trail.

William's legs weren't in sync with the rest of his body as he lurched and wavered his way, complaining about his feet sloshing and sliding in those wretched boots.

Malaria? Surely not. We were taking pills for that.

Yellow fever? No way. We'd been vaccinated.

"We should have asked Ruben to cut you a walking stick," I said, peering up the trail, but there was no sign of Ruben or the kids.

And then it got worse. When we finally made it to the river crossing, the rope was gone.

❁ ❁ ❁

Seattle— William fell in the night: His legs gave out on his way back from visiting the portable commode we'd set up in our bedroom. We'd thought he needed his wheelchair only for longer distances. We'd been sure he could manage inside the house with his walker.

Keeping up with William's disease was a moving target: Once we got used to a level of disability, William would get worse and we'd be forced to readjust everything we'd been doing. Those time bombs on William's spinal cord had come of age—he'd recently had another MRI—and they were now detonating. Damaged myelin and frayed nerve axons were disrupting signals from his brain to his limbs. William was sinking into his illness, sometimes quickly, sometimes slowly.

The crash in the night—and his shriek—woke me. "William? William?"

Nick called from the other room. "Dad?"

"Help!" William gasped from somewhere he shouldn't have been. "Help!"

"Are you okay?" I jumped out of bed, flicked on the light, and knelt by him on the floor. He lay sprawled and twisted, one leg under our bed, his head inches from the corner of the dresser. "Did you hit your head? Honey? How's your neck? Did you break anything?"

"No. Help me up." His voice sounded frail.

I sensed Nick hovering in the doorway. "Can you pick up the walker?" I asked. "Straighten Dad's legs too. Gently now." I turned to William. "I need to know if you hit your head."

"No! I didn't!" William struggled to sit up; then he leaned

against the bed. "Damn it, Emily, I can't even take a piss on my own."

He wasn't injured, except for a tennis-ball sized bruise on his hip and an aching shoulder, but getting William back in bed wasn't easy. We did it in stages: I buckled the gait belt around William's middle. Nick and I hauled on it as William heaved himself to his knees, flopped onto the bed on his stomach, and lay panting as we swung his legs up and around.

There has to be a better way to do this, I thought, *but what it is, I have no idea.*

This was the future we were so frightened of, only two years since his diagnosis. What would the next two years look like? The next five?

❊ ❊ ❊

Amazon Jungle, Peru— We stood by the river, staring in disbelief, wondering where the rope had gone.

"What the *hell*?" said William.

"We're at the right place. See?" I gestured at the oddly shaped stone to which the rope had been tied. A frayed green remnant dangled from it. Where were the kids?

"The rope must have worked loose after they crossed. Ruben!" William put his hands around his mouth. "Ru-*ben*!"

We held our breath, but all we heard was the call of an oropendola.

"Laura! Nicky!" I yelled. And then I saw something. "The rope!" It was about five yards downriver, snaking in the slow current just below the surface of the water, and entirely within reach. "It must still be tied to the tree on the other side. I'll go get it."

"No, let me," said William.

I stared at the rope, then at him. "But, honey, that doesn't make sense." I flinched as something shrieked in the not-far distance. It would be dusk in a few hours. Hadn't Ruben seen jaguar tracks a few weeks ago? "You're not feeling well. I can do it."

Something jumped in the river. A fish. Nothing but a fish.

But William was on a mission. He handed me his day pack, then picked his way along the bank, barely slipping, to where the rope fluttered a few feet from shore. He peered into the water. "It looks okay. A little siltier here than where we crossed. Muddy." He leaned over. "I think there's a layer of dead leaves on the bottom. The water's dark. It's hard to see."

"Be careful. You don't know what's hiding in that mess."

He took a step so squishy I could hear it from where I stood. He paused. "Wow. The mud is kind of deep here. It's… um…sucking at my boots." Holding his arms out, with a grunt he lifted his foot—his boot muddy past the ankle—and took another step, this time into the water. "See? I can almost reach the rope." He took another step, then reached into the water. "Not yet. It's moving away." Calf-deep in water, he freed his boot from the mud and took another step.

Where did he get the energy for this? Five minutes ago he'd barely been able to walk. "William! Come back. Ruben said there were bad areas here. We'll cross without the rope."

"Ugh. This mud, it stinks. In a second, honey. I've almost got it now." He pulled at his right leg with his hands. William's boot tops were out of sight now. He strained mightily and moved his right foot about six inches, but in the meantime his left leg sank *way* too far into the mud. It made him lopsided; at any moment he would fall. He windmilled his arms and looked wild-eyed at me over his shoulder. "Emily? Emily? I think I'm stuck."

"I'm coming! I'll help you."

"No!"

I stopped short at the panic in his voice.

"If you come over here, you'll get stuck too." He stopped thrashing, wet up to his waist. He was right, but how could I stand there and watch him sink into an Amazonian river?

"I'm coming." I looked wildly around. "I'll…I'll snap off a tree limb! I'll get you something to grab onto!"

"Wait," he said, catching his breath. "Not yet. I have an idea. Just watch."

William seemed to relax. As soon as the silt and mud settled, he allowed himself to slump into the water, sitting down on the muddy surface, treading water gently with his arms. In a single long graceful move, he extended his upper body and lay down on his stomach, pike position, his legs still buried in the grasping mud.

"William! What are you *doing*?"

"Wait," he said calmly, his face tight with concentration. "Watch."

I clutched a nearby tree as he lay on the water. And then I noticed something: He was wriggling and pulling his legs and body and, little by little, he was freeing himself. First one boot broke the surface of the water, and then the other. He squirmed on his belly toward me, half swimming, half mud-skating. I leaned over. He took my hand, rising to his knees, then his feet. Dripping globs of foul-smelling mud, he staggered into my arms.

"William! How did you know to do that?"

He grinned. "I saw it on a survival show about quicksand.

The trick was to go from vertical to horizontal. It actually worked."

"You were amazing." I smoothed his hair and rubbed mud from his cheek. "But that wasn't quicksand. That was quick-*mud*. You almost drowned in quick-mud."

And then the two of us were laughing. Holding on to each other, without the rope, we slipped and slid and squished our way back to the river crossing. We were debating whether to cross on our own when Nick, Ruben, and Laura appeared, waving and hollering. A moment later Ruben was splashing his way across the river toward us, pulling the green rope through his hands. He secured it to the rock so Nick and Laura could cross too.

William sat on the stone for a well-deserved rest, telling his story to an enthralled audience. Ruben listened, his face abashed, horrified, admiring in turn. "Wait one moment, please," he said shyly when William finished. "I wish to make something for you."

Ruben walked back to where William had been mired in the mud, where the riverbed still churned angrily. With three mighty whacks of his machete, he cut down the sapling I'd clung to. He trimmed its branches, smoothed the pole with a straight-edged stone, and, with quick flicks of his pocketknife, whittled an anaconda head on its top.

With a formal bow, he presented it to William. "A walking stick, with my apologies, sir." He took a breath. "I should not have left you. It was a terrible decision, but Laura was stung many times by fire ants, and she had pain. I went to my boat for medicine for her." Ruben was contrite. "I did not know the rope was broken. I thought we would make it back in time."

"It's okay; don't worry about it." William took the walking

stick, hefted it, balanced it on his palm. "It's beautiful," he said, looking up at the young Peruvian who'd spent the past week with our family, helping us, showing us his world. "Thank you, Ruben." William's eyes were wet. "This will help me on the way back. I'll treasure it always."

❋ ❋ ❋

Seattle— William depended on that walking stick more and more during the year to come as he began his slide into the disease men his age weren't supposed to get. Three and a half years later he could barely stand, much less walk. I would lie awake in bed for hours after William fell asleep, tormenting myself with what-if scenarios from our as yet unknowable future: He was pretty disabled now—how bad would it get? Would he need a power wheelchair? What if he became so disabled I couldn't take care of him by myself? How would we afford it all? How would I deal with everything?

One morning, as the room filled with dim gray light, William stirred. He rolled over onto his back. He stared at the ceiling for a long while, then turned to me. "I've been thinking," he said, his voice low, serious, fragile-sounding.

"Yeah? Me too. What about, honey?"

"That walking stick."

"Oh?" I glanced to where it was propped, gathering dust in the corner. "What about it?"

"I'm glad we went there. I'm glad we met Ruben." He paused. "And I'm glad we have all those memories. Good memories."

"Yeah," I said. I took his hand. It got lighter in the room, and the details on the anaconda head came into view: the blunt nose, the depressed eyes, the sinuous neck.

"It's more than just good memories, though," William said ten minutes later. "The stick could be a symbol of struggle, of overcoming shit that life throws at us. Overcoming some of it, anyway. We ought to display it somewhere downstairs, as a reminder."

Something relaxed inside me. I nodded, squeezed his hand, thought about how nice the stick would look if we hung it horizontally on hooks under the framed picture between our easy chairs in the family room. William was right: We needed to be reminded that he—and I—were stronger than we gave ourselves credit for. He'd gotten mired in quick-mud and then freed himself. He'd trekked through that sweltering jungle on slippery trails with already compromised balance, and made it back safely.

Like that journey through the Amazon, the future wouldn't be easy. He would falter; I would give him a shoulder to lean on. He would stumble; I would help him up. He would grow ever more disabled; I would be unable to do a damn thing about it. We would, both of us, be stung by fire ants, get stuck with too-big boots, and be forced to navigate unfamiliar territory.

William would sink into stinking mud. He would struggle to pull himself out, again and again.

It might not be pretty. But if we looked for them, there might be waterfalls along the way.

First Comes Love

By Nancy Bonnington

They met at a community college in Mr. Anderson's math class—a class for playing catch-up before entering a degree program. Neither of them liked math, as it did not come easily to them, and neither knew what they wanted to do scholastically—so from the start they had that in common.

Loren was thin, with wispy blond hair that was somewhat greasy, and bound to go bald in old age. Her mother had paid for her first quarter at the community college, simply to spite her father—an unskilled, intense alcoholic—who was out of work and out of unemployment checks. This caused further tension in the constantly enraged environment in which Loren had grown up. She realized, too late, that she should have turned down the money.

Randy was a bit chubby yet still rugged in appearance. He managed to climb tall trees—which would later astonish Loren—at a frightening speed, hauling the chain saw up behind, which dangled like an oddly lethal clock pendulum well beneath him. He was a tree topper—generally for private landowners—when not attending classes, a job title he enjoyed explaining, especially to women. Loren would eventually refer to him as Monkey, although the nickname didn't hold forever.

His home life, too, was fractured. His mother, an untreatable schizophrenic, lived with his grandparents, all of whom he barely knew. His father was a long-haul truck driver, rarely home. Since the age of thirteen Randy had been ostensibly on his own, and with the ever-present fear that he might also be carrying in his own genes the seed of some incurable mental illness.

They began kissing at the back of the math class—the other students ignoring them—whenever Mr. Anderson turned to write out equations on the whiteboard. They thought it was funny, partly because they had fallen into each other's lure even before an official first date—starting with chatting and holding hands at the back of the class until one day they both tipped their chairs far enough toward one another to reach lips until Randy's chair slipped out from under him—and partly because it was so lusciously juvenile to snatch feels and kisses while Mr. Anderson suspected nothing and droned on about innocuous matters like "a negative times a negative equals a positive."

"Do you suppose he's talking about us?" Loren whispered one time.

Randy smiled, one side of his lips quite higher than the other, as always. She was never sure he got the joke, but he always responded.

Neither of them would pass the class, nor continue with college. Within a few short months Loren would prove to her father's satisfaction that college had been a waste of money. She took a waitressing job at a twenty-four-hour restaurant and eventually paid her mother back. Randy was bumped to a supervisor position in the tree-felling business and received a hefty raise. Somehow the two of them moved into an apartment, sharing their lives without really discussing it. Ever since the back of Mr. Anderson's class, it just seemed natural they would always be together.

By the following year they were married. Loren thought it was necessary to express vows until death, and Randy followed suit without complaint. Their respective families both voiced concern that they were marrying due to a pregnancy—much too young—but that was far from the truth. In fact, Loren wished she were pregnant and had not been using birth control, and Randy was not inclined to use condoms, as they were "like having sex with a raincoat."

They had a brief honeymoon, camping in the Olympic rain forest. They bivouacked to a remote spot in the back country, ignoring the requirements for registration and passes, until they found themselves in a circle of tall heathers within old-growth Douglas firs; the smell of wet foliage and musky off-season floral scents were epic to Randy and like another world to Loren. They pitched their tent and donned hiking boots. Randy was good with a compass and had brought with him a shotgun for protection.

They were lucky to run into no one. In the hours they tromped through virgin lands, or at least laid down the first human footfalls in a very long while, they grew closer to each other. Their relationship was, Randy guessed, on a new plane.

"The beauty of nature…it makes me love you even more," she said to him, perhaps the most poetic thing she had ever said. "Or maybe the smell of the woods is an aphrodisiac."

And Randy felt the primal instinct of a man wanting to care

for his partner, as though they were the only man and woman left on earth. And in a way they were.

"Hello!" Randy screamed as they rounded a bend that jutted out above a fertile valley. There was no echo, per se, but a stark silence, then Loren yelling, "Yodel, yodel!" And the silence that ensued was deadening. They were alone. There was no doubt.

They made love on that very outcropping, the ground still damp in late summer. And then Loren cried in Randy's arms for hours. She couldn't explain it, except that she was happy and had never been loved before.

"I want a baby," she cried. It was not logical but instinctive and necessary. She needed the unconditional love that even a perfect man couldn't give.

She wept about her childhood, her parents, her lonely existence before Randy. She wept about the first time a boy had rejected her. She wept about dropping out of school and other failures. And he held her and longed to give her everything she needed, but which he knew, perhaps in the recesses of his mind, was not possible.

They returned home renewed but different. Loren knew that the next step in life was to start a family. "Three or four children," she told Randy. He remained noncommittal, though not opposed to the idea.

For months they tried. They had sex as often as new lovers, but Loren had taken to superstitious thoughts and activities. Her aunt had given her a homemade bedspread, and Loren decided, since her aunt had nine children, it would bring them luck to make love on top of that bedspread, and so none other would do. She had taken to reciting her own prayers before an orgasm, and in the throes of love she would scream, "Oh, God, oh, God, make us a baby!" For she had begun to think that sex for pure pleasure would only bring bad luck, and that one needed to be of the proper spiritual mind.

It annoyed Randy a great deal, but he soon began to believe that they had no chance of getting pregnant anyway. Several of their friends had children, and it seemed like a thing that anybody could readily do. Indeed, he had a younger brother who was already three times a father by three different women.

Finally Randy announced one day that it was perfectly okay to adopt.

"I'm not going to raise someone else's child when you're the one I love," Loren cried. It was a furtive way of saying she wanted to continue her own lineage.

"But we might bring another schizo into the world," Randy argued.

"Don't bring that up. Every family has crazy people, but that doesn't mean we will."

Although he couldn't appease her, he didn't really have to. They could no way afford any artificial means of reproduction. So for a while they dropped the subject. Loren screamed for pure pleasure again during sex—no more entreaties to God, thank God—and Randy believed they would always be a couple without children, which was okay with him.

❁ ❁ ❁

One day Randy came home to their modest apartment smelling like evergreens and perfume—a mild but toxic mix that seeped into her pores when he hugged her.

"Where have you been?"

"What d'ya mean? Working."

"Uh-huh." She curled her lips in a catlike scowl and rolled

her eyes. He took off his work clothes, threw his heavy boots that were caked with mud into the corner of the coat closet.

"I wish you wouldn't," she began.

"Are we going to start?" Randy swung around and glared at her, but he could hardly hold her stare.

"Who is she?" Loren asked, her heart appearing to break, her breath held back like a dam was in her throat.

He'd never been unfaithful—never. She knew that. But for the past few weeks he worked too long and too hard, came home too exhausted. And a tree topper didn't smell like perfume.

"Who?" Randy asked. He pushed his way into the kitchen and scrounged for sandwich makings.

"She—"

"Who?" Randy asked again.

It went like that for a little while—the first real argument in their marriage—and nearly all monosyllabic.

"Sue?" That was Loren's best friend.

"No!" he said.

He tried to calm her down by admitting that he'd stopped at Earl's Bar for a drink, shot some pool. But that was it.

He cracked open a beer and bit down on a bologna sandwich. "You can come with me next time, you know. I'll stop home and pick you up."

The truth was, Randy had brushed up against Ted's girlfriend. Ted was the newest tree feller. He was a bit of a dolt, but likable enough.

When Ted went to the bathroom, Randy closed in on Alicia and bought her her third beer.

She was curvy—not like Loren—and flirtatious in a mature way. She had a few years on Randy and was the kind of forbidden fruit he once thought was out of his league. But at Earl's it became possible. She knew how to smile and brush his thigh with an allure that brought a quiver to his knees.

Ted took Alicia for granted. So when Ted came stumbling out of the men's room, still zipping up his fly, he didn't even ask his girlfriend if she wanted to go outside with him for a smoke. Ted said he had to catch up on several smokes because he'd been having a nicotine fit for an hour, which was what ruined his game. He nearly broke his hand punching the back door open with a strong jab, for no particular reason, except that Ted did everything too big. He drifted out to the alley, along with the smell of grilled burgers and the strains of an Ed Sheeran tune about love.

Randy told Alicia that Ted was crazy. Alicia agreed and they both laughed. That's all it took, a shared laugh at Ted's expense.

Randy set down his pool stick across the table, then lifted Alicia's hair off her shoulders. He felt a twinge of desire in his belly, just at the touch of her hair.

He leaned in to kiss her and she smelled soft and fruity—a bit mysterious. She kissed him back, neither of them glancing at the rear door, now closed to Ted. It was more than Randy could handle.

They made love in the back of his truck. He had to move aside the chain saw, boots, ropes, tree-topper equipment—and it smelled of old mud. There was barely room beneath the canopy for the two of them, but they seized the moment. It was purely carnal—nothing that meant anything more to Randy than great sex. He didn't want to look Alicia in the eyes or know anything about her.

When it was over, they went back into Earl's Bar, Randy only escorting her lightly with a hand that could be mistaken for a platonic gesture. They shot pool again, soon joined by

Ted, who never glanced at them sideways or appeared to suspect anything.

It troubled Randy later. Back in the cab of his truck, heading home. It troubled him that he could not satisfy Loren these days, for nothing short of a baby would be good enough. Loren always asked, "Do you love me?"

It was a terrible, acidic question. What was she trying to pull? He always said, "Yes," but she would lift one eyebrow or expel that little stream of air, like a child trying to whistle.

"I love you," he would insist, but she was so damaged she couldn't believe it.

He did indeed love her but began to loathe having a damaged wife. She was no more fixable than his mother's illness.

Coming home to their apartment, Randy felt flushed with shame, largely because he'd cheated on Loren, but partly because he'd used Alicia. She was nothing more than a bar whore to him—an attractive whore who was kind enough to make herself available. Still, she didn't deserve the come-on. He didn't want to ponder—for even a brief minute—what kind of disastrous relationship lay between Ted and Alicia.

Loren was suspicious. Only a woman has that keen sense of smell, Randy thought. Was he really permeated with Alicia's odor, that mild fruitiness that had made him crazy? He couldn't duck out of the way when he came home, for Loren had been waiting for him.

He hugged her, kissed her. Then for a long while, he tried to defend himself.

He grew angry. It was Loren who made him cheat. She wanted one thing in the world, a baby, and he couldn't give it to her.

He felt like screaming at her when she asked, "Who?"

He felt like shouting, *You made me do it!*

Instead he denied and denied, until she half believed him. And they went to bed on an awkward truce.

"Would you turn off the damn light?" he said. He vented this little bit, and had the last word as Loren made her way to her side of the bed, careful not to touch him.

✻ ✻ ✻

At an early hour, when it was still dark, Randy awoke to a strange sound. He opened his eyes and squinted. There were muffled bumping noises coming from the bathroom.

He reached out for Loren; she was beside him.

The sounds were faint but detectable. Someone was snooping; then they moved through the hall and appeared in the bedroom doorway. There was a black shadow, like an animated oil smudge, moving slowly into the room.

Randy squinted and feigned sleep for a moment. He wondered what to do. He was sick with fear for his wife, who was sleeping on the side of the bed nearest the doorway. The blinds were shut tight on the tiny bedroom window.

It had crossed his mind that it might be Ted intruding, Ted having learned about his tryst with Alicia, Ted there to kill him. And so he was mildly relieved that the size and shape of the encroaching shadow didn't seem right to be Ted.

He lay still and thought to reach for his cell phone on the nightstand. But if the intruder was armed, what could Randy do?

His shotgun was locked in the back of his truck, his pistol in the glove compartment—stupid places to store them, but Loren would not have them in their home.

Randy squinted to see the intruder moving close to the bed, the dark silhouette now hovering over Loren.

Suddenly Randy knew he would die for his wife. As if last night had never happened. He would take a bullet for her.

He kicked off the bedcovers and flew across Loren's body, propelling headfirst into the stranger. The two of them crashed to the floor; Randy felt his elbow crack, but the pain would wait.

"No!" Loren was awake and frantic, sitting up in the bed. "Help! Help! Get out of here!"

He was on top of the intruder, pummeling his face and head with both fists. Sometimes he would miss, and his knuckles would ram into the bare floor.

The stranger managed to roll out from under Randy; he was shorter and smaller. Weaker. Randy realized he had the strength to kill the man, and apparently the intruder was not armed.

The intruder gave up the fight, bolted down the hallway and out the front door.

Randy yelled at Loren, "Stay here!" He grabbed a set of keys from the entryway table.

Loren was up and pulling on a long overcoat and following him. Randy, in nothing but his shorts, fled the apartment and stood for a moment looking up and down the dark street.

The parking lot was long and narrow. Randy heard a car start and quit. Then again. The intruder was having engine trouble.

"Randy!" Loren grabbed his arm. "Don't."

"Stay here!"

He ran several yards and rounded his truck to the driver's side. He opened the car and climbed in. Loren opened the other side and scrambled to get her seat belt on while Randy yelled at her to get out.

But she was with her husband, where she belonged.

A black, beater sedan skidded forward, nearly hitting them. Randy thought he saw two people in the car. Then the sedan flew over a speed bump and out onto the thoroughfare.

Randy took off after them, straining to see the make, the model, the license plate of what he was following—something to identify the intruder's vehicle in case he lost them. But there was no license plate.

They sped through the near-empty streets; his truck clock read 3:15. The black sedan, only a few car lengths ahead, skidded around a street sweeper.

Randy reached for the glove compartment and retrieved his pistol. Just for defense, he told himself. But his blood was boiling, and he knew he was headed for his very first out-of-control rage.

How dared a man enter his home and stare down at his wife's sleeping body?

Suddenly the sedan jumped a barrier into a 7-Eleven parking lot; no doubt the intruder was trying to cut through to the freeway entrance on the other side. The black car rocked like a boat, its blunt wheels spinning on pavement as the driver tried to turn too hard to the right. Then it ran head-on into a parked recycling truck. The sedan's hood flew open, steam escaping like a creature let loose.

Randy pulled into the 7-Eleven. He jumped from the truck, the pistol in his right hand. He pointed it at the black car, whose driver was already halfway out of the vehicle. A woman was screaming. She was in the passenger seat. She rolled out of the car and onto the pavement, stoned or inebriated, picked herself up and screamed to her husband, "What the fuck!" She swayed and dropped to her knees, then stood up again.

The man ran for the woods behind the store. The woman

looked at Randy wide-eyed and shouted, her face lit up by the store lights, "Don't shoot!"

She was ugly—gaunt and pockmarked cheeks, an awkward, knobby-kneed stance—and she cried out again: "Don't, don't!"

"Get out of here!" Randy yelled. Was she stupid?

"No, no—" She waved her hands. "I can't—"

"Run," he yelled, "or I'll kill you!"

He was about to pull the trigger and blow away this woman who possibly meant something to the intruder. He was about to pay the intruder back for invading his home. What was the stranger doing in their bathroom anyway? Looking for pills? A couple of drug addicts? And how dared the intruder enter his bedroom where his own wife lay half-naked atop the lucky bedspread!

The woman knew she had no choice. He could see the momentary confusion in her eyes turn into instant determination to survive. She kicked off her pointed shoes and ran, stumbling back and forth, barefoot after her man, falling once more before disappearing behind the building.

Randy didn't bother chasing them.

Loren remained in the truck the whole time. Randy knew she'd watched it all and he was afraid for her. She would want him to call the police; perhaps that's what they should have done back at the apartment. Call the police. He stared at his wife's lone shape behind the windshield. Loren didn't move a muscle.

As Randy walked past the hissing black sedan, he heard a small cry. In the backseat he spied a baby, perhaps six months old. It was lying backward, head angled toward the floor, and sobbing. There was no seat belt, no booster seat. A miracle to be alive.

The baby's tender legs were poking out from a disposable diaper. The pink skin tones shone from the store lighting.

Goddamn drug addicts ran off and left their kid!

He opened the car and lifted the child out. The soft flesh dazzled him a bit. As he held it, it stopped crying and stared at him.

He glanced at the front doors of the 7-Eleven. For some reason nobody emerged. Perhaps the employee was in the back room taking stock. Or maybe calling the cops. Or the whole incident just hadn't stirred any interest.

Randy climbed back in his truck, but in no great rush, and with the baby. He placed it in Loren's lap and stowed the pistol. His blood pumped hard. It was the first time he had ever known such satisfaction.

Neither of them spoke. The baby cooed like a dove. And Randy started up the engine.

They sat there for quite a while in the parking lot. Maybe he was waiting for a police siren that never came. Maybe Loren meant to say something but was not sure whether she was dreaming. Maybe if he turned off the engine, it would break the spell.

At daybreak, the sun rose and the pickup was still quietly running, though it hadn't moved. The 7-Eleven was empty of customers. Randy was lying with his seat titled back a few inches beside Loren, who cuddled the sleeping infant in her arms. A reddish-orange sheen brightened the whole hood of the unwashed truck. Although Randy knew it was only a mirage from the dawn's light, he thought it was one of the most beautiful colors he'd ever seen.

Eat This

By Susan Whiting Kemp

My friend Jamie holds out a thistle bloom, her fingers curved gingerly around the prickles. "Eat this," she says.

I've never once acted on one of her off-the-wall demands. But now that we're sixty-three, I worry that I might someday. I imagine the purple work of nature poking my tongue, cheeks, and roof of my mouth while I try to figure out how to chew without impaling myself. Then I imagine succeeding, and watching Jamie's eyes widen in surprise. It makes me laugh.

I set the wheelbarrow handles down, reach into its basin, and pick up a cabbage. Its outer leaves are falling off; suddenly it seems to me to hold the entire work of the spring and summer within its tight green orb. "Eat this," I say, opening my mouth wide to indicate it should be done in one bite.

Jamie pulls her lip up into a sour-taste sneer. "Eat my shorts." She hikes the thistle onto the lawn; it disappears into the ankle-deep grass. I make a mental note to wear shoes outside until I've found the thistle.

I drop the cabbage back into the wheelbarrow; a tiny bit of dust blooms upward. "Eat my dust," I say.

"Eat it," she says, ending our wordplay. She turns and walks over the hazelnut-shell path toward my house. The breeze has picked up, so that all forty-two of my whirligigs are turning. It makes the house look like it will lift off its foundation. It makes me happy.

A car pulls into my roundabout, sending up more dust for somebody to eat. A customer who has seen my sign on the highway about handmade gifts for sale, pulling in to do some shopping on her way to Seattle. She's a young girl, maybe twenty-five. I direct her to the flower garden, where glass ornament–topped stakes nestle among white hydrangeas. "I'll give you ten dollars," she says of a blue beauty that cost me twenty dollars to make.

Jamie bristles and starts to speak, but I interrupt before she can tell the girl off. "I've got earrings for ten dollars." I direct the girl to a table where I've set out some of my wire-twist earrings. She exclaims over the treble-clef pair, and hands me cash.

As the girl is driving off, I tell Jamie not to even think about scaring my customers away. But suddenly I'm confused. I'm not at home. I'm sitting at a table with a white tablecloth and a fake plastic rose in a narrow plastic vase, and Jamie is there too, and she looks old, and she is handing me a spoon. "Eat this," she says.

"Eat my shorts," I fire back. But my voice is scratchy, like I've eaten a thistle. I look down and there is soup in front of me. I am a little hungry. I dip the spoon into the bowl, but I'm too far away. I need to scoot up, but the chair feels stuck. I look down; it has huge wheels. Jamie loosens the brake and pushes the chair closer to the table. The soup is bland. They don't use salt or a lot of spices. I don't want to be here. I think of where else I can be instead.

Jamie and I are sitting in a Mexican restaurant for our thirtieth birthdays, and the staff has gathered around. One of them is holding out a hot pepper in a bag. It's smooth and green. He says, "Eat this." Jamie takes the bag, all cocky and confident, and folds its edges back.

Everybody is chanting now: "Eat this, eat this, eat this, eat this." Jamie takes a bite out of the pepper. Not a small bite. Half the pepper. She's chewing and swallowing and smiling, and nodding like it's no big deal, but then she's leaning a hand on the table, then both hands against the wall. She's holding her hands over her mouth, bending forward, bending backward, grabbing the glass of milk, stuffing a cracker in her mouth. Then she's got a hand against her sternum, saying she can feel it like fire, and she's lying in bed, moaning.

But it's me lying in bed moaning. Jamie sitting watching me. I ask her whether her stomach is better now. She says she's fine. And I realize that I'm not getting things right. Something's wrong with my brain. I'm not thirty. I'm older. "Can they fix me?" I ask.

"Of course," says Jamie. But I always know when she is lying. Except once.

"I can't go get Halloween decorations," Jamie says. "I have to go home and do laundry." She's not looking at me; she's looking at the TV in my living room, at president Jimmy Carter standing at a podium, and she's fiddling with the loop on one of the eight zippers on her leather coat. She goes home and I drive off by myself, but I just don't get it. Halloween is Jamie's favorite holiday. She would never pass up a chance to shop for scary skeletons to do laundry.

Halfway to the store I realize I forgot my purse. I go back for it. Jamie's car is in my driveway, and so is my husband's. Warren was supposed to be working at the store, but he's not, and Jamie had driven home to do laundry, but now she's back. I go inside and hear laughter and squealing in the bedroom. I put my hand on the doorknob and pause. A piece of coal sticks in my throat, burning.

Jamie is still trying to get me to eat. But the tablecloth is blue, and I'm at the table with the fake daisy, not the fake rose. I yell at her for ruining my marriage, but the wrong words are coming out, and the staff members are there calming me, and Jamie is calming me, and I don't think they understand what I'm angry about, because they keep telling me that I've always liked applesauce.

My hand is on the doorknob. I turn it, push the door open, and enter the bedroom. The rush of air blows twenty purple and pink orbs about the room. Warren looks crestfallen at the sight of me. Jamie lets go of the balloon at her mouth on purpose; it screeches around the room and drops to the floor. So does Jamie. I've ruined my own surprise party.

I'm sitting at the blue table, and they are still trying to get me to eat my applesauce, still telling me that I like it. I take a spoonful and feel its smooth, wet graininess in my mouth. It's true. I do like applesauce.

I'm lying on my beach towel at Sand Lake Park, alone on a Saturday. All the girls I hang out with are in dance class, and I've tried it but I'm the most uncoordinated twelve-year-old there is, and anyway I can never remember the steps. Jamie, the girl in my math class who always has a funny comeback for John Eventhaller's comments, lays her towel beside mine. We watch people do cannonballs and flips off the diving board.

Jamie hands me a red delicious apple, saying, "Eat this." She's taken bites out of one side of it. I turn it around and bite into the virgin side. The water sparkles. The sun feels hot on my shoulders. I chew and swallow, and take another bite.

Fronds of Mercy

By Evelyn Arvey

"My posting is to a nothing-planet," I tell my loved ones at our evening meal. I've put off this announcement for days, for weeks, until the news could wait no longer. This is not the triumphant posting we'd expected. No, this is rancid, reeking *disaster*. I rock on my belly, sucking on the tip of my smallest frond.

My two husbands and three wives swivel their eyes at one another, and then at me.

"What?" demands Third, my favorite wife. "A nothing-planet? The Universal Friendship Corps is sending you to a *nothing-planet*?" She slaps the table, making a flute-candle fall to the floor, where it sputters and goes out. "Fronds of Mercy! What's wrong with them, you?"

"I don't know." I sink so low on my belly that my cheek skims my knee. "I don't know!"

My mates fling the remnants of our lovely meal to the floor—natterfish legs, seagrass slaw, and a platter of miniature salt-demons in hoary sauce—but the lost food doesn't matter because no one is hungry now. At their customary places at the far side of the table, Second and Sixth, my husbands, stand up in unison, lift their fronds in a cry of solidarity, then sink to their bellies again, a malodorous cloud hanging above their heads.

Fifth slaps the table. "Tell us, you! Where are they sending us, then?"

I worry at the cilia under my lower fronds, rolling them, pulling them, teasing them, until First knocks them away. "You've probably never heard of it," I say, wincing because I've hurt myself. "It's bad, you."

"I spit acid on them!" yells Second.

"I pinch their fronds!" First shouts. "I raise a trumpeting war call on them! So I do!"

Sixth points at First. "Shut up, you." Then he points at me. "Tell us, Fourth."

"Then listen, you." I lift myself from my belly, just a little. "The Universal Friendship Corps is sending me to one of those awful fringe planets." As always, I supplement my spoken words with a silent language made entirely of aromatic scents emitted from my Leelee gland, scents that my mates parse with their own twitching Leelee glands. My scented message hovers in the air between us, billowing, flowing, dissipating: *I don't care...I don't care...I don't care...I don't care...*

A lie, of course.

Second touches my biggest frond, then blasts me with his own scented message. *I love you, wife...I love you, wife...I love you, wife...*

Fifth's teeth clack. "Where are they sending us for the next four years? Tell us, you."

I hang my head. "Then listen, you. Its official designation is PP77. Peculiar Planet Number Seventy-seven. I'm to be their first Universal Representative." I don't have a single aroma in my Leelee gland to augment the words, because how could such a planet not be an outlier, an oddity, a universal laughingstock?

Third slides along the bench, wraps me in a warm hug.

"What's wrong with the corps?" murmurs Second. His scent suggests that the idiot who did this to me should put his droppings in their morning tea and brew them up for breakfast.

My mates. Oh! How I love them!

I might be leaving my home planet, but I am not leaving *them*. We are a team, the six of us. We are four females and two males, six parts of a whole. Like all Familias, we are legally, psychologically, and substantively tied to one another once the marital bond is triggered. Our unions are like none other in the settled universe: If we leave the immediate vicinity of our mates for more than a few hours, we will sicken.

Malaise, it's called. It starts as simple confusion and a general feeling of unease, then descends through well-known stages: a tingling in the tips of the fronds, a dulling of the sense of smell, a loss of balance. It ends an hour later, having transformed the stranded wife or husband into a urinating, weeping, speechless creature who, if not reunited with his or her Familia, will fall into a coma and, ultimately, die. Occasionally a person in the last throes of Malaise will go insane: raising our people's ancient trumpeting war cry, attacking and spewing stomach acids on the very people trying to help. Even so, Malaise is a small price to pay for something as magnificent as our plural marriages.

My mates and I are called Maalia Toorda, which means "beautiful matrimony" in the old language. Our secondary names are selected by lottery: we are Maalia Toorda *First*, Maalia Toorda *Second*, Maalia Toorda *Third*, and so on.

My name is Maalia Toorda Fourth.

I am female, neither the youngest nor the oldest. And I am entirely, quiveringly, frond-shakingly happy. Or I was until I received my posting to a nothing-planet.

My couchmates agitate the burrow's humid atmosphere with their fronds, bewildered and upset. I wave mine also, trying for a sip of clear air, but Sixth, the sweetest-smelling of my mates, has just emitted a smog so intense it makes my nostrils quiver. I don't have a favorite husband or wife, but if I were forced to choose a *favorite* favorite, surely it would be my honey-fruity-spicy husband Sixth, the youngest of us all. "But, Fourth!" he shouts, splattering me with a half-masticated salt-demon. "Your translating skills! What about your translating skills?"

"And your simultaneous interpreting ratings!" says Fifth, her middle fronds quivering. "What about them?"

"No one interprets scent-to-verbal as quickly as you!" adds Third.

Fifth turns bulging eyes to me. She slaps the table. "What's *wrong* with them?"

"I don't *know*!"

Second caresses my largest frond, his touch warm and full. "I spit on them!"

First rolls off her belly and lumbers to her feet, and everyone falls silent. I gaze up at her and find I can see the bristly hairs growing on the undersides of her fronds, a tantalizing view that in other conditions might make me giggle and pull her aside for some private time. But right now all I want to do is to bury my tear-streaked face in her belly and feel her fronds caress the hurt away. Instead I sit, trembling, as First clacks her teeth once, twice, three times, our people's way of indicating, *I have something to say, so listen, you, and parse my scents!*

Five attentive Leelee glands waver in her direction.

"Listen, you. This is no mistake. There must be a reason they want Fourth to go there."

I blink. "You think so?"

"Yes! You're too valuable for a nothing-planet. The corps is sending you right where they want you." She looks around the table. "Familia Maalia Toorda, parse my words! They need our wife for something special. Something secret. That's what I say."

"First is right, you," says Fifth. She scoops a plump salt-demon from the floor, brushes it off, pops it into her mouth. Its carapace shatters between her teeth and even from where I sit I can smell the creature's peppery-spicy juices, reminding me why a gift of a single large, perfectly formed salt-demon is the traditional way for our people to propose marriage: The risqué little things smell exactly like our word for (excuse my coarseness, if you will) *to fuck*.

"Of course I'm right," First says, looking at Second with narrowed eyes. "The corps needs her."

I'm not so sure it's a good thing to have the Friendship Corps need a person.

❋ ❋ ❋

A package comes for me.

The title engraved on my new bracelet-of-office reads, in coiled calligraphy, *Maalia Toorda Fourth, Universal Linguist and Wife.*

"And *wife*?" demands Second. "Don't they mean *wives*, plural, and *husbands*, plural?"

"It's a mistake," I say, rustling my fronds. "They know we're all of us going."

"They'd better." Second underscores his statement with a

puff of turpentine scent that suggests that he'll set them straight if they try to separate us.

Our departure date is announced.

We tell one another this is an honor, dubious planet or not; of *course* we are going. We sell our burrow, deal with the slag heap of our belongings, run about bidding good-bye to friends and family. As for me, I finish teaching my Advanced Alien Linguistics course, resign my post at the university, set aside my manuscript, *Profanity and Vulgar Language: A Treatise*, and begin my duties as a member of the Universal Friendship Corps. I set myself to learning the three alien languages of Peculiar Planet 77, and I tell myself I will be the best lingüist the Friendship Corps has ever seen. I will show them what marvels can be achieved by the best scent-to-verbal translator in the world!

So I will!

I will make Familia Maalia Toorda proud.

According to the Friendship Corps, the three primary languages of Peculiar Planet 77 are, in order of usage: African Termite, Java Script, and Mandarin Chinese—and what delights the languages turn out to be! What convoluted syntaxes they have! What primitive structures and odd rhythms, so far removed from any other language in the settled universe.

A pleasure, indeed, and I know: This is what I am born to do.

I throw myself into my studies, my fronds quivering as I babble dynamic strings of object-oriented codes that form Java phrases, as I drill myself on the lovely tones of Mandarin, and as I tackle the overly specific Termite vocabulary.

I love it all.

Especially Termite. Such a lovely, rich language! What other alien culture is so attuned to their surroundings that they have eighty-seven words for *dirt*? None other! My favorite dirt word—*tchmor*—is defined as *fine-textured, light-colored earth suffused with the subtle perfume of elephant dung*. Elephant-dung perfume! My Leelee gland quivers: I must make an opportunity for Familia Maalia Toorda to experience this wondrous thing, this elephant dung.

I only wish I were certain that what I told my Familia is true: that the corps truly understands about our plural marriage. For we are a rarity, even on our own planet.

❋ ❋ ❋

They come for us at dawn.

Vehicles painted the corps trademark green and dark green churn up great clouds of dust that the Termite Nation of Peculiar Planet 77 must surely have a name for.

"Come, you!" cries the driver of the first vehicle, a captain of the corps. He waves his green-uniformed fronds in our direction. "Maalia Toorda Fourth! Maalia Toorda Fourth! Come forward, you. Climb the ladder. You will ride up front with me. The rest of you will ride in back." His fronds unroll and stand straight out, pointing at us.

Why can't Fourth ride with us? someone scents.

We want to be together!

The captain waves away our rising scents. "Because I don't want my vehicle all stinked up, that's why." He blares the truck's horn once, twice, making me cringe. "Come, come! Put on your name patches. Why don't you have your name patches on?"

"I already know my name, you reeking Greenshirt!"

"Yeah!" someone adds. "Plug your mouth with your toileting frond, Greenshirt!"

What lovely insults; my mates are in fine form. If I weren't so nervous, the tips of my fronds might turn pink with pleasure.

Drink shit tea, Greenshirt! Drink shit tea!

This last burst of scent is from Fifth. Always the crudest, my pretty little Fifth.

"Names! I need names!" shouts the captain.

"Look, you." I open my pack. "I have the name patches."

"Good," says the captain. "Put them on. Then you"—he points to me—"*you* will ride in front, with me. There are things I need to tell you."

"Fine," I say, although it's not. Why must I be separated from my beloveds when I most need them? As soon as everyone has a badge slapped to his or her belly, I call for my husbands and wives to gather close. "Hurry, hurry, you! Scrum!" I look behind me. "That odious driver is clacking his teeth at us."

What got under his fronds, do you think? someone scents.

Third makes a deliciously rude gesture, crossing two fronds.

Ignoring the captain, turning our backs to him, Familia Maalia Toorda presses together, fronds wrapping fronds; so tightly do we cling to one another that not the smallest breeze can pass between us. Warm, soothing scents rise from our midst as we murmur loving words and caress one another's fronds. Our voices rise, chanting our people's famous hymn: "The Cherish Blessing of Sister Seven." Surely you've heard of it.

The sweet voices of my loved ones calm me. But still I am troubled. I raise my head from the scrum and eye the personnel vehicle. The journey to the space station will take most of the day—will we stop every few hours so my Familia and I can replenish our togetherness? Why can't I ride in the back with the others?

"Get in, you," the captain demands. "Take the seat on the right, Maalia."

"It's Maalia Toorda *Fourth.* My name is Fourth."

He flicks the tip of a single frond. "Whatever."

It is time to join him, but I can't move.

Sixth lays a frond across my back.

Third smells my unease also. With graceful fronds she traces the sign of the traveler over my head. *Don't worry, Fourth*, she scents after she finishes her blessing. *You are cherished. You are not alone. We are with you always.*

I make the sign of the traveler back to her, remembering with a rush of affection that of all my spouses, she was the one with whom the marital bond had been triggered the quickest. It still makes my fronds swell to remember how indelicately soon after we met she presented me with a matrimonial salt-demon.

"Go *on*, you," First says, giving me a gentle push. "Stop worrying. We'll be right here. The driver will let us be together when we need it."

I clamber with distress-paled fronds into the impossibly high cab of the personnel carrier, imagining my beloveds climbing into the back without me, dusting themselves off, taking their seats, arranging fronds, buckling on restraints. We are separated only by a thin metal wall, but they might as well be on the other side of the universe.

I tell myself I'll be fine without them. For a while.

Deep inside the vehicle a rumble starts up. I peer out the window, where dust billows so thickly I can't see the entrance to our home burrow as we pull away. *No matter*, I tell myself. As we top the hill beyond the town, the captain begins to speak. "Listen, you. We have much to cover. So listen."

I listen. And then I wish I'd never left home.

❊ ❊ ❊

I reek of bitter betrayal and sour cowardice.

My beloveds and I have today arrived at the gates of a new world—be it Peculiar or be it Fringe matters not—but as I stand at the viewing windows to gaze at it for the first time all I can think is: *I am not the person I thought myself to be.* For months I lived frond-to-frond with my husbands and wives inside our cramped interstellar transport module without telling them this rotten-smelling thing that caused my soul to putrefy more with each day that passed. How is it that *I*—who calls herself a linguist!—do not have words when they matter the most?

There is no language that would serve this cruel announcement I must make.

Fronds of Mercy.

Now we are there and it is almost too late.

As we step off the transport module and sniff the air of Peculiar Planet 77, I ignore the tantalizing scents. I tug on First's largest frond, clutch at Sixth, wrap one of Second's fronds in my own. "Scrum! Scrum!" I squeal, "Family scrum, right now. I have something to say before we go any further. Scrum up, you!"

"What is it?" says Second, his fronds still for once.

My stomach threatens to expulse as we huddle in this cloud of foreign aromas. I reek of shame, of sorrow, of embarrassment.

What's wrong, dear one? someone scents.

I can put it off no longer. "We're, ah…"

My mates, my mates. How can I do this to them?

Sixth tugs on my smallest frond. "We're *what*?"

"We're no longer married!" I gasp. "The Friendship Corps annulled it! They say the natives of PP-seventy-seven are religious—abnormally religious! They…they don't accept plural marriages. Especially multigendered ones." A shudder goes rippling through my fronds. "We're to consider each other no more than *friends.*" My fronds roll up so tight I think they are trying to withdraw right into my body. "I'm sorry! I'm sorry! I didn't know!"

"Friends?" whispers my sweet Sixth. "I can't be…friends with you."

First narrows her eyes, furling and unfurling her fronds. "You didn't *know*?"

Unbelievable! someone scents.

I am suddenly, shockingly alone, for my wives and husbands—my *former* wives and husbands!—have jostled and shoved and elbowed me right out of the family scrum.

Third pokes me with a stiff frond. "Fuck being friends! Fuck that!"

(As a linguist specializing in profanity, I should like to point out that *to fuck* and its countless permutations have been found in 96 percent of languages in the known universe. Many years ago I wrote a scholarly paper about this ubiquitous, multipurpose word. Under different conditions I would have loved my family's creativity: "Fornicating fuck-fronds!" "Fuck their fuck-beds!" And the plain but simple alliterative "Fuck your fricking feces, Fourth!" But now isn't the time to admire their profanities. Now is the time to wallow in abject misery.)

"We'll go into Malaise if we're separated," cries Sixth.

Second whirls to face me. "Or maybe we won't because we've been *annulled*?"

"I'm sorry!" I wail. "I'm so, so, so sorry!"

Fifth snaps her fronds this way and that. "They can't do that! They *knew* about us. They knew we were married."

Second scowls at me. "We never would have come if we'd known."

I wipe away tears. "And I wouldn't have asked you to. I'm sorry."

We huddle in a not-scrum, not sharing togetherness.

"You knew about this?" says Sixth. "You knew, and you didn't tell us?" His aroma has lost four or five strains of sweetness, and that hurts more than anything.

Liar! someone scents.

Coward! someone else scents. I can't tell who lobbed the insult.

Really, it doesn't matter, because it's true.

"Look, you," says Second, staring over me.

I turn around. Not far away, a crowd of natives seethes behind a barrier, oblivious to our family crisis, cheering and waving and calling out to us. I am their first-ever corps representative, the first delegate from the universe to visit in person, the first who is to stay on their planet. According to my mandate, I am to live with them and learn their ways. I am to pave the way for more interaction between our peoples. I am to teach them our language and compile usage notes on theirs. Of *course* they are excited. Of *course* they have prepared an official welcome for us. It's not their fault the corps has just torn apart my Familia.

Or was it me who did it?

"We have to go to them," I whisper. "And I'm so, so, so sorry! It wasn't supposed to be like this." I throw in a powerful aroma of contrition.

First takes me by a frond, hard. "You're not getting out of this so easily, you."

"Let her go, you," says Second. "We'll deal with Fourth

later. What I want to know is, how do we deal with *them*?" He gestures to the natives. "Wasn't someone supposed to greet us?"

"Yes, of course someone is going to meet us," I say, trying to pull away, trying not to panic. My stomach still feels on the verge of expulsing. "The Friendship Corps selected a native liaison for us, but I have no idea where he is. Stop twisting my frond, First! That hurts, you."

First pinches me and then lets go, but first she scents something quite rude in my direction and crosses her fronds at me. I scowl at her as the scrum breaks apart and we begin to make our way down the walkway. *You're such a bully, First.*

And you're such an idiot, she scents right back. *War trumpeter!*

Frond licker!

Acid spewer!

"Stop it, you two," says Third. She rubs at her Leelee gland, wincing.

Sixth nudges the others out of his way until he is at my side. He takes my smallest frond in his own, and I catch his *I-am-mad-at-you-but-I-love-you-anyway* scent, a private aroma meant just for the two of us. The soft buttery fragrance reminds me of his formal proposal to me, when, with an extravagant bow from the waist, he'd presented me with the traditional silver tray with one perfect salt-demon in the center.

Ah, that plump little salt-demon!

It was a beautiful specimen, aromatic, pinkly sexual, carnal even, laid out like a prize with its tiny legs fanned just so on the paper doily, its tail arranged in an enchantingly suggestive manner—*fuck me, my beloved*, it's message seemed to say. How wonderful that salt-demon smelled! Like a promise of things to come!

Sixth smells angry and disappointed, yet he loves me still.

Maybe I *do* love him best.

Now he caresses my frond, soothing away the hurt inflicted on me by First. "Fourth," he says. "You're supposed to be our leader. So lead us, you. Tell us what we should do. The poor things are trying to get our attention." Sixth points. "See, you?"

I see.

More natives are here to welcome us than I'd realized, many more. The shrill sound of their language rises around me, but to my dismay I don't understand a word. How can I, when so many of them are nattering all at once? I emit a horrified scent: Are they speaking Termite? Or Mandarin? It can't be Java!

I can't tell. I ought to be able to tell. But I can't.

The native greeting party has aimed strong yellow lights and visual recorder units at us, and banners too. Off to the side they've erected a decorated stage that reminds me of a matrimonial platform.

Third hisses. Second clacks his teeth.

I realize with a stomach-churning start that the natives have quieted and are watching us intently. Watching *me* intently, for I am the one wearing the silver bracelet-of-office.

"Fourth?" says Second. "We have to do something, you."

We're pressed together again, united against the onslaught.

Tell us what to do! scents Sixth. *You can do it, Fourth.*

I peer at the natives, feeling woefully unprepared. Where is our liaison? "Um. I've read about first contacts. This counts as a first contact, don't you think?" My fronds twitch. "We need to demonstrate good intent. We should wave to them, you."

As one, in perfect unison, Familia Maalia Toorda spins around to face the natives. We hold our largest fronds high over our heads in greeting. Our many upraised fronds make a lovely undulating motion, the best synchronized wave we've ever managed. I would be proud if I weren't so upset.

The natives at the front of the crowd raise their slender, too-short arms in the air and imitate our wave. "Look!" I say. "They're copying us!"

"Fourth!" Second is waving at double speed now, spoiling the effect. "I don't care about the idiot natives right now. You let us come all this way—*and you knew*?"

"No! I didn't know! Not at first! And then it was too late."

First's teeth clack so hard I fear she'll break one. Still waving, she turns to me. "*Was* it, Fourth? Was it really too late? Or were you just counting your underfrond cilia?" First rolls up her fronds, holds them high, then lets them slap at me as they fall—*whack! whack! whack!* My shriek of surprise is greeted by a swell of chatter from the natives, and clapping, and flashes of light.

First puffs her chest. "Fronds of Mercy! They liked that." She whacks at me again.

"First!" I holler, covering my head as best I can. "Quit that!"

The natives roar their approval.

"*Stop* it!" I howl, trying to avoid her by ducking between Sixth and Third. "Leave me alone!" I gasp for air, but it smells so strange here, I end up gagging.

Sixth and Third have joined First. They're flapping their fronds at me too.

"Ow! Not so hard, you! I already said I'm sorry! I didn't mean for it to be this way." I give Third a nice twisty pinch, and she jumps away from me, fronds flailing.

The natives, predictably, love it.

"Fourth," says Second, his voice grown loud and braying. "How could you *do* this to us?" He bobs up and down in place and I know what's coming, but he's too fast; I can't escape the spit he expulses at me. It's not stomach acid, just saliva, but it's unpleasant all the same—I mean, it's stinking smelly *spit*—and I howl at him and wiggle my hips and shake my fronds in anger. I can't help it.

He spits again, jeering and spewing insults from his Leelee gland.

I spit back, landing a nice big wad *smack* in the junction between his upper and lower fronds, even though I know I oughtn't. First contact is proving to be much more difficult than I'd been led to believe.

The natives break out in wild cheering. I turn an eye toward them. They are wiggling their hips and howling. A few spit in my direction.

Are they *copying* me?

Fronds of Mercy.

"Leave me alone, you!" I run away from Second, shaking my fronds to rid them of his saliva. "I didn't know what to do, Second. The driver said once I signed the contract it was too late; he said I couldn't back out." I spin in a circle, my fronds flying outward. "I said I was sorry, Second! What could I do? I signed a *contract*!"

Now all of us are spinning and flapping our fronds. We're like that sometimes, Familia Maalia Toorda. What one of us does, the others are soon doing also. Perhaps our marital bond isn't broken after all.

"Hey! Look at the natives," says Sixth, slowing down, his fronds coming to rest on his belly and back. "They think we're putting on a show."

"They think we're *performing* for them?" Fifth gasps. Smelling of acidic disbelief, she slaps two of her fronds over her head.

The natives clap their thin little hands over *their* heads.

Idiots...idiots...idiots... Fifth scents.

"Fuck this!" interrupts Third. She stomps her foot, which makes the natives cheer again. She stomps her other foot, then turns around in a slow circle, still stomping, fronds swaying. I can't help but think that my wife is stunning in this moment. Maybe *she* is my favorite wife.

Even though I don't have favorites.

The natives clap, and hoot, and call out to us. Some of them have joined hands and are kicking their legs and wiggling their middles, still imitating us—or are they *dancing*?

"Fuck the contract!" Third says when she is facing me again. "*I* didn't sign a contract. I think we should go back home. The transport module is still here. It's automated. We could, you know." Her smallest fronds are flipped up and pink at the tips, and she looks ravishingly beautiful, even though her mood smells ferocious.

First contact has gone wrong, so very wrong.

What am I supposed to do?

And then *he* shows up: our contact on Peculiar Planet 77, our guide, our liaison, our new best friend. I know right off who he is. He wears a green-and-dark-green Friendship Corps shirt, the twin of the shirt the captain was wearing back on our home planet. I find the familiar colors comforting in this alien place.

We call him Greenshirt.

* * *

Peculiar Planet 77 natives are smaller than we are, but they aren't *entirely* unlike us. Compatibility studies have been performed by our scientists: The aliens breathe the same air we do; they consume the same sorts of food and drink; they even reproduce in a similar manner.

There are differences, of course.

They smell strange. They sprout hair in the wrong places. They look so much the same that it's impossible to tell them apart one from another, or to tell male from female. Their limbs are stubby and their arms have squiggly little fingers instead of nice strong pincers—but the biggest difference, of course, is the crippled lives they lead due to their unfortunate lack of fronds and Leelee glands.

My mates and I lower our fronds and watch Greenshirt's approach. I slide between Sixth and Third, and they let me. They even drape protective fronds over me. There is a nervous twitching from every member of the Familia as we press together, almost but not quite scrumming. For the moment they've forgotten their anger.

"That's a male one, right?" says Second.

"I guess so…" I say, not sure at all. We've studied the human anatomy schematics the corps provided, but seeing the aliens in person is not the same.

He's awful, Fourth, someone scents.

They all are, someone adds.

I agree. I know I shouldn't. What kind of Universal Representative am I if I can hardly bear to look at the natives I am supposed to be making friends with?

Greenshirt begins to speak.

My fronds curl. Why don't I understand a word he says?

He speaks again, slower this time. Then, perplexed, he looks from one of us to the next.

"Go up to him, Fourth," urges Sixth. He nudges me with a frond. "Talk to him!"

Fourth! someone scents. *Do something! Say something!*

I step forward.

The crowd of natives has fallen silent, as have my husbands and wives. It's just me and Greenshirt.

"Greetings!" I croak in the Termite language, even though I am quite sure Greenshirt isn't speaking Termite. "This is truly a momentous occasion for our two peoples! My Familia and I are honored to be your guests!"

Greenshirt just looks at me, frowning.

"The *tchmor* of your world pleases us!" I yell, louder than I intend. All those lights, all those alien faces staring at me, making me forget half the words I've memorized! I take a half step closer to our liaison. "I say, what lovely *tchmor*!"

His smile fades. He shakes his head slightly.

"Greetings," I repeat, my voice shaking. I am still speaking Termite, and I know I am overpronouncing the clicks and glottal stops, but I can't help myself. "We are so very pleased to be here."

Greenshirt says something else, but still I don't understand. Maybe he isn't speaking Termite? "Good day, sir!" I say in Mandarin. "My family and I are delighted to meet you at long last."

He frowns.

"Hello?" I say in Java—even though I know it isn't Java he's speaking—but I try anyway, enunciating each marker of the sequence as precisely as I can, just in case, before giving up entirely. The Friendship Corps has given me the wrong languages to study.

Nice job, Fourth, adds Fifth, who is pointing a frond tip at me and sneering.

It's not my fault, I scent, and I know it smells pathetic.

Now what? someone asks.

"I have no idea," I say aloud, because who but my loved ones will understand me in this terrible and malodorous place? Is this what *tchmor* smells like? If so, I am sorely disappointed. "No…fucking…idea."

❁ ❁ ❁

Greenshirt leads us toward the raised platform, chattering at me as if he's forgotten I don't understand his language. Or maybe he doesn't know. He bobs his head and makes chuffing sounds that might be laughter, or might be digestive sounds, or might signal that he is about to break into an alien war ritual—how am I to know? Greenshirt smells nervous, and excited too, but what do I know of alien body odors? I know *nothing* about these natives, thanks to a Universal Friendship Corps that hasn't been friendly since the moment I climbed onto that personnel vehicle.

I will send a letter of complaint, I decide. A strongly worded letter of complaint. I may even have to add a profanity or two.

We follow Greenshirt away from our interstellar transport module and across a wide, open space. We cling to one another, surrounded by our own muggy scents—bitter alarm, sour apprehension, rotten fear. Clutching the fronds of the person in front and behind, exactly as youngsters do when playing Frond Train, my husbands and wives and I fumble and stumble our way up a much too steep staircase and onto the platform I'd noticed earlier. We huddle together as lights flash, flash, flash at us. I wonder: *Why* have the natives set up a matrimonial platform for this historic meeting of our two peoples instead of a more appropriate ziggurat?

What am I missing? What am I not understanding?

Sixth steps on my toes in an effort to get closer to me, and then I do the same, unwittingly, to Second. We are all of us reduced to a milling, many-fronded, many-scented mindless creature. Greenshirt has also mounted the matrimonial platform, and many other natives, but the bulk of the crowd stays below and does not join us. One of the aliens approaches the front edge of the platform, grips a vocal-augmentation device with his stubby, ineffectual hands, and begins to shout at us. A new round of flashing lights starts up.

"What is happening, Fourth? Why are we on a matrimonial platform?" Sixth whines.

"Maybe this isn't a matrimonial platform," I say. "It could be their embassy. Or a place of worship."

It's a gallows, someone scents.

"Fronds of Mercy, this place reeks." Third's voice sounds small.

"Oh! Oh!" cries First. "My Leelee gland! It's burning!"

"Mine too," says Sixth.

I look at him with one eye, and swivel the other toward the native who is still blatting and yowling at the front of the platform. It is an ugly language the native speaks, nowhere near as nice as the playful, expressive Termite—but oh, how annoyed I am that I cannot speak it.

The corps can brew shit tea.

And then drink it.

It's frond cancer! someone scents. *That's what it smells like here! I figured it out!*

"I want to go home, Fourth," says Fifth.

"Me too!" says Second.

"I do too," adds Third.

"Scrum! Scrum, you! Quick!" I holler, but it is too late.

A raucous banging of hands rises from the crowd; the speaker is no longer screeching into the vocal-augmentation device. We watch as he (or is it a *she*?) steps back from the edge of the platform and is lost to us, an alien face among many other alien faces. Familia Maalia Toorda shuffles closer to one another, our poor Leelee glands tucked as far as possible away from the stench of this place. I cling to Sixth, to Third, and I smell their fear, but my fronds quiver and shake: I got us into this but I can do nothing for my loved ones! I am powerless!

Fronds of Mercy.

Natives push in on us. With mouths open to display upper and lower rows of teeth—such displays are a sign of aggression on 86 percent of inhabited planets—the natives rudely shove their way between me and my mates, separating us even as we cling to one another, and I find that as oddly shaped as their bodies may be, these natives are surprisingly strong, and insistent too. It comes over me like a fecund fog, and finally I understand: These natives are *alien*. They are not *like us*. How did I not see this before? What kind of Universal Representative am I for not understanding this most fundamental of concepts? These natives are not funny-looking, funny-smelling, frondless versions of *us*. They are *other*. And now I am truly frightened.

"First!" I holler into the morass. "First! I can't smell you!"

A native gesticulates too close to my face with his twiglike fingers, making chuffing noises. He shows me his teeth again and again. He chatters at me in his impenetrable language. He tries to force me to take a drinking vessel with my toileting frond. How disgusting. How uncouth. Do these natives know nothing about *us*?

They want, want, want!

All *I* want is to scrum with my family. And to leave this place.

"Second!" I call, but he too is surrounded by natives. "Third! Fifth!"

First reaches for me. The tips of our fronds meet, then are torn apart by a passing native, a rudeness that would never happen at home.

"Sixth!" I cry. "Sixth! Where are you?"

Black-garbed natives move between us, shoving foul-smelling drinks and malodorous bite-size edibles at us, but I am not hungry. I am not thirsty. Eating ought to be done in the privacy of one's home, just like bed games. Can't these natives see that my fronds have lost their color and my stomach is a cilia width from expulsing? I reject one offering, ignore another, shove away a third—why do they think we would be hungry at a time like this? Why do they think we would eat in public, when such a thing is a gross display of rudeness?

And then the crowd parts, and Greenshirt is walking toward me.

I fluff my smaller fronds. I step forward. "Listen, you, Greenshirt!" I announce in my own dear language, not caring that the native will not understand. "I hereby give you formal notice: My family and I are leaving!" My voice does not shake; my words do not degenerate into growls. At this moment I do not care what the consequences may be. Signed contract be damned! "Greenshirt! Listen, you! I resign my post!"

"Nice!" calls Second, waving a pink-tinged frond at me. "Well said!"

But Greenshirt is not paying attention. Bowing from the waist, he presents to me a small silver plate with a paper doily on it. In the center of the doily is a salt-demon.

❊ ❊ ❊

A salt-demon!

What is this? Is this native mocking me?

It smells exactly right. The presentation is spot-on. This salt-demon is bigger than those at home, its coloration a more exuberant pink—but no doubt about it: This is a matrimonial salt-demon. It lies curled on its side with fanned tail, all charming and innocent, and erotic too, the very embodiment of love, of fornication, of all things sexual and amorous. Everyone knows this! People don't just...*eat* matrimonial salt-demons!

It cannot be clearer: Greenshirt—an alien!—wants to marry me.

My Leelee gland quivers. The salt-demon smells luscious and tempting, and familiar, just like a salt-demon ought to smell. Through my stunned haze I realize that Greenshirt is speaking to me. Baring his teeth, bending his lips in a most frightful manner, he tips the plate toward me, the better for me to see his offering.

The salt-demon slides toward me. I take a backward step. Greenshirt takes a step too. I do not understand Greenshirt's words, but to me his meaning is clear: He must be declaring his intent! He must be saying the formal words of proposal, quoting the marriage liturgy, reciting the nuptial poetry. We *are* standing on a matrimonial platform. I was right.

Fronds of Mercy! My stomach is about to expulse.

Suddenly it is all laid before me. I understand everything.

This is why the Universal Friendship Corps insisted I deny my plural marriage. This is why I wasn't properly trained, or briefed on local customs, or given the correct languages (although as a linguist, this makes precious little sense to me). It's been there all along, engraved on my bracelet-of-office, plain as the smell of rain, only I have been too blind to see it: *Maalia Toorda Fourth—Universal Linguist and Wife.*

And Wife. I am being sacrificed to a political marriage between our peoples.

"No!" I shriek. "Never! Never!"

I smack-smack-smack the plate from Greenshirt's hands with a frond, and the horrid salt-demon skids to the floor with a wet plop. I stomp on it! I dance with fury! I mash it to pulp under my heel! And then I spin around and whack Greenshirt across his ugly tooth-filled face. He throws up his hands and falls screeching to the floor.

"No!" I stand over him, pointing with all fronds. "We *will not* marry you!"

Shouts! Movement! Flashes of light!

"Fourth! Fourth!" calls Sixth from somewhere behind me. "What was that?"

What happened? someone scents.

I don't answer. I can't. Because I'm not sure anymore.

I stare down at Greenshirt. I'm panting, trembling, with fronds that don't know where to rest. What have I done? Oh, what have I done? These natives are more delicate than I had thought. How badly have I hurt our liaison? Have I created an interstellar incident?

He's not getting up.

And now Second is at my side, his fronds tight and red. "Fourth? What happened?"

"I'm…I'm…" I take a ragged breath. I point a trembling frond at Greenshirt. "He…he…that native, he proposed to me!"

"*What?*" Second spews a string of *fuck*-laden profanities. I cling to my husband, gazing down at the Greenshirt. He isn't dead; I haven't killed him; his chest rises and falls.

"We have to get out of here," I say.

I brought my beloveds to this place; I must take them home again.

But how? How am I supposed to help my beloveds in this incomprehensible place? I spin in a frantic circle. There are many, many more natives than there are of us.

You are our leader, Sixth told me not half an hour ago. *So lead!*

I fan my fronds high over my head. "Familia Maalia Toorda!" I bellow. "Make a train. To the transport. *We are leaving!*"

Quicker than I would have thought possible they are with me, my mates whom I love more than life itself. This whole thing is a mistake, this whole journey. I must make it right! I must beg their forgiveness for bringing them here. I feel all atremble with embarrassment and worry, but I can't fret about that now, not yet, not while we are escaping, not until we are safely on the transport and away from this rancid place. My wives and husbands gather in line behind me and I smell their excitement. With fronds held high and Leelee glands tucked in, and feeling grand, oh, so *grand*, we leap off the edge of the matrimonial platform.

"Fucking foreigners!" yells Sixth as he jumps.

I rather wish I'd done the same.

Frond-to-frond, we run to our transport. Natives shout after us, but we don't care.

Laughing now, my mates and I throw ourselves into the transport hatch.

"Take *that*, Greenshirt!" hollers Second, sticking his head out of the hatch. "You can't have her! She's *our* wife!"

And then I know.

They're mad at me, yes. And I have much to apologize for. But we are Familia and their anger is but a grain of *tchmor* lost in a mountain of love.

And it smells divine.

Crossing Paths

By Nancy Bonnington

My neighbor was a very religious man, which I overlooked in order to care for him.

The first time we met, he told me he was born and raised in the Northwest, and never had any notion of leaving, since we were living in God's country.

If we were in God's country, I thought, what did that say for the rest of humanity who were not as fortunate? Were they living in Satan-land?

I had that way of taking offense where none really existed. I know, looking back on it, that I was not a caring person, though a caregiver, and not a particularly forgiving person, though I expected forgiveness from others.

I was sullen mostly, overweight from a diet of white foods, and hated people for the sake of it. I figured life was a chore meant to be barely tolerated, and the point of it all? We would never find out.

I had not yet been in love. In fact, I had been accosted in a vacant lot at nine years old, brutally raped, my clothes torn from me, my attacker weighing three times my weight, pinning me to the ground and asserting himself amid threats of death or further harm. Having thus lost my virginity—which is how I saw it—I no longer had any need of a man in my life.

At eighteen I found myself alone, though not lonely. My parents had split up two years earlier, my mother moving to California, my father to Georgia, both inviting me to live with them, but neither actually caring whether I did or not.

I stayed put, therefore, found a room in a house, and my father sent me money from time to time. I lost touch with my mother, and for the most part I scraped a living by waitressing, phone soliciting, data entry—I had wicked fast fingers—and occasionally taking on a client for the simplest of caregiving chores. After all, I was not a real nurse, just almost a kid.

Jack's religion always struck me as a crutch for a weak mind, though I didn't dislike him. I learned he was ill when one day I met him at the mailbox. I hadn't seen him for some time. He was pale, skinny, and wearing a bathrobe that swamped his old body, his bony legs sticking out below.

"Cancer," he said, nodding at me. And he smiled.

I blushed because it was so obvious that I wondered what was wrong with him.

Pretty soon he had me over to cook and clean and do errands, like mail packages of his stuff to relatives. He said he would dole things out before he died rather than having them fight over it. He laughed about them fighting over it, so I knew he wasn't serious; I guessed he came from a close family.

Jack told me about the church he had attended when healthy, and how religion had saved him.

"I came home from the Vietnam War," he said. "Couldn't find work, couldn't fit in, took up drinking and just wandered around the streets looking for a fight. One day I was so down on my luck I wandered into a soup kitchen. They made us say prayers for our meals, which upset me a great deal, but I didn't turn down a free meal."

After about six weeks of praying and eating, Jack explained, he didn't mind the prayers—actually found solace in them. Then one day he was offered a chance to be baptized and save his soul. He felt the Lord move within him, which meant he would go to that church and get dipped into water—a grown man stripped of his dignity, like a baby, I thought.

"I wept before I even got to the altar," Jack said. He looked long and hard at me, like my father used to look when I came home late and a bit drunk. "It wouldn't hurt you to try it," he said. Apparently religion saved him. He found a job, married, raised a daughter, and lived happily ever after. Except that his wife and daughter were killed in a plane crash. But even that didn't shake Jack's faith. He turned his grief over to God and believed they would all be together in the end.

Jack made it sound simple, and at that age I thought maybe it had been for him.

"Let me give you something," Jack said the first day I had to help him walk to the bathroom. He closed the door and I waited, hearing him pee, and then led him back to the bed.

He reached into his nightstand and handed me a fistful of tickets. He could barely hold his arm up long enough for me to grab them out of his hand, he had grown so weak.

"Season tickets to the Seattle Symphony," he told me. "Have you ever been to a symphony?"

"Fuck, no," I said. "Sorry, I mean, I don't exactly get into classical music."

"Have you ever listened to it?"

"Yeah, like the theme from *Star Wars*, maybe," I said.

"Huh." Jack wasn't impressed. "Promise me you'll go to the symphony and use every one of those tickets for yourself."

"You mean if you can't make me a Christian, you're gonna make me a classical music lover?" I laughed.

Jack was too tired to laugh, but I knew he was amused.

"You remind me of me, back in the day," Jack said. "I carried a concealed weapon everywhere, didn't trust anybody, and hated. Hated, hated, hated."

"A gun?" I said.

"From the army. A souvenir of my former life," he added.

"Did you kill people in the war?" I asked.

"I have to assume I did," he said.

"You don't know?"

"I was a pilot," Jack explained. "I dropped bombs." He closed his eyes and wouldn't answer any more questions.

I snuck out of the room and let the nurse, Alyssa, in, who had been knocking quietly at the front door.

"How is he today?" she asked.

I liked Alyssa because she asked me questions about Jack as if I were more than a kid.

"He's tired," I said. "And pretty weak."

"It won't be long," she whispered to me.

I almost offered the symphony tickets to Alyssa, but then I figured it was sort of like a dying wish from Jack that I use the tickets myself. How bad could it be? I thought.

Several times that week I forgot about the tickets. But I had told my roommates about them. They were all 420-friendly and had nothing to do with culture, only because they were too stoned to hop the bus downtown, I guess. But they said, "Cool." Every one of them.

So that Saturday I washed my hair and pinned it up, put on a black sweater that showed some cleavage, black pants that weren't too worn-out, and looked in a mirror. It looked like I was going to a funeral, but it was the best I could do.

I took the number seventy to Benaroya Hall. I got there early and was nervous, my stomach churning, which was crazy. I was nervous about walking into a symphony hall. Maybe like an old lady would be nervous going to a Young Thug concert. I'm not sure.

It was crowded. The elevators opened to a long lobby, where there was a place to buy coffee and tables and chairs to wait for the show to begin.

I sat down, not wanting to spend money. Then I changed my mind and stood in line for a latte. I needed something to do with my hands.

"Excuse me," a man said. He bumped into me from behind. I swung around and looked at him. He was tall, slightly overweight, muscular, and had a fancy woman hanging onto his arm. He was looking over my head, trying to get the barista's attention.

I turned back quickly. I got my coffee and rushed to the women's bathroom, my heart beating aloud. I dumped the coffee down the toilet. I was so nervous I couldn't drink it. I was nervous because the man I bumped into was nobody ordinary—he was the same man who had raped me when I was nine.

In my wildest dreams I never thought I would be crossing paths with him again.

I didn't believe there was any mistaking it. I knew his face. Not that I dreamed about it recently, but seeing it suddenly there, hovering over me at the coffee stand, the same eyes and brows, the same narrow lips and pointed chin…I knew it was him, staring at me from half a lifetime ago!

I sat on the toilet for a few minutes and took deep breaths. I hadn't thought about him for some time. I even thought I was over the whole incident. Shit happens and all that.

He looked rich. Jesus. And with a lady who was all decked out like a princess.

He hadn't noticed me.

I heard a bell. *Ding-ding-ding.* And I wondered why it was ringing.

I peered through the stall crack as all the women in the bathroom gathered their purses, finished up their lips, and so on, and made a beeline for the door.

I hesitated, not knowing what to do.

The man hadn't recognized me. I could follow him, learn his name. I had never reported the rape to anyone, least of all my parents. I wasn't about to go through a sexual interrogation at the age of nine.

I checked my watch; the concert started in two minutes. The man would already be in the theater.

A woman wearing a red vest came into the restroom and began wiping down the counters.

I left the booth and brushed past her. Out in the lobby there were only a couple stragglers. Doormen were ripping the last tickets.

Without giving it any further thought I walked through the theater door, handing my ticket over, and hung back, pretending to search for my seat.

I saw him again. There he was, near the front. I recognized the lady for sure; she had her hair in a fancy tangle atop her head and a fur-lined collar on her coat, which was hung over her seatback. She was pretty, but mostly because she had money. Without all her expensive trappings, she might have been plain looking.

I sat down three rows behind them; that's where fate and these tickets had put me. I tried to take deep and slow breaths. Instead of relaxing, I began to think of murder.

Yes, murder.

I found that I was clenching a program, though I don't even remember how it got in my hands. I tried to focus on the concert notes, to glance up occasionally and make sure the man didn't bolt. No reason he would, of course.

It was an all-Mahler concert. I glanced over the program. Mahler, Mahler, Mahler.

The program said Mahler was a Jew born in Bohemia who rose through the musical ranks of Europe. He converted to Catholicism to secure a post as director of the Vienna Court Opera.

What would Jack think of that? That was more audacious than praying for a meal. That was really using religion to get what you want.

I glanced up and saw the man who hurt me put his arm around the woman, who probably didn't know she was sitting with a monster. I wondered whether they were married.

The lights dimmed, the conductor walked out, and the music began.

I have to say, if I had not been so obsessed with the sighting of my rapist, I would have liked Mahler. There were even moments when the music swelled with such force and emotion that I believed Mahler really got me. Sometimes it was beautiful, sometimes dark and scary. He knew right where my head was at!

But how could Mahler know I was sitting there contemplating murder?

There was an intermission. I knew it was coming because I'd seen it in the program. I made my way to the aisle as quickly as I could, and well ahead of my rapist and his lady. They were stretching by their seats, politely waiting for others to exit.

I cruised across the lobby, glad I wasn't wearing heels, and sat on a chair, which was conveniently hidden behind an architectural column. I could spy the exit of the theater without being seen.

I was developing a plan. I would follow him after the concert, the rapist and his lady. I would see where he lived. I would stalk him and murder him.

Then it dawned on me that they probably came by car, maybe even limousine. I was on foot. How could I follow? Hire a taxi? Tell the bus driver to "follow that car?"

And what would I do even if I could follow them? Hit him over the head with my purse? Shove his nose into his brain with my girly fist? Get real!

I became enraged by the hopelessness of my situation. I was too upset to be nervous any longer. The last moments of Mahler's symphony actually rang through my head, echoing the rapist's demise…then my own. Gustav had a way of ending a piece with such finality, like a person saying, *Just do it! Bam! Bam!* And then *Uh oh!* Fading into a disastrous future.

I glanced at a table to my left. A man was buttering a roll with a plastic knife. *A knife.* Could I stab the rapist to death with a plastic knife? Would I have to stab his lady too?

The thought of murder didn't bother me, but my inadequacies against a full-grown man…it was like being too short to reach some kind of lifesaving medicine on a high shelf.

Desperate, with my pulse throbbing in my neck, I thought about Jack and his medicine. He had morphine, which I knew could be deadly in a high enough dose.

While my feverish thoughts raced, the rapist came out of the theater, laughing and whispering to his lady. They stood in line for champagne. I could tell they were close, like new lovers. Definitely not married. They touched each other a lot, flirted like juveniles.

I could put morphine in his champagne, I thought. If I had a bottle of it right now, I could distract him, pour it in his champagne, and run away. Would that work?

I played the scenario through my head. Or course it was wretched. It wouldn't work.

The rapist and his lady were oblivious to my concerns. He kept leaning into her, rubbing her shoulder and brushing his lips against her cheek, as if he needed to whisper something in her ear too sexy to say aloud.

My stomach turned. I didn't want to watch him smiling, laughing, enjoying the evening any longer.

I left the theater. Outside it was drizzling and the wet felt good on my face as I waited for bus number seventy to go back to the U District. I didn't even care if he came out right then and saw me. I almost wanted to confront him without a plan. Just get it over with. Perhaps shove him in front of the bus. A cliché, but I did think about it.

❊ ❊ ❊

That night I didn't sleep. I had lost the opportunity to face my enemy. Maybe I could hire a hit man.

I thought about Jack and his religious zeal. I thought about

Jack fighting in a war and dropping bombs on villages. Men, women, and children. Maybe even American soldiers. They made mistakes over there, didn't they? And just now Jack was sleeping soundly, knowing he'd be dead soon and reunited with his wife and daughter because Jesus loved him.

"Heaven," Jack had told me, "is an amazing place. So much so that Jesus said it's beyond our comprehension."

Jack would have been useful to me before he got all religious. Jack could have killed the man for me, back when he was practically a mass murderer anyway.

I rolled over and over throughout the night, and twisted in the sheet and couldn't find a way to sleep. I wondered whether I would ever get a chance to see the rapist again. The bogeyman, the asshole, the big prick. I had a lot of names for him, but mostly I just called him the rapist.

By morning I was crazy tired and didn't want to see my roommates. I stepped under the shower and closed my eyes and felt the water flow down my head like a cracked egg. I felt my breasts and wondered whether I would get cancer there someday. I wondered whether I would someday find a huge lump too big to do anything about. Would I hire someone to clean the house and watch me die?

❊ ❊ ❊

"Did you enjoy the concert?" Jack was acting brave, propped up on a pillow. He turned his attention to me and smiled. His face was gray; his cracked lips were stained red. He had some drool in the corner of his mouth. He was talking low and slow.

"It was Mahler," I said.

"I know. What did you think?"

"I think he's pretty badass."

Jack pointed with his spiny finger at his bureau. "Open up the top drawer."

I wondered whether he needed a change of underwear. If so, that was going to have to wait for Alyssa.

I walked over to the bureau and opened it.

"That little book," Jack said. "Get it."

It must have been his old army pistol I spotted. It was black, cold, and heavy, and I had to shove it into a pile of socks to reach the book.

"It's a Bible," Jack said.

I hesitated.

"Go ahead; it won't bite you."

I grabbed the Bible, shoved the bureau drawer closed, and held it up. "This? This is a Bible? It's ridiculously small," I said. "Is it a Bible for midgets?"

Jack smiled, though he quickly dropped the smile and closed his eyes. "It's yours now," he said. "I wanted to give you something."

"Is it, like, condensed, with just every other word?" I should have said thanks, but I was on a roll. "Or was it written by little baby Jesus...in little baby handwriting?"

I should have objected to the gift I would never use, but it wasn't like he said it was a hundred-year-old family heirloom.

As if reading my thoughts, Jack said quietly, "I lifted it from a hotel in Hanoi some years after the war was over. It was the first one I ever read. It's pretty dang cute, isn't it?"

I thumbed through it, while Jack seemed to be falling asleep. The whole Bible fit in the palm of my hand. The edges of the pages were gilded gold. I glanced at my hands to see whether any of the gold had rubbed off. It hadn't. The typeface was small but very crisp. I could read the words clearly.

"Puh-salm One," I said.

"Psalm," Jack said. "The 'P' is silent." He tried to laugh, which came out as a crackle of spit stuck in his throat. "Psalm One… 'The way of the ungodly shall perish.'"

I snapped the Bible shut. "You better sleep now," I said. But I couldn't help thinking about those words after all: "The ungodly shall perish." It was like God was saying to me, "The rapist deserves to be killed."

Jack barely opened his eyes and shut them again. He was silent long enough for me to leave his bedroom. It was always good to get out of there, because Jack's room had the lingering smell of dank decay, even though I tried to keep the place clean. Sometimes I'd be home and still smell it on me.

I tottered around Jack's house, did the laundry and the dishes, took out the garbage, and swept the porch.

I was leaving his place just as Alyssa was arriving.

"Good morning," she said in the driveway. "How is he doing?"

"Being very religious," I said, holding up the small Bible.

"Anytime now," Alyssa said, shaking her head sadly.

I didn't want to remind her that she'd said the same thing the day before. And the day before that.

I went home, which was a short walk through the neighboring hedge. I danced up the porch steps, aware that I was hungry, and I bounded into the kitchen, full of life for no reason.

"Someone's happy," said my roommate, Shaun. His bloodshot eyes probably had just opened from a long night, though it was noon. He didn't seem very happy with himself.

While I ate, I tried to come up with a murder plot. I even

switched on the TV, because somebody is always killing somebody on TV.

Then Shaun asked whether I liked the concert and would I be going again. "You have season tickets, right?" he asked.

Oh, how stupid I am! How dumb! Season tickets! That's what rich people do...they go to every concert in the season. That meant the rapist would be there again, probably with his red-headed lady. If I just showed up to every concert, I was bound to spot him again.

Now all I needed was a plan.

❁ ❁ ❁

Three weeks after Alyssa started saying, "Any day now," Jack died. I was sitting in the living room thumbing through old magazines that Jack said long ago I should throw out. He was on a large dose of morphine. I got up to turn off the kettle and decided to go see whether Jack would want to sip some weak tea.

He was peaceful enough, his head turned slightly on the pillow, mouth partly open, face...well, relaxed, I guess. What are you going to do with your face when you're dead? His eyes were shut. I think that helped me a lot, because I was a little queasy. If his eyes had been open I might have thrown up.

"Oh, my God, Jack," I said out loud. "You're the first dead man I've ever seen."

I lifted one of his hands, because it was dangling off the side of the bed. His skin was room temperature, his arm a bit stiff. I laid it on the bed beside his body.

I had not expected to be the one to find Jack dead. I don't

know why not. I was there more than Alyssa, because she was the high-paid help and I was the inexpensive girl next door.

For a minute I wondered what to do.

Duh, call 911.

I glanced at my cell phone and thought to maybe call my roommates, or maybe call Alyssa. Finally I just called everyone.

After reporting Jack dead, I looked around the room for the first time, and I mean I really looked around the room. Jack had no pictures on the wall, save one shot of him in a uniform with a uniformed buddy, probably in Vietnam, and a tilted painting of Jesus. The Vietnam picture was a three-by-five wrinkled black-and-white, stuck with a single pin into the wall beside the small closet. Both men—Jack and his war buddy—wore rifles over their shoulders and looked younger than me, little boys on a scout trip. The rest of the bedroom was worn carpet, slightly yellowed wall paint, a table with a TV set, and a single bureau. On top of the bureau were a few get-well cards from Jack's church people and a pot of flowers that were wilted.

The emptiness of Jack's lonely death chamber struck me cold, and I almost cried.

I glanced at the bureau again as I heard approaching engines, and I swallowed. It's not that I hadn't been thinking this terrible thought, maybe all along, but now it was real.

I opened the top bureau drawer and rummaged for the gun. I glanced back to make sure Jack was really dead and not watching me, and of course he was really dead. My pulse quickened, as I knew what this gun would mean to me.

It was where I'd left it, tucked beside the socks. I pulled it out as engine noises drew closer. I headed to the living room. The police and ambulance and coroner—or whoever the 911 lady had notified—would be here soon. The engines now sounded a block away.

I grabbed my jacket off the back of the couch. I stuffed the gun in the jacket pocket and put the jacket on. I tried to act natural. The jacket felt heavy on me, as I realized I was now a felon.

Everything went okay. Alyssa came, because I had called her, and two of my roommates, and we all tried to stay out of the way as the coroner took Jack's body out on a stretcher. An elderly neighbor asked whether we wanted to say a prayer. I shook my head. I let him put his arm around me, though, because he really wanted to comfort us. He was the oldest one in the room. He was wearing a damp overcoat, which made me shiver.

That night I thought about Jack and, in my own way, I said goodbye to him. Not a prayer, but just a little conversation spoken to the ceiling in my bedroom. "Hope you were right about everything up there," I said. "I mean, I hope there's a God and that he's taking care of you."

The next evening I was in my low-cut black sweater and black jeans and my hair up and handing a ticket to the usher at Benaroya Hall. It was kind of like a dream, because inside my purse was the weight of Jack's gun. I'd checked it, after Googling how, and I knew it was loaded.

The rapist was there…his arm over the same lady, her same fur-lined coat slung over the seat a few rows in front of me, her intricate bun gleaming like a piece of waxed fruit.

This time the concert was movie music, and I almost laughed at the program in my hands, because on it was "Theme from *Star Wars*." I thought about Jack and how he might smirk, and I actually wished I could go home and tell him about it.

At intermission I hid behind a pillar near the bar. People swarmed around to grab a glass of red or white wine. I looked at a water pitcher brimming with ice; I was uncommonly thirsty but I didn't dare show myself.

The rapist emerged with his lady. They stood off from the bar some ways. They looked a bit bored, and nodded and mouthed words to each other that I couldn't hear. I was suddenly afraid that they would leave the concert. Maybe movie music turned their stomachs, and they would never come back again. Maybe I'd never have a chance to kill him.

The lady, dressed in a long silk skirt and bright green blouse, seemed to be excusing herself. Then she headed toward the double doors. Probably a bathroom run.

I might never get a second chance.

Not knowing what I would say, I trod across the patterned carpet and approached the man. He was wearing sharp trousers, a dark navy jacket, and a white dress shirt. Had he dressed for the concert or was he coming from a posh job?

"Excuse me," I said. I had to repeat myself, because the first time actually stuck in my throat.

He looked down at me, his expression of boredom now seemingly fixed for the evening.

This isn't going to work, I thought. *He's dressed way too nice.*

"I have to go home and...my car battery...my car..." I hesitated. Were others watching us?

We seemed to be alone in our own bubble. Most of the crowd was gathered in little twosomes or circles of four. Nobody was looking at us.

"My car won't start. I have jumper cables, but I'm not quite sure how to use them. If you could just show me... You won't have to get dirty—just point," I added. "Do you have a car here?"

He frowned and glanced around. I was clearly a nuisance. He still didn't seem to recognize me, for which I felt both relieved and angry.

"There's a really long line in the women's bathroom," I added. "If you're waiting for…And this will only take two secs. I mean, if you know anything about attaching jumper cables." I found myself blushing, fearing that I was too bad an actress for this role. Growing a bit desperate I tugged at my sweater so that it would reveal a great deal more cleavage. To my chagrin a boob nearly popped out.

It worked, because he stopped looking about for his date. And I doubt it was compassion for me that had him quickly following me to the elevator.

We got in, and I punched the button to the lowest level. He didn't look at me, but stared at the panel of numbers flashing by. I realized, as my pulse raced, that I was going to kill him.

We reached my target floor and got off. My heart was beating so loud I feared he could hear it. I brushed damp hair off my forehead.

He followed behind me a pace. I walked around in a semicircle toward a dark corner where one lone car was parked. I was lucky, because the corner of the garage was unlit. I glanced up at the ceiling without tilting my head, and noted that a length of lighting was out. How perfect. *Once again*, I thought, *it's like God wants him dead too.*

We stopped near a four-door car, which in the dark appeared gray.

"Open your hood," he said, catching up to me. "Let's make sure it's a dead battery."

"You can pull the latch," I said, pointing at the front of the vehicle. "I think it's in the middle. It's my dad's car."

The man stepped in front of me to find the latch. As he did, I reached into my purse; I had already unzipped it, and at home I had practiced reaching for the gun. I was able to have it in my hands before he even looked up.

I pointed the gun at him. He fiddled with the hood so long looking for a latch that I actually had to clear my throat to get his attention.

When he looked over at me, he straightened up and gasped. He raised his hands in the universal response to a holdup. "Jesus fucking Christ, you can have my watch, my car keys, whatever. What the fuck is this?"

I remembered all those years ago, me begging him, "Please don't kill me; I'll do whatever you want."

Suddenly I was more than just a felon; I was on a mission to teach this man a lesson. But I was breathing so heavy and scared, I started losing my spine. I started feeling sick to my stomach. Someone could come out from the elevator at any minute. Even though we were in a dark corner, the man could yell, and I could be caught and go to prison for life.

"Okay, throw me your wallet," I said, trying to improvise. I was aware that snot was rolling down my upper lip. Certainly I was more scared than he was. "And your watch."

He took off his watch—his hands were pretty steady, considering—and he reached out toward me.

"No," I hissed. "Throw it on the ground."

We both listened to the watch clatter on the cement floor, probably broken now.

Then he threw his wallet at my feet and raised his hands again.

I had one of those out-of-body experiences. It didn't last

long, but I saw myself holding a gun on this well-dressed man, who was amazingly cooperative. He didn't even move a muscle, while back inside my own body I felt my legs quaking and sweat dripping from my armpits.

This is going to be noisy, I realized. *Shit!* I hadn't even thought of that before.

What the fuck am I doing?

If I pulled the trigger, I'd have a minute maybe to rush up the ramp and out onto the street. Then I would run down Second until I could catch a bus. There were a lot of buses on Second. It wouldn't matter where the bus was going. But, of course, someone might see me.

I was shaky and nearly in tears. If I killed him I wasn't going to get away with it. And I'd seen those real-life prison shows. It was an ugly prospect.

"Take off your clothes," I said, shifting to an escape plan.

"Look here..." He shook his head like I was crazy. "Just let me walk away. Whatever is going on...I won't tell anyone."

"Shut up! And take off your clothes."

If the rapist were naked, he couldn't chase me through the Benaroya atrium. Not with all those polite ladies sipping wine.

He sighed and said, "Suit yourself."

He began to undress, and I felt a sense of peril, like I was a little girl again. I didn't want to see him naked. Somehow standing here with a gun, no matter what I said or did I felt like I was the victim again, not him.

"Throw the clothes over here."

He did. He was soon stripped down to his shorts, and without questioning it he stooped and removed them. "Is this what you want?"

He stood in front of me naked, with a brazen look on his face, dangling his underpants from his right fist.

Then he dropped them, raised his hands again, and stared at me. I caught a few feverish glances around the garage, still empty of other people.

I looked into his eyes, his dark eyes. Even if we were in sunlight, I knew those eyes would be black as eels.

"Get down on the ground," I ordered, trying to hold my commands steady. "And face the wall. Don't look at me."

"Why are you doing this?" he asked, too calmly.

"Because I know you," I said.

He drew his head back and gave me this look—not of recognition, but of pure spite. The light snapped on above—perhaps from a timer, or a motion sensor, or faulty wiring…or maybe it was all God's plan. Because I knew it was him then. For sure. My rapist. There was not the shadow of a doubt as we locked eyes.

❁ ❁ ❁

He was new in town, he told me. A new neighbor.

He was a stranger, true, but terribly friendly.

I had just hopped off my bicycle because the hill was too steep for me to ride. I pushed the bike and grunted, and then he had appeared by my side, as if by magic.

"Here," he said. "Let me help you with that."

He was exuberant, handsome, a toothy smile that nearly filled the lower half of his face

He pushed and we chatted. He thought I was very pretty, smart, and was interested in my life.

Near the top of the block we stopped. The neighborhood was quiet and near dusk. My mother would have dinner waiting.

"...a great big fort, for the younger kids," he was saying. "Do you like forts?"

"I love them. I used to have one."

"I was thinking of building it in that field." He pointed to the vacant lot beside us. "I'm an architect," he said. "But I could use your help picking out the best spot to build it. In fact, I'll hire you as my assistant."

As he pulled a $20 bill out of his pocket, my eyes widened, but I tried to downgrade my excitement. "Sure, I can help."

Minutes later we were stomping out a clearing in the tall grass and racing each other to make the most of it. The lot was sparsely treed, but yellow weeds and grasses as high as my head had grown unchecked in this undeveloped spot for as long as I could remember. The lot was, as the man had pointed out to me, a perfect place to build a fort.

We stopped stomping, broken stalks pasted to the tops of our shoes, and the stranger lay down in the clearing and heaved a great sigh of satisfaction. "Wow, perfect," he said.

He smiled and waved his arms and legs side to side, like making a snow angel, only there wasn't any snow.

"Try it," he invited me.

I caught his enthusiasm bug. I laughed too, and landed in the flattened weeds beside him. I made my own invisible snow angel. I noticed the sky was full of drifty clouds that were easy to make pictures out of.

I was just going to tell him about the Mickey Mouse hat I saw...

I don't remember all that happened next, except the sudden weight of him was on top of me and I couldn't breathe. I gasped for air as he covered my mouth. Buried beneath him, I was completely paralyzed by his strength. For a split second, maybe I thought it was a game.

But then my lungs were fighting too hard, and it was very serious. I tried to budge: I tried to roll over, turn my head, free my hands that were pinned above me. The friendly fort builder—the stranger, the architect, the new neighbor, whoever he was---was suddenly showing me a knife that had a serrated blade. He ran it past my eyes, back and forth, then he set it against my throat.

I felt the mild prick of the blade and wondered he if he'd drawn blood. There was no need for a knife; his weight alone would kill me.

"I'm just going to hold this next to your skin," he whispered in my ear, "for your own good. And if you're very quiet and don't shout, you won't get hurt."

His charm had fallen away as quickly as if the earth had opened up and swallowed it. He let go my hands long enough to reach for his pants, but I didn't move. I was too scared.

Our eyes locked, and all that remained of the stranger was a steely look of evil. That, and his scar. The scar was faint but it was there. It was an inch long from the side of his nose to his upper lip. And I remember wondering what had caused it.

Had some other child scratched him?

❁ ❁ ❁

No. There was not a shadow of a doubt. There was the same steely eyes and faint scar that had marked him as the robber of my childhood as our eyes met under the garage lights.

Now the man knelt down and took one last look at me—his

eyes narrowed to enemy slits—then he lay on his stomach atop the oil stains in the staff parking spot. He didn't move. "You'll regret this," he growled. "*Whoever* you are."

"You don't get the privilege of knowing my name, you son of a bitch."

"You're making a mistake," he hissed.

"Shut up!" I heard my voice ricochet off the concrete walls, then pure quiet. I kept glancing around the parking level. How strange that it was empty and quiet.

I was grossly aware of the silence mixed with the smell of a dank garage. Not the odor of urine, as you might expect, but stale, dank corners where bad things hide and never completely dry up. Like memories that stick forever in your mind.

I realized I was burning up. I looked toward the elevator and saw a large, industrial dumpster. I had to think, to not *lose* it. Panic would destroy me.

"If you move, I'll blow your head off," I said. I hoped my words sounded stronger than my nerves.

I backed up, one hand full of his clothing, the other pointing the gun at him. He lay still and compliant. Calm. Almost peaceful. Was he going to make a snow angel in the oil slick?

I walked backward, as fast as a person can without tripping. He didn't move. And when I reached the elevator I threw his clothes in the open dumpster. One of the trouser legs caught on the edge, and I struggled to free it for a moment. I tugged and tugged; then it came loose and I flipped it past the open lid.

I glanced about then stood in front of the elevator and punched the up arrow. Five, maybe six times. Then I listened for the sound of the carriage coming down, the familiar creak of pulleys in an echo chamber. But all I heard was a soft scuffling on the ground behind me.

I swung around to the blur of a shadow racing toward me—as fast as any mythical demon. *I had only taken my eyes off of him for a second, hadn't I?*

"You *cunt!*" he screamed, nearly on top of me with his outstretched arms. The insult shuddered down my spine like a lightning strike.

He came at me so fast I had no choice but to pull the trigger. I lifted my arm and squeezed all in one motion. Automatically...instinctively...purely to save myself, I opened fire.

The blast was the loudest thing I'd ever heard in my life. In my head, all the atoms around me shattered. My ears thundered, and the power of it all—the bullet, the noise, the emotions—unleashed tears that ran unchecked down my face.

At the same time as the blast hit my eardrums, the man's eyes widened—dilated pupils haloed in white registering the shock—and then he flew backward and hit the pavement. Eyes shut.

I wondered whether Jack had ever seen a man fall like that, but then Jack had probably never seen death from his airplane. Up close, it is something unreal that you wait to catch up with you. Something that you know will stay with you forever when it does.

I stopped breathing as time froze like a still-life painting. I waited for the man to jump up and kill me, a cheap stunt in a bad movie, but he didn't. I could see where the bullet had gone straight through his forehead. Blood spilled on the gray concrete. Blood spattered my shoes. Had I hired a professional hit man, the shot would not have been any deadlier.

For some reason, I couldn't move. I waited for the hand of a cop on my shoulder. I waited for my destiny, knowing the script of my whole life had already been written. But nothing touched me.

Finally, I willed myself to take a breath. I breathed in slowly, then exhaled. My pulse quivered. My head buzzed. The elevator door opened and I climbed inside. Halfway to the lobby I realized the gun was in my clenched hand. I shoved it into my purse with difficulty, my hands were shaking so hard. There was moisture on the edges of my purse where I had clutched it.

I exited the lobby onto Third Avenue and stepped on a bus. I didn't look at the number, because it didn't matter where I was going. I gazed through a stupor at the gray urban-scape that slid past my window—lit-up storefronts, homeless tents pitched under bridges, and traffic jams on overhead passes—and regular people. People had regular lives and were going about their regular business, but that would never be me again. That sudden separation from the rest of the world was perhaps the hardest feeling of all.

It would be a long while before my legs were steady enough to get off the bus and find my way home.

❁ ❁ ❁

Slowly and in a daze, I picked myself off the wilted grass. A rust-colored circle the size of a dinner plate marked the very spot that had changed me. My underpants were stained bright red and draped around my ankles. I pulled them up and drew on my flimsy trousers.

The man was gone. The road was quiet. The air was thick with a potential storm. Every bit of me hurt. My wrists felt broken, my knees displaced. My thighs were bruised and I ached in places that were new to me.

I sniffed and shook, every bit of me shook, as if a cold snap had hit our neighborhood. I couldn't stop shivering. Something was all wrong. Something was terribly wrong.

In the distance a dog barked twice. It was an unfriendly bark—mean-spirited—or maybe it was just very afraid.

I climbed up from the short embankment to the street, to find my bicycle leaning neatly on its kickstand. I blinked back tears, licked my lips, which I had bitten raw, and tasted the metallic flavor of my own blood.

Stupid, I thought. *Stupid, stupid, stupid!*

I touched the handlebars, rubbed the cold smooth steel on my palms, until my stomach dropped away. The wave of shame that hit me bit down almost harder than the rape, and I knew…I knew from that day on…I would never tell a soul.

❁ ❁ ❁

I went to Jack's funeral. In the news I had learned that the rapist's name was Kevin Wright. Of course, they didn't call him the *rapist*; they called him the *victim*.

I was scared, even at Jack's funeral, because there were probably cameras at Benaroya, and I would hear a knock at my door, and I would be arrested.

I had been so stupid. For a premeditated crime, it sure as hell wasn't *meditated* very well!

Jack had many people at his funeral, probably from the church. I didn't know why he died alone, or why those people visited only once or twice with flowers. Maybe even religious people got the heebie-jeebies around cancer. It occurred to me that I would not mind caregiving, maybe even being a nurse someday. I figured cancer was the worst of the diseases and I'd seen that already.

Alyssa sat beside me, wobbling on an unstable chair, and wept. She was patting my hand while tears came down her face, and saying, "Jack was one of the good ones."

Although I was invited to stand up and speak, I didn't. I wasn't sure what to say about my experiences with Jack. He was my first dead man. But not my last, obviously.

❁ ❁ ❁

The next day, I was arrested. Nobody had to knock on my door. I was strolling down a sidewalk in my neighborhood and a police car picked me up. It was that simple. I squinted at a bright sun and then ducked my head into the back of the squad car, knowing I wouldn't see the sun for a long time. I was in handcuffs, though I don't even remember them cuffing me.

Was it murder or self-defense? That was the question in court. I told the story of how Wright took advantage of an innocent child. In the end, I didn't want to kill him. "Even if he was raping other little girls," I added. In the end, what I cared about was my own skin. I would never have harmed the asshole, *Puh-salm* One or not, except that we crossed paths. And crossing paths—I looked up and down at the jury—may have been God's plan all along.

I would have gone to school, I think, and learned to be a nurse, yes, or a nurse's assistant. I would have let him go to the next concert and the next, with his lady on his arm, had he not lunged at me. He should not have lunged at me. It was poor judgement on his part.

And as for other children, they would have continued

getting hurt—transformed into their own bleak futures, untouchables in their own heads, and on and on. Ad infinitum. For I'm certain that throughout this world, where sin is a permanent fixture, the beasts of mankind rarely perish.

Despite what Jack would have said about all this.

Evolution, Accelerated

By Susan Whiting Kemp

A threespine stickleback fish crawled out of the lake on its stubby fins as awkwardly as a slug on crutches. It sucked at the air through thin lips while its gills gaped uselessly. The sticklike fins gave out, and the stickleback flopped to the sand. The fall—a scant two centimeters—didn't seem dramatic to us, but was fatal for the fish, since it couldn't organize its fins to lift itself once more.

The moment the stickleback expired, three more emerged. These three drew long, slow breaths, as if they'd always lived on land and were happy to be back. With their club-shaped feet, they plodded over the sand with more seeming self-assurance than the first stickleback.

We didn't realize the ecological importance of the walking stickleback fish immediately. After all, any deep ocean documentary portrayed amazing species that biologists had only recently discovered. Transparent, pulsating creatures that lit up like Syfy channel spaceships. Worms that endured thousand-degree temperatures. An octopus that could shape-shift itself into a snake or an angelfish in an instant. In the realm of spectacular wonders, the three-inch gray stickleback was barely noticeable, even taking into account the three tiny dorsal spikes to fight off predators.

However, the sudden evolution of the stickleback was momentous not only in speed, but in volume. Within a few days many more threespine sticklebacks climbed out of the lake. Some survived; some died. Birds, cats, dogs, and raccoons tried to eat them, but got stickle-stuck. We wore shoes at the lake to keep from getting speared, and walked carefully even with shoes on to keep from squashing the desperate-looking crawlers.

Within a week so many sticklebacks had emerged, scientists calculated that all the sticklebacks had now evolved and left the lake. By then politicians and the media speculated that their evolution was caused by some kind of toxic chemical.

The lake was quarantined. We had already stopped going there because the odor of rotting sticklebacks remained on our skin even after we rubbed ourselves with soap or lemon. Instead we frequented the beaches on our glacier-carved estuary, where there were no prickly fish bodies on the shore.

However, one day a purple starfish crawled from our estuary onto the beach. It traveled quickly, unlike a normal starfish. Then an orange one emerged, traveling over the sand smoothly and efficiently, as if it had purpose. A cocker spaniel barked and nipped at it until it flipped over. Its multitude of tube feet were abnormally long and rippled in a single direction, like wheat stalks blown by a west wind.

The ratfish emerged next. We had never heard of them and were astonished when a biologist told us there were 200 million of the snouty, green-eyed fish in our estuary. Once they began trudging out, however, we believed her. The ratfish kept coming, in masses and clumps. We backed up off the sand and onto the road for fear of being engulfed by the pale, slimy creatures.

From the height of the road we examined the water, hoping to discover a clue as to why the starfish and ratfish had evolved. Many of us assumed radioactive materials had contaminated the water, and thought if we saw the water glowing, we would be right.

The water didn't glow, but snow globe–size bubbles rose from its surface and floated above the salty water. Odd, coagulated strings hung from the bubbles. When we realized the bubbles were jellyfish and that they were floating toward us, we headed for our cars, bicycles, and homes before the stinging tendrils could trail their poison across our bare shoulders and faces.

Other creatures emerged and traveled overland. For a time we watched the waves of migration from our windows, not daring to step outside. We were afraid of many of the creatures, like the sea slugs, because their audacious color combinations signaled that they might be poisonous. Baby blue and hot pink. Basketball orange and punching-bag red. Neon green and grape-jelly purple.

The wolf eels and moray eels terrified us as well. Some evolved feet and legs. Some didn't. All slithered and slinked and looked at us with evil intent.

The deep-sea creatures were the most disturbing. They traveled at night, the sun too bright for their bulging eyes. Headlight lanternfish with bioluminescent lures staggered along, confused in the streetlight glare. The fanfin sea devils worked their oversize jaws, and walked on stilted legs, like fishy zombies.

Other sea creatures didn't frighten us. Rather, they threw off the natural order of things. We weren't used to seeing salmon and trout crowded around puddles, ponds, streams, and swimming pools to drink, looking in rather than looking out. To us, that was like seeing a photograph negative.

We weren't used to seeing hordes of seahorses climb into our trees and bushes. They preferred evergreens, self-ornamenting them as if they were Christmas trees. They nibbled the pine needles and holly leaves until something startled them, then camouflaged themselves, like lights turned off.

We tried to match the fish we saw to photos from our computers. We excitedly identified the yellows of the copper rockfish, the reds of the painted greenling, the whites of the grunt sculpins, and the domino spots of the kelp greenling. After days of this we grew weary and stopped marveling at the diversity of colors, sizes, and shapes.

We also tired of thievery. Sea creatures were particularly adept at squeezing through the holes and cracks in our buildings. The octopuses roamed through our houses and opened drawers, cupboards, refrigerators, and jam jars. Tiny fish scuttled like cockroaches through our walls and hid in our cupboards, boring into packages and feasting on the contents. Plankton hovered in our living rooms like gnat clouds, filling the space and chasing us to other rooms.

The noises the new land inhabitants made disconcerted us. Roars, clicks, grunts, squeaks. Some called to one another with mournful cries that carried for miles. Sometimes the human ear didn't register the sound consciously, but when a chill came over us we could tell that some odd creature or other was making its way along the road or through the yards, fields, or woods.

We weren't alone in our plight. Communities throughout the world experienced the same problems we did. Places more distant from water had fewer fish visitors at first, but it didn't take long for them to become overwhelmed as well. Mathematicians explained the lack of space by comparing ratios of the two-dimensional Earth surface with the three-dimensional ocean that covered three-fourths of the globe, but we could see it for ourselves by the masses of fish that jostled about for space.

We debated about what caused the sudden transformation. Some said global pollution; some said God. Some made hopelessly elaborate theories involving a combination of natural selection, internal chemistries, and water pH.

Scientists tested the water and descended in submersibles to look for the cause of the mass exodus from the world's water bodies. They had plenty of theories but needed time and data to substantiate them.

We demanded help from our local government, which supplied snowplows to clear the roads. We called them fishplows, and watched them slowly urge the complaining fish off the roads.

We emerged from our houses to resume our lives, carrying umbrellas to fend off the jellyfish, and tying perfumed scarves over our noses to mask the smell. We accidentally stepped on cuttlefish, which were experts in camouflage and liked to snuggle themselves into gravel, lawns, and gardens. We misstepped and they sprayed ink on us and scuttled off.

The fish left bits of themselves everywhere. Bright red scales glittered in ditches. Shards of transparent skin, like fairy wings, were draped across bushes. Discarded fins stuck up from lawns like tiny boat sails. A gelatinous goo of fish eggs lined paths, like piping on a birthday cake.

Just as it seemed we would be able to cope with our newly changed world, larger fish began to emerge from the water, some as heavy as five hundred pounds. Tuna, swordfish, and marlin evolved hooves, and charged like buffalo through our cities and towns. Swordfish and marlin snouts caught in fences that ultimately couldn't hold them back, even when electrified.

Land mines and other explosives were barely effective against so many fish, so we fortified our houses with concrete and steel until we felt as if we were jailed inside. We cheered when each type of fish moved to more promising territory, and fretted about the ones that refused to move on.

Then came the sharks. At first they only attacked other former marine animals, but soon they favored cows and pigs. As was the case when we used to swim among them in the sea, they avoided humans for the most part, but attacked us when we were at our most complacent. We paid shysters large sums of money for shark repellent that made us stink like chemicals, rejoiced when it worked, and raged when it didn't.

Pods of hundred-foot-long blue whales staggered through our towns on stegosaurus-style legs. They destroyed any remaining fences and gardens, and crushed our wooden houses in search of the plankton that fluttered in our living rooms no matter how hard we'd tried to eradicate them.

With time the most reclusive ocean inhabitants emerged, the ones we'd known as sea monsters. Some of us had once denied their existence, while others had hoped and made documentaries with grainy photographic proof. Now thousands of dragon-headed creatures emerged as if to prove the eccentrics right. The creatures' long, scaled tails had a tendency to curl themselves around light poles, tree trunks, and overly curious biologists.

By the time scientists calculated that all the fish in the world's water bodies had evolved and climbed onto land, our lives and homes were in ruins. We were crowded into shelters. Our normal food sources were cut off, so we ate the fish, but evolution had made them tough and bitter-tasting. We'd been poisoned, poked, shocked, sprayed, bitten, and nibbled. We were tired.

We plotted ways to un-evolve the fish and force them back into the water where they belonged. We watched for signs of weakness and talked of taking back our land, but it was all talk. We were too demoralized, traumatized, and fractured to act on our grandiose plans.

We had always loved the sea. We built our cities next to it, and made sure our houses had a view of it. We marveled over the endlessness of length we couldn't see across, and the depth we couldn't plunge to. Now we loved and marveled over it even more. We went to its edge and watched it, presumably to find a reason for the mass exodus, but in truth to be close to it. We gazed into it as if we might be able to see the kingdoms the aquatic animals had left behind.

Hordes of us crowded the water's edge, soaking our tired feet and scooping the water with our hands, heedless of any damage it might do to us. The stinking air was thick and stifling. We felt filthy, dried out, heavy. We desired the shimmering emptiness of the water. We longed for the feeling of compression it would bring as it surrounded our bodies.

We swam in the water, weightless and free. We dived underneath the waves, remaining longer and longer, until the day we no longer needed to surface. The light beams filtering through the water cut and stung us, so we descended from the sunlight zone to the twilight zone, and from there still further to the midnight zone.

We felt our eyes enlarging, growing to a proper, more comfortable size. Parts of us that we didn't have a name for opened up and invited the water in, while other parts pulsed it out. Our sense of separateness dissipated, and we understood the water as if it were a part of us. We comprehended its currents and temperatures as if we had generated them ourselves, and perhaps we had.

We descended still further, to the abyssal zone, where we cavorted in underwater waterfalls. We gravitated toward the heat of underground steam vents, watching their crystal chimneys and black smokers, and brushing against feathery, long discarded, tubeworm plumes.

We slipped down into the ocean trench, finally feeling that we'd come home. We became luminous and transparent. We spent our days delighting in our radiance, and feeling the cooling comfort of the water pressing on us, holding us together, giving us a reason for being.

Laura's Island

By Evelyn Arvey

"All subjects claimed that an important function of their daydreaming was twofold: a disconnection from the pain of living and a magical transformation of misfortune into desirable experiences."

From "Maladaptive Daydreaming: A Qualitative Inquiry"
By Eli Somer, PhD

It was Mitch who gave me the island. He gave it to me on a damp and listless Thursday, a Thursday so hot that his body mostly refused to function, as happens to people with multiple sclerosis. He was miserable. Because he was miserable, so was I. The two of us were slumped on our recliners, waiting for the afternoon to drag to its sorry end, waiting for me to muster enough energy to haul both of our pathetic selves to bed.

"Mmm," Mitch said, waving a *Neurology Today* at me. "Look at this. It's about that new MS drug."

He handed the magazine to me. The medicine was meant

for the other, more common type of multiple sclerosis. The type Mitch didn't have.

"Did you read it?" he asked a minute later. "What are you looking at?"

"This." I held up the magazine, folding it so only the glossy advertisement opposite the article showed. "The island is pretty, isn't it?"

"Mmmm."

I stared at the image: a low-lying island, an atoll maybe. A line of palm trees leaning over a strand of golden sand just wide enough for walking. Turquoise waters rippling in a wide lagoon. A fallen palm lying half-buried in sand and pebbles, the perfect place for me to sit and contemplate the breakers on the far side of the lagoon.

See? I was already picturing myself there.

A pharmaceutical advertisement was splashed across the sky of this idyllic place: *A New You! Try Our Herbal Drugs.*

Mitch interrupted my reverie. "We should go to bed. You turned on the air conditioner?"

Of course I'd turned on the air conditioner. Had I ever forgotten?

I took very good care of my husband. In a few minutes I would help him to bed, which was quite an undertaking: I'd grip his gait belt and help him from his easy chair and into his wheelchair. I'd help him from the wheelchair to the stair lift and then into his upstairs wheelchair. I'd help him relieve himself. I'd help him change into his nightclothes. I'd make sure he took his handful of pills. I'd lift his legs onto our bed, and then I'd gently manipulate them, stretching his tight-as-piano-wire hamstrings while trying not to hurt him. Then I'd massage the knots out of his shoulders, his arms, his legs.

I'd do all of that and more.

But not quite yet. I wanted to do something else first.

I went up to our room and taped the picture to the wall beside the bed. *I just want something pretty to look at*, was what I would have told Mitch if he'd asked me what I was doing. *I want to fall asleep pretending I'm there on that island. Not here.*

On the other hand, maybe it was better if he didn't ask. There were things Mitch didn't need to know: I was so very tired. I was so very unhappy. Worse, I'd begun to realize I didn't like my life anymore and I felt guilty for even thinking that. It wasn't Mitch's fault that his disease had made him dependent on me. My life revolved around Mitch's illness; it had to. I was his caregiver.

It wasn't his fault. It wasn't.

I sighed; the picture I'd just taped to the wall wasn't straight—the right corner hung low. I unstuck it, bent the paper forward to put another piece of tape on the back, and then I saw it: a handwritten note on the top right corner—*Laura asked for it three times, and she was heard.*

What was this?

A message scrawled in felt-tip marker on the back of my beautiful island?

This might be a good place to mention my name: Laura Wilson.

My name is Laura.

❁ ❁ ❁

I stared at the picture of the island when I woke up the next morning, careful not to squirm because as soon as I moved, my day belonged to Mitch. I lay on my side, studying the image

I'd taped to the wall. I counted the trees: eighteen in the foreground, many more in the background. I took note of every color in the lagoon: the luscious blues, the impossible greens, the succulent turquoises.

Such a beautiful place. If I were there, I would spend an entire day doing only what *I* wanted. How novel that would be, to do nothing at all! How long had it been since my time had been my own?

I want to go to there, to that island, I thought, yawning, still half-asleep, eyes closing on their own. *I really, really want to go there. I want to go to that island so badly.*

❁ ❁ ❁

And then I did.

When I opened my eyes everything was different. My bedroom was gone. The hallway was gone. The window looking out on the Douglas fir was gone.

What?

I reeled out of bed, yanking the covers with me. "Mitch! Mitch!" I shrieked, but he didn't answer because *he* was gone too.

The island, I thought. *I'm on the island. This isn't possible!*

I fell back to sit on the edge of the bed, clumps of sheet still gripped in my fists—my bed, minus my husband, was the only thing that had followed me to this place. I sat there taking in my new surroundings, reminding myself to breathe. The air smelled exactly as I'd imagined it would: of sunshine, of ocean, of warm growing things. I reached out and ran my fingertips over the woven matting that now covered the wall near the bed. The bumpy, knobby texture and soft *rat-tat-tat* of my fingernails convinced me more than anything that something marvelous had just happened.

Except…maybe it hadn't.

It all seemed so very real, but what if it wasn't? I'd been desperately wishing for my dismal reality to be replaced by something better, something tropical, something where multiple sclerosis wouldn't be a part of my life. So…maybe I was hallucinating. It all looked so real, but maybe I'd tumbled into a powerful daydream?

I stared out the window, taking in glimpses of glimmering ocean through the trees, following flickers of brightly colored birds as they darted here and there, watching a green gecko with yellow toes scramble up a palm tree, and then down, and then up again. No daydream included geckos clambering in palm trees, or wall-coverings that left tiny bits of rattan under the fingernails, or the salty-tangy smell of the ocean.

This was no daydream. This was real.

I looked around. What had been my bedroom was now a one-room, light-filled cabin. My bed and a small bathroom with a half-open door were at one end, a kitchen and eating area in the middle, and a sitting area opening onto a covered lanai at the far end. Screened windows on all sides let in warm breezes and golden light.

In the same place where I'd taped the picture of the island last night was an image of my own home. I leaned forward. Written in the sky over the house was another message: *Welcome! Tell no one. This place is for you alone.* In smaller writing, underneath: *Laura, you already know the way home.*

I stared at the picture, twisting the bedsheets in my hands.

The picture was wrong. I didn't know the way home!

I looked away, anywhere but at the wall, and noticed things

about the room I hadn't seen before: a coffeemaker, a pair of yellow flip-flops beside the door.

Maybe I do know the way home. I took a deep breath and sat up straighter. I got here by saying I wanted to be on the island. Maybe I just had to say I wanted to go home three times? I gazed at the picture, knowing I was right. *Okay. I can do that. Only…only I can't tell Mitch where I've been.*

Which made me gasp.

Mitch!

I'd all but forgotten about him! Was he okay?

What kind of caregiver was I? Was Mitch lying in a broken heap on the floor because I'd stolen the bed out from under him? I had to go back home! I'd been on the island for about five minutes; anything could have happened in those five minutes. I put my hands flat on my knees and stared at the image of my house.

I want to go home. I want to go home. I. Want. To. Go. HOME!

And I went home.

❊ ❊ ❊

It was easy. I closed my eyes and when I opened them again I was home. Mitch was exactly as I'd left him, sprawled on his side of the bed, asleep still.

How many times did I go to the island that first day? Twenty times? Fifty? Like a Ping-Pong ball, I bounced back and forth, back and forth. No matter how long I lingered on the island, only one second passed at home.

Mitch never noticed a thing.

❊ ❊ ❊

Or maybe he did.

"There's something about you..." Mitch said as we were eating breakfast. "You seem cheerful this morning."

"Do I?" I sliced a strawberry and slid the pieces into his bowl.

"It's nice."

He ate his cereal. I buttered my toast.

"Laura," he said after a while, "we need to start looking again. This time for real."

We needed to find a new place to live, a wheelchair-accessible place. The locations we'd already visited—the condos with cheap wooden paneling, the apartments that were even less accessible than our own house, the senior retirement complexes with roving old ladies and bingo nights—they made me wince, but Mitch was right. The house we'd lived in for twenty years was still functional for his needs, but only just barely. Soon it wouldn't be.

"I guess so," I said. "Okay."

Mitch looked out the window, then sighed. "How about when it's not so hot out?"

"Next month, maybe."

"Next month."

We shared a look. It was the same thing we'd said four weeks ago.

All day long I stayed near Mitch and helped him with everything he wanted or needed until it was time to go to bed and I could go back to my beautiful little private island that was most decidedly *not* wheelchair accessible.

❁ ❁ ❁

Welcome, Laura, read the first page of a book called *Laura's*

Island Paradise that I found in the cabin. *Make yourself at home. You will find your kitchen to be restocked every morning with fresh selections for your enjoyment.*

I looked up as a brilliantly plumed, long-tailed bird landed in the tree next to my lanai. It regarded me with a tilted head, as if it had never seen such a thing as a too-pale woman in a cotton sundress sitting on a deck chair with her feet up, sipping jasmine tea, nibbling on sliced fruits, and humming.

"Hi, you," I said.

The bird chittered.

Something moved at the base of one of the palm trees—a coconut crab? It was huge, as big as the pillow on my bed. I recognized it from my new book.

"Hi," I said.

The stalks on top of its head waggled.

You will be glad to know there are no mosquitos, sand flies, rats, snakes, lionfish, jellyfish, or sharks on your island nor in the surrounding waters.

"You won't bite me, then?" I asked the bird. It fluffed red and blue feathers and came closer. I plucked a grape from my fruit dish and set it on the far edge of the table.

The animals of your island are tame and will leave if you clap your hands. None will enter your cabin uninvited.

The bird hopped closer.

"Are you tame?"

It chirped.

"You know what? Mitch would love you. He really would."

I had plans for this, my first full day: As soon as I finished my tea I would go exploring. I'd circumnavigate the island on a network of trails, a hike that, according to the book, would take an hour or so. When I finished that, I'd find the location where the original photograph of the island had been taken. Perhaps I'd dip my toes in the ocean. Perhaps I'd do some sketching in the blank-paged notebook I'd found in the cabin.

Perhaps I'd start coming back to life.

Was this the reason for the island's existence? For me to find happiness again?

A nice thought, but I was sure there was more. There had to be more.

The bird fluttered to the table. "Go on; take the grape," I said.

He made quick work of the grape. Just to see what would happen, I clapped my hands softly. He hopped backward; then with a final chitter he flew away. I knew he'd be back; he was my first friend on the island.

I read the final words of the introduction.

Make this island your own. Come as often as you like. Stay as long as you need to, so that you may be a good caregiver to the one who needs you. May you and those you love be forever healed.

That last line? It may be the most beautiful thing I'd ever read.

❁ ❁ ❁

Over the next few weeks I learned more things.

I found out that small items tucked inside my bathrobe pocket, such as ginger candy or a packet of tea, would make the jump to the island with me.

I learned that the island animals would come to me for minor injuries, and I would try to help them by following the first-aid section of *Herbal Remedies*, the second book I found in the cabin.

I discovered that I enjoyed making simple poultices following directions in the book. I used the leaves and twigs of bushes that grew right outside my cabin, and I loved the way the concoctions infused the room with an earthy, spicy aroma as they bubbled on the stove.

I learned that I missed Mitch terribly, especially at night when I was alone in my little cabin in the palm trees. I learned that I never stopped feeling guilty for leaving him behind, for cheating on him emotionally with a magical island, for leaving him out of a huge part of my life.

Most of all, I learned that lounging on my lanai, walking the trails, playing with the wildlife was wonderful, but it wasn't enough. Where was my mission?

I needed a mission.

A mission would give me a reason to be on the island, a reason for everything.

❁ ❁ ❁

"No, really, you do seem different," said Mitch, peering sideways at me from the passenger seat of the car.

"Oh?"

"I can't put my finger on it exactly. But you do."

Mitch and I were on our way to visit an assisted-living place, but I had my doubts. How could we possibly live there? We were far too young to be sidelined in such an institution. But if not there, where? How long could we manage in our house? How long could I manage without help?

No wonder I escaped to my island every night.

The assisted-living facility was on the other side of town, so we had time to talk. "Mitch, um, let's play fantasy," I blurted.

"Let's pretend you could do anything you wanted. What would you do?"

"Okay, fine. I could do anything? Hmm. Do I have MS?"

"No. No. Of course not."

He thought for a moment. At a red light he turned to me. "Okay. If I wasn't messed up, if I wasn't like *this*, I'd own a bookshop. With wooden floors. With couches and a cat. Two cats! And a coffee shop." He pointed to a café with blue awnings across the street. "It would look like that place over there." He paused. "Hmmm. There are condos above those shops."

The light changed and I drove on. "I didn't know you wanted a bookstore, Mitch."

"I guess I didn't either, until just now."

We drove in silence for a few blocks.

"How about you, Laura? What would you do if you could do anything?"

If I could do anything?

Anything?

The world slowed down. I made a choking sound.

"Laura?" Mitch asked, sounding worried. "What's the matter?"

With a roaring sense of destiny, with my hands clenched white-knuckled on the steering wheel, I told him. "Mitch. Honey…I would…I would find a cure for you."

"Good one," he said, nodding.

I'd found my mission.

❊ ❊ ❊

I was sitting cross-legged on the bed in my island cabin with my animal friends, trying to figure out how to help Mitch, but my eyes kept wandering to the gray kitten who'd shown up that very morning, limping, whimpering, hungry. I gave him a bowl of cool water and fed him from my own breakfast of eggs and ham. Then I cleaned the angry wound on his front leg, wrapped it in the soft leaves of a pantan bush, gave him a few mashed-up oceanberries to combat infection, and then made him a nice nest of two blankets and a pillow. *Herbal Remedies* had helpful advice for everything, it seemed.

Everything except for curing multiple sclerosis.

I opened *Laura's Island* to the plant-identifying section, leafed through sketchbooks full of my own simple drawings of island flora, reread the chapter in *Herbal Remedies* on creating and testing poultices. I studied the notes I'd jotted down about my attempts to help my animal friends. I frowned. Why were the animals so prone to accidents? And so sickly?

I'd think about that later.

"But what should I *do*?" I asked a gecko. He'd climbed up onto the bed and was sniffing at *Herbal Remedies*. "Tell me. How would you make a cure for MS?" I scratched the gecko under the chin, where he liked it best. "Mitch has primary progressive MS. His nerves are damaged. Are you listening? That's why he can't walk. The axons that link the sections of his nerves are gone. What should I do?"

My island friends had no answers for me. The bird I met on my first day flew down from the headboard to land at the gecko's side, fluffing his feathers so that I could see the smaller blue ones underneath. The kitten batted at the gecko's tail as it swished back and forth, a game they both seemed to enjoy. After a while I clapped my hands and they dispersed, all except for the gray kitten. It was time to study *Herbal Remedies*.

For real this time.

I had a mission.

❁ ❁ ❁

"You're going to the library?" Mitch closed the pamphlet we'd been looking through. *Salmonberry Creek Residences*, it said on the glossy front cover. He shoved it so far across the table it nearly fell into my lap. "It's been a long time since I've checked out anything from the library," he said with such a low voice I could barely hear his words. He looked out the window at the drifting October clouds. "Help me to the bathroom?"

I pushed his wheelchair into the too-narrow bathroom, banging it on the door frame, giving him an unpleasant jolt. "Sorry, honey. We ought to get someone in here to widen it."

"Later."

"Later." I put on the brakes of his wheelchair. "Besides, we might be moving."

"Moving. Right."

"You know what?" I helped him pull down his pants and underwear. "We passed some nice-looking condos on the way to that assisted-living place, remember? Above the place with the blue awning? We should look at those."

"Sure. Fine."

I helped him onto the toilet, both of us silent. As often as we'd done this awkward dance in the bathroom, we never got entirely comfortable with it. We never got comfortable discussing our impending move, either. Neither of us wanted to acknowledge that the hard work would necessarily fall mostly on me. I hadn't even started going through our house to sort and clear the detritus of twenty years of marriage. I could barely bring myself to think about it.

That afternoon I checked out seven books. Most were about herbal healing, but one was a history of the Civil War, a subject Mitch had been interested in before being stricken with MS. I had an idea: Before going to the island each night I'd read aloud to him. It would be a surprise we'd both enjoy. It would be nice.

We needed nice things in our lives.

❁ ❁ ❁

I collected samples of every plant on the island. I studied their life stages. I sketched leaves and stems and flowers. I dissected buds and collected seeds. I sat for hours testing plant sap for inherent healing properties, as directed by *Herbal Remedies.*

I made myself an expert.

❁ ❁ ❁

My fingers turned palest green, and the color followed me back to the real world.

"You've been *gardening*? When do you have the time?" Mitch asked one morning as I helped him dress. He followed my hands as I pulled on his socks and smoothed out the toes, as I tugged his soft knit pants with the drawstring over ankles, knees, hips. Working in tandem, his arms slung around my shoulders and me clutching his gait belt, we transferred him from the bed into his wheelchair, and once again I was grateful for my sturdy frame, and for my height, and even for the fact that I was somewhat overweight. I tried to be careful, because what would Mitch do if I hurt my back? My knee nudged the Civil War book where it lay on the bedside table, reminding me that we were almost through the last chapter and it was time for me to find another book for us to share.

He loved reading time. We both did.

He was right: We'd been busy. Amazingly, there had been a unit available at the place above the coffee shop with the blue awning, and—lucky us!—it was ADA compliant. There was an elevator. It had a roll-in shower. Mitch's wheelchair would fit in every space—no more crashing into door frames. There was nothing wrong with the condo. It was relatively new. It was in a decent area. There was a community garden out back. There was a restaurant—and a coffee shop—only steps away. How could we not take it?

But oh, that condo was small.

❁ ❁ ❁

I cleared out the house with help from two college-aged boys my neighbor had recommended. It took three weeks. On the last day I called for pizza after they left because I was so exhausted my bones hurt. Mitch told me he was useless. Utterly, completely, disgustingly useless. I said, "*Please* don't talk like that, honey; it's not true." Mitch said he was only telling it like it was, and would I just shut up and let him be?

Mitch wasn't worthless—he *wasn't*—but I'd seen how miserable he was as he watched me and my helpers packing, labeling, carrying boxes. I turned away so he wouldn't see me cry. I went into the bathroom.

It wasn't his fault.

I didn't come out for fifteen minutes, even though I knew I'd left him stranded in the kitchen. I swabbed at my eyes with my T-shirt, hating myself for being upset when I didn't even have an excuse, not when compared to Mitch.

Or maybe I did.

The deal for the condo was closing in three days and our house was going on the market soon after; that must be why I couldn't stop crying. Or maybe it was because my life was spiraling out of control—because I was on the brink of not being able to care for Mitch on my own.

What would happen then?

Deep down I knew that the worst of it was because I *still* hadn't found a cure for his MS. He was losing ground. How long until any cure I made didn't matter anymore?

❊ ❊ ❊

So I worked even harder.

One evening on my habitual walk around the island, I sprained my ankle on a root. As I limped home I gathered herbs, choosing them from memory, amazed at the knowledge I'd managed to amass. When I got to the cabin I made a poultice—using a recipe from *Herbal Remedies*, but adding a touch of nerve-fern to encourage the tendon to heal and six spears of pulverized sawgrass for bruising—and spread it liberally on my ankle. It wasn't a total failure. The bruising and swelling went down, but the pain persisted for several more days.

Even so, it was encouraging. I wrote it down in my notebook.

❊ ❊ ❊

Mitch and I moved into the condo.

He called himself the master of ceremonies. He directed every piece of furniture, every box, every lamp and television and bookshelf, rolling himself around our new accessible home as if he'd built the place himself, wheeling circles in the entry to the bathroom, and looking—I couldn't keep my eyes off him—like he was enjoying himself.

After the movers left and we were alone again, he came up behind me. "Laura," he said, "I'm sorry I was such an ass the other day."

"It's okay."

"I was thinking. Maybe we should look for a caregiver to help you out?"

I was smiling, but the tears flowed anyway.

❁ ❁ ❁

On the island my animal friends were having a hard time. Every few days one or another of them would come to me for doctoring. It didn't take many poultices or ointments for me to realize that the island must approve of my agenda and was helping me in its own way. One golden-tinged evening, after I'd been frolicking in the lagoon with my sea turtle friends, a yellow-toed gecko showed up on my lanai. The poor thing had a broken spine—I was certain of it from the way his hind legs dragged and his tail hung limp. I scooped him up carefully and placed him on the kitchen counter, and set about making a special targeted massage oil. I cooed to him as I rubbed it on, hoping he wasn't in too much pain, hoping that my ministrations would heal his nerves, axons, and all the rest.

The next morning he flicked his tail at my sweet gray cat.

This was it. This was Mitch's cure.

❁ ❁ ❁

"Let me rub your back, honey," I said to Mitch as soon as I was home. I sat down on the bed, clutching the small tub of massage oil as if it were worth its weight in gold. Maybe it was. I'd brought it home from the island in my bathrobe pocket. "I made a nice massage oil for you. With special herbs."

"Really?" Mitch gave me a dubious look. "Massage oil? Since when do you make massage oil?" He took a deep sniff. "It smells like that stuff you bought at the farmers market."

"It does?"

"Mmmm."

I spread the fragrant oil on him, thicker than I had put it on the gecko. Mitch was right: The oil did have a familiar smell, and I had to admit that the pale green tub looked just like the market-purchased one that had sat on my bedside table since last summer and was now missing. Coincidence. Pure coincidence. There *had* been an island! I *had* made this massage oil! I traced the knobs of Mitch's backbone once, twice, three times, knowing from multiple MRIs that his MS was in his spine and not in his brain. I rubbed the oil in, my fingertips willing the healing herbs to pass through his skin and work their island goodness on him. Because I *had* healed a yellow-toed gecko the same way. Because the gecko *had* run off into the palms as if he'd never been injured.

It had all been real. Right?

"That feels nice," Mitch said. "I feel better already."

❊ ❊ ❊

After his special massage, we fell asleep for a short while, holding hands. Which hadn't happened since, well, I didn't remember when. Maybe never.

"Hi," I said when I awoke, lying next to him, watching him. The island seemed far away, a dream almost, the cabin, the palm trees, the animals, all of it. "How do you feel?"

"Fine. That was the world's best massage you gave me." He

sounded sleepy. "Laura. The shop below us. Right by the elevator. On the first floor…"

"Yes?"

"Get this. It's a bookshop." He squeezed my hand. "With wooden floors."

I sucked in my breath. "Is there a coffee stand inside?"

"There is."

"No joke. And a cat?"

"Two of them."

I thought for a moment. "Couches?"

"Soft leather ones."

"Is it accessible?"

"This whole building is accessible!" He picked up a lock of my hair, twirled it around his finger. "I bet we're going to spend half our waking hours in there. They'll love us."

"Or they'll hate us."

We laughed.

"Is it for sale?" I asked.

"Not yet."

"Not…yet," I repeated, still laughing. "Well. We can wait."

"We'll have a little money left over from the sale of the house," he said after a cozy silence. "I think we should buy a van with a wheelchair ramp."

"Yes! Good idea. And we'll look into getting caregiver help, like you said."

"I'd like to get a cat. A gray cat."

"Me too!"

We lay on the bed, dreaming, planning, closer than we'd been in years. Had I cured him? Maybe. Maybe not. He seemed different, but maybe it was the effects of this new home, this new beginning, that we were feeling. My eyes landed on the picture of my beloved island—I'd carefully removed it from our old bedroom and replaced it on the wall of this room—and I realized it was different. The image was the same, but the caption had changed.

"What is it?" asked Mitch, lifting his head to look over my shoulder.

"Nothing." I turned toward him again, snuggling closer, allowing myself a private little smile. The new ad copy had been written just for me: *Enjoy your life; it's the only one you've got.*

Well. Maybe I would.

I didn't need the island anymore. I had everything I needed right here.

Out of the Flames

By Nancy Bonnington

I always remembered the fire—the rush of yellow, red, and gold flames licking up the walls of the nursery and voices screaming. A woman's face as she scooped me up into her arms, a woman who was not one of my aunts. The face had a strange, long shape, with pouting lips and high, dark eyebrows that weren't real. Her face was close to mine as she carried me in her arms—I was three, maybe four—and bolted with me out the front door of the house. A man was there too—a tall man in a dark suit—and not one of my uncles. He hustled in and out of the house, and finally came to the car with my little sister, Ellie. She was two, maybe three. She was crying, and screaming, "Mommy." We were bundled in blankets that soon smelled of smoke. I coughed a lot. Snot ran down my sister's chin. I told her everything would be okay. Everything would be fine.

We were placed in the backseat of a long, dark car and whisked away into the black night—a cold and solid ebony across a dark, moonless landscape, save the fiery flickering of my parents' house, where they died.

From then on I called her Mom, that woman with the fake eyebrows. And her husband Dad, who haunted the house like a junkyard ghost. He was usually covered in crumbs and an uneven, short growth of whiskers. There was something about him that smelled, so even when he said, "Get over here, Amy, and give me a hug," I cringed. I did it because he was Dad, but I always visibly cringed. The smell of his tobacco and body odor could linger on my T-shirt all day long.

"We saved you, you little brat," Dad said, as I set a bowl of Cheerios in front of him and told him we were out of milk. I didn't know what saving me had to do with being out of milk—I didn't use up the last of it—but I said, "Sorry." I said sorry because I owed him my life. And also because he was mean, I did what he asked—I crawled up on his lap to light his cheap cigars when he told me to, and I let him tell me what a useless waste of their hard-earned money I was.

My sister was a year younger and also obedient. Eventually the two of us took it upon ourselves to divide up the house chores, and we'd keep an intricate schedule of duties, which shifted from week to week so we wouldn't get bored. We made up a game where we put a sticker on the other's side of the board if their chore wasn't done right. The one with a sticker had to do the chore over again. We made up this game so Dad didn't hit or yell. I hated his yelling worse than his sharp swats, maybe because it broke into hysteria at times. He cussed a vulgar stream of profanity and threatened to kill you. You could say that was just his way, but by his tone you knew it could actually happen someday—he could stick a knife in your belly. Too lazy to get out of his easy chair, he'd order us to go stand by him and he'd swat at our butts with his hand or a belt. It stung enough to make me wish I knew my real father.

Mom became the money earner after Dad lost his job. She worked at the local country store, owned by the Drakes—Mr. and Mrs. Drake—the only adults I could say I knew anything about.

Sometimes, on a slow weekday, I'd walk over to the Drakes' store to buy a candy. Mrs. Drake never asked me questions, which is apparently the reason I was allowed to go there. Mom said, "Anybody ever asks you anything, you just nod like an idiot and come back home and tell me about it."

"Won't take much for them to believe you're an idiot," Dad said.

Mrs. Drake never charged me for the candy, but I'd shove a nickel across the counter anyway, so I wasn't beholden to anybody. Dad always said if you owe someone a favor, no matter how small, it'll come back and bite you in the ass.

They fought a lot—Mom and Dad—and I knew it was because of me and my sister. Things fell apart a couple years after the fire, and by the time I was seven I knew grown-ups can love and hate each other at the same time. I knew they can harbor a lot of pain that makes them growl like whipped dogs. That was my dad, anyway. My mom threw in the towel when he got fired and she had to go to work. They should have gotten some kind of government check, they said, but for some reason they couldn't, and she had to work, and that pissed her off. Sometimes they talked about working under the counter, and I didn't know what that meant.

Some nights the house erupted into so much savage noise, it was like a shrill voice-bomb had gone off in the small living area. They'd accuse each other of drinking too much or not being a good enough husband or wife. But between the lines there was this feeling that me and my sister were the real burden. And sometimes it wasn't even hidden between the lines.

"It was your idea to take these children," Mom said to him. I was listening through the bedroom door, in the room I shared with Ellie.

"You wanted children!" he screamed at her. "I saved our goddamned marriage by giving you what you wanted."

"You should have saved your job, too. How the hell do we raise kids if you can't hold a job?"

"Shush… Shut up, the kids have ears."

"You're lucky Ray Fucking Blackstrom has a heart; otherwise, you could have landed in prison for lining your pockets." Then with a lower voice: "You could have landed *both of us* in prison…"

"If I hadn't been caught you'd be singing my praises." Then dad's voice dropped too. "You would have thanked me for it," he hissed. "You would have said, 'Do it again—'"

"Amy and Ellie can't be explained, Greg! You can't fuck up and get the police asking questions because of petty crime… you don't even know how to do *that* right."

Whenever Ellie asked me why Mom and Dad were fighting, I'd say, "They have a lot of weight on their shoulders." But that was just me not understanding it any more than Ellie. What did Dad do to get fired? What did it mean to line your pockets?

"Something's not right," Ellie would whisper. "Amy…are you scared like I am?" And her fearful little voice would send shivers up my spine.

Our new parents hadn't always been cold and hard. In the beginning we got a lot of attention—as good as pampered lap dogs—and sighs of relief that me and my sister were alive and well. I remember getting hot chocolate with miniature marshmallows in it, and Mom reading me stories by the fireplace. And Dad would whistle some tune along with the MP3 player—we weren't allowed to watch TV—and he'd be in a good mood and head out the door because he was retired and going to hang at the tavern. He had been a bean counter before me and Ellie came along. Whatever a bean counter was.

In the beginning, I cried and cried—for days or weeks or even months—about my dead parents. But Mom did her best to comfort me and somehow I adjusted. It was like walking through a painful fog to go back and remember anything. And I tried not to, because it made me sad.

Ellie didn't remember our parents. Maybe that's why she was relatively happy and laughed a lot. According to Mom, Ellie had a "shitload more life in her" than I did. My new parents favored Ellie over me, but I didn't mind, because I cherished Ellie.

Every Saturday Mom picked up the paper from the corner store, whether she was working a shift there or not—the local free paper—to line the birdcage. There was a parrot that didn't talk in the corner of the main room and sat on one spot all of its life. Mom didn't read anymore, and the soiled bird papers piled up out back in the green bin below their bedroom window until the garbage truck came. There were times later, after I learned to read, that I would try to pick out the stories—spying through the thin bars of the birdcage—on pages blurred by parrot dung. There were only a handful of books in our house—a Bible gathering dust on the mantel (I suspected it had never been read) and some romance novels that I was forbidden to look at.

When Mom wasn't working and wanted her newspaper for the bird cage, Ellie would go with her, skipping carefree and holding Mom's hand. Mom rarely asked me to go, because I was too sullen and she couldn't trust what I'd say to people, because the store could be full of people on a weekend.

People were a big threat. Mom and Dad explained it like this: *You two were rescued, but the law says you should have gone into a crummy foster home. You wouldn't like that—being passed from home to home with a bunch of strangers. So you have to mind what you say to people. People can be your worst nightmare."*

People was why me and my sister didn't go to school, apparently. Mom kept saying she'd homeschool us, but she did a fairly slipshod job of it.

"Did you go to school?" I once asked them.

"Your dad tried to go to school," Mom said, "and dropped out twice."

"Because the teachers were lamebrained idiots," Dad said. "The way it is nowadays, nobody knows what they're talking about. You want an education, you're best off educating yourself."

I didn't bother pointing out to Dad that educating myself was a bit difficult, since I'd been forbidden to go anywhere or do anything for the past four years. I had not been allowed to have friends since I was five years old. I had distant memories of playdates with the neighbor kids. Plastic swimming pools, computer games, and balloons at a party. But we'd moved twice since, until we landed in a country area at the end of the lane, eerily secluded, where Dad said, "the trees don't whisper."

Dad was wrong about that, because some nights Ellie and I could both lie in bed and hear the trees whisper. Long *shhh's* like a librarian's voice, but more like in a scary movie— where the wind quietly rises and falls, rises and falls, then the boogieman suddenly jumps out at you from the screen. That would be a limb striking the eaves.

"What do you suppose the trees talk about?" Ellie asked me.

I admit I could have belayed her fears by explaining that trees don't talk—Ellie had been too scared to watch the forest scenes in the *Wizard of Oz*—but instead I said, "I think they talk about the world before people. The good times."

"Your father's smarter than most people," Mom added, in a rare moment of pride.

"She didn't marry me for my looks," Dad quipped. I thought he was kidding, but I took it to heart; he must have been pretty smart, because he was quite ugly.

When I was eight and a half, things took a slight turn for the better, because Ellie found a lost puppy that wandered into our yard. It had no collar, so Ellie claimed it. I was certain we'd get in trouble for asking, but Dad took a shine to it as much as we did.

It was a brown mutt on the small side. Healthy and happy. Made Ellie's enthusiasm look like plain dirt on the bottom of a worn out shoe in comparison. Ellie named him Chipper.

He was soon learning a great deal, because Dad said he'd kick the shit out of it if it did anything wrong. But one morning I saw Dad wiping pee off the kitchen floor with a bath towel. And all the while he was muttering at Chipper, "Yeah, yeah, I know you couldn't help it, little guy." I made sure Dad couldn't see me; I was so happy that he was fond of our dog. In fact, I was thrilled to discover Dad had a secret soul inside of him, proof that deep down he might be okay.

Dad started taking Chipper for walks in the woods. Sometimes Ellie and I were allowed to tag along. The three of us taught Chipper to fetch. We could throw any old thing out ahead of us—a rock, a stick, a frozen discarded sock—and Chipper would go all out for it. He'd run at top speed, his puppy feet splayed and comical like overgrown boots, his ears flopping with excitement, then he'd bring it back, whatever it was, pride clearly busting out of his heaving chest.

Eventually Dad got the idea he'd buy a rifle and shoot squirrels or something. We didn't live in a place where shooting was allowed. But Dad said the government had no right to tell people what to do. Besides, we were near a forest. And folks around there pretty much minded their own business.

Mom said it was too risky, which sparked an argument between them, for which me and Ellie had to leave the room.

"Don't shoot an animal," Ellie pleaded on the way out. *"Please."*

"Don't worry," Mom said, "he'd miss the side of a barn."

All night, Ellie kept me up with fear for the invisible animals that lived in the woods—in her mind, Dad was going to slaughter all of God's innocent little creatures that made the bushes shudder from time to time, or that squawked from the skies, or slithered through the tall grasses at the end of our yard. Ellie loved every living thing.

Ellie's love for the dog grew as fast as the weeds that Dad couldn't keep out of our lawn. Ellie taught Chipper all the low-brow circus moves and even put on a show for our family—roll over, play dead, shake. And so on. It was natural that she would take charge of Chipper when Dad was finally ready to hunt.

I tagged along, mostly in the back; Ellie trotted beside Dad holding Chipper's leash. The grass was high and wet and soaked through my jeans. The woods deep on federal lands were a mix of elm and fir, so that the ground was a soft bed of green leaves intermingled with needles. Sometimes there were thick bushes that Dad would stomp a path through, us following, picking our way slowly and carefully to avoid thorns. Sometimes the trail was wide-open and the three of them—Ellie, Dad, and Chipper—would walk abreast, with me still taking up the rear.

It was early, past dawn, but not yet to where the sun could cut through the upper branches of the trees. It was gloomy dark green all around. Every once in a while Dad would stop and put up his hand; he'd say he spotted something—a grouse or a wild turkey—and he'd take aim at the dense foliage and pull the trigger.

I hated the sound of the shot but had to admit it thrilled my heart like a jolt of electricity.

Ellie was delighted every time Dad missed. In my opinion there had been nothing there to shoot anyhow.

Ellie began to get bored by the long hike and the lack of animal sightings. She began tossing sticks up ahead for Chipper, who bounded through the woods like a wild thing, knowing how to pick his way in and out of the trees and brush.

It was starting to sprinkle. We talked about going home. Dad pulled his hood over his head, as if to answer that we were equipped just fine.

At one point Chipper dropped a stick at Ellie's feet, as the sprinkle turned into a steady drizzle. Ellie didn't have a hood. She shook her head rapidly like a dog drying off, and laughed.

"It's fun, but it makes you dizzy," she said.

Dad lifted his gun and took aim up ahead, with Ellie not paying any attention to him. Ellie flung the stick for Chipper as far and hard as her skinny arm could muster.

The puppy took off at full speed; Dad pulled the trigger. Perhaps Dad saw the movement in the bushes that was Chipper's tail, the blur of brown and white fur, and thought it was a turkey, or maybe Dad didn't care what it was. In any case, we all heard the blast, then the silence that followed—silence like a deafening hush that reminds you of being vulnerable. That blast would clinch Ellie's view of Dad forever.

She ran screaming full force after Chipper.

Dad stood tall and still, scowling, his jaw was punched forward pointing at his own mistake; rain dripped from the hood of his yellow slicker, as he slowly drew the rifle down to his side.

I ran after Ellie. When I caught up to her she was crouched in a thicket—her arms scratched up from retrieving Chipper from the thorns. The dog was still on her lap, a gunshot wound bleeding into Ellie's jeans.

"Oh, God, Ellie," I said.

"Do something," she pleaded with me. But she made no move to give him up. Chipper was tightly held in her arms, his glassy eyes staring off at nothing.

When Dad caught up to us, Ellie looked at him furiously. "You killed him!"

There was a pause, and to his credit Dad looked worried and stunned, but then he burst out, "What kind of an idiot hunting dog runs in front of a bullet, goddamn it? What kind?"

Ellie let loose great sobs and I could only stand by and watch.

Dad used the butt of his rifle to dig in the soft soil and we buried Chipper right where he'd fallen. I remember a funny smell in the rain-soaked air that evening—like burnt metal and fresh dirt.

Back at the house, Mom tried to comfort Ellie, but soon ordered her to buck up and stop crying. Dad munched on a sandwich and stayed out of it. Nobody seemed to get that Ellie was not just crying over Chipper's death—bad as that was—but over Dad not caring a lick.

There was nothing I could do about Chipper, but I told Ellie that night that Dad cared a lot and was just too stubborn to admit it. By then Ellie was saying Dad killed Chipper on purpose.

I told her about the time I saw Dad in the kitchen with a soft spot for the puppy. How he actually wiped up Chipper's piss like it was no big deal.

Ellie didn't believe a word of it and never forgave Dad. "He's not capable of caring…about us or a puppy," she cried. "He's a monster."

"He rescued us," I reminded her. But we'd been told that so often, it had lost its power.

I let Ellie climb into my bed that night, and I caressed her head, like a mother might do, as she rested against my body and sobbed herself to sleep. I lay awake. It was a weird feeling that I had defended Dad. I thought about the look on his face as he laid Chipper in the shallow grave; it was as hard a look as fired clay. Maybe Ellie was right.

As years passed, Ellie and I grew even closer. Mom called us *Siamese twins*. I suppose it was unnatural that we didn't have the usual quarrels of siblings. But we were so isolated, it just made sense that we'd be each other's best friend. We trusted each other with our deepest secrets and longings. Ellie wanted to be a vet when she grew up. Ever since she'd held that dead dog in her arms she wanted to help animals—keep them alive if possible. She told me later that she felt Chipper's last heartbeats throbbing in her palms and then quivering to a dead halt. And how it tore her in two that she couldn't help him.

I didn't know what I wanted to be, but I was certain something would strike me when the time was right.

We often slept in the same bed so we could whisper in each other's ears and not wake Mom and Dad. We picked out each other's clothing from the assortment of options that Mom brought home from time to time, some from Walmart and some from the secondhand shop. Our parents didn't care what we wore, so long as it wasn't revealing, now that we were maturing into young women.

Ellie and I got our hands on all sorts of magazines about mechanics, motorcycles, and men's fashions. It was for the photographs, of course. We would pick out which men would be the best lovers and which would make the best husbands—and they often weren't the same.

We did each other's makeup, though we had to hide our made-up faces from Dad. And Mom was no help, since she was all about being natural, other than drawing in her eyebrows. (I never asked what happened to the ones God gave her.) She didn't even color her hair when it started coming out all gray. Ellie had such beautiful large brown eyes, I adored emphasizing them with black eyeliner; and Ellie, in turn, liked to rub out my imperfect little blotches and pimples with gobs of concealer and foundation. About the only difference between our faces was that my eyes were always a bit puffier, and I wore pink lipstick while she loved bright cherry.

One autumn day, when were high school age—though we weren't enrolled—Ellie and I took a walk to the new trailer park about three miles down the road. Mom and Dad grew less and less concerned about our talking to strangers, since we had upheld years of sworn secrecy about our truancy and dubious heritage. As far as we were concerned, we got what we got for a mom and dad, just like it was a crapshoot for anybody.

And as far as schooling went, Ellie and I had discovered the local library by the time we were twelve, often grabbing a bus on the weekends—so as not to arouse suspicion from strangers about children loose on a school day—to the outskirts of town, where a humble brick building beckoned to our growing curiosity.

We lied about our names on the library card applications. It just came naturally by then to deny our true selves.

We picked out our books very carefully, as though each were a block of gold or a high-paying lottery ticket. And we always chose the same subject to study between us, so that we could bounce our newfound knowledge off each other. I recall reading about Amelia Earhart, the Civil War, and black holes in space, as well as a music dictionary and the history of rock and roll. You would think the library would have made us want to expand our knowledge outside, in the real world, but for quite some time we were content to check out books and stay up late at night reading and sharing thoughts until are our eyelids dropped and our voices ran dry.

The other thing the library gave us, finally, was access to a computer. The old library lady showed us how to get on the internet, and then there was no stopping our abilities. In fact, the internet was where we learned that the town had a new mobile home park.

We got there near dusk. The place was set up on an old dump site that had been cleaned up and converted. There was a dozen or so homes of various types and sizes—old and new. A man who said he was the owner of the place lived in a fifth-wheel at the entrance, sat on his porch, and sang out-of-tune songs that we'd never heard before. There was a huge dog—a husky mix, Ellie told me—that was tied with a long rope to a tree. It was all bark and no bite, but if you didn't know it you'd be scared plenty to mess with anybody's home. The owner said, "He's a war dog—trained to sniff out bombs and bad guys."

I didn't know if that was true, but I steered clear while Ellie went up to it and made friends.

At the very opposite end of the park there was a single-wide mobile with its door perched open. Outside, a woman was hanging some sheets on a line, and a young man, probably her son, was pounding some kind of metal on a concrete slab.

Ellie was the first one to speak to him, so in a way she had first dibs. That was fair in our world.

"Bruce," he said, when she asked his name. He stopped pounding and smiled. He had yellow crooked teeth, but otherwise the handsomest smile you could find, because it was friendly and not all judgy like some people can be. I could tell by the way Ellie exhaled that she was instantly in love. She blushed and asked him what he was doing, while I hung about like a dumb shadow at her side.

"Replacing an old axle," he said. "On my bike."

Over the next twenty minutes or so Ellie took such an interest in axles, you'd think she was going to get her PhD in motorcycle maintenance.

Bruce went along with it all, even letting Ellie take swings at a piece of metal with a heavy, blunt hammer. I got bored and went home.

Over the next several months Ellie spent most of her evenings and weekends at the trailer park—Bruce worked at a body shop during the week. And I was jealous, I guess, because Ellie was a year younger than me and had her first boyfriend before I did.

I got on my high horse one night and told Ellie, as she was sneaking out the back door, that she'd get in a lot of trouble for seeing Bruce and the she should wait until she was older. A lot older.

She got fired up, like I'd never seen her. "How dare you tell me what to do?"

"I'm your older sister," I said, pulling that card for the first time in my life.

"Then you should know what it feels like to be in love," Ellie snapped.

It hit me in the gut, so I shot back immediately, "You keep seeing him and I'll tell Dad."

I didn't mean it, of course, but I wished I could get me and Ellie back to the way we'd always been. She didn't seem to need me anymore, and certainly not the way she needed Bruce.

"I'll never speak to you again," Ellie spat. Then she left.

I'm not saying it was my fault, but at the time I felt certain I'd never see Ellie again. Indeed, a day passed, then two, then a whole week. It became clear that she'd run off with Bruce.

Mom and Dad said if Ellie thought she could run away with a boy and then come back home, she had another *think* coming. I had told them what happened, because I couldn't invent a lie quick enough to cover for Ellie. They acted worried, and for a bit that made them softer in my view, but then I heard Mom say to Dad, "She damn well better get hit by a bus rather than bring us trouble."

I frequented the trailer park day and night asking questions. "Where'd they go?" I asked his mother. She was a waitress at the local coffee shop. She always looked worn-out, but she was generally nice. And she'd say to me, "Don't you worry—Bruce is a good kid and your sister will be okay." But I wasn't much comforted when she added, "Let's just hope Ellie isn't pregnant."

I missed Ellie terribly, like a hole in my gut was opened up, and there was nothing to smile about anymore. As the days went by I longed to see her face pop up outside my bedroom window, as if the whole thing was just a lark.

I badgered everyone at the trailer park; I couldn't call a cop, of course. They might ask questions and get Mom and Dad in trouble. But I could play detective—I could ask every resident of that park when the last time was they'd seen Ellie and what had she been doing and what had she been saying. I even took a notebook and pen with me and spoke to each of them at their doors like a reporter. But they all shrugged; they knew and liked Bruce and Ellie, but nobody had anything to offer as to their whereabouts.

I was at the park so often that I happened to be there one night when a badly dented Buick pulled into the lot and Ellie climbed out, yelling at Bruce to grab their bag of clothes from the backseat.

Bruce saw me first, apparently recognizing my shape in the darkness of a low-watt porch bulb. Then he waved.

Ellie saw me and rushed over. We hugged like it had been years—Ellie seeming older, like she'd outgrown me. She stood taller—or was it my imagination? She had makeup on—eyeliner the way I would have drawn it, and beautiful cherry-red lips.

"Oh, Amy," she said. "I'm sorry for worrying you. I'm so sorry." Her eyes were teary.

"It's okay," I said. "You're back safe." I didn't want to scold her; I didn't want to lose her again.

Bruce's mom came out and greeted them, and then some neighbors said hello—and it was obvious me and Ellie couldn't be alone. Finally everyone but Bruce left us, and Bruce and Ellie and I walked over to the fire pit at the far end of the park.

While Bruce started a fire, I asked Ellie where she'd been.

She was silent, until Bruce looked up at her and prodded, "Tell her."

"You always said we were born in Seattle," Ellie said.

"Yeah? So?"

"I just wanted to see it," Ellie said. "I wanted to see where I came from."

I nodded. Ellie had asked me throughout the years to tell her about our real parents and I had struggled to come up with much of an answer. Little bits and pieces of them came to mind—hanging onto my mother's hand, the back of my father's head as he drove. But it was mostly just a feeling of there being people around who loved me.

"Bruce has a cousin there," Ellie said. "And we stayed with him and met a lot of cool people, and we partied and stuff… And Bruce taught me to drive." Ellie glanced down at her hands and paused. "I'm sorry you weren't there, Amy."

I shrugged. I supposed if I spoke it might come out shaky, because I was feeling choked up that my sister had such an adventure without me.

"Anyway, I was like some creature from outer space to all of them." Ellie pulled Bruce to her side, now that he had squirted some starter fluid on kindling; soon, we'd have a roaring campfire. "People kept asking questions—Bruce told them I'd never been to school."

Ellie looked up at me as I took a sudden breath. It was nothing, really—why should anybody in Seattle care?—but we'd lived all our lives by the oath that we'd never tell this secret.

Bruce lit a cigarette and opened up a half rack of beer. "It's warm, sorry," he said.

Ellie said, "That's okay, sweetie," and took a bottle of Miller from his hands and drank from it. Bruce opened another and handed it to me.

I had never tasted beer, a fact I would not admit in front of Bruce. I was careful to drink without making a face. It really didn't taste bad anyway.

Bruce lit a cigarette and handed it to me, then did the same for Ellie.

The three of us drank and smoked in silence. The fire pit was far enough from the mobile homes we knew nobody could hear us. And most had gone to bed anyhow.

"Ellie, I have to go," I said. "You know I'm already in big trouble. And frankly Dad still has his rifle. I think Bruce better watch out too. Dad might kill him. I won't say anything until we figure out what to do with you."

"Amy, don't go," Ellie said.

"I have to—are you kidding? It's soooo late!"

Finally Bruce said, "Sweetheart, tell your sister."

They shared worried glances. I knew what the big news would be. I just knew it—that Ellie was pregnant. That they were going to have a baby together, maybe get married, maybe not, but run off somewhere and start new lives together.

I braced myself. I heard nothing in the dark but the sound of the fire—a crackling deep in the heart of the logs.

"Amy..." Ellie pulled a small stack of folded paper from her back pocket. In the firelight the papers looked yellow. "I printed this out at the Seattle Library. You know, Mom and Dad aren't our real parents...." Ellie gasped and stopped talking. She cracked a new beer and wiped her nose on her sleeve.

"Ellie, duh. I've always told you everything I can; I just can't remember much about our real parents. I was too young... almost as young as you were."

"But you remember the fire."

"Of course. I told you about it, how Mom and Dad rescued us. I've told you that a million times. Mom and Dad were friends of our real parents…and they risked their lives to pull us out of the house…"

"They weren't friends of our parents, Amy. They've been lying to us all these years."

"Then why did they run into a burning house to save us? I remember it, Ellie. That's no lie. I remember Dad carried you out in his arms. He could have been killed, or worse.…"

"Yeah, they rescued us from the fire…but that doesn't mean shit, now that I know everything." Ellie's voice was high and agitated. Bruce pulled her close and whispered, "It's okay, Ellie…Take a deep breath."

"They weren't friends," Ellie repeated. "Haven't I always told you something's not right? They're the ones who set the house on fire!"

I let out a long whistling breath like a kettle of steam. "Jesus, Ellie. I know you hate them but that's crazy."

"Amy, we have proof…we brought you proof, and I was afraid you wouldn't believe me, but we researched it through old newspapers. It's all here."

My breath came shallow, and I felt dizzy. I felt my face break out in a sweat, but I tried to act cool as Ellie shoved the papers in my hands.

"You're crazy," I said, but I stared at the fire and didn't dare open the papers.

"I can't read this in the dark," I stammered.

"Enough light from the fire," Ellie said.

I drank from my fourth beer and Bruce handed me a whole new pack of smokes and said, "Keep 'em."

"There's just no way..."

"Amy, they don't work under the counter to avoid taxes. They're on the run! They must have changed their names back then."

I longed to turn the clock back a month or so. Before Ellie ran away. I knew Ellie was smart and she'd have evidence for what she was saying.

"Mom and Dad are wanted," Ellie said. "for arson, kidnapping...and *murder*!"

In the hours that followed, I drank and smoked and the surreal night sky spun above me in big circles like a tilted canvas at the end of a parasol. Around and around.

Ellie talked on and on about how Mom and Dad had to be certified psychopaths.

"I had to come back for you," Ellie explained. "Me and Bruce...we want the three of us to go to the police together. Tomorrow. Don't you think it's a little weird that Mom and Dad have no relatives...no brothers, no sisters, no parents... bullshit!"

I couldn't take it in. I had thought I was braver than that and was ashamed to learn that I was still a little girl, easily bewildered and not in control of the knot that had taken up all the room in my stomach. I shrugged without saying a word. How I wished that I could dredge up some courage!

"You can sleep here tonight," Bruce said quietly. "We have a couch."

"You've gotta come," Ellie said. "To the police station. Tomorrow. Promise me. And you can't go back to...*their* house. We don't belong there anymore."

I only half nodded, with my stomach doing a whirly

dance, because I knew that in the morning our worlds would change forever.

"Don't you get it?" Ellie shook me. "They killed our parents and they stole us!"

❁ ❁ ❁

That night I slept off and on, hearing the loud snores from Bruce, and surprisingly Ellie as well. Oddly, I didn't even think about Mom and Dad, who they really were, who we were. I just laid on the couch and watched the porch lamp flicker as, one after another, curious insects hit the hot bulb and sizzled to death.

I dozed maybe an hour and woke up knowing I had dreamed of my biological mother. I could see the details of her face as never before, a kindness that radiated from an open-lipped smile. And she even smelled of a lotion that was like sweet flowers. I longed to know what that lotion was, stock up on it, and rub it all over me and have her with me again. Before I forgot that scent again. Before the smell and the face retreated into my blurry dreams again.

Her eyes were open wide as she blew sloppy kisses on Ellie's belly. Then she put down Ellie and picked me up and hugged me, her soft cheek against mine as I rested on her hip, and she was like no other human, because I could feel this one really important thing about her: She loved me more than herself. *That die-for-you kind of love that me and Ellie had been missing ever since!*

I allowed a few quiet sobs to escape, but soon confusion welled up in me. It made no sense: Mom and Dad had their troubles, but…it had started out okay. They loved us. Though, through the years, their lives had become too stressful for them—Dad not able to keep a job, Mom not getting whatever it was she wanted from me and Ellie.

I sat up and moved quietly to the kitchen table, where I could read Ellie's papers by a task light.

The article said the fire was started with gasoline. Arson was the undeniable conclusion. And the couple who lived down the street had been seen climbing into a dark vehicle and disappearing with the children. Two bodies were found inside the house.

Two bodies.

I tucked the papers back in my pocket and lit a cigarette. The logical thing to do was to confront Mom and Dad. Find out what really happened…

They must have changed their names. In the beginning, we moved and moved and moved. We didn't go to school. And they worked…under the counter. And Dad…I knew he had stolen. But what had he stolen? Besides us?

I imagined being brave enough to go to the police, brave enough to take on the task ahead for Ellie, because I was the older one. But I closed my eyes and slumped my not-so-brave head in my hands.

And then I saw him too—shirtless, tanned, and mowing the lawn, pausing to lift me into a swing. The chains of the swing set were smooth except where there was a bit of rust, and I could feel it rough on my hands. The swing set was erected on a bed of bark in the corner of our yard, and the smell of fresh-cut grass drifted close in the air.

He was tall, towering above me, yet he always crouched low or knelt down to speak to me, to tie a stray shoelace, or to brush my head with a love peck. He was a gentle giant, at least that's how I remembered him. *I remembered my real dad!*

❁ ❁ ❁

Sometime before four a.m. I slipped out of the trailer. I made my way quietly out the door, but the need for stealth was negligible with all the alcohol consumed during the night. Even Bruce's mother looked passed out, as I could spot her motionless legs and torso, dangling off the bed, through the open bedroom door.

It was a long, dark walk down the country lane. The road that dead-ended at our house was rarely used, except for a gravel turnaround halfway there, where people would pull over to smoke a joint or make love. But that night it was completely still.

I took deep breaths to calm myself. I squinted in the dark and prayed for guidance. I didn't pray to God, in particular, but to the forest, the trees, the dark, the night…the animals. I prayed that I could be a stronger person than the puny soul who was plodding down the road. Strong, like a wild thing, driven by natural instincts.

At first I traveled only to the sound of my own footfalls on hard dirt, but soon enough there were sounds like a large cougar behind me, following me and gaining. I'd never seen a cougar around those parts, but I knew the jagged sounds of its breath catching in its throat like shards of glass. I got the feeling I was being stalked—not just by any wildcat, but by the queen of all wildcats.

The forest turned medieval on me.

Was that the effect of a hangover?

"Go away," I shouted, alarmed to hear how timid my plea sounded. "Get out of here!" I raised my voice more, though it quavered, and it seemed like the dark forest on either side was judging me a fool.

It was useless to turn around or stare into the woods after the cougar; for one thing, it was too dark to see her, and for another, I knew the creature was invisible. A spirit.

Reality tilted on its head, as I stood still in the road and closed my eyes. My head pounded.

After a moment it was quiet. And the sudden hush calmed my mind. The cougar sounds disappeared, but left behind something deeply primal in my heart—something instinctual, something natural, something wild.

I knew the country road, of course, though it was dark. I knew each turn of it from over the years. I knew the largest potholes, the deepest, rain-catching ruts, the jagged stones that you must steer around to not stub your toe. And yet it all seemed fresh to me that early, predawn morning; it was like I had awakened in a somewhat familiar skin but the world around me was totally new.

Eventually I arrived at their house and circled to the backyard. The moon, as if on cue, revealed itself—the shape of a toenail clipping—and I could see the familiar yard where Ellie and I had spent so much time tumbling; catching moths, naming them and letting them go; and playing made-up games with a deflated soccer ball. Such was our otherwise friendless but sisterly existence.

I was awed by the quiet of the night, interrupted only by creaking trees, and I almost wished that Chipper would come racing into my arms. But of course he didn't.

Mom and Dad were likely asleep. Their small bedroom window was just above a clump of dead juniper bushes, beside the plastic container of old bird papers.

I felt a loss so deep, it penetrated my chest—a loss that made me collapse in a tired heap to the brown, summer-dried lawn. My head began to reel again, even as I gulped down sorrow that hurt my throat—sorrow that choked me and threatened to break me in half.

Mom and Dad had lied to us our whole lives.

Again, and no longer to my surprise, I was remembering my *real* parents vividly and aloud. I watched them touching each other before sitting down to dinner—my father whispering a quick made-up prayer, my mother laughing, but her head still bowed in reverence. I was in a high chair kicking the underbelly of the table with my feet. It felt so good, those rubber toes on wood. *Kick, kick, kick.*

Then they almost appeared before me—my imagination boiling over to the surface of all my senses—almost as visions, shimmering beings in the still night.

He took her hand. She got up from the table and nodded at me from the past. "You'll do what's best, Amy."

My father nodded too. "You know what you have to do, Amy."

I wished I could show this vision to Ellie! But how can one transmit conscious waves? I wished I could solidify them, capture them—print them out on cold, hard paper, just like the truth of Ellie's research. But I was powerless because I was, and always had been, inconsequential.

I got up off the lawn and lit a cigarette. After two puffs, deeply inhaled, I lit a wad of Mom's bird papers with the tip of the cigarette, then I touched the papers to the tiny, dry juniper branches which immediately took flame.

It was like déjà vu, how the flames grew—as I fanned them with more bird papers—and how they began to lick at the paint on the cedar siding of the house. In the dim light of that slivered moon, the tongues of fire were brilliant and mesmerizing.

I tossed the cigarette into the bin and looked over my shoulder at the yard where they stood.

Their faces began to fade, my *real* parents, as I balled up another handful of dirty bird papers and stuffed it in the junipers.

They were both young. In fact I was quite stunned because I realized I would be their age in the not-too-distant future.

Even my little sister circling around the house, out of breath and yelling, "What are you doing?" didn't seem to matter.

My father's arm was wrapped around my mother's shoulder, as if they were about to walk out the door into a thick fog—a dense and shifting fog like a living smoke screen. The same fog that had buried them to me and Ellie long ago.

Cerebrospinal Fluid Leak

By Susan Whiting Kemp

This story is dedicated to Dr. Wouter Schievink, Dr. Menahem Marcel Maya, and all the caring people at Cedars-Sinai Medical Center who helped me fight the octopus.

The steampunk octopus turbans his legs around my head. Channeling graceful strength into each iron tentacle, he squeezes. I try to remove him, but loosening an appendage only leaves room for another to take its place. He is stuck fast, compressing my skull, tightening like a vise. As a mechanical creature he must have an on/off switch; I reach up, but he contorts his leather-metal head, hiding the switch, revealing it, hiding it. Or perhaps I am mistaken about the switch, and he is a perpetual-motion machine: once started, never stopping.

I insult the mechanical beast, calling him calamari, shark-bait, Octopunk, and all manner of names. If my tirade wounds him, he doesn't show it, except by squeezing more tightly. Octopunk's head looms over me. I'm unnerved by what I see in his eyes. The black of smoldering, the red of burning, and all the stages in between, an automaton soul so deep and terrifying, I fear I might fall in.

Octopunk touches behind my ear with his suckers, and at the base of my head, testing, probing. Is this the way in? How about there, or there? Each contact prickles. How many legs does Octopunk have? I would have thought eight. But a steampunk octopus would have as many legs as its designer pleases.

And its designer would give it the skills of an octopus, one of which is to unscrew a jelly jar, so why not a skull? Octopunk tries to unscrew mine in an attempt to reach the delectable liquid pools in my brain ventricles—there, deep in the very center. When he finally finds his way in, he'll siphon my cerebrospinal fluid completely. He'll steal the precious fluid that guards my gray matter and bathes my spine.

Then a bright burst of understanding. Octopunk has already gained entry, and is entwined with me now. His probing, his squeezing, is a calculated effort to remove my fluid slowly, so that it continually replenishes. He needs me to survive. And further: He views our relationship as symbiotic. But how can it be, when it's take, take, take, and no give?

But yes, he has given me something. The images I see on the backs of my eyelids: vivid patterns with acoustic-tile contours. And he has given me the sound of the ocean. My inner ear is a vast, distant seascape, faraway crashing waves interrupted by sudden, quick buzzes, steampunk mosquitoes whizzing past my head.

Octopunk touches a tentacle tip to my quadriceps. Not to get my attention; he already has that. To set off a muscle cramp. Now he stabs my rotator cuff. Three different places, three different pain types. I see now: Octopunk is a pain artist.

A pointillist, but not a minimalist. He adds pain for balance the way a painter adds a mountain in the background.

Or maybe this is how Octopunk communicates. Through pain rather than words. And in that case what is the alphabet? The sentence structure? Verb, noun, punctuation? How could I possibly decipher it? What gave Octopunk the idea that I could decode his message, and how do I dissuade him of that conviction?

I seek out the Cephalopod Removers to rid me of Octopunk. He is invisible to them, but my brain sag tells them he is secreted in my nervous system. A remover injects caffeine and morphine directly into my veins, telling me Octopunks abhor these. Octopunk barely reacts. Next the remover injects my veins with tiny steam engines, which zoom throughout my body, their heat injurious to steampunk octopus precision machinery. Octopunk flees for a time, or so I think. Hours later, when the steam engines deplete themselves and are no longer zipping back and forth to my extremities, Octopunk is there. I realize he never left. The steam engines merely made his presence bearable.

The removers continue the search for my invisible Octopunk and his mysterious entry point to my system. To flush him out, they inject my spine with liquid fire, then tilt me so it flows upward, lumbar to thoracic, thoracic to cerebral. Bathing my spine and brain in lava.

Is that the sound of Octopunk sniggering?

I won't stand for that. I insist on the nuclear option. A lead canister boasts a radioactive warning symbol proclaiming the danger of its isotopes, but I insist they be injected into my cerebrospinal fluid. That their half-lives be used to investigate me so that I don't have half a life.

The removers tell me that the isotopes didn't work. But I know better: Radioactivity unleashed turns a tiny lizard into Godzilla. So I become a caricature of myself, a Godzilla of sorts, and I battle Octopunk. It's a glorious battle fought amid pain waves rather than ocean waves, lasting months rather than days. A battle that Octopunk wins. We sink below the sea, Octopunk still clinging to me, ever more entwined. I see civilization above, but the sea's surface distorts it, distances it.

I was sure that a machine couldn't think, but now I know otherwise. I can nearly hear Octopunk's thoughts: bland, indefinite musings—no black and white, no yin and yang, no this or that, only the other. He is still trying to deliver his message.

But I refuse it. And though Octopunk tries to hold me back, I travel. From the land of pine to the land of palm, to see a different set of removers: Octopunk-ridding specialists. They show me jellyfish—a promise, of sorts, that soon my brain will float with such grace. And they tell me of their weapon: cephalopod glue.

The mere mention of it makes Octopunk tremble. A small bit of the stickum, strategically placed, would destroy him. Its touch would bring his clinking, clacking, probing to an abrupt halt.

Where to inject the stickum? Near the thoracic vertebrae, back-scratcher level. Octopunk squeezes as hard as he possibly can, but fear ultimately takes hold of him. He unfurls a leg. Then another, then another. He detaches completely, hovers for a time until he sees it is no use. He escapes.

I am free. Octopunk is gone, leaving the residue of his mechanical-grade ink on my psyche. It is only now that he is gone that I can decipher the message he had been trying to give me. And that message is: Look.

And so I look, and so I see them. Millions of people, each entwined with their own steampunk creatures. All invisible except to the bearers—and now to me.

I think to myself: So many are suffering; where are their removers? I remain to stand sentry. Surely they will come soon.

Number Three Is Missing

By Evelyn Arvey

They're worms, when you come right down to it: wriggling, squirming *worms*.

They're disgusting.

Right now they are crawling around inside the stump of my left leg. I try to convince myself that it's okay, that these worms are not the parasites that gave me such vivid nightmares when I was younger. No, these worms are million-dollar wonders of modern medicine: partly robotic, partly bioengineered, and wholly alive. There are ten of them, these builders of my new left leg. I want a new leg. Therefore I want *them*.

Only they're revolting.

Dr. Soraya inserted the worms into my stump this morning at eight o'clock—as she's done each of the three days since my medical trial began—through the Hickman worm port in my thigh. Twelve hours later she's back, clicking the nozzle of the worm habitat to my port with a magnetic *clunk* that makes me shudder even though it never hurts as much as I think it will.

"There," she says. "Now we wait for them to come out."

They take their time, my worms.

Dr. Soraya keeps busy while we wait. She cleans the skin around my port. She takes photographs of my stump. She sits at the hospital's computer in the corner of my room and enters clinical notes. Finally she turns off the room lights, takes the under-skin flashlight from its charging dock, and sweeps it over my leg. Dr. Soraya says the same words every time she flicks on the flashlight: "Let's take a look, shall we?"

I don't know if it's the power of suggestion, but suddenly there's a maddening itch under my skin, right where Dr. Soraya is aiming her light. The worm? It must be. I think I feel it squirm. I sit on my hands to keep from scratching. It's a good thing the worms don't stay in my body at night or I might do something stupid in my sleep, like gouging them from under my skin with my fingernails. Or something.

Dr. Soraya turns the room lights back on. "Look! Here comes the first one."

The worm, slick and reddened with my body's juices, noses its way blindly through the port and slithers into the habitat. Another squirming worm leaves my body, then another, and I wonder: Do they think limb regeneration patients *want* to see this? Why must the hardware be transparent?

The better question might be, why am I watching?

Counting the worms is not as easy as it might seem. Sometimes two or more of them tumble out of my port at the same time, curled around each other in a single wriggling mass, and then I worry we've missed one. Dr. Soraya assures me that each worm carries a locator chip and that she knows exactly where each one is at all times.

After a while she leaves, taking my worms and their habitat with her. Now it's time for the other part of the team—the researchers and bioinformaticians down in the basement lab—to leap into action. They'll work with my worms through the night, collecting and studying data, making minute adjustments to the robotics, and doing whatever else it is they do.

Does Dr. Soraya know how much I loathe these worms? Is that why she and the others keep such a close eye on me? I have signed a sheaf of contracts and nondisclosure documents, and I know there are many things they are not at liberty to share with me. I've promised to stay in the clinic for the entire thirty days, in bed mostly, under constant observation and video surveillance. Maybe they're worried I'll sell classified information to their competitors. Or maybe they're concerned I'll turn on my worms and ruin their expensive trial.

They needn't worry.

I'll do anything to have two legs again. I'll even let them put Guinea worms into my body. *That's* how much I want a new leg.

❁ ❁ ❁

Guinea worms are parasites. They prey on humans, and sometimes dogs.

I've been horrified by the things since I was a sophomore in high school, when my then-favorite teacher—who'd spent time in Africa in the Peace Corps—held my science class in spellbound disgust with tales of Guinea worms he'd seen extracted, in person, *with his own eyes*. He even helped. He knew infected people, some of them his friends. My teacher got way too much pleasure in telling us these vile stories in graphic detail. Or maybe he just liked hearing the girls shriek and watching them clap their hands over their ears.

Midway through my junior year, I thought I had a Guinea worm. I really, truly did. Late at night I felt it chewing on me, digging tunnels through my flesh, and itching, always itching. I told my best friend, who told my mother, who had a furious confrontation with our teacher, who sat me down—with my mother and the principal in the room—and told me that no, I was not infected; there were no Guinea worms in North America. The next day the whole school knew I'd succumbed to worm hysteria. Everyone called me Worm Girl until the day I graduated.

So here I am. Worm Girl, in the flesh.

❁ ❁ ❁

My worms are tame.

I constantly remind myself that they aren't really Guinea worms anymore. They're little more than transport vehicles and assembly factories; all parasitic tendencies and reproductive abilities have been scienced right out of them.

Here's how it works: The worms eat a nutrient-rich slurry called Mix Number 72 that is injected into my port every three hours. I think the slurry looks like regurgitated oatmeal, but Robbie, my fiancé, has a better description: He says the slurry looks like half-congealed pudding made of ground-up gopher guts, just like that old campfire song. *Great green gobs of greasy grimy gopher guts…*

Inside their long, sleek bodies, the worms separate the slurry into microscopic particles using their own natural organs. These particles are further refined by robotics coded with the world's most intricate programming. The worms spit the compounds out at the work site and, following their detailed programming, they painstakingly cobble my new leg together—bone, muscle, veins, skin, tendons, toenails, all of it. All I ever feel is an occasional itch or a vague tickle.

It *is* cool. Even I have to admit it. I mean, they're *worms*.

❋ ❋ ❋

I looked them up on Wikipedia. Guinea worm disease is properly called Dracunculiasis. Due to past efforts of health organizations such as the Carter Center (run by former president Jimmy Carter), the disease is all but eradicated. Today only a handful of cases are reported each year. Back in 2014 there were 126 cases. Twenty years earlier, there were *3.5 million* cases.

I wonder: Does limb regeneration by Guinea worm count?

How about hysterical infestations in high school students?

❋ ❋ ❋

Dr. Soraya gives me a gift this morning, this fifth morning of my procedure: a worm puppet longer than my arm. It has enormous googly eyes with long black lashes, and a red-lipped mouth I can open and close with my fingers and thumb.

For a worm, it's pretty cute.

"I made it myself," the doctor says, helping me thread the puppet over my hand and up my arm. "I'm nowhere near as accomplished at sewing as you are—I went online and looked at your line of clothing. Very impressive!" She pauses. "You have to name him."

"Thanks. He's great." I make the puppet yawn, then get the hiccups, then nip at her wrist. "Quincy. I'll call him Quincy."

Dr. Soraya runs her fingertips over Quincy's soft pink fabric and, laughing, tries to evade his bites. Turning serious, she holds up a camera. "Let's take a look, shall we?"

I sling the puppet over and through the bars beside my hospital bed, clanging its plastic eyes against the metal rails as Dr. Soraya tugs the knit wrapping off my stump and begins snapping pictures. Frowning, she sets the camera down and prods gently at the very end of my stump. "Localized puffiness and edema. Here. Here. And here also." She looks at me and grins. "Beautiful. This stump is absolutely beautiful. It's starting!"

* * *

My stump.

First of all, it isn't beautiful. My leg comes to an abrupt end six inches above where my knee should be. The skin is puckered and discolored with surgical scars and trauma scars and burn scars, and there is one pesky area that my prosthesis rubs raw no matter how hard my prosthetist works at it. To me, the circumference of my stump seems far too big to have ever been the mirror image of my right leg—but how is that possible? I try not to look at it. I try not to touch it more than absolutely necessary. I haven't grown used to my stump in these six years since the terrorist attack, even though everyone said I'd eventually accommodate to it.

I got over the trauma and moved on with my life. I went back to college in a power wheelchair, then with Canadian crutches, and later wearing a series of prosthetic legs with knees that were promised to be almost as good as the real thing, but weren't. I finished my degree in fashion design and went into business for myself. I found a niche: clothing for people with disabilities. For the sight-impaired I created clothing with sewn-in descriptive Braille tags and luscious textures to delight the fingertips; for people with sensory disorders I developed a line of seamless clothing made of the softest fabrics. Most exciting of all were the skirts and pants and dresses I designed to be comfortable with prosthetics, that don't snag or pull or drape in odd ways, that help you forget you're different from everyone else.

People loved it all.

I met Robbie through mutual friends. I fell in love with him, we got engaged, we moved in together, and he finished his doctorate in bioinformatics—a far cry from the teenage computer hacker he used to be. According to his friends, Robbie had once hacked into his high school computer system and changed the grades of every student in the school. He waited a half hour, just long enough for them to be seen and a buzz to build; then he changed them back again and sat back to enjoy the hysteria. Funny guy, my Robbie.

Six months ago Robbie urged me to apply for a trial of an astonishing new medical procedure called worm-assisted limb regeneration. Everyone at his lab was in an uproar over WALR, Robbie most of all. He was convinced WALR had a better-than-average chance of success, mainly because several people he'd known from his doctorate program were working on the project.

He told me I'd be a moron if I didn't apply.

If I was selected for the medical trial we wouldn't have to pay a thing. For twenty lucky people the psychological evaluation, the procedure itself, the monthlong clinic stay, and the four-month cycle of physical therapy afterward would all be free. What kind of idiot would say no to all that? Didn't I *want* a new leg?

"But, Robbie," I told him, rubbing the sore spot on my stump. "What if something goes wrong?"

"It won't." He had a sheaf of paperwork in his hands. "You show up for the psychological testing," he said. "Only don't tell them about the imaginary Guinea worm infestation you had when you were sixteen, okay? They don't need to know about that."

"Okay."

"I'll take care of the rest. I'll fill out the paperwork for you. I know exactly what they want."

Apparently he did know exactly what they wanted, because here I am—Worm Girl all over again. I was selected to be the thirteenth WALR trial case, and the first above-the-knee leg regeneration. I cried when I got the news. Worms or no worms, I am thrilled to be here…but no one will ever convince me that this stump that used to be my leg is beautiful. Not even Dr. Soraya.

But—hey—it is starting.

Edema! Puffiness! Finally, proof that the worms are doing their thing. The countdown has begun; in twenty-five days it will be over and there will be no more worms inside of me ever again. Even *I* can wait twenty-five days if there is a brand-new leg at the end of it. I high-five my doctor, and then Robbie, who's been sitting in his customary seat by the window, but has now set down his laptop and come over to my bed to admire the puppet and see the changes the doctor is so excited about.

I put my hand on my stump as if it were an old friend who will soon move away forever.

And it isn't awful.

❁ ❁ ❁

The adult female Guinea worm is as thick around as a strand of spaghetti. She grows in her human host (who has unwittingly ingested standing water containing water fleas tainted with her larva), and she will normally achieve a length between two and three feet long. From the host's gut, she will travel under the skin toward the legs, where she will make a horribly painful ulcer in her host's knee or calf or ankle, then poke her reproductive glands out into the open so she can spew her eggs into a community's drinking water and perpetuate the cycle. Male worms are much smaller and thinner, at around two inches in length, and are not known to be parasitic.

My worms are juvenile females. They are no thicker than a strand of angel hair pasta, and are a scant six inches long. But it doesn't really matter what they look like, because they're tame.

They're *tame*.

❋ ❋ ❋

Robbie has claimed the chair by the window. He sits there for hours on end, his legs thrown out, his chin on his chest, frowning at his laptop as he scrutinizes screens full of tiny-looking code and punches keys so fast I can barely see his fingers move. He's working on a data set that he's just gained access to, and he's pretty sure he's already found a malfunctioning line of code. He's idly messing with Dr. Soraya's data wand, mindlessly flipping it end over end through his fingers as he stares at his computer screen.

"Robbie," I say. "Hey. You shouldn't do that. That's for the worms."

"What?" he says, sounding distracted. Then he laughs and sets the wand aside, rubbing the back of his neck.

We watch the evening news.

Tonight Robbie stays all night with me, on his chair that can be pulled out to form a makeshift narrow cot. I invite him to join me in my hospital bed, video cameras or no video cameras. We cuddle and watch TV for a while, but when Robbie pulls the covers up to our chins and reaches for me, I gently push him away. "Sorry, honey. I can't. I know they're in their habitat right now…but I just can't."

He tickles me with Quincy the worm puppet instead.

"Ouch! Careful!" I say, rubbing my forearm where one of the hard, sharp-edged googly eyes has slashed me. "Let me see that, will you?"

Where did Dr. Soraya purchase these eyes? They are in no way child-safe, especially since one of them has a cracked edge that is sharp enough to draw blood. I regard my cut arm in dismayed surprise, but Quincy has taken to pestering me and nibbling at my ear, and I am forced to wrestle the puppet to the bed—keeping well away from those lethal eyes—and to give it a severe trouncing.

* * *

"Why worms?" I ask when Dr. Soraya comes in to do the morning worm insertion.

She pulls the privacy curtain closed. "What do you mean?"

"They explained it to me when I signed the papers, but you know, I still don't get it, not really." I pause. "I mean, why couldn't you do limb regeneration with, I don't know, little robots? Why not ditch the worms?" I watch Dr. Soraya set out supplies: habitat, cleaning cloths, slurry syringe, under-skin flashlight, data wand. "It makes everything more difficult, doesn't it? Keeping them alive and healthy?"

Dr. Soraya snaps the habitat nozzle onto my thigh port. "It comes down to DNA."

It turns out that my worms...*are* my worms.

They carry my DNA; they were engineered especially for me, for this one job and for no other—which explains the million-dollar price tag that luckily I don't have to pay. My body recognizes them. It doesn't attack them. Limb regeneration by genetically altered worms is a simple yet incredibly complicated idea that was decades in the making: Everything the worms create for me carries my DNA.

No rejection. End of story. Clever little monsters, aren't they?

"Let's take a look, shall we?" Dr. Soraya says, wielding her special flashlight as if it were the Olympic torch.

❁ ❁ ❁

They're up to something.

I gingerly trace the lumpy new contour of my stump as I talk on the phone with my mother. I tell her that I've been sketching for my new clothing line for heat-sensitive people with multiple sclerosis, and that Robbie and I are going to host a party to celebrate the grand unveiling of my new left leg—can she and Dad come? But my mind is wandering: What *is* that flap of loose skin on my stump that my fingers have just found? It wasn't there a few hours ago.

Are there worms in it? What are they doing?

When I set the phone down, I ask Robbie to bring me the hand mirror and the under-skin light—Dr. Soraya said we could use it whenever we wanted, just to remember to put it back on the charger afterward.

Carefully we take the blanket and pillow away from my leg. Robbie props up the mirror and we study the flap of skin. It's much larger than I'd thought, and it has pink nubbins protruding from the outermost ridge. Toes? Are those things *toes*? I lean forward, trying to get a better view. We turn off the room lights. Robbie aims the under-skin light, and then we see the worms, glowing a lovely cobalt blue, swarming the bottom of my stump. Some of them are inside the flap of new skin. One worm is rooting around inside what might be the big toe.

"Gross," I say. "There's a worm in my toe. That's... really gross."

"But those toes are gonna be real cute. Right?"

We watch the worm back out of the big toe and visit the next one in line. I look at Robbie, and then suddenly we are laughing, big snorting laughs that will surely bring someone from the nurses' station to investigate.

"Um," I say. "I suppose we ought to call Dr. Soraya."

We're still laughing, and flicking at the toe nubbins to see them wiggle, when Dr. Soraya and Gwen, the evening nurse, come in. Dr. Soraya is pleased with the toe buds. Very pleased.

She takes more pictures.

❁ ❁ ❁

According to Wikipedia, there is only one way to safely remove an adult Guinea worm even though it's hardly ever necessary these days: tug gently on the worm's exposed uterus, which will eventually poke out of the host's flesh in order to spew her larvae, wind the uterus around a matchstick, and then pull the worm out of your body an inch at a time, winding as you go, a process that can take many grueling, painful weeks. The process is exactly as my high school teacher described it all those years ago.

The images are seared in my mind; I cannot unsee these things.

Did I really need to know that Guinea worms have uteruses?

Why do I do this to myself?

* * *

Robbie orders six carryout pizzas with roasted garlic on them—he says the garlic cloves look like my toe buds, which I think is both ridiculous and hilarious. He walks the pizzas past the nurses' station and invites everyone to drop by my room for an impromptu celebration of the new toes. My room fills up with the many people involved in my care: Dr. Soraya, Gwen, Corazon (the tech), Miles, whose job Robbie and I have never been able to figure out—and of course the data and robotics guys from the basement.

Robbie gets along great with the night owls, which isn't much of a surprise. They are deep in conversation as I munch garlic pizza and show Dr. Soraya the fashion designs in my sketchbook.

"I think I've figured it out," Robbie says after everyone is gone, even the worms.

"What? Your new toe fetish?"

"Very funny." He smiles. "No. I'm talking about that messed-up line of coding I've been working on. The basement guys helped me find a workaround."

"Oh, that's good." I eye the pizza box. "Hey. You want to share the last piece? Or can I have it?"

They didn't tell me that growing a new limb was such a hungry business.

❁ ❁ ❁

I have toes!

They look just like real toes now, and they have darling little toenails that are the exact size and shape of those I lost. I also have a new foot, an ankle, a calf, and a knee. I keep pulling the blankets down to admire the new parts of my body. It's not what I expected, though: The leg is…empty. It's just skin. It's a bag of too-pale flesh that dangles from the end of my stump like an underfilled water balloon or a flesh-colored knee sock. If I tilt my head just so, it looks like the pattern for a legging, or a leotard. Dr. Soraya says there is a small amount of gelatinous fluid inside the skin, and a network of blood vessels, and not much else except for worms at this point—but it is alive! I can feel it when Dr. Soraya pricks the ankle with a pin! I am thrilled with my flat new leg, but there is no getting around it: Having this unwieldy, flapping *thing* attached to me is downright weird.

The leg must be kept clean just like any other part of me. Robbie has decided he is going to help me wash today. It's something Gwen—my favorite nurse—would normally do, but Robbie says no, let him do it. He picks up the leg, swings it over his arm, and lets it dangle as he suds it up with a warm, soapy washcloth, a sight so weird that it's pretty much beyond description. He says he likes the toes especially, confirming the whole toe-fetish thing. Laughing, he says next time he's out he'll buy nail polish and paint the toenails.

❁ ❁ ❁

Really, I should have stopped looking at Wikipedia days ago. I shouldn't have followed those links. I should never have read that entry on Dracunculiasis on the Centers for Disease Control website. It is doing me no good to know these things about my parasites—about how they reproduce, about how the females spawn hundreds of larvae at a time. I didn't need to know that sometimes a worm will die inside a host and can ruin the host's hip joint (or knee joint, or ankle joint) with their disgusting putrefying bodies.

I did *not* need to know that.

❁ ❁ ❁

I'm alone in my room but for the video camera, something that doesn't happen very often. I pull the bedcovers off my leg and peer down at it, lying there all pink and squishy-looking, full of wonderful and awful things. Dr. Soraya says the delicate scaffoldings of bones are appearing now—all over, and all at once—and muscle tissue, and the lymph system, and tendons and cartilage, and all kinds of other stuff I don't know about.

I tilt my head and regard the leg.

I decide the foot is not as flat as it was earlier; it's starting to fill in and is looking more like my other foot, which thrills me no end. I would take pictures and post them on the internet like a baby announcement—*Look at my new foot, everybody! Robbie and I are going to call her Samantha!*—but my contract absolutely forbids any leakage of information, so I don't.

For the first time I feel like this is *my* leg. It doesn't belong to Dr. Soraya anymore, or to the lab guys.

It's *mine*.

What will it be like to have two legs again? What will it look like when it's all filled out and curvy? How long will it take me to learn to walk again?

I run my fingers lightly over my new knee, relishing the sensation.

❊ ❊ ❊

When Dr. Soraya does the evening extraction, the amber buttons on the data wand don't all turn green. She punches buttons on the wand, repeats the test, gets the same results. "Number three?" she says, sounding distracted, as if she's forgotten I am in the room. "Now, that's… really odd."

"What's odd?" I ask. I set down my sketchbook. "Is it a worm? Did a worm go missing?"

"Of course not. No. Don't worry. We'll take care of everything. I think I'll ask the others to take a look. And I'll bring in a few specialists." She pauses. "We'll discuss it and then I'll fill you in later."

"Why can't you tell me now? What's going on? Please!"

Dr. Soraya doesn't answer. She's tapping notes into her computer in the corner of the room, consulting handwritten pages she'd written earlier. Abruptly she stands, grabs her data wand, and leaves without saying goodbye.

And then I realize: Being a patient in a medical trial of this scope might have a few drawbacks.

❊ ❊ ❊

"She's lying," I say to Robbie. "I think she's not telling me something."

I'm leaning over my belly, arms crossed, and I'm shaking.

The movement is making Quincy the worm puppet swing back and forth from his perch on the bed rails. Robbie closes his laptop. He's been struggling with his big project—his data set still isn't performing correctly—but now he sets his frustration aside and gives me his full attention. "Really? Lying? About what?"

"The worms." I scratch my thigh, near the port.

"Scoot over, Worm Girl." Robbie sits on the bed next to me and massages my shoulders. "I don't think she's lying. She's bound by confidentiality clauses, just like you are. She'd tell you if something was wrong." He runs a finger lightly down my thigh. "Your leg looks great. We're at the halfway point; did you know that? Look at that sexy ankle! I can see the shapes of the bones under the skin, I swear I can."

"She lost a worm. Number three. She said number three."

"Honey. No. She didn't lose a worm."

I don't argue. But what does he know? I'm the one who knows what worms feel like as they move through your body, not him. I know the horrible itching just under the skin, the squirming feelings, the ache of flesh that has been invaded by parasites. I *know* this feeling. I've felt it before.

I don't sleep at all. Whenever I close my eyes I am plagued by the slender, wriggling forms of Guinea worms. Robbie, kindhearted Robbie, sleeps next to me in his pullout cot.

* * *

They take me for tests. Ultrasounds, MRI, CAT scans, X-rays, blood work. Are they routine, part of my scheduled care? Or do they have something to do with worm number three?

"Dr. Soraya," I say when I'm finally back in my room. The

doctor has stopped by to do a quick scan. "Listen. I have itches under my skin." I rub my arms and my rib cage and my waist. "Why? Why am I itching?"

She looks up at me, frowning slightly. "You're itching? You shouldn't be itching. We'll give you Benadryl."

"Is it the worm? Tell me! Is it worm number three?"

"Of course not. Why would you think that?" Dr. Soraya flashes me a smile as she leaves the room. She must think I am joking.

"When are the specialists coming? You said specialists are coming!" I call after her, but she doesn't hear, or doesn't bother answering. Take your pick.

"Dammit," I say.

Robbie stands up. "They'll come. They're probably waiting for those test results." He comes close and drops a small paper bag onto my lap. "Honey, look. I bought you that toenail polish I promised."

Sighing, I open the bag and lift out the bottle. "Midnight Eggplant." I smile at him, trying to put some warmth into it. "Where do they get these names? I like the color. Thanks."

He pulls over one of the visitor chairs and sets about painting my toenails a lovely semi-matte black with plum undertones. First he paints the toes of my new foot, and then of my old foot, and he does it so neatly and carefully that I find myself wondering whom he practiced this on before me, and how I never knew this about him.

As he paints, he prattles on and on about that pesky code of his, how it's not behaving the way he expects it to, how he thinks it might be impacting several other threads of work, how he's going to look at it more tomorrow, how he might fix what he'd done. It occurs to me that it sounds an awful lot like the prattle the basement guys were saying about their work with the worms. I shift my good leg, rub my shoulder, scratch my cheek. I'm still itchy. Why am I so itchy?

Finally Robbie screws the lid back onto the nail polish. "There," he says. "What do you think?"

I know what he's trying to do. He's trying to distract me.

"It's great. Thanks," I say, even though it's not working. It's hard to be distracted when a worm might be loose inside of you.

How long can I take this?

* * *

Gwen brings dinner for me and Robbie: spaghetti that looks way, *way* too much like worms. What were they thinking? I'm still pushing the noodles around my plate when Dr. Soraya comes with her specialists. The lab guys from the basement file in also, and two men Robbie and I have never met before. They circle the bed and lean over me, murmuring, speaking their science language. They ask Robbie to move, not caring that he'd been holding my hand for moral support.

"Let's take a look, shall we?" Dr. Soraya positions my leg flat out on a clean sheet, smooths the skin with gloved hands, and invites her guests in for a closer look. They stare at it, point at various locations: the inside of my knee, my lower calf, the outside of my ankle. They prod at the underside of my foot. They don't seem to know what to make of…whatever it is. They share notes and computer printouts with one another. Gwen brings in a larger version of the under-skin light, and the doctors go back to studying the patch on the inside of my knee.

A violent burning itch has started up on my left hip. The rogue worm? I bite my lip and try not to squirm.

"Mmm, yes," one of the new doctors says.

The tallest lab guy scratches his chin. "Right."

"There they are. That's what I'm talking about," says Dr. Soraya. "Right there, by the knee."

Robbie appears at my side; he must have pushed his way to the bed. He takes my hand.

"What?" I say, near panic. "*What's* right there? What are you talking about, Dr. Soraya? It's number three, isn't it?"

"We've found several small anomalies. Like I said before, nothing to worry about." Dr. Soraya turns away. "All right, let's meet in the conference room," she says to her team, and just like that, she's done with me. She's holding the door to my room open, letting the others file out ahead of her. Robbie and I are not invited.

"Wait!" My voice comes out somewhere between a shriek and a howl. "Come back. *What* anomalies? Is it the worm?"

Dr. Soraya's hand rests on the door, but she turns around to face me again. "Please. We'll know more when the tests come in. Wait until tomorrow, all right?"

"No! I don't want to wait. Get number three *out of me*!"

She frowns as if I've said something baffling. "I'll come back and extract the worms at eight o'clock, just like always."

"That's not what I mean and you know it." I glare after her. "You're not telling me everything!"

"Honey," says Robbie, patting my arm. "Calm down."

Dr. Soraya turns around, and her face isn't unkind. "Believe me. It's nothing to get upset about. We'll know more tomorrow."

My hands are clenched so hard my fingers hurt. "Then *why*"—my voice goes up an entire octave—"why are all of you so fucking worried?"

❊ ❊ ❊

What does "several small anomalies" mean, anyway?

Dr. Soraya gives me a sedative when I go to bed, and Benadryl also, but they do nothing for me. It's way past midnight, and just like last night I'm wide-awake. I feel the rogue worm squirming under my skin. There are phantom itches, and real itches too. The area around my thigh port burns with the itching, and my hip. The damn Benadryl isn't working. My fingernails make long ribbons of red scratch marks all over my skin, and still I scratch. I wish Robbie were here, but he's gone down the hall to take a quick shower.

What has Dr. Soraya so baffled she had to call in specialists? I throw the covers off and stare at my leg. Suddenly it all becomes clear: Guinea worm number three...has *spawned.*

Inside of me.

Usually spawning doesn't take place in the host's body. Usually standing water and fleas are involved in the worms' complicated breeding cycle. This wasn't supposed to happen—something *made* the worm spawn. My glance falls on Robbie's laptop. All at once, like an avalanche, pieces fall into place, and suddenly, horribly, I know. It was Robbie.

Robbie did this to me. He hadn't meant to, but it was him.

The timing fits, all of it: that enormous code he "got access to"—a fine euphemism for hacking, only I hadn't seen it. The broken line of coding. The fix that turned out not to be a fix at all. Robbie messed with the worms' programming; I know it like I know the itching underneath my skin. Because of Robbie, worm number three took off on her own. Because of Robbie, she spawned.

Of *course* Dr. Soraya has no idea what the anomalies are! How could she?

I swallow. My hands make fists on top of my covers. I'm too hot; then I'm too cold. I'm feverish. I press my nurse call button, only nobody comes. I feel sick to my stomach. I'm sweaty. I'm sweaty *and* itchy. *And* nauseated. Where's Robbie? I need to talk to him! Itchiness is a symptom of Guinea worm disease! I know this from my research.

My *God.*

Guinea worm larvae are loose in my body—I can't sit around and wait for Robbie. I damn well am not going to wait for Dr. Soraya and her consultants to get rid of them. I have to *do* something. I yank Dr. Soraya's puppet off my hospital bed and fling it to the floor. Its plastic googly eyes hit the floor tiles with a surprisingly loud clatter.

Worms. I *hate* the slimy things. I think I might throw up.

I was going to tell Robbie to kick that odious puppet across the floor for me, stomp on it a few times, then stuff it into the garbage when he got back from his shower…but he's not back yet; he's probably at the nurses' station, or has even gone down to the basement to find his pals. It's just as well he isn't here, because now I have a better idea.

I will fix the larvae problem myself. Robbie created the problem; *I* will fix it.

No one else needs to know that Robbie hacked the WALR program.

I lean over and snatch the puppet up by those outrageous eyelashes and study its eyeballs. I nod. My idea might work. It has to. I grasp the puppet by its long wormy body, swing it around, and slam its head against the bedrails once, twice, three times, until a piece of white eyeball flies off and skitters across the floor.

Both googly eyes now have sharp edges, just as I'd intended. I stare at my leg, holding those eyeballs between my fingers as if they were brass knuckles. My hand shakes.

My…beautiful…new…leg.

You were almost mine, I think, *you are lovely, and wondrous, and I was beginning to love you.* I blink back tears. *I'll miss you. I'll miss your sweet toes with your black nail polish. I'm sorry. I'm so, so sorry. But I just can't live with worms.*

With great heaving sobs, I begin to do what must be done. I use the sharp, jagged edges of the puppet's broken googly eyes on my poor leg: I tear! I jab! I slash!

I will kill those larvae.

Fury rises to the surface, a rage I hadn't known I'd been holding on to all these years. I feel that rage now—oh, *yes*, I feel it now. Worm Girl harbored years of resentment toward her high school science teacher for having told those horrific Peace Corps stories in the first place, for having planted seeds that led to hallucinations and hysteria. I cry for Worm Girl. I cry for myself. It's not fair to lose a leg to a terrorist…to get it back… and then *this*. Not. Fair.

Out! Out! Damn worms!

Out!

Blood wells up from the deep scratches on my left leg. The blood is full of larvae; I just know it is. How did I *ever* think it was a good idea to let them experiment on me with *parasites*? Why did I let Robbie talk me into this? I was getting along *fine* with my prosthetic; I really was. And now where am I? I'm fucked, that's what: If I don't do a thorough job exterminating this nest of larvae inside my knee—this *anomaly*—a thousand baby Guinea worms will colonize my body.

Maybe they already have.

Tears mar my vision, but I swipe them away with the back of my hand. I *won't* think about my leg; I *won't*. Holding my breath, I wield the sharp edge of the puppet's bloodied eyes and slash at my new leg, and I slash, and I slash—it hurts like hell but it's not enough—*it is not enough.* My leg is bleeding... but I need to get inside the leg. I need to tear it open and *get at those larvae.*

Now! I need to do it now! I need to do it before the people come. I'm surprised they're not here already—but I've been fairly quiet; it's the middle of the night, and they must not be paying attention. Their video surveillance is failing them, and they don't even know it yet.

I frown at the bloody googly eyes.

I've used eyes like this before, in my own work. I know how to make a better weapon out of them. It takes only seconds to arm myself: I turn the puppet inside out and find the two clamps that hold the eyes in place. I pry them loose with my teeth. I turn the puppet right-side out, and the eyes, now loose, fall into my hand. Each eye has a sturdy metal pin on the back of it.

My weapons.

I'm through being quiet. With a pin in each hand I stab at my leg. I stab; I scream with pain; I stab some more. Delicate things inside my leg fall to my assault, and I hear their small crunching sounds. And then suddenly Robbie is at my side, trying to still my murderous hands, but I am stabbing-stabbing-stabbing, and I almost stab him too.

"Stop! Stop!"

"Robbie?" I say, blinking.

"Honey! Stop it!" he cries. "What are you doing?"

"They spawned! They spawned!"

"No, they didn't! They can't—you know that." He draws in a sharp breath. "Oh, God, what have you done to yourself?"

Dr. Soraya is here, and others too, and before I know it they have me by the arms. They pry my weapons away, and it *hurts*, and I see that my palms have been slashed by the sharp edges of the eyes.

"Give those back!" I shriek. "I need them! The worms *did* spawn! They're spreading all over my body! Let me *go*!" I try to twist away. "Robbie! Robbie! Tell them what you did. *Tell them to let go of me!*" I gasp for breath, writhing in my bloody sheets, and I see that my left leg is in tatters and that there are deep gouges radiating from my thigh port; when had I done that? I look up at Robbie, pleading, crying. "Number three got loose! It was a female and she spawned in my knee! Dr. Soraya said so! The larvae are already on the move, Robbie! We have to stop them. Let me go, *let me go*!"

Frantic now, I bite the nearest arm.

Robbie makes a wet, muffled sound. "No, honey, oh, no, don't do that."

Dr. Soraya's voice is all business. "She's hallucinating. And going into shock. Gwen, start the IV. Miles, hold her down. Good. Get the boyfriend out of here." Dr. Soraya yanks bloody covers off the bed and peers at my leg. "To the surgery suite. Stat. I may still be able to save the leg."

Save the leg? She thinks she might have to amputate it?

"No!" I scream, and fling myself half off the bed. "No! No! Not my leg!"

Robbie's face hovers in front of me. "Honey," he says, and then his voice breaks.

I turn on him, barely noticing that someone in a white jacket is swabbing my arm with an alcohol pad. "Robbie. You…you… you messed with their programming, didn't you?"

"No! What are you *talking* about?"

I struggle against the arms holding me down. "You did this! You hacked the WALR computer! It was *you*, wasn't it? That code you were working on—"

They stab me with a hypodermic needle.

I scream.

If Robbie says anything more, I miss it.

❁ ❁ ❁

There is a new Wikipedia article about Guinea worms. I'm in it.

I've read it so many times I've memorized entire paragraphs. There are so many links to outside sources that the page is speckled blue. There are pictures, lots of them. Halfway down the article are the three pictures of me: a "before" picture of my leg stump, looking pale and exposed; a picture of Dr. Soraya leaning over my hospital bed, light wand in hand, examining my new leg when it was in the flat, floppy stage. The last picture is of me and Robbie a few months later at our celebration party. In this picture I am wearing a purple miniskirt, and I look radiant and whole. My toenails are painted Midnight Eggplant and are an exact match to my skirt. My new worm-generated leg—the caption points out—is perfect in every way: an exact mirror image of the other.

The article has a footnote: This patient nearly lost her leg due to a serious adverse reaction to one of the regeneration medications. It was only through the heroic efforts of Dr. Soraya and her team that the patient's "miracle leg" was saved. The patient—the footnote goes on—has recovered fully and has no lasting effects.

Except.

Except in the middle of the night, when number three wakes up and I can feel her moving underneath the skin of my new leg, and the unbearable itching begins.

Happening with the Gods

By Nancy Bonnington

[Notes compiled for The Complicated Greek, by Richard Mild.]

Zeus does not rule from a petty house of chaos, as so many think. Nor is he as unpredictable and unmalleable as some say. Perhaps he once was, stirred up by the richness and fame of the land, less than subtle in his indignation. Perhaps he did overreact, punishing Prometheus by eternally ripping out his liver, and for what? Because Prometheus gave us fire? Absurd! Overrated! It has been said that Zeus took revenge on men by creating women. But I don't believe it. Look at how his sculptured hand caresses Harmonia's golden locks as they laugh and play by the river. He touches her breast and there is not a hint of vengeance in his heart.

No, Aeschylus was wrong about Zeus—he didn't mean to be the oppressor of mankind; he never wanted to be the god of all gods. That day they came to him, he tried to hide beneath a rock but lacked the fortitude to stave off the masses. Their adulation rose as in one voice, beckoning, then naming him king. So he stood, first in the form of a bull to gather courage, then that of a man. His bent head took the laurel, and nobody can blame him for that!

He is passionate but growing fairer in his judgment each year. Of course he has always envied his own son, Dionysus. Zeus wishes that he, too, could give ecstasy all day long. While Zeus' pleasures have been limited, proportioned to time as his schedule demands, he has shown a virtuous amount of restraint. That Hera slayed the mother of Dionysus, that in bitter jealousy, after pacing for a fortnight, she threw a bolt of lightning at Semele's head, shows who has the quicker temper. Not to mention that there are those who think Zeus is not even Dionysus' father. Hera never even bothered to check the facts.

N.B.—Remember to thank Hera for the magic fruit tree. The juice of the golden apple appears to have cured my eczema.

The night I first met Hera, she was making love with Poseidon, old man of the Sea, at the oracle of Apollo at Delphi. Initially I registered horror at the sight—let's not forget the stench—of the old man, land-logged in the summer sun, whose sea smell permeated the air. And I am not a voyeur, but peering out from behind a large gray stone, I began to witness with fascination the play between these two immortals. Hera, whose dewy skin shone like the inside of an oyster shell, was granted each request she made of this unlikely old man. It was the first I had known of the metamorphosing talents of Poseidon. He could with stunning agility change his shape into that of any creature. What would shock a mortal woman was merely titillating to Hera, however, whose requests for the seven-headed sea dragon of Cyber caught even the old man by surprise. And how remarkably she kept up with him!

When they were through, and Poseidon had slid back to his underwater hiding place on a bed of seaweed, I stepped forward and greeted Hera.

We walked together through an open wood. This place, sustained by a certain lushness of vegetation, salient streams, and tidy camps of peaceful worshipers, was—and I admit a sense of awe—the most beautiful place I had ever seen. Hera, who moved sometimes as fluidly as the rivers or the wind through the grasses, was continually touching my shoulder, darting glances at me, and posing questions. How did I like the modern world? My job? My wife? Did we have any children? "What is it like," she asked, her huge eyes growing even huger, "for mortals to make love? They still do, don't they?"

I hesitated to answer for all men.

But then we talked of Vera, and how my wife and I were drifting apart, and how, when Vera first heard me speak of the gods, she loaded up the bathroom cabinet with valium and purchased a self-help book entitled *Living with a Dangerous Man.*

But I was not dangerous, and Vera had to admit the possibility of the gods (and give some credence to my vocation, as well). The fact that this happening with the gods began on the night before our twentieth anniversary was, I believe, a grand coincidence. For Vera to suggest anything more, without evidence, is what I call pure feminine conjecture. I only wish she would suspend her disbelief long enough for a proper discussion. What I ask of her is nothing more than the skill of a child.

Hera listened without judgment. Morality is different among the gods—right and wrong are more like directions, like north, south, east, or west, existing as possibilities from which to choose. Thus, Hera was an exquisite listener.

"Go on," she coaxed.

Vera had accused me of trying to kill myself. "You're jumping and saying you were compelled," she huffed at me. "I don't know if you really believe in these gods of yours, or if you're trying to drive me crazy, but *you need help*!"

"If you would only hear me out—"

"And if you don't get help"—she spun and looked me in the eye—"then you've got a hell of a fast fall coming...."

If Vera believed my brain was performing with less agility, I must say my students had quite the opposite opinion. This happening with the gods had enlivened Mythology 101 to such a degree that my class had perfect attendance. After all, education is in the details, and I have been blessed to observe the little things. Like the way Zeus clears his throat every time Hera rests a hand on his shoulder. I call it Zeus' anticipatory grumble. Hera has a way of turning the barest touch into foreplay. At times sparks will fly from her fingers so that she need not even touch her husband flesh-to-flesh. It is a joy to watch them when they are in their better moods.

"I would never have told you about the gods if you didn't mean everything in the world to me. For God's sake, Vera..."

But she is distant. I do not tell Hera that my wife and I no longer make love. When things fade, I adjust. Is that a strength or a weakness? Vera has even said she lives with an unconscious man. How can I touch her after that?

There was nothing I enjoyed more than observing the gods. From them I hoped to become more human, perhaps to admit my own frailties beside the superior shortcomings of supreme beings. A praiseworthy goal. It was never my fault that Vera suffered a common lack of classical training, and yet she had once respected me. I admit it was an obsession—my book. But Vera had not married a couch potato. What exactly she wanted from me I could not tell. I had tried. I had refrained from conversing with the gods as long as possible. I do not even consider it a talent, more of a sublime gift. That Vera could not be happy for me is a continual source of shame. I have told her that marital bliss does not thrive even on Mount Olympus. At that she slapped my face and wept.

On a typical night: The strangeness of the night comes from the clouds—that it is cloudy, that there are no stars, that it seems like we are trapped underneath a nutshell. You can feel the roundness of the sky when it is close, the roundness of everything, the planet you are on; you can feel your own otherwise imperceptible soul; you can write a song about circles in life, cycles, implosions, how things get turned in upon themselves, but on a typical night it feels like a trap. Standing on the deck of the ferry, it is wrong that it should be so hot. It is wrong that the sky is illuminated by the city lights, a perversion of nature, where the source of all light and life should come from above.

I tried for months to refrain from my visits. But this happening with the gods was out of my control.

One night (I don't know how many times before; it is all a blur; it is all the same. Vera has asked for a reckoning, a sort of time line with the intricate details that no biography can accurately provide, while I can offer only this), I was too tightly bundled. I took off my jacket to the sound of ripping Velcro. Others were gathered around me, more passengers huddling under absurd layers of clothing, as though we were at the

North Pole rather than floating on Puget Sound. "Brr," said mothers and children, while fathers muttered hypotheses about high-pressure zones, cold fronts, and the origin of supercooled water droplets on the ferry deck. They all sounded foolish. This much I did not imagine.

We would reach Seattle soon, five minutes to go, with the smell of the sea getting stronger as it does near the wharf. I felt it happening and didn't question it. The bubbling up inside my stomach, the rush to the brain like gas, like something lighter than air and invisible, the spirits holding a shindig in my skull.

As it usually happens, my head swells or seems to. Greek letters flash by like the countdown images on a picture screen. The gods and goddesses crowd into the temple. I am not overworked or prone to fancy, as Vera insists, but open to all possibilities. I am an open jar, while Vera's lid is on too tight. When her anger reaches a fever pitch, I remind her that I am faithful. For all of that I receive no points. Only the heartache of belittling glances and angry shrugs.

Four minutes to the dock and my waist was pressed tightly to a railing. Vera was in the cabin where I had left her in midargument. I leaned over, searching for the water below. I peeled off my shirt. I could see the water, but faintly. It was flat, grayish, dancing teeny waves popping up and down, flittering like the balls in whistles. Larger waves, I knew, were there beneath, somehow supporting the ripples, huge and rolling like a mother's belly. Through it all the ferry moved squarely and smoothly, a knife through icing, and there is no reason to believe the water felt no pain. All matter was charged with such feeling. My lips buzzed with electricity as I licked them. It is possible that I heard Vera's voice, but more likely that I felt the tug of a higher friendship and longed for it to be ours, only to know, in my heart, that the gods are capable of far greater understanding than my own wife.

I was compelled to jump by the force of invisible hands. From above I heard a brief gasp, then nothing more. As the water closed in around me I sank, my wet pants and heavy-soled shoes pulling me downward. I had not even waited to fully undress myself, such was my utter contempt for the argument with Vera. (Take a break from the book? Had she lost her mind?)

It was bliss. Was it the third time? The tenth? The twentieth? I sank into the always welcoming hands of the gods—warm, cozy, and accepted. As usual I found brilliance and friendship in the blond meadow beside a temple where Zeus was receptive to me. "Greetings, Richard," he said, and we shook hands. His eyebrows lifted in a question and I began to answer, "Vera…"

"Women!" he said, and, "Don't get me started."

Then I watched well into the evening, his animated speech beguiling all around the table with the myth and lecture of feminine evolution. When Zeus speaks of women, his eyes water. "Of course, Hera, my dear and anointed one, is by far the loveliest," he concluded. And Hera held up her glass, a toast to the god she adored above all. I felt the distance between myself and Vera ever widening, and yet I confess the feeling of warmth and self-acceptance of one who is growing beyond his roots. I confess, too, that I got mightily drunk on nectar and did little thinking about my marriage.

The experience came to an abrupt end when suddenly I shot upward, breaking through the surface of Puget Sound like a fist punching through taut cellophane wrap. A life raft had been lowered at the sound of a man-overboard drill, and the ferry was shrinking into the Seattle skyline, the lifesaving dinghy rushing my way. The gods were gone, one shoe was lost at sea, and my head was clear—remarkably clear. It always happens that way—that clarity, that feeling of euphoria, a cleansing of the jittery, overactive synapses.

A crowd had gathered at the waterfront, happy to be present at a crucial struggle of life over death. "Thank God," some said. Complete strangers. It is not that I don't care for my fellow man (Vera is so wrong about that), but I suspect there is little genuine concern left in the world for one stranger about another.

"Thank God you're okay," a woman said to me. She was beautiful, her scent as profound as the texture of a tree, and my hand mechanically slicked back my wet hair.

Vera was angry. She made this accusation that I turn off my senses when we argue. I don't know what it is about me. If only Vera could see that all couples argue, even the gods. She is prone to exaggeration and melodrama. I have come to an acceptance of the situation, while she riles against the confines of an imperfect joining. There is indeed, in my opinion and in the opinion of my brighter students, a tendency for women to expect too much from men. There is also—and I say this without pride—an advantage to a man's natural coping skills. While Vera weeps day after day, I move forward. I have asked her to do the same, to no avail. That very night I climbed into bed beside her and she turned from me. I stroked her back and she shuddered, letting out a dismal sigh, long and low. We have become like shadows that erase each other. Zeus told me that Hera once spit a blinding venom into his eye as they argued over his extramarital activities, and yet even that, I told Zeus, would be preferable to Vera's trained aloofness.

Another time we were conversing and Vera was strange. When I touched her, she smiled sadly at me and said I didn't get it. She shook her head and said we were falling apart. If only Vera could visit the world of the gods, she would see how trivial our problems are. I tell her that even those with omnipotence can't always smooth the waters. When I feel impotent and Vera is a shrinking bud so far off... Aw, sometimes my research is a pure longing....

"I mean it," Vera said to me another day, her eyes blistering. "Consider this an ultimatum."

I heard the door slam and felt the house reverberate with Vera's anger. I knew even before reaching Elliot Bay that I was imploding. It is a feeling of utter powerlessness and self-contempt.

I stood on a fishing dock with several loners reeling in their lines to empty hooks. At first my head began to tingle. Then my arms. If I were not already experienced at this I would have thought I was having a heart attack. The water was calm and flat. This time I could see Hera sitting at a marble table just beneath the surface. She appeared to be drinking something.

I fell hard. My stomach and thighs slapped the salt water with a loud *thwack!* The distance from the dock to the water had been farther than I imagined. But again it was not by choice that I plunged into the drink. In a way I was just accepting an invitation. I cannot blame one single god or goddess, but I was mysteriously drawn to Hera sitting so coyly at that marble table. Had her powers overwhelmed my better judgment, I can't say, though I could see a sparkle in her eye as she raised her cup to me.

That afternoon the gods were playing a kind of bowling game. Zeus was there along with Harmonia, his mistress, and other minor figures. Live sheep were used as pins, and the gods bowled with a ball of fire. It was a sight to see. While Zeus showed off his near-perfect form, I visited with Hera.

"Do you notice," she asked me quite suddenly and with amusement, "that your wife's name is very similar to mine?"

And I had to admit that I fell in love with my wife's name even before I fell in love with my wife. It is a strong name—yes, perhaps because of my association with Greek mythology and the similarity of Vera to Hera.

"It is mere coincidence," I assured Hera.

She laughed and touched my cheek as she spoke, a touch that seemed to melt my face. "How ignorant and beautiful you are, Richard Mild. You can't deal with things, can you?"

"Vera never understood me. I question that she even knows what love is," I began. But an ache in my heart cut me short and I quickly asked Hera whether Dionysus had visited and in what health.

Hera shoved a jug of wine my way in answer to the question. On the surface Hera is a motherly goddess, but beneath it all she seethes with jealousy of the younger generation. It is not unlike her to suggest her children are due for punishment. Only with luck, and that she is fascinated by my plight, do I stay on her good side.

"What do you truly want for yourself?" she asked me.

My mind went blank, shut off like a light. Then my thoughts dwindled into obscurity. After nearly licking the last drop of nectar from the bottom of my clay mug, I bade farewell to the gods and promised to return.

"You may work it out with your wife," said Hera. But she turned to look at Zeus and they both laughed. (Laughter of the gods can light up the sky.)

"Even still," I began.

"O mortal!" Hera sang, "You may even find solitude *victorious*!"

More dreary laughter. I did not wait to hear the end of her thoughts, for a sheriff's deputy was pulling me from the bay by my coat collar and I was coughing and sputtering—such a mess. I was checked over, rebuked, and released to the custody of Vera, who spoke only four words to me on the way home: "We need to talk."

After that I visited the gods often, took voluminous notes, invoked their personalities for my students, and bathed in the satisfaction of making great progress on my book. What Vera was up to I don't know. I had since moved into the spare bedroom.

One night Vera and I were involved in our usual one-way discussion. She was chastising me and I was perplexed. Suddenly she burst out, "You are going to have to deal with the fact that I want a divorce. I don't care how sick you are—I can't stay in this. I want out!"

I was speechless. She could just as well have cracked my skull. The fact that we were stuck in neutral by no means necessitated a declaration of complete failure. It was possible that Vera and I needed counseling or a vacation. But divorce? I would put the book on hold, I told her.

The next morning Vera was gone. The house trumpeted with my dejection. The rafters shook. I stormed up and down the hallways, in and out of the rooms, observing with care what items were missing, what mementos Vera had felt compelled to take in this first round of our undoing.

I quickly drove to the waterfront and boarded a ferry, a peaceful route unburdened by encroaching ships. The sound appeared deceptively shallow and slow. The wind spoke like a child's whisper as I stood by the rail. I listened to the rich bellow of the ferry's horn as we slipped away from the dock.

How could I separate myself from Vera? We were intertwined, regardless....

I felt the uprising of the happening with the gods. But this time I closed my eyes, took deep breaths, and counted to ten. The fluttering in my head subsided. For the first time I won the battle. No invisible hands clawed at me; no temptations beneath the sea drew me away from this limited dimension.

I could feel my heart pumping slowly and methodically, lending its blood to all portions of my body. A seagull flew past. Then I was momentarily alone, in the bigger sense of the word—alone in a universe of absolute and utter vastness. Alone with no obligations. I could almost feel Vera removing her tendrils from my spine bit by bit, like peeling cooked spaghetti off the walls.

I swung a foot over the railing, and for the first time I wondered whether the gods would be there to meet me. This time I jumped of my own accord, however. I cannot deny it.

[Further notes compiled for The Complicated Greek, by Richard Mild.]

He is older now, calmer. We talk about women with less animation. He has even run a weave across the old loom for Hera—some sort of a throw rug for her birthday. Hera's face is timeless, unchanging; she sits and watches us, smiling like my mother used to smile. I think Hera is wiser than Zeus. All these years and she never let on.

The only thing that still bristles on occasion between them is Hephaestus. Hera conceived him by herself, without her husband's permission or participation. Dear, angry Hera, strong-willed Hera. Born weak and crippled, Hephaestus was rejected by his mother. Angered, he temporarily imprisoned her. Who knows what went on between the two in those long months? Zeus on the patio shakes his head. But Hephaestus, who was given Aphrodite for a bride, no longer complains. And in the eyes of his stepfather, Hephaestus' own brilliance burns with unspoken respect.

And as for Hera's part, she no longer mentions her father. The subject is not taboo, only comfortably forgotten in this household. Cronus, who has spit up all the children he once swallowed—strange Cronus, conquered by Zeus—has probably already regretted the queer, maniacal handling of his paternal affairs. So Hera believes. Eating his children was just an instinctual act. And Zeus and Hera are really no worse for the wear.

Yes, to see the pair, aging yet ageless, forever shaping the lives of lesser undying gods, musing on the plight of men, to see this, and to see it in person, is an experience I cherish too much to give up.

I only regret not being able to convey these notes to my editor….

"Checkers?" Zeus asks, scratching his beautiful square jaw. Still there is that same amusement on his face. "Is that anything like chess?"

"I've known you so long now, Zeus." I hold my poker face. A bee is scratching at my leg. "This is a game I believe I can beat you at."

With my finger I am creating boxes in the sand at the god's feet. He picks up a handful of flat stones and, with a single breath, colors them black and red. He asks me how Vera is doing. I tell him I wouldn't know.

"Don't you think it's time to be going home?" Hera whispers. Her voice is a soft breeze that ruffles the fig leaves. I am in my underwear, and still I sweat. But this is hardly a problem with the great blue pools of water built around the temple. One could refresh himself all day long and never grow weary here.

"Home?" I ask. "I used to have one of those." I snort with laughter and the others laugh with me.

"Beautiful Richard, our fixture," says Hera. She snaps the back of my shorts and all the gods snicker. But I don't mind her affable gestures. I deal with each emotion as it arises.

When Night comes forth, sweeping her coat of jewels across the sky, it is a pleasure to watch. Zeus gazes upward, smiling. I am going to ask him a question, but then he looks at me, lifts a finger to his lips, and shakes his head. Harmonia, goddess of marital bliss, is returning to her husband, while the god of gods climbs silently up the worn path to Mount Olympus. Hera turns and waves goodbye as well. More often, I am thinking, mortals should seek some setting as primeval and pure as all of this. Surrounded by such beauty, I cannot even remember the lovely hills of the Puget Sound region. I only vaguely recall Vera on that day, dressed in her Sunday finest, waiting for me to sign some papers. At the moment, I can't even recall her face.

Sinkholes

By Susan Whiting Kemp

When the sinkhole opened up in Mullen Sofer's yard, Aunt Jennifer told me, "Grace, it was God's work." She didn't have to continue on to say "…because Mullen is a sinner." She'd said that so many times I knew the drill. She didn't like the way he farted in the store whenever he saw her, then told her she was jealous she didn't have fart-on-demand skills. She didn't like the way he called her Weasel Face, though, to be fair, he said it lovingly, and anyway she wasn't anywhere close to looking like a weasel.

She didn't like the way he didn't have a steady job but sponged off of the various women who lived with him for a week here or a month there, or in one case (the one who only giggled and adjusted her bra strap constantly) a full three months. She didn't like the way his yard had one Toyota and two Subaru carcasses that he wouldn't dispose of properly. And apparently neither did God, since the sinkhole took the Toyota.

I gasped when I saw the photo. The sinkhole was so big,

whole cedars lay inside it. The Toyota sat at the bottom, so small. It never had a chance.

Aunt Jennifer wasn't the only one who said it was God's work. Lucille, one of Mullen's ex-spongees, said that she hoped the sinkhole would widen until Mullen dropped through straight to hell.

Uncle Mark was one of the few people who didn't think Mullen had it coming. He had always been more accepting of people, especially me. Aside from my parents, he was the person I loved most in the world.

Still, Uncle Mark was deeply devout, and talked of the sinkhole as part of the Lord's plan. I often wondered why I didn't believe in God the same way others around me did. Maybe there was only so much belief to go around, and when people like my aunt and uncle carried buckets of it, that left only a teaspoonful for me.

As it turned out, if God had created the sinkhole, He did it indirectly, through a broken water pipe. After it was discovered the utility company turned the water off and rerouted the pipe, and the sinkhole stopped sinking. They told us it was a washout and not technically a sinkhole, but every single one of us still called it that.

Mullen said God gave him the sinkhole for golf practice, and I heard he putted garbage into it with a certain glee that most people didn't find contagious. He refused to let the county do any repairs because, "That utility man said Al Gore visited that City of Shoreline sinkhole in 1995. Nobody's filling mine in until I get my very own vice presidential visit."

"Grace, you stay away from men like Mullen," Aunt Jennifer made sure to warn me during one of my frequent visits to see her and Uncle Mark. "He would chew up a nineteen-year-old girl like a piece of Fruit Stripe gum."

"Give me some credit," I said. "He's twice my age, has Bozo hair, and howls at the moon." At this, Uncle Mark raised his eyebrows, and that was all it took. I doubled over laughing. He could always make me laugh quicker than anybody else.

Then another sinkhole opened up in a different part of town, in Addie Sampson's yard. Another known sinner. The term you heard the most from everybody was, "It certainly is a coincidence," said either as if they really meant it was a coincidence, or it most certainly was not. Aunt Jennifer said flat out that God was giving us hints so big only a blind man could miss them.

I visited the new sinkhole, which was threatening Addie's house. The opening under the back porch didn't seem that big, maybe as wide as a washing machine, but it was too dark to see how deep it went. I didn't think it was a punishment from God, though its sudden appearance did seem like a message. Like someone upstairs was trying to tell Addie something.

The county engineer said this latest sinkhole was from an abandoned coal mine. I'd thought coal mines were found only in places like Kentucky, but apparently plenty streaked through the Cascade Mountain foothills of Washington State. The county rushed an engineering company out to address the problem before it ate up Addie's house. Inside the hole they rigged up a rebar cage that looked a lot like the playground equipment the elementary school had to replace because it was too dangerous for children. They pumped goop into the rebar cage. It looked like marshmallow cream blobs yellowed with age. They covered that over with concrete and a layer of sod. Presto, no sinkhole.

I knew all this because Addie showed me the before, during, and after photos. "Big hole endangering house. Big hole filled with goop. Lawn with sinner standing on former big hole." She beamed at her own image; she knew where she stood with my aunt.

The day after the coal mine sinkhole was filled, Mullen came to the Vege-Lation, where I waited tables. He'd been hiking in the woods and told us the ground out there was on fire. We thought he had been drinking. He insisted he hadn't. So after our shifts, tired as we were, four of us set off with Mullen. We hiked about a half hour, and sure enough, we came across a depression in the ground that was smoking like somebody had just put sand on a campfire. Some of the trees around the smoke plume had tilted toward the depression.

As we watched the smoke rise, I couldn't help feeling like somebody was trying to send a message through smoke signals.

"It looks like Satan needs some vent holes," said Mullen.

Janna, the restaurant's bookkeeper, sniffed the air with her gem-studded nose. "Smells like they're cooking rotten eggs down there."

"That's sulfur," said Mullen. "Hell's full of it."

"You should know," said Janna. Mullen just grinned.

"You found another sinkhole," I said.

"Looks that way," said Mullen joyously.

Later on, a government mining expert named Pete took a look and officially certified that the ground was indeed on fire. To be more specific, an underground coal seam had ignited. Turns out coal seams are notoriously hard to put out. Pete told us that they can burn for a long, long time, and that a place in Australia had been burning for two thousand years.

He gave us informational pamphlets that told us to stay on the trails so we wouldn't be overcome by carbon dioxide and other deadly gases. And also so we wouldn't fall into any invisible sinkholes eaten out by the fire.

"Our third sinkhole," said Aunt Jennifer to me, shaking her head and accepting a stack of pamphlets to distribute to local businesses. "First Mullen's place, then Addie's, then the one in the woods."

Somebody brought Mullen a pamphlet. I heard he made a paper airplane out of it and flew it into his sinkhole. I was nervous for him. Surely it meant something that he'd now found two sinkholes.

But nothing happened to Mullen. It happened to Uncle Mark. Out of nowhere he died from an aneurism.

Aunt Jennifer held up as well as could be expected. She said she had God to lean on.

I didn't hold up nearly as well. I couldn't reroute my thinking to believe he was gone. Surely he was still off at school teaching the sixth graders, or mowing the lawn out back, or building an osprey nest. And every time I thought about my uncle, gone for good, the ground under my feet felt hollow, as if a sinkhole were hiding there.

A month after Uncle Mark died, I sat down with some corn garbanzo curry after my shift at the restaurant. I looked out the window and saw steam rising, as if a dryer were venting, on the other side of the building. Outside I discovered that one of those hell vent holes had opened up at the edge of the parking lot, frighteningly close to the Vege-Lation.

Pete, the government expert, held a community meeting. He told us that the whole town and surrounding area used to encompass five different coal mines, all long ago abandoned. "You're living near a maze of underground tunnels and coal seams, and it's hard to say where the coal fires will turn up next and create more sinkholes." He showed us maps from the early 1900s, which were incomplete, making it impossible to identify every coal seam running beneath the ground. "If your town keeps expanding like it has been, you might stumble across a few more."

Pete called it the Mullen Sofer fire in his official notes, because Mullen had discovered it. Mullen wasn't at the meeting, but I heard later that Mullen laughed so hard when he heard a catastrophe was named after him that he nearly fell off his riding mower.

"You should name the Vege-Lation coal-seam fire after Grace," suggested Addie Sampson, giving me a proud look, as if finding the fire were something special. Luckily Pete had already submitted the report calling it the Mullen Sofer fire, so he couldn't name it after me. Besides, Pete said it could be the same fire, all connected underground.

"Maybe Mullen actually started the fire," said Lucille, Mullen's former lover. "Is that possible?"

Pete shrugged. "Sometimes humans start them, but if mining exposed the coal seam, lightning could have caused it. Or spontaneous combustion—minerals oxidize, which causes heat, which makes a seam start burning on its own."

I finally spoke up to state the obvious: "Why don't you just put it out? Then you don't have to name it after anybody."

"We can't," said Pete. "We could try, but it usually doesn't work and would cost more than the gross national product of Japan."

Lucille spoke again. "I think we should take advantage of the fire and sell tickets to see it."

"I wouldn't advise it," said Pete. "It's very dangerous. The gases can kill people. Anyway, a coal fire is an environmental disaster, but not something unique. There are thousands of coal fires all over the world. In fact, there are so many, they actually contribute to a big chunk of the greenhouse gases."

The Vege-Lation had to close. The owners took it in stride and left for Eugene. I took it harder, because I needed the money. Plus I hated change and having to start over. Just when the ground under my feet was starting to feel solid, it turned hollow once more.

Aunt Jennifer told me, "I'll pray for you."

"Okay, you do that," I said. The nice thing would have been to tell her I would pray for her too, but when I prayed, it felt about the same as chanting magic spells. I didn't mind her praying for me, though, if it made her feel better. And maybe it would work in my favor after all.

Six months later I got a job at Food Market. The day I started, Aunt Jennifer came in to the store. Mullen came in soon after.

I was busy fronting stock, pulling the cans forward on the shelf nice and neat, when I heard an odd noise, a cross between a shriek and a moan. I wondered if a raccoon had gotten into the store, but then I heard it again, and it was definitely somebody in pain.

I ran. There, in one of the aisles, Aunt Jennifer was on her knees, a can of dog food clutched in her hands. Mullen, who had just reached her, laid his palm on her shoulder. "What's wrong?" he asked.

"I don't need this," said Aunt Jennifer.

"Need what?" asked Mullen.

"What's wrong?" I asked.

"I forgot Otis is dead," said Aunt Jennifer. Otis was Uncle Mark's slobbery St. Bernard. He had been completely devoted to Uncle Mark, but never let anybody else touch him. Otis loved to pee on Aunt Jennifer's strawberry plants and dig holes in the yard. "I was on autopilot." She cradled the can of dog food like a baby. "I'm so tired."

"Do you want me to take you home?" I asked.

"I'll take her," said Mullen. He put the dog food can back on the shelf.

His offer was a relief to me. It was my first day on the job, and I feared I'd be fired if I left suddenly. I watched Mullen herd her out the door and into one of his Subarus, which, surprisingly, was running now.

The rest of my shift, I worried about Aunt Jennifer. Finally, after clocking out, I tore over to her house. Mullen answered the door. Putting his finger to his lips, he let me in. "She's sleeping."

She lay on the bed, a comforter over her, slightly askew. Mullen pulled it up over her shoulder, like you would for a sleeping baby.

A month passed. I'd been working a lot of overtime at the store, and though I would occasionally give Aunt Jennifer a call, I hadn't seen her. When I finally got a day off, I stopped off at her house and she wasn't there. I passed Mullen's place on the way home, and saw Aunt Jennifer's car parked in front.

When I knocked, Aunt Jennifer answered the door, telling me Mullen wasn't home. She got us some soda pop and led me out back to see the sinkhole. Up until now I had seen Mullen's sinkhole only in pictures. I knew it was big, but the size of it in person struck me silent.

We sat down on frayed orange lawn chairs overlooking the natural wonder, using a broken-down air conditioner as a table.

"So. You and Mullen Sofer," I said. It was obvious. She was welcoming me into his house as if she owned it, and wearing one of his shirts.

She nodded, a slight smile on her face. "Surprising, isn't it?"

"Especially since you said he was a womanizing moron and that any woman who went within three feet of him should be sterilized, just in case."

She shrugged the way Mullen shrugged, shoulders forward. "He's not the same as I thought. You would like him," she added, as though I'd never met him.

"I guess I just never pictured you hanging around with anybody who badmouthed God so much."

"I don't believe anymore," said Aunt Jennifer. "I just can't."

I felt as if the wind had been knocked out of me. This was a new development. Another change I didn't welcome. I didn't know how to respond. Finally I said, "I miss Uncle Mark too."

"That's not it." She squirmed a little, as if she were sorry she had brought it up.

"Then why?"

"Otis…" She didn't finish.

"I don't get it. What does Otis have to do with anything?"

"I'll never get it of my head." Aunt Jennifer stared straight ahead into the evergreen trees beyond the sinkhole.

I put my hand on hers. "Tell me. Please."

"I think Otis was the last straw, Grace. It was just so awful. We were playing fetch. I let him go farther and farther into the woods. I threw the ball over some bushes. Otis chased it. I didn't see the smoke coming out of the ground until it was too late. A chunk of ground gave way under his weight, and he disappeared into the hole. He yelped, and then it got quiet. One minute he was here; the next he was gone. And there was nothing I could do. All those things Pete said about the ground collapsing under you and the gases being poisonous were true. It was horrible…."

"Why didn't you tell me before?"

"I thought Mark's death was a test," Aunt Jennifer continued. "And I persevered. And I was so proud that I kept my faith. Proud that I bore my grief in silence. The sin of pride, you might even say. I thought I was as strong as a rock."

"So did I, Aunt Jennifer."

"But then Otis met such an awful death. And he wasn't a sinner, just an innocent creature. And things that I thought made sense didn't anymore."

If you asked anybody, including me, what was the most unlikely thing to ever happen in our town, they would have said sinkholes or the ground catching on fire. But they would be wrong. The most unlikely thing was Aunt Jennifer losing her faith.

"You'll find God again." I felt stupid saying something I wasn't sure of, and so offhandedly. Like I'd just told somebody their lost keys would turn up somewhere.

She nodded. "Maybe, Grace. But right now, it's like I had this rubber band inside me, stretching more and more with every loss or pain or obstacle…until it finally it just snapped. It's hard to explain."

"I used to count on you holding me in your prayers," I said. "Even though I didn't believe, it felt good."

"I'm sorry, sweetie."

I felt like my heart had rolled into the sinkhole in front of me and lodged beneath the Toyota. I had to change the subject. "So, you've been seeing Mullen since that time in the grocery store?"

"Yes. He's been my rock. He helped me through a bad time. He says he never thought he'd get a woman like me, so he'd better find a way to keep me. He went out and got a job." She laughed. "Can you believe he's tutoring children?"

Suddenly I knew that the sinkholes were indeed a message. But not for Mullen or anybody else. For me. A message that things change, and denying it won't do me any good. And when I really thought about it, there were more ways for things to change than there were for things to stay the same.

I didn't yet know what to do with this knowledge, or who had helped me gain it, but it did feel good to have turned a corner. The ground under my feet felt solid, for now, and that was all I could ask.

Stories Based on Writing Prompts

Sister of the Bride

By Evelyn Arvey

(Based on the prompt, "Saturday at 6:25 p.m.")

I haven't seen my dad for years, not since my college graduation. There is a good reason for this: My dad is what *Cosmo* calls an "Energized Energy Suck," the worst kind of energy suck of all. Just thinking about being around him brings on exhaustion; I've never met anyone else who prattles on and on like he does, whose voice gets raspier and louder the longer he talks, who gets so caught up in his own stories that he doesn't see his audience's eyes glaze over or their surreptitious inching away from him. This boorish behavior is only the beginning of what's wrong with my father—believe me!—but I, unlike him, am not the type of person who would put anyone to sleep with the tedious details.

Le sigh. He is *so* annoying, though.

Dad is meeting me here at SeaTac airport even though I told him not to, that I would call Uber. I'd been careful to use "Straight, Strong, Sassy" language with him, as recommended by *Ms.* magazine, but for someone who talks so much, he isn't all that good at listening. So here I am, forced to wait for him instead of hopping into an Uber and going on my way. I grab my suitcase, follow the crowds down a short ramp to the double doors, and emerge at the Arrivals pickup area. It is an unremarkable Seattle day: sixty-three degrees with a slight drizzle and just enough breeze to make my hair tickle my cheeks. I take a deep cleansing breath, counting *one, two, three*, and tell myself I can get through a car ride with my father—soon enough there will be plenty of other people he can bother. I call Gabby, my best friend and roommate, to fill her in on my flight.

"Samantha! Sam! Over here!" Dad pulls up to the curb, waving and hollering, not caring that I'm on the phone. His pewter-color suit is wrinkly, the fabric so cheap that his sleeve is corrugated at the elbow. He's not planning to wear that to the ceremony? I hope? I let him hump my suitcase into the car as I slide myself into the front seat and resume my conversation.

Dad pats me on the knee, then pulls away. "It's good to see you, honey."

I shoot him a look. Can't he see I'm on the phone? I'm trying to deal with Gabby. She's wigging out—our cat, Clancy, has just barfed on the living room carpet and Gabby *does not do barf.* "Leave it," I tell her. "Cover it with a paper towel and we'll tell the housekeeper to get it on Monday."

"Why didn't I think of that?" she says. "You're amazing, Sammy."

"No. You are."

"No. *You* are!"

Dad clears his throat. Already annoying.

I shoot him a "Personal Power Look," complete with audible sigh. I *love* the new Personal Power movement; it's done amazing things for me.

Dad ignores the sigh. "How's life in Santa Barbara?" he says, switching lanes, oblivious.

So freaking annoying.

I give up. I do my *kissy-kissy-goodbye* thing that I've done with Gabby since the day we first met freshman year; then I shove the phone in my pocket. "Fine."

"How's Gabby?"

"Also fine."

"She should've come! Mom and I would love to meet her."

"She has to work." I'd told her not to come.

"Well, I'm so glad *you* came, Sam. It wouldn't be the same without you! We didn't know for sure if you'd be here until you talked to Aubrey yesterday."

"I had plans." *One, two, three, let it be, be, be*, I tell myself. "Dad. I had plans. Important plans. I had to change them."

"It's your sister's wedding. In under two hours."

"I know that." A wedding at seven o'clock on a Saturday evening—at least Aubrey is on-trend with the timing. Last month's *Bride* magazine had a six-page spread about evening weddings and how glamorous they were. Not that hers would be anything like the ones in the magazine, but at least she's trying; I'll have to say something about how she's finally putting on her big-girl panties and attempting to be stylish. *Give compliments when they're due*, the magazine recommends. *Be kind. You never know when you'll want someone's help with your own wedding.*

"You cut it awfully close," Dad says.

I glare at him. Who is he to criticize? "It was the only flight I could get on. And my plane was late."

"Well, you're here and that's what matters." He leaves the

airport access highway and merges onto the freeway. "Hey. I bought you a four-pack of that coffee drink you used to love. It's in the backseat. Did I get the right flavor?"

"Oh?" I grab the closest one, a mocha in a stubby little bottle, wishing my dad had bought me something good, a sparkling water flavored with acai berries maybe, or a gin and tonic. I'm thirsty, though, and I drink the too-sweet stuff down in one long gulp.

"Like it, huh?" Dad asks, sounding proud of himself.

I toss the bottle into the backseat. "It's okay."

"Good. I'm glad. The things cost enough." He laughs. "Hey, did I mention we're picking up the flowers? It'll be quick."

"What the hell, Dad?"

"It'll be quick," he says again. He glances at his wristwatch. "It's just after six. We'll be fine if we hurry."

It takes *way* longer than it should take for me to realize that my "Personal Power Look" doesn't work if the intended recipient isn't looking. "But I've been traveling all day, Dad. I'm tired! My hair is flat! I need to take a shower before heading to the church."

One, Two, Three. Breathe! One, Two, Three. Breathe!

Straight, strong, sassy.

"You should have gotten the flowers before picking me up," I say.

Idiot, I add silently.

"I couldn't." He sighs. "Your plane was late, remember?" And then he goes on and on about detail this, and plan that, and your mother's a wreck, and Aubrey broke down in tears at breakfast this morning, and John's car has a dead battery, so he couldn't go to the airport to get you, and the photographer lost the address of the church, and one side of the wedding cake got a little smashed…and on, and on, and Dad doesn't even realize I've tuned him out. Finally we leave the freeway at a downtown exit and head toward First Avenue, toward the seediest area of the city. He glances at me. "I'll be fast at the florist, I promise." We drive over a pothole and the ridiculous decoration hanging from his rearview mirror, a sharp-edged guitar made from a cut-up Coke can, swings from side to side, making small metallic sounds.

A tasteless idiot, I revise.

"Whatever," I say.

We park in a three-minute loading zone in front of a store that looks like it hasn't been painted in fifty years. In the display window is an enormous poster of a white-clad young man in a kung fu stance—obviously not a floral shop. "It's around the corner," Dad mumbles when I glare at him. "C'mon, Sammy, come with me. I need your help with the arrangements. Please?"

"It's six twelve," I say. "Six *twelve*."

"I know that, Samantha."

He beeps the horn to lock the car; then I follow him down the sidewalk, which is booby-trapped with disgusting garbage: piles of dog shit, a hoodie-wearing young man lounging against a shop wall, three crumpled cigarette packages, a packet of French fries all smooshed and moldy—a nice neighborhood, this. Why are we buying flowers *here*? What's wrong with a nice shop in a mall closer to home, closer to the church? Then I get it: Dad must know the owner. Someone from his church, most likely. "Throwing business her way," I can almost hear him say. "She's a real nice gal. Too bad that kid of hers got cancer." Dad's done this before. Everyone knows he's a sucker for a sob story.

There's a man passed out on the sidewalk, in the doorway of a closed shop—how utterly repulsive. I hold my nose and give the man a wide berth, but Dad has stopped. He bends over and touches the man's shoulder, then gives it a quick shake.

"*Dad!*" I hiss. "Get away from that!"

The man reeks of cheap alcohol. He's pissed himself. He has a seven-day beard, a T-shirt with an apple-size hole right over his left nipple (*framing it*, how revolting), and he wears a baseball cap so filthy I can't tell what its original color might have been. The vagrant clutches a banana—a banana!—in his right hand. His breath is labored, rattling in his chest, ugly.

I step back.

Dad shakes the man again. "Hey. Hey! Are you all right?"

The man's mouth gapes open. He grunts.

"Dad! What are you doing? Let's go."

"This man needs help."

"Let's *go*," I say again.

But Dad digs his phone from his suit pants. He dials.

"Dad!" I say, tapping my foot. "The wedding!"

The man belches. He's dropped his banana.

Dad turns to me. "An ambulance will be here in a few minutes."

"Okay. Let's *go*, then. Flowers, remember?"

He peers at me, his eyebrows bunched. He gestures at the drunk. "But, Sam. He's sick."

"He's drunk."

"We can't leave him. Someone could…"

"Could *what*, Dad?"

"I don't know! He's incapacitated. Someone could hurt him! Or steal his belongings. See, honey? He has decent shoes. Someone could rip those right off his feet."

Gross, I think.

"We should stay with him." Dad glances up the sidewalk.

"You saw what kind of place this is." Dad hunkers on his haunches next to the man, not waiting for my opinion, not caring one iota about what *I* want, about how tired *I* am, about how I *damn well* am not wearing my travel clothes to Aubrey's evening wedding. He puts his hand on the guy's shoulder again. "Hey. You okay?"

The drunk farts long and loud.

I step back. Put my hands on my hips. Bite my lip. This is vintage Dad—he's so out of touch with reality. Always doing weird things no one else would do. Just *look* at him: He's managed to muss his hair. His face looks blotchy. Even wearing a suit he looks almost as ragged as the flotsam of humanity lying on the sidewalk. I almost wish I hadn't come to Aubrey's wedding after all. "It's six twenty," I say, but my "Personal Power Voice" isn't as powerful as it should be. I clear my throat, open my mouth to try again.

"Sirens," says Dad, cutting me off. "I hear sirens."

Thank God.

He stands up and squints over my shoulder. "I see them. They're coming." He gives me a long look. "As soon as they get here, Sam, we can go."

The ambulance pulls up, bigger than life, all sparkling white, all red and blue flashing lights. Two unbelievably handsome men get down—tall, dark, and uniformed, each of them, like magazine models; what more can a girl ask for?—but they don't see me even though I've taken a pose right in front of them. They only have eyes for the man on the sidewalk; they barely even listen to Dad's overlong story of how we found him.

I take a last glance at the vagrant. I can't help myself; it's like staring at a gory freeway accident even though you don't want to. His face is screwed up as if he's about to heave again, but one eye is open and it's staring straight at me, and I see that this wretched slob of a man has the brightest, most beautiful blue eye I've ever seen. What a waste.

"Let's *go*, Dad," I say, and this time I approve of my voice.

We're going to be late. It's already six twenty-five and we still have those damn flowers to pick up. We have a wedding to get to, but they'll wait for us.

I'm the sister of the bride. They'll wait.

Saturday at 6:25 P.M.

By Nancy Bonnington

(Based on the prompt, "Saturday at 6:25 p.m.")

Detective John Drake sat at the dimly lit table in the Chicago basement diner and checked his watch. He stared at it for more than a minute, nodding slowly. Finally he looked up at his partner.

"Do you have the time?" he asked.

Detective Lisa Marlow frowned, brushed a stray blond lock across her forehead, and said, "Damn it, John, you've been so preoccupied with the time lately."

"The time," John shouted, looking back at his watch. "Tell me…right…exactly…now!" He lowered his free hand like a flag at a car race.

"It's six twenty-six p.m.," Lisa blurted. "Jesus, when are you going to share your problem with me?"

"I'll be goddamned; there's no more doubting it," John said. He stood up suddenly and threw his crumpled paper napkin on the table, followed by a small wad of cash. "Let's go," he barked. "Get in the car."

"John, what..." Lisa began, but she knew it did no good to argue when the detective was in a mood. She watched him make a beeline to the diner door, only to stop for a split second, slap a hand near the cheap diner wall clock, and yell, "Shit!"

In the car Lisa turned to John, put her hand on his arm, and was just about to ask if he was okay. Perhaps inquiring after Mary's welfare would calm him down. "How's your wife—"

"Lisa, listen to me." He turned to her and stared hard. "This might be difficult for you to take in. For at least three weeks now...maybe longer...I haven't a clue really how long..." John took a deep breath, then shook his head. "It's just too unbelievable, Lisa. But it's a fact. Saturday at six twenty-five p.m. no longer happens. No...longer...happens! Saturday at six twenty-four p.m., yes, six twenty-six, yes, but there is no...I mean *no* goddamned six twenty-five p.m."

He switched on the engine, laid an arm behind Lisa's head as he swung his own head around to back out of the parking stall. "I know it's unbelievable. But I've been checking it over and over, and not just me."

He pulled into traffic, nearly sideswiping a semi. He darted a look at the sky from under his visor; it was dusk, but clear. He rolled down his window and sniffed the cool breeze. "Everything else seems so...normal."

They rode in silence for a moment. Lisa didn't ask any questions, not yet. Finally she said, "Where are we going?"

"There's this guy, this doctor at the university. Dr. Peter Laskey."

"Are you ill?"

"No, no. A doctor of physics. A Nobel prize doctor of physics."

John put a heavy foot on the gas and passed the next three cars on the crowded thoroughfare.

Lisa kept quiet, because when John was like this you couldn't push him for answers, but he'd spill his guts in his own good time. They'd been partners for four years, and John couldn't keep a mystery to himself. Even one as absurd as the disappearance of one minute every Saturday.

Time, Lisa thought, doesn't work like that. You can't just lose a minute. Likely it was related to a mistake in some kind of world clock that everyone's fancy watches were syncing to these days.

"You realize there's some rational explanation," Lisa said, finally breaking her silence.

"Exactly." John swerved onto the university exit as Lisa grabbed for the dash. "Rational. That's why we're going to see Dr. Laskey."

* * *

Laskey was an amiable fellow, low-key, young, and not what Lisa had expected of a Nobel prize winner.

"Since you called last week," Laskey said, "I've made my own observations. In fact, I brought in a whole gaggle of scientists. I want you to meet them."

They entered a small auditorium, where a dozen or so smartly dressed men and women sat in theater seats quietly chatting to one another.

Laskey led the detectives to the front of the room. "The best minds in all of geekdom," he whispered to them, and smiled.

Lisa smiled, then watched Laskey bound onto the stage, taking two steps at a time. She and John sat down in the front row. The lights dimmed and a white screen lowered at the back of the stage.

"Ladies and gentlemen, this is what we know so far." Laskey ran a video clip showing a close-up of a clock—its second hand ticking loudly, and the minute hand slowly progressing from 6:23 to 6:24…to 6:26!

"And here again," Laskey said, "No six twenty-five!" He ran another video clip, same scenario, different clock.

"And then again." This time Laskey showed a clock high up in a tower above a palace. "Big Ben, ladies and gentlemen. Last Saturday evening in London. Video thanks to Dr. Burke."

The camera zoomed in to show the minute hands of the clock. The auditorium was dead silent now as Big Ben's biggest hand clicked from 6:23 to 6:24…to 6:26.

Loud murmurs erupted.

"My God, Chris, do you know what this means?"

"So far we only have a few theories," Laskey continued. "Number one, the Russians are tampering with our clocks. We don't know how—magnetic energy? Sound waves? It fits with speculations from the CIA."

"The CIA?" Lisa cried out.

Laskey nodded at her and John. "Yes, they're on the case. It could be a national security crisis as well. The NSA, the FBI, even the ASPCA is interested. Hell, every government agency that has gotten wind of this is trying to understand—"

"The ASPCA?" Lisa asked. "For God's sake…"

"Number two," Laskey said, ignoring her, "A spike in solar flares has been known to effectively decalibrate sensitive equipment." He ran a video of a bright red and yellow sun with swirling gases erupting into giant explosions. "Dr. Dabber is here and will later discuss the solar storms, also known as coronal mass ejections. The most powerful of this decade happened only three weeks ago. Coincidence? We'll see.

"Number three," he continued, "the rise in ocean temperatures."

Laskey displayed a weather chart showing hurricanes gathering over the Atlantic Ocean. "Could it be an atmospheric disturbance?" he asked, raising his voice as if speaking over a storm. "Some unknown attribute of global warming?"

A man in the audience raised his hand.

"Yes, Dr. Deiter?"

"The Department of Theology at Cambridge has postulated that the time anomaly disproves the existence of God. For example, it can now be shown mathematically that light can escape a black hole, since during a missing minute gravity would not exist…ergo—"

"Yes, yes, I've read your email, Doctor, and I understand your interest in theology. But we have to first consider what is causing the missing minute and the immediate ramifications to societies across the globe…No Saturdays at six twenty-five p.m. in Seattle means no Sundays at eight twenty-five a.m. in northeast Asia, and so on and so forth."

Lisa's head swam as the meeting became a dry debate regarding the shifting calculations of the planetary time zones. Would the time differentials remain the same? And even so, what effect would the missing minute have on the calendar year? Would they need to add one leap minute every year, as it were, to offset the missing minute? Or perhaps a five-leap minute every five years…and so on and so forth.

Outside, it was raining. Lisa lit a cigarette under the cover of an eave and questioned John. "These scientists—these so-called experts. Aren't they overlooking something?"

"What's that?" John asked.

"I mean, you know, like…" Lisa exhaled a ream of smoke. "Who gives a flying fuck, for instance?"

"What? Lisa!"

"Does it really matter if we lose a minute once in a while, John? Shit, you know yourself nothing ever starts on time anyway."

The weather became brutal, the rain battering the pavement. Their car was surrounded by deep puddles. Lisa and John got in the car and watched sheets of water slide down the windshield.

"I'm sure you want to get to the bottom of this as much as I do," John said. "You're a damn good detective, Lisa."

❋ ❋ ❋

Six weeks later, the missing minute had been verified by enough people and leaked to the media that national news was focused on it around the clock. As far as the clock was reliable, that is.

At exactly what should have been Saturday at 6:25 p.m., and was therefore Saturday at 6:26 p.m., crowds across the globe stood beneath the public clocks and marked the occasion of the missing minute with candlelight vigils that lasted exactly one minute. Some, as Lisa had, shrugged it off as a rather trivial event. But most citizens of the world now suspected something huge was happening, and suspected it was probably not a good thing.

Conspiracy theorists surmised everything from a connection to JFK's murder to the destruction of the New York Twin

Towers to the curse of daylight saving time simply catching up with the whole world.

When the Super Bowl rolled around, a hushed crowd watched while at 6:25 p.m. the long pass to the end zone simply dropped out of the air and fell straight to the ground. Meanwhile, airlines noticed their engines faltering for a whole minute in the air; a man bending on one knee to propose to his girlfriend would never hear her answer; a surgeon would drop one whole minute of stitches in open-heart surgery—nothing fatal, but damned annoying.

It appeared that one minute was not missing, per se, but existed in some way outside of the normal time-space continuum so that events that were meant to occur on Saturday at 6:25 p.m. were simply swallowed up.

A baby born at exactly 6:25 p.m. might disappear the moment it cried out. But where had it gone?

Certainly it was not a Russian plot, for that no longer seemed feasible. Besides, Russian marriage proposals, airplanes, and babies were all experiencing the same fate as those across the globe.

In fact, what was once a trivial anomaly became a cause for nervous anxiety. So scary was the missing minute at each 6:25 p.m. on Saturday that businesses closed, dinner dates were scheduled to a later time, people held steady in their homes. Traffic signals were set to turn red for a whole five-minute interval before, during and after the missing minute.

After a year had passed, the only good that came from the phenomenon was that every human being could boast, and technically be correct, that they were fifty-two minutes younger than they would otherwise have been. But it seemed a small gain for such a mysterious, weekly interruption of normalcy.

❊ ❊ ❊

Detective Chronus was no hungrier than usual. He was planning to escape with his family from Gamma Z quadrant, where time had been depleted from overpopulation. The other gastro-chroners were starving too. There was no time left to eat—no nanoseconds, no minutes, no hours, nothing, the time-space continuum having been nearly depleted by their own ravenous time-eating species. Some had already left the galaxy, but not all were healthy enough to travel. They had waited too long as a whole, there being so many naysayers surrounding the question of global waning. Though it was known the time was slowly disappearing, some said, it was a natural event, and not something that the hungry gastro-chroner creatures had perpetuated. In fact, it was Glob's will that the world wax and wane in time privilege, and it was seen by some as sacrilegious to declare otherwise.

It was true that during widespread illness, when so many of the species became nauseated and vomited up their fourth-dimension meals, time was restored a little bit, but one couldn't count on it; nor would a whole species want to count on being ill to slow the progress of global waning.

"We're out of seconds," the waitress said, snapping her gum. "The shelves are bare. You might as well get off this planet while you can."

Cronus, who was salivating and almost rolling the imaginary, sweet taste of a split second over his tongue, gathered his family together and headed for the Torota Spaceship, Flight 610. It was a small ship but it got good mileage.

They were among the last to leave Gamma Z. His poor children had not eaten in days and had begun to appear younger.

They could not digest what little raw time was given them. And they were rather weepy, as they had had to leave behind their beloved flesh-eating pet, Static, because there was no room for animals.

"We've destroyed our world," Chronus told his children, "by greed and gluttony. There is no more time in Gamma Z and we must find another galaxy to consume."

"But what else would a person eat, Papa, if not time—roasted time, time soup, time over easy…?" Big Ticker asked.

"We used to eat plants, sweetheart. Before we discovered we could eat time and thus live forever."

"You mean people used to *die*?" Little Digitick, the youngest, almost exploded with mirth. "You're kidding me, right?"

"Don't laugh, sweetie. The time famine has severely decimated our planet, and for the first time ever, pardon the pun, many of our people have run out of time and thus starved to death. To death, honey. But don't worry, we are going to a solar system that has twenty-four hours in a day. More than enough to live forever."

"Holy cow," Minor Pause said, brushing her gold locks from her brow. "That's a lot of time!"

"How many days are in an aeon?" asked Little Digitick.

"It's all relative." Chronus cleared his throat aloud, as he always did when he needed to ignore a question he could not answer.

"You see, honey, as gastro-chroners consume only one-millionth of a second per annum, the new solar system will be like the land of Edith to us. Where we're going," Cronus continued, "there is still a lot of time. Oodles of it. It's a place called Earth. We'll feast on time like there's no tomorrow. In fact, we probably won't arrive at tomorrow for several generations."

"How many seconds are there on Earth?" young Chronus the Second asked his father. He rubbed his tired noodle brain and paused for brief moment, which of course Minor Pause quickly gobbled up.

"Three hundred sixty-five days in a year…twenty-four hours in a day…sixty minutes in an hour…sixty seconds in a minute—"

"Oh, Papa," Digitstick said in a quavering voice, "it sounds like the most wonderful place in all of the extraverses."

Chronus frowned, shame causing his antennae to wilt. "Yes, but we won't be alone. I have to tell you something, children. Earth is inhabited by creatures—human beings. They won't be able to see us, but they coexist in the time container. They bleed, they have material bodies, and they have no ability—absolutely none—to function without time. We will be eating into their very futures, I fear. Unless they can evolve."

"Oh," Chronus the Second said sadly. "That's not right."

"Well, it's us or them," his father said quietly. "And the High Council made its decision, right after Chronumbus discovered the New World—a world largely covered in oceans—which we now call the Blue Plate Special. But don't fret, my little darlings—time for the Earthlings will dissipate so slowly they won't even notice it. A second here, a second there…perhaps there will be no consequences at all. Indeed, the High Council has probably taken all of this into consideration. It is not our intention to harm others."

"The earthlings are not smart enough to detect the missing time?" Digitick asked.

"Um, no." Chronus cleared his throat loudly. "I don't think so. Now fasten your seat belts and take out your forks. The space-time continuum is just up ahead. We'll pull over for lunch."

Era of Trolls

By Susan Whiting Kemp

(Based on the prompt, "Saturday at 6:25 p.m.")

I was sitting at Heathrow airport, tired. So tired. The voices of hundreds of other travelers flowed by me, interrupted by gate announcements about not-my-planes. I couldn't wait to get home, so I'd gotten to the airport early. I always do that at the dentist's office, hoping they'll escort me to the place of pain a few minutes early, and get me done early. Sometimes it works out. Not that I thought that would happen with an airplane, but arriving early is a habit with me. As Dad would say, "Matilda, it's how you roll." And now it meant that I had to wait longer. Waiting seeps into you. Or out of you. I don't know. My thoughts wouldn't make sense until I'd gotten some real sleep.

I'd worked so hard the whole week. Set up the booth and chatted with conference attendees about essential oils. Gave out little samples of Stay Bright, Learn Bright, Sleep Bright, and so on. I enjoyed it the first hour, maybe two, each day. But then it morphed to what it really was: a means to an end, earning college money so I could major in public health someday and do something meaningful with my life. Breathing in the patchouli-lilac-sandalwood mixes. Watching people suck aerated health into their lungs and react with a smile or a shake of the head.

And now the flight was delayed. I looked at my watch. It was 6:25 p.m., and the plane that was supposed to be taking off right now to take me to Seattle hadn't arrived from points south. It wouldn't be here for another hour, and even then they would have to unload it and clean it before getting us aboard.

The woman in the seat across from me was staring at me. "God, you're a mess," she finally sputtered, smoothing her asymmetric-styled hair—shoulder-length on the left, earlobe-length on the right.

I looked down at my outfit. I hadn't spilled anything on my tan pants and avocado blouse. What was she talking about?

"No really," she said. "What were you thinking when you got dressed this morning? That frumpy was a good look on you?"

What was her problem? I sat up straight, stifling the urge to tuck things in a bit. I wouldn't give her the satisfaction. Her silk top and fashionable leggings didn't make her better than me. And that pretty face didn't either. She resembled somebody famous, but I couldn't pinpoint who.

I searched my brain for a good comeback. Something to make her understand that she wasn't entitled to belittle me. In fact, let her work as hard as I did all week and then see how she looked. Unfortunately I was so tired I could barely put a full sentence together, much less lob a kick-ass retort. I could only glare.

She leaned forward conspiratorially, hand to the side of her mouth. "You know, you could have that nose fixed."

I took a sharp breath in. That crossed the line and zoomed way past it. The woman had hit a sore spot. It took all I had not to shout at her. I spoke slowly and carefully. "It's been a really long day, and I'm not in the mood."

"Yeah. I bet you're never in the mood. That's why you're alone."

Lucky guess that I was unattached, I thought. Out loud I said sharply, "Stop insulting me." I looked around. Yes, they'd all heard. A mother and child to my right, a man in a suit to my left, and several people sitting on either side of the nasty woman, all looking at me. Maybe somebody would jump in, tell her she was out of line throwing shade at me like that.

Nobody did. The woman pulled the kid from the seat next to me into her lap. The man in the suit got up and left. So did the people sitting next to the nasty woman. I thought about leaving too. I felt I shouldn't be the one to have to move, but I wasn't up to this right now. And besides, what if she was crazy? Was that why everybody had left?

The woman's face pixelated briefly, then returned to normal. And her asymmetric hair changed from shoulder-length on the left to shoulder-length on the right.

The woman wasn't real. She was a holographic troll.

I'd heard about them. Just like regular internet trolls, which taunt you just to get a rise out of you, but these could appear in three dimensions. I didn't expect one to look and sound so real, like she was right there with me.

So this was a prank. I was a random traveler being videotaped for a reality show, and this was the part where they told me it was all a setup, and I laughed with relief. Hell, no. There would be no laughing, no slapping palm to forehead. And especially no signing of waivers to air it.

How had they managed to do this? I looked around for the projection source, but it was a big place, with lots of possible hidey-holes. "You don't get it, do you?" the troll asked. "That's because you just can't fix stupid."

I snatched up my purse and carry-on bag and headed for another seat. The troll strolled along behind me. "Matilda," she said. "You can't do anything right."

I turned, stunned. She knew my name. This was no random encounter in an airport. The troll was targeting me personally.

"Who set this up?" I asked, running the possibilities through my head. My parents—absolutely not. My friend Elsa—no, she wasn't a practical joker. My workmates—no, too mellow. My roommate Janine, maybe. She was a firecracker sometimes, but how did she find the time with her new job?

The troll just smiled knowingly, making me feel dirty somehow. I went to the bathroom to wash my face, thinking I would lose her at the door, but when I looked up she was leaning against the tiled wall. I caught a glimpse of myself in the mirror, my mouth hanging open. Embarrassing. I couldn't understand how this all worked. Had somebody planted something on me that was projecting the troll?

"How did you get in here?" I asked.

"I'm not in here. You're imagining me. Because you're crazy."

I did consider that I might be hallucinating. Being overtired and all. But there were two other women in the bathroom, both looking at the troll. I began examining my things for a method of projection. "I'm going to shut you off," I said. "And then I'm going to figure out who did this. And they're in big trouble."

One of the women said to the other, "Oh, shit, she's got a

troll." The other one said to me, "Honey, it doesn't work that way. You won't find it." And they both cleared out, scooting around the troll as if she were radioactive.

That was when I first started to get an inkling of the danger I was in. The two women had seemed so fearful. My seatmates back in the waiting area had been too, now that I thought about it. What did they know that I didn't? I splashed more water on my face. I swore at the electric hand drier when it didn't work and patted my face dry with my shirt, listening to the troll laugh derisively at my predicament.

The troll followed me back to the seating area. "You're a failure. Just a salesperson. And not even very good at that. It's because you're not the sharpest tool in the shed. Just another idiot. Imbecile. Fool. And gullible too. Not very perceptive, either. There've been a few things in your life you didn't see happening, even though they were right in front of your face. Am I right? Did you learn from your mistakes? No. You make the same gaffes over and over again."

The troll kept on and on. Sometimes it was wrong, but sometimes spot-on. It had me remembering some troubling times in my life. Things I thought I'd moved past. When my flight was finally announced over the loudspeaker, I was so relieved I nearly cried. I could finally leave it behind.

And for a few minutes I did. Then she reappeared. The enormity of it all really struck me then. The troll could follow me anywhere. Even onto a plane. And while she didn't need a seat technically, when she glared at the man next to me, he vacated his for the troll, and fast.

The troll now began lying, announcing that I was racist, a thief, a pyromaniac, on and on. People gave me such evil looks. Either they believed the troll, or blamed me for having one, or both. I held it together pretty well, I thought, through the flight, and made it home to the apartment in the Fremont area of Seattle where I rented a room from Janine. I dropped into the blue velvet couch, nearly knocking over the books that stood in for its broken leg. When Janine's opera career took off she would be able to fix it. And get a music stand that didn't tilt slightly.

I called the police and they said they'd send somebody. Instead I got a call from an officer who took the details and had me send a photo of the troll. While the officer sounded sympathetic, she said she couldn't do much without more information, and to call her if I learned anything new.

That whole weekend was a blur. Even at home the troll wouldn't let me sleep. Earplugs helped, but only to a point. Janine was out of town on a singing gig. It was just me, the troll, and a growing sense of shame and anguish. You can't have somebody—or something—picking out your faults so continually without starting to believe them. I already knew there were plenty of other people around who were smarter, prettier, and more clever, but having this drilled into me for hours made me feel like the lowest of the low. It had me crying sometimes, screaming other times.

I couldn't go to work on Monday. Not with that thing around. And I couldn't figure this out by myself. I'd gone to coding camp for a week one summer when I was a teenager, but that was only enough to show me how much there was to know.

I walked past the Fremont Troll statue, a huge ogre clutching an actual Volkswagen Beetle in its enormous hand. How ironic it was that I lived blocks away from such an icon. Farther down, near the Lenin statue, I entered Giant Statue Secure, a cybersecurity company I'd often passed by and never thought

I'd need. The lobby was decorated in tangerine. When I told the receptionist why I was there, she said, "You can't bring that in here."

I wouldn't take no for an answer, so the receptionist made some calls, and a woman—also decorated in tangerine—came out to the lobby.

"I need help," I began.

"That's obvious," said the troll.

"We can't do anything," said the woman, taking a step back. "We'd be inviting trouble."

"Just tell me where to start. I don't know the first thing about three-D trolls."

She backed up another step. "They're from overseas. You pick them up like a virus, and the creator of the virus is the only one who can cure it. You can't get to the programmers. Just pay the ransom. That's the only way."

"What? What ransom?"

"They haven't asked for a ransom? Well, usually they do. If they don't, well…"

"Well what?"

"Then somebody's just doing it for fun, and it's impossible to know when it will end. It's a bot that runs automatically. It could go indefinitely." My anguish must have shown on my face, because hers softened. "You'll just have to ride it out. Please go now."

"At least tell me what programming language I need to learn to fix it myself."

"You could start by fixing your face," said the troll. "Oh, never mind. Losing battle."

The woman held up her hands. "No, no, no. Don't learn any tech at all. That would be feeding the troll. The troll sees what you see and hears what you hear, and in that way it learns what you learn. You'd just make it stronger if you learned something its creator doesn't know."

Janine came home earlier than I expected that afternoon, while I was packing once more. "I'm going," I said. "Trolls are catching."

"Yes, go," said my troll. "Nobody wants you around."

"Stay," said Janine. "We'll figure this out."

I was so thankful. Only then did I realize what a true friend I had, not willing to abandon me.

Janine gazed at the troll. "She looks like a famous person. Who does she look like?"

I shrugged. I hadn't placed the face yet. Janine began searching my clothes for a projecting device, finally packing up my suitcase with everything I'd brought back from the trade show. Clothes, purse, ID, papers, everything. These she put in her car trunk and drove off. In spite of her effort, the troll stayed with me.

When Janine returned and found out I still had the troll while she was gone with my things, she ordered me to get naked. So I did.

That gave the troll plenty to say. "When's the last time you went to the gym? I thought Flopsy was a rabbit."

"What are we looking for?" I asked.

"No idea," said Janine. "Electronic chip? A funny mole? Skin-colored patch?" We searched my skin. Janine poked some moles on my back until they bled. I took a shower and Janine scrubbed me, the troll cracking up at my pleas to be gentle.

The next thing she tried was to out-insult the troll, but no insult fazed it. Janine was a pistol. She really was. But just like a champion Go player couldn't beat Google's AI, she couldn't outdo this bot. She only taught it new phrases, which it picked up and spit back at me.

I went outside for a walk to get some air and to give Janine a break, trying to believe that one day I'd be free of all this. I walked past the Rorschach Blot, a bar Janine and I frequented. They had a nobody-sits-alone policy, and we always met fun artist types there. There was a husband-and-wife performance art team, Lilly and Willy, who made mile-wide diagrams in the desert and then videotaped their choreography in it. "Crop circles, with rocks instead of crops," Lilly described it.

There was a man who called himself Ringo and only sang Beatles songs. He brought his own microphone, which was miles better than the bar's mic, and sometimes let Janine use it. Not me. I couldn't sing worth a darn.

There was a whole group of body painters who came in naked; the last time the theme had been "universe," and they'd come painted with planets, stars, and swirls.

I passed the party store, with its balloon archway, where I'd bought a mini helium tank and balloons for the birthday party I was going to throw for Janine. But there would be no party if I couldn't get rid of my troll.

After crossing the Fremont Bridge I strolled along the canal, feeling sorrier and sorrier for myself. "Remember that thing you said?" asked my troll. "It was so stupid."

I flashed back to the trade show, when I'd told a man to try some Relax Bright because he seemed like he could use it. He hadn't been openly annoyed, but left quickly, and now I was kicking myself for being so rude. That was the evil genius of the way this troll worked. It didn't always need to be specific. It could just lead me to the water of self-disgust; I would do the drinking myself.

A man was standing on the grass, looking harried. Another man was walking around him, badgering him the way my troll badgered me. So he had a troll too. He would understand what I was going through. He would be my comrade in arms. I walked toward him, my troll calling me an idiot, my heart beating fast. If we compared notes, maybe we could figure out how to stop this together.

The troll victim waved at me, and at first I thought he was as excited to see me as I was to see him. But he yelled, "You can't bring trolls together. It's dangerous. They learn from each other. You'll make it ten times worse."

Worse than this? I thought with horror, feeling cursed, cursed to my soul. I ran away, up a pathway and around a building. I leaned against it, huffing loudly to catch my breath, my troll berating me for being an out-of-shape slob. I vowed that I would beat this troll somehow, some way. For me, but also for others suffering through this. Nobody should have to endure such a thing.

The thing about vows, though, is that they're just vows. They're not an answer in themselves. I had no idea what to do next. It was so hard to think with the constant berating.

How was the troll attached to me? And who had attached it?

I sat on a bench and pondered what I'd learned so far. Trolls were bots. Their creators were overseas and often demanded ransoms. They were catching. They learned from one another.

How could I know what was true and what wasn't? It all seemed like HIV in the 1980s. People were afraid they would catch HIV like a cold. Later, people got educated. What if that was the case now? That people were misinformed? That trolls weren't that catching? Janine didn't seem to believe they were.

And the truth was, I found it hard to believe that a computer virus could jump from person to person. Sure, swine flu could jump from a pig to a person. But computers and people weren't made the same. This felt more intentional. And after all, the troll knew my name from the beginning.

I took my shoes off and stood in the grass while the troll prattled on. Finally I said, "Shut up. The grass feels good. I want to enjoy it."

The troll started talking about how ugly my hands were, as if it thought I was feeling the grass with my hands rather than my feet. Did that mean the troll was reacting to my words rather than my actions? Could it hear me and not see me?

I felt as if I were on the verge of something. I needed a little boost. Some caffeine. Putting my shoes back on, I went into a restaurant, sat at a table, and ordered a Coca-Cola. The waitress brought it to me, not yet realizing I had a troll.

"That pop will go straight to your thighs," said my troll.

I nearly did a spit take. The cybersecurity expert told me the trollmeister was in a foreign country. But my troll called a can of Coke a "pop." In other parts of the United States, the casual term was *soda* or *Coke*, or something else. What if the programmer was in Seattle?

I'd been thrown off because I'd been in Europe when this had all started. I had thought somebody attached a troll projector to me while I was there. Now it seemed possible I already had it when I left, and it just hadn't been activated.

I started home to tell Janine about my revelation, and then had another one, right on its heels: I'd been so glad I had a good friend to help me get through this, who wasn't afraid of my troll. The *only* person who hadn't been afraid of my troll. There was a reason for that.

Janine had attached the troll to me. Three months ago she had advertised for a roommate. But she had really been looking for a victim.

My mind whirled. We were tight, but the reality was, I didn't know her as well as I liked to think. Our new, strong friendship was a sham to enable her to attach a troll to me. Somebody could be paying her to do this—she needed money; she was barely scraping by.

The more I thought about it, the more it made sense. If there really was some kind of hologram projector, she could have put it on me. Taken it off me while she scrubbed me, then transferred it back on. She was so touchy-feely, always hugging me hello and goodbye. It would have been easy.

I stomped homeward, grunting in fury along the way. This was going to be the confrontation of all confrontations. I would be on her like white on rice. Like a dung beetle on shit. Like…I couldn't think of any more, but I would have no mercy. She was going tell me where it was, and I would destroy it. Then I would destroy her. Or something.

When I arrived, a woman I didn't recognize was in our apartment. Tall, narrow face, red dress, black hair swept into a volcano. Telling Janine in a melodic voice, "Isn't it about time you went to the smarts department and picked up some brains?"

Now Janine had her own 3D troll. It occurred to me that Janine could have given herself a troll to make herself seem innocent. But I knew from her expression that she hadn't. That anguish was real. And it was my fault. Trolls *were* catching. I felt terrible that I'd blamed Janine for something so evil when she was suffering so much because of me.

I considered running away—for Janine's sake, if not for

mine. In case the trolls really could learn from each other. But it was important to solve this, and I couldn't do it by myself.

"It's only been here an hour and I'm already going crazy," said Janine. "I've got to get it out of my hair."

"What's wrong with your hair?" asked Janine's troll. "Have an accident with the lawn mower?"

"All right," I said. "We'll figure this out together." I told Janine what I'd learned and deduced about my troll so far. "And what we need to know is, how do they stay with us? We know there's nothing on our skin. So how does it project from us? What's it attached to?"

Janine thought and thought, finally bursting out, "I don't know!" Her troll's colors brightened.

"You're a know-nothing," said Janine's troll.

"It just got brighter," I said. "Emotion strengthens it."

"Okay!" Janine picked up her metronome. "It wants emotions? Well, here are some emotions for it." She threw the metronome and it made an unsatisfying clunk against the wall.

"Calm down and help me brainstorm."

Janine took several deep breaths in, then blew several out, as if prepping for a deep dive. "Okay, okay. Brainstorming."

"Lamebrain, lamebrain, lamebrain," sang Janine's troll.

"You're right. It's just reacting to what it hears," said Janine.

The troll said a final, "Lamebrain."

"Brain. Brain!" I said. "Maybe something to do with our brains! How would a troll projector get into our brains?"

"Neither of us has had brain surgery," said Janine. "What if electronic worms crawled into our ears while we slept?"

I cringed. "I think I would have noticed that."

"True," said Janine, "you're a light sleeper."

"Light sleeper?" asked my troll. "Not with that snore."

"It doesn't have to be in our heads. We emit brainwaves. Actual energy. Maybe it does something with that."

We rushed to the kitchen and got the aluminum foil. We fashioned helmets and tucked them onto our heads. "Make it so the foil covers more," I said.

"Oh, you're cooking?" said my troll. "I think I'll eat out today."

The word *foil* triggered talk of food, though our actions had nothing to do with cuisine. This seemed to prove they couldn't see us. The insults kept coming. The foil did nothing to stop them. But then how did the troll know that my ugly nose bothered me? Was it a lucky guess?

"Okay, okay," Janine removed her helmet. "It could be attached to something else that's unique about each of us. Like our fingerprints."

We both looked at our hands. A troll projecting from our fingerprints. It seemed just as likely—or unlikely—as anything else. I began to understand why people used witch doctors. I got a fingernail file out of the bathroom, sprayed my finger pad with antiseptic, then rubbed it with the fingernail file, fast and furious, as if I were filing away my troll—which I hoped I was.

"Stop!" said Janine. "Oh, God, Matilda, how can you do that?"

Janine had had her troll for only an hour. I'd had mine for days. What Janine didn't understand was that at that point I would have sunk a knife in my gut to rid myself of the troll. Sanding away a fingerprint seemed minor in comparison. It hurt like hell, but I kept going until I removed the whorls, dancing around the room, saying, "Ow!" and trying to shake off the pain.

"You big baby," said my troll. "Cry all you want. Nobody cares." I began sanding another fingertip.

Janine grabbed my wrists to stop me. "That didn't fix it," she said. "What else can you think of?"

I squeezed the words out through the pain. "DNA. DNA is unique."

"True, but I don't know where to start with that. We can't scrub DNA off. Keep brainstorming."

"Facial recognition," I blurted.

"Okay, okay." Janine nodded. "In facial recognition, the computer calculates depth and length between your features. So what if we change that?" Janine retrieved some transparent tape. She taped her nose to her cheek, pulling the tip to the side.

She looked absolutely ridiculous. I began laughing. I continued laughing. I couldn't stop. I must admit I let myself become a little hysterical. I'd like to think I was testing my troll to see what it would do. It brightened, then said, "It's true. Hyenas do laugh."

When I'd calmed, I said, "I don't think it's how we're seen. It's something projecting from us." I motioned outward.

"Voices," said Janine. "Voices project."

"Yeah," I said uncertainly. "But how can something attach to a voice?"

"You said brainwaves give off electricity. Voices must give off something too."

I glanced over at the helium and balloons I'd bought for Janine's birthday party, sitting on the table. I filled a balloon with helium, then sucked it into my lungs. "I hate trolls. They suck," I said in a silly helium voice.

What happened made me drop the balloon in surprise. At the sound of my altered voice, the troll changed. It smoothed out, losing all its features. Then something resembling ants began scrolling down its body.

My mouth dropped open. I'm sure Janine's did too, but I wasn't looking at her; I was looking at the answer to our problem. "That's code."

We scrambled for our phones and took photos and videos for a few moments until the code ran out and we seemed to have captured it all. In minutes, the troll morphed back to a simulated person once more. Then we loaded the images on my laptop and examined them for clues.

"Look for a line break; that might show where the heading is," I said. "And then something after 'slash asterisk.'" It wasn't easy. There was a massive amount of code and I wasn't sure how much we'd captured. The coder had not been stupid enough to leave his name embedded. There was a long stretch with nonletter characters that we thought might have been a secret code of some kind. We spent some time replacing those characters with letters, but couldn't get it them make real words.

We had no real clue. And we still didn't know how the code had attached to us.

"We've been focusing on the trolls themselves," said Janine. But what about the trollmeister? Think serial killer."

"Oh, my God," I said. "You think he's toying with us before murdering us?"

"Not literally, but he gets joy out of our pain, and he's destroying our lives. Just like a serial killer. In one of my classes I learned about geographic profiling; people who commit serious crimes have patterns. Where they go to work, where they shop. They don't go that far out of their way to commit their crimes. They strike within two miles of their homes."

"He might be in that apartment building, looking at us," I

said. We looked over at the neighboring apartment. The nondescript windows. I shivered.

"Nobody wants to look at your repulsive face," said my troll.

"Let's circle back," I said. "We know it has something to do with our voices."

"Somebody recorded us singing," suggested Janine.

"You, yeah, but not me." I had serious stage fright and a fear of microphones so bad I knew it was called microphonophobia.

"Last week at the Rorschach Blot. You were drunk. You sang 'We Are the World.' Ringo let you use his mic."

I had forgotten, but now blurry memories returned. Of feeling like I was actually changing the world though my very voice. Of people egging me on. Of the encouraging look Ringo gave me when he handed me the microphone. I remembered telling Ringo I wouldn't sing in public until I'd had a nose job, which was never, but then I sang anyway. That was how the troll knew to needle me about my nose. "Ringo did this to us," I said with contempt.

The mention of the Rorschach Blot triggered something more. I studied my troll's face. The cheeks, the eyes. Rather than somebody famous, my troll looked like somebody I knew. "You know those body painters at the bar? My troll looks like Saturn."

Janine looked at her troll. "Mine looks like Lilly." The wife from the performance art team Lilly and Willy. Ringo not only got his troll victims at the bar by recording them, but also used the patrons as templates for his evil designs.

I fumed. And felt ashamed. "I've been so naive," I said. "So stupid."

"Now you're getting it," said my troll. "Stupid. Stupid. Stupid."

"This isn't our fault," said Janine. "We didn't do this to ourselves. Don't forget that."

"It's your fault," said Janine's troll. "Just accept that you're to blame. For everything."

Janine bowed her head. I knew what she was feeling. Each word was a twist of the knife. Each insult became easier and easier to believe, until they all felt true.

I called the police officer I'd spoken with before and explained what we knew. She sounded excited and told us to sit tight; they would take action and get back to me as soon as they knew anything.

I hung up and stared at Janine's music on its tilted stand. For a short time I'd thought this was her doing. Things could have been different if we hadn't solved this together. Tears came to my eyes. The notes on Janine's music blurred slightly, so that they looked a lot like the characters in the code that we hadn't been able to decipher. They had the same repetitive patterns.

"They're notes," I whispered. "The characters are notes."

Janine caught on right away. "In the code," she said. "But why would they be notes? What would they mean?"

Janine grabbed up her phone and studied the photos we had taken. She began singing. I recognized the Beatles song immediately as "Octopus's Garden," one of my childhood favorites. As she sang, her troll's colors dulled, so I jumped in too, my bland voice blending oddly with her rich operatic tones.

The trolls began to fade. We sang as if a stadium of cheering fans were spread in front of us. Our evil nemeses looked stonewashed, then shrank like bathtub vortices; then, one after the other, they popped out of existence with champagne-cork noises.

Our evil parasites were gone. We stood quietly for minutes,

feeling reborn, tears running down our faces. Then we bounced up and down like two kids jumping on a bed. We hugged. We laughed. We shouted, "We're free, we're free!"

When we sobered up, we talked about thankfulness. And how we would never be the same. And how our discovery would help other 3D troll victims. And how Ringo must have programed the troll to expire when the notes were sung, and that it was genius to have that as a failsafe. We wondered how the mechanism actually worked; there was so much to know, so much to figure out.

An hour later we got a call from the officer. They'd moved fast, ferreting out Ringo's real identity and tracking down his residence, but he'd moved the week before. He was still free. He, and others like him, were still out there.

I recognized that this was just the start of a new era. The Era of Trolls. New holographic innovations were coming. And with them great peril. I saw it as clearly as if it stood in front of me, taunting me with insults.

I didn't know how, but I was going to stand up to it. I vowed I was never going to let a troll attack me—or anybody I knew—ever again.

The thing about vows, though, is that they're just vows. They're not answers in themselves. I had no idea what to do next. But I did know that whatever it was, it was going to be a whole lot easier without a troll telling me I was a few slices short of a sandwich.

I hooked a red balloon up to the tank, filled it, and sucked in the helium. "I am going to save the world," I said in a ridiculous tiny voice.

We laughed and laughed and laughed.

Clouds and Tubers

By Evelyn Arvey

(based on the prompt, "Rivalries, Portals, and Footfalls")

We flew with the clouds, my stepbrother, my parents, and I. With breath that steamed and danced and dissolved into fog; with footfalls on pebbles, then on mud, then on carpets of strangely shaped leaves; with percussive hearts that proclaimed first joy, then awe, then the heavy ache of our bodies, the four of us followed our Peruvian guide along a narrow trail up, up, up, then down, and down, then up, *up* again, always, forever climbing. Through tendril clouds and soft dampness the trail coaxed us ever closer to—

"*Damn*, that's cool!"

Andrew, my not-really-my-brother, shattered the green silence. I shot a look at him, the same look I've been aiming at him for two long years, from the day my mother married his father and we became stepsiblings. How many times had he ruined moments like this? How many times had his loud voice and his effusive gestures stolen attention from where it ought to belong? A person's first glimpse of one of the wonders of the world was a momentous occasion, but he'd ruined it. I'd never have this moment again, this precious first glimpse of Machu Picchu.

But Andrew hadn't noticed my look. He never noticed.

His voice boomed and echoed. "Hoo-*wee*! Would you look at that. Just … look at that."

"Wow…" said Mom, her voice trailing off. She held her arms tight around her waist, as if to hold the magic of this place close to her heart.

Dan, my stepfather, ran his hand through his hair. He was breathing hard. We all were. "Who would have thought we'd end up above Machu Picchu, looking down?"

Our guide laughed. "Is beautiful, no?"

It was. The wispy clouds we'd been hiking through had settled over the ancient ruins as dense fog blown by a brisk wind, revealing or hiding now the lone tree in the central plaza, now a terrace, now a flight of stairs, now the peaked ends of dwellings. I easily recognized the residential quarter; I'd done my due diligence on Machu Picchu before leaving home: six books checked out of the library, a National Geographic special on cable TV, two scholarly videos, and a handful of YouTube videos that ranged from surprisingly informative to so bad they made me want to laugh and cringe at the same time—so the view below me seemed familiar, as if I'd been here before, or as if I'd lived here in a previous life. What had it felt like to discover this magical place back in the summer of 1911? I imagined Hiram Bingham III hiking the same trail I was on, pulling his leather jacket tight against the chill, seeing these same overgrown terraces for the first time, how breathtaking it must have—

"Dude!" Andrew said, pointing, "A what's-it-called, an alpaca! Over there!"

"Llama," corrected the guide, pronouncing the double L like a Y: *yama*.

"There's hardly any people," said Dan, squinting, holding his hand over his brow.

Our guide nodded. "This is good time to tour. Off season."

Ten minutes later, with fine cold rain dappling our faces, we'd descended a staircase made of neatly trimmed stones and entered the site proper. I breathed deeply, and again, and again, inviting the air of this place into my body, into my soul. Besides, it smelled good. Mossy, earthy, full of petrichor. A frisson ran through me, scalp to toe and back up.

I touched my mother's arm. "You go on ahead." I cleared my throat, wondering how it was that my words could seem both too loud and too timid in this place. The site felt holy to me, like a wilderness chapel in a fantasy novel, or the birthplace of a goddess, which, who knew, it might have been to the Inca priests who built it some five hundred years ago.

Mom looked at me dubiously.

"I want to take some pictures." And to be alone.

She nodded, somehow understanding my unspoken words; then she, Dan, and Andrew walked off between rocky walls, listening closely to their guide.

I entered a room through a tall portal with a stately light-colored lintel stone and found myself in a narrow, roofless space, a rectangle of stone masonry lit by three trapezoidal window openings. I knelt and ran my fingers along the lower stones, the original ones worked by Inca commoners, not the darker-colored stones near the top of the wall that had been set in place by modern restoration teams. Human remains had been found in or near this room—not the human sacrifices that titillated the masses, but the bodies of lowly workers who had evidence of bone-nibbling parasites and broken limbs; the very people who built this room, perhaps. I could almost see them chipping and smoothing and lifting and measuring. I closed my eyes, listening for their ancient voices.

I listened; I held my breath; I heard. A small wind made the quietest of susurrations as it crossed the open ceiling, the open portal, the open windows. The speech of ghosts.

When I opened my eyes I saw a delicate blue flower growing in the cracks between stones in the window, framed by stones, set against one of the most majestic views on the planet. Most of the fog had lifted; what remained made the scene even more enchanting. I set my camera on its nifty folding tripod. Focus: sharp mountains, dense greenery. Focus: tiny blue petals, mossy stone. Focus: Huayna Picchu on the far side of the citadel. Focus—

Andrew.

Just outside my window, framed beautifully. Waving and grinning. Being an ass.

"Get out of here!"

But instead of heeding my most ferocious glare and going elsewhere, he took hold of the window ledge and tested it by jumping up and down. No, he couldn't—he wouldn't. Not even Andrew would—but I was wrong. I stood speechless behind my camera, hand clutching my remote shutter button (shooting who knows how many images) as he jumped up one last time and, feet flailing, *wriggled his way through the window and into my Incan sanctuary.*

He brushed gravel off his palms and stood up, his face shining. "I did it! It wasn't even that hard."

"You can't come in through the window, Andrew! You have to stay on the paths and go into rooms through the door openings." *Like anyone with half a brain would.* "Do you want to get us kicked out of here? This is one of the wonders of the world. You could have knocked a piece off the windowsill or…or…"

He brushed something off his jeans; I didn't want to know what it was. "This place is awesome, sis."

"You could get arrested for stunts like that."

He looked out the window. "Naw. There's no guards around. No one saw."

You crushed my pretty blue flower, you boob. "It doesn't matter that no guard saw you. This is a protected site!"

He shrugged.

"Go away," I said. My camera took one last shot as I released the remote cable. I frowned, staring at the small image on the back of the camera. It was a gorgeous shot of my not-brother framed by the stone window, contemplating the majestic view; I'd be sure to delete it as soon as we got back to our hotel room at Aguas Calientes at the base of the mountains. Or…maybe I'd print it up and offer it to Dan, a gift, a portrait of his son, a thoughtful thank-you for taking us all on this trip meant to help the four of us bond as a family.

Andrew trailed his hand over the stone that formed the bottom of the window opening. "How did they make these?"

"Stonemasons chiseled them one at a time, each stone meant for a particular place."

"No kidding."

He paced slowly around the perimeter of the room. I stood beside my tripod, wondering how long it would take for him to grow bored and leave.

"Did…um…people live in this room?"

"That's what they think. Yeah."

"Who?"

I sighed. Did he really want to know? Or was he finding new ways to annoy me? He looked expectant, so I told him about the workers' quarters (of which this room was a part) and about how workers and soldiers and farmers had come from all over Peru to live and toil here in the mountains. "Machu Picchu pulled in experts from all over."

"Experts? Really?"

"Sure." I went to the window and, pointing, told him about the terraces and how they were meticulously constructed to halt erosion and to drain heavy mountain rainfall and could easily have fed thousands of residents with potatoes and other foodstuffs.

"Really?"

"They stored their surplus in warehouses." I joined him at the window. "On the other side of the slope."

We stood in silence, taking in the view. The fog was gone.

"Look!" he said, his voice as quiet as I'd ever heard. "Over there. My dad and your mom."

They were climbing a short staircase, shoulder-to-shoulder, holding hands.

"Doesn't look like they're worried about us," I said.

"Forgot we came."

"We could have fallen off a terrace and they wouldn't notice."

He smiled. "Or ridden one of those llama things down the mountain."

"Or been abducted by Inca priests."

Andrew laughed. "See that stairway over there?" He pointed sharply to the right. "I ran up and down it three times. The people must have been in amazing physical shape if they had to carry things up and down those terraces." He frowned. "Like potatoes. You said they grew potatoes here, right?"

He'd been listening to me. Surprise, surprise.

"Not only grew them." I turned away from the view and leaned against the windowsill. "Listen to this, Andrew. It's my favorite thing about the Incas. They were master botanists! They took eight varieties of poisonous tubers and from those eight plants, over who knows how many hundreds of years, they developed *three thousand* different types of potatoes."

"Seriously?" He whistled. "From poisonous plants? Wow."

"Yes! Some of the potatoes were grown in ultra-microclimates—like they'd only grow on one or two terrace levels on the side of one particular mountain facing one particular direction—and that was all."

Andrew stared at me. "You are *way* more interesting than that guide!"

I couldn't help it. I liked Andrew in that moment.

"Follow me," I said, gathering up my camera and tripod, stepping out of the dwelling. "There's something nearby I want to show you."

He walked faster than me, a bundle of pent-up energy, touching a stone, kneeling to look at something near the ground, jumping to peer over a wall, walking toe-to-toe along a narrow ledge alongside the pathway, turning around every so often to make sure I was still with him.

And me? I told him stories of this place.

And as we walked, I realized something: Maybe my stepbrother was exuberant and excitable and, well, often obnoxious, but *maybe* he wasn't a boob. At least all the time. As much as it hurt me to understand (because maybe, just maybe, I am a little self-centered), Andrew loved this wondrous place as much as I did.

Just *differently*.

And the thought occurred to me right as we reached the little grassy plaza in the middle of Machu Picchu—where not one, but three llamas grazed near the lone tree—that maybe, just maybe, if I had had a natural brother, he might have been something like Andrew.

My Nemesis, My Muse

By Nancy Bonnington

(Based on the prompt, "Rivalries, Portals, and Footfalls")

I haven't written a poem since I read those of the Great One last week. My unfinished collection is buried in the cloud.

He taunts me—my indelible rival—as I hear his footfalls in the night and snap on my light. He is quite visible standing in my doorway, the portal to my sallow universe. Welcome to the deep end, friend. The deep south…south of hell.

You are my new favorite, Pablo, and I rue the day I read you. You reprimand me without knowing, while your words drip with the romance and lushness of a savage king. I put my mind to other things. I wash my clothing and sort my tax returns and rearrange my furniture. And there is always something to vacuum up.

The keyboard is obnoxiously silent, the keys almost all dusty, except for the backspace, which I punch and punch and punch, erasing anything that I had started, time and time again, since a week ago.

"What are you attempting?" he asks, his voice raspy like a ghost's is meant to be.

"A poem. Poetry."

"A poem in the dark? Ah, yes, I wrote like that at times."

"Never like me, though," I answer. From the darkest corner of my heart I try to write something about the stillness between each breath...but nothing comes out. There are no words for the moments that matter.

I turn to him, and I say, "It hurts, man. You asshole, you bastard." My language, not even translated, is dirt-poor and burns and reeks of trying too hard. "I ache to be as brilliant as you."

I lie back in bed and pull the covers over my head. He should go away if I will him to. Each time I blink and peek, indeed he appears and then disappears—like an irony that doesn't stand on its own, or maybe like fate after it proves its existence.

He comes and goes.

Then one special day, I gain courage and steam. I get out of bed in the night. What can be more invigorating than his words? I pick up *Twenty Love Poems and A Song of Despair*. It is weighty in my hands, even more so in my heart. The words literally come in ounces and pounds, and leave me knowing what it means to be a heavyweight in the literary world.

Leaning into the afternoon I cast my sad nets toward your oceanic eyes—

Who writes like that?

He does.

I feel the soft wind of him behind me, as he reaches around and drops a pen on my desk. It is black with a metal tip, the kind that needs an inkwell. I smile for a moment, but then I remember he has been dead as long as there have been computer keyboards. He has been a figment only in others' minds, until I filled my nightstand with his tomes…so full I cannot close the drawers.

Now he comes to me in the night, when I prefer to write, and he flattens my self-esteem like a pancake under a steamroller. The words catch in my throat as sure as they become lodged within the inkless pen.

If I could speak his language… Oh, but all I know is "*hola*" and "*sí*", not even enough to begin a haiku.

Then one night he is like an animal, standing there over my bed after breaking into my home and roaming around in my head, pacing like a leopard. He is a cagey laureate knocking at the window of my insanity. Before, the only dead I saw did not speak, did not question me, and did not argue when I rolled over.

I glance toward the shadowy door and beg him to leave. The dead usually lie still and hard in their coffins while women weep.

He seems restless.

I am more attracted to his soulful language than his form, so I close my eyes when I gain the courage to ask him for a love poem. And he speaks close to my ear, in the language that I don't understand, but the beautiful rhythms rise and fall, then snap to the shore like ripples in a pond.

"More," I coax, when he hesitates, even for a breath. "Don't stop."

I'm a whining child, and there is silence for a length of time that would fill the whole *Song of Despair*, and then he says, "Ask me why I am here, Belinda."

"Why?" I ask obediently.

"Because they killed me," he whispers, his soft voice glancing off my earlobe but ringing within the ear canal long after it stops.

"Who? Jesus, why? How?" I ask.

He is haunting in his glow, for his face lights up brighter each time he says he was murdered. And I can't help but open my eyes and gaze at his face, like watching a lightning storm or a tragedy at the side of a highway.

"They killed me. They killed me."

Now he is the whining child.

"Tell me your love poems," I interject to distract him, and for a moment his dark figure begins to shake and shudder, so aggrieved he is, I think, by the memory of love. I imagine him trying to recall what it is to soar over the rooftops of the earth—above all else, as he once did in life.

"Love is so short," he moans. "Forgetting is so long."

That is all I get from him. And I feel sorry that I brought it up.

Soon enough, he fades. I ache to have him back, though I'm humbled and afraid...and though my writing life might be over.

In the darkness after midnight, I have a thought like a stone moving slowly down my throat. He once was a baby; why can't I start simple and wean myself from the benign, and ever so slowly, slowly, slowly progress toward the brink of a mature relationship with the muses?

For a moment then, I have hope.

Ordinarily a bird lover, I seethe when the first ones begin to chirp outside my window—the sparrows and starlings, their short, sharp voices moving toward one another's to a point of certainty and clarity, announcing that the world is about to begin another day.

My desk and computer appear in the daytime not so romantic, and my walls bleed with water stains like old ladies who can't help it, and my rug is soiled where the cat must have peed. And I am back in my own reality.

Pablo is gone. He is gone forever, I know with my intuition. Perhaps it never happened.

And then I pick up the morning paper, which I peruse less often than the internet these days, and unceremoniously in some latter page and down in the right-hand corner there is this story headline: *Cancer didn't Kill Pablo Neruda. Was it murder under Pinochet?*

When the phone rings, I'm not ready for it. My agent asks me if I'm going to meet my deadline, and all I can say is, it's too early to tell. "Half of the poems have been written," I explain. "But the other half are still at bay, awaiting my nemesis, my muse. I might even have to begin them all again. And anyway, it is almost almost impossible not to plagiarize."

Are You Really Marilyn Monroe?

By Susan Whiting Kemp

(Based on the prompt, "Rivalries, portals and footfalls")

Me: unassuming, forgettable, scrawny, blond.

Marilyn Monroe: the opposite of me, except for the blond.

Neither of us: thrilled to be there.

Well, Marilyn was, at first. She thought she might be able to go to Hollywood, but the Séanz program doesn't work outside of the séance room. So she was naturally surly. Dead people often are at first, or so I understood—I had just started working at Séanz, so I didn't know how bad it could be.

Séanz had furnished the séance room like a 1950s living room to put Marilyn at ease. White-and-gold plush sofa. Side tables with ashtrays. Writing desk with ceramic peacock paperweight. They had given me paper and pencil so that we could progress to the interview without wasting time explaining computers. Séanz was a start-up, and needed usable information from dead people to prove that this wasn't some kind of parlor trick.

So far they hadn't gotten that information, and I could see why. Marilyn was throwing pillows and lamps around the room, emoting anger in the wriggling way she used to do in her films. "You can't push me around," she said in that high, breathy voice.

"I understand completely," I said. "People like to tell you what you can and can't do. That's got to be difficult."

Marilyn looked over at me, wide-stanced on stiletto heels, chest heaving, glass ashtray in hand. She wore a yellow flowered dress that fit her frame perfectly. A lock of hair fell tauntingly out of place in front of her eye. "What did you say your name was?"

I had to admit that Marilyn was absolutely riveting. I'd admired her movies, much as I didn't want to, since she was the type who had bullied me throughout my childhood. In person she was even more marvelous. In spite of myself I knew I could watch her endlessly, but our time would be brief. We had only ten minutes for our entire visit, and then Marilyn would have to return to…wherever she was before. The dead never talked about that, so we didn't know anything about the afterlife itself.

"I'm Clarita," I said. "If you tell me a few things, then I'll find out whether there's a way to get you to Hollywood next time. No promises, but I'll ask." I tried to word it so she wouldn't haunt me later. I didn't know whether she could, but we knew so little about the dead.

"Well, I suppose." She breezed over to the couch and sat on the one cushion she hadn't thrown at the wall. "What do you want to know?"

The way she waited for me to speak, lips slightly parted, as if the world hinged on what I was about to say. I wanted to be her.

Suddenly and forcefully, a wave of jealousy the strength of which I'd never known surged through me.

She was so vulnerable. So heartbreaking. So Marilyn. I wanted to comfort her. Give her a cookie or something. Maybe this was why people offered her Valium back when she was alive. They just wanted her to feel better. Oh, and get the movie filmed, I suppose.

I gathered myself together. *Be professional.* "What is it like in the afterlife?" I knew I wasn't likely to get an answer about that one. But it was worth a shot.

Marilyn pursed her lips. "Ask me something else."

Five minutes left. I asked the big one. "Why did you kill yourself?"

I expected Marilyn to get angry, but she merely batted her eyes. "A lot of reasons, but the last straw was a voice mail from Joe...."

"A voice mail from Joe DiMaggio?"

"Yes. I divorced him but we were still friends."

"There wasn't voice mail in 1962."

Marilyn stood and wandered to the desk. She picked up a ceramic peacock and stroked it. "I'm bored. Let's talk about something interesting."

"Of course," I said. "Let's talk about your favorite role out of your...how many movies did you make?"

"Ten," she said. "Give or take."

"I could have sworn it was a couple dozen at least," I said. "Are you really Marilyn Monroe?"

Marilyn threw the peacock against the wall. It broke into several pieces. "You are the most annoying little creature I've ever met. Of course I'm Marilyn Monroe."

She never stopped emoting. Next she morphed from angry

to sad, and I could see it in her face every step of the way. She knelt at my feet and said softly, "You have to believe me. It's just so different after you die. Some details aren't as important. You start to forget them. You hear things about the world and things all mix together like a big ol' pot of soup. Tell me you believe me. Tell me you know I'm Marilyn."

"I believe you." I did. I couldn't help smiling back at her. She stood, buoyant, obviously pleased with herself.

"So…what *is* important in the afterlife?" I asked.

Marilyn avoided the question. "I didn't want to do this. It's horrible coming back here. It's so…limiting. It's like you're squeezed into a funnel." She clamped her arms against her sides and shimmied. "And you come out as a tiny piece of what you really are."

"So the afterlife feels more expansive?"

"No. That's not it at all." Marilyn slipped out of her shoes, gave a sigh of relief, and wiggled her toes. "You know, I was a good person in life. I cared. I donated. I volunteered. Then I got to the afterlife and found out that wasn't the point."

I held my breath. Was I really going to be the first to know something about death? My heart pounded. Marilyn looked off at nothing for a long time. Two minutes left. "And?" I said carefully.

She gazed at me then heaved a single, big sigh. "What the heck. You might as well know. In the afterlife, fame is all that matters. And it's cutthroat, dearie. You think it's hard to go viral in the earthly life, just you wait."

I took this in. It wasn't at all what I expected to hear. "So the afterlife is like life, but more intense."

"No, no, no." She held up a manicured finger. "The afterlife is nothing like life. But it's the only context you have, so that's what I've got to work with. Let me put it this way. What you do in life prepares you for the afterlife. And if you aren't famous in life, you can't hack it in the afterlife."

That couldn't be right. But there was something absolutely honest about her and the intensity with which she spoke. I was drawn into her being as if we were starting to share a soul.

What if she was the devil?

I turned away. It was my turn to go to the desk. Trying to think. Before I took this job I didn't believe in the devil. But I also hadn't believed in ghosts. Things had changed. I needed to allow for anything to be the truth.

One minute left. I pulled myself together. I had a job to do. I turned back. "Tell me more."

"I shouldn't. But I just don't care anymore. So I'll tell you that you'd better get famous if you have any sense at all, because being famous is the only thing that prepares you for the afterlife."

"How could fame be all that matters?"

"Because that's what the earthly life is for. Why do you think there are so many people? I'm telling you, nothing else is important." She grabbed my notebook from my hands and tossed it onto the ground. "Stop writing. It's not that hard to remember. You need to get famous."

I stared at her. Her emotion was so compelling. Jealousy flowed through me. Why couldn't I be like her? Was she the devil, inciting that in me?

Or maybe there was more to her message. "So I need to do something noteworthy now. Make a difference. Change the world."

"No. Just get famous. That's it. How you get famous and what you do with it is of no consequence whatsoever, except that a lot of footfalls help."

"Footfalls?"

"Oh, right. That's not a concept here. How do I explain?" She wiggled a bit. "The more places you go, the more people see you. In-person fame is important too. Singing stars do quite well in the afterlife, because people see them in the newspapers but also in person. Touring evangelists, same thing, although religion has nothing to do with it."

"Why should I believe you?" I asked.

Marilyn started to fade. She looked down at her arms, then back at me. We were out of time. "Take my advice before it's too late. Go out and get instantly, utterly, irreversibly famous. Everywhere."

"Wait, don't go," I said, leaping to my feet.

She blew me a kiss, then faded some more. "Remember me," she said. "Remember I did you a favor."

And she was gone.

I had some thinking to do. Whether I believed her and how much. What to put in my report. And mostly, what to do with the rest of my life. In my mind's eye I saw Marilyn blowing me a kiss in a repeating loop, over and over. I picked up the broken peacock pieces and put them back on the writing desk. I replaced the couch cushions. I looked at the spot where Marilyn Monroe—or perhaps the devil herself—had knelt at my feet.

I asked myself, How would I go about it? How would I become instantly, utterly, irreversibly famous—everywhere?

Before leaving, I turned back for a final look. Though the room was empty, it didn't feel that way. I put my fingers to my lips, blew a kiss, turned away slowly, and stepped over the threshold.

Jesus on a Rocking Horse

By Evelyn Arvey

(Based on the prompt, "But unfortunately, that's illegal.")

At first Carmen didn't realize it was Jesus. The smudges and oil spots, the paint drips in the exact hue of old mustard, the tread marks of a long-ago car's sudden stop—all these things, and worse, sullied the alley behind the apartment she shared with two roommates that she barely knew, but the alley's detritus held no interest to her other than to make sure that her wheelchair's wheels didn't roll over something disgusting that might then be transferred to her carpet.

At first Carmen saw only a filthy alley. And the occasional rat. And Mossy Rivers, the equally filthy homeless man who lived in a stairwell at the far end of the street. But on a chilly March evening when she turned the corner into her alley, she saw it: a face, several times larger than life, rendered on the ground in the middle of the alley like a charcoal drawing made with the street effluvia she tried so hard not to notice. The face was like one of those trick posters, Carmen decided, one of those computer-generated pictures where you could see the New York skyline only if you squinted and unfocused your eyes and gave yourself a headache.

Carmen hesitated at the entrance to the alley, rolling her wheelchair several inches back and forth, back and forth, watching the face grow fuzzy, come into focus, grow fuzzy again. If she rolled too far in either direction the face disappeared into its component smudges, spills, and grime. If she rolled to the perfect spot, the face was so clear she could see a stray hair on its forehead.

The hair became a single ramen noodle when she rolled forward.

"What you looking at?" Mossy Rivers was slouching against the nearest wall.

"Nothing." She shook her head. "It's nothing."

It really was nothing. The face was gone. The noodle was only a noodle.

Mossy Rivers belched. "Excuse me."

Carmen reached around her chair to the book bag she always slung over her chair's handles. She dug out a brown paper bag and held it out to Mossy. "Tuna salad today."

"Half?"

"Half. You know I can't eat a whole one."

Mossy executed an extravagant bow complete with an arm flourish so graceful that Carmen could almost see the plumed velvet hat he pretended to hold. He took the bag from her hand. Turned away. Strolled down the alley. Disappeared into his stairwell. Pulled closed the gray-upon-gray wool blanket that served as his door. Mossy always ate her offerings in his stairwell; he'd never once opened the bag in front of her to see for himself what she'd brought.

She wondered: Were the half sandwiches the only food Mossy ate all day?

What about the weekends? What did he eat on the weekends?

For the next two weeks the face in the alley welcomed her if she took the time to search for it. The individual components might change—the noodle hair was replaced by oil-stain shadowing on the face's forehead, for example—but the face itself, with its serene gaze and kind eyes, never did.

"I know you're looking at something!" Mossy Rivers said on the Monday of the third week. He clutched a bag (with half a roast beef sandwich) close to his chest. His knuckles were white. "Tell me what you're looking at!"

Carmen almost didn't. She almost left. But some small part of her wanted to share this secret treasure, wanted someone else to experience what she was experiencing.

"Okay." She closed her eyes. Opened them again. "Stand right behind me. Yes. Right there. Now, um, kneel down to my height." She waited while he did so. "Okay. Now I'll move out of your way."

She rolled next to him. How could Mossy look so darn *elegant*, crouched as he was, dressed in clothes that were almost rags, reeking of stale cigarette smoke and old urine?

"Now what?" he asked.

Carmen pointed at where she knew the face ought to be, although she could no longer see it. "There. On the pavement. Before that dumpster. Take your time; squint; move your head slowly until you see it."

She waited. Had it taken her this long to see the face the first time?

Mossy jerked. "What the *hell*!"

"You see it? You see it?" Carmen leaned forward in her chair. "Do you?"

But Mossy, still clutching his brown bag, rose to his feet and sprinted down the alley.

Carmen stared after him, a smile twitching at the sides of her mouth: On the way to his stairwell, Mossy Rivers had altered his path. He'd deviated to the far side of the alley to avoid running over the face. He'd seen it.

❊ ❊ ❊

The next day Mossy was waiting for her. She gave him a half turkey on rye; then they took turns gazing at the face in the alley.

"How is it possible?" Carmen asked, not really expecting an answer. "I mean, by all rights it should be gone by now. It rained last night, for God's sake! But there it is. Same as ever."

She made a move to leave, but Mossy stopped her. "Wait," he said. He crammed his sandwich into a gaping pocket in his jacket, then pulled out a small Phillips screwdriver from the same pocket. Without saying anything, he knelt onto the pavement at her side and began tightening the screws that held her wheelchair together. He motioned for her to take her arm off her armrest and tightened that too.

"Thank you," she said when he'd finished.

He shrugged, not looking at her, looking for the face in the alley probably. "It was wobbling," he said finally.

❊ ❊ ❊

The next day the face had a neck. A few days later, shoulders.

"Who do you think it is?" Carmen asked Mossy. It was Friday. The face wasn't just a face anymore; there was a vague suggestion of clothing now, folds of cloth that rounded the face's neck and draped artfully down the figure's chest.

"Who do *you* think it is?" Mossy straightened up, both knees cracking. He peered at her.

She didn't answer.

"Your tires need air," he said finally. There was a bicycle pump in his hands. Had he stashed it nearby, waiting for the perfect moment to offer? It took longer to fill her tires than she thought it should, but she didn't mind.

"It's Jesus," she whispered as he stood up, his knees cracking again. The nozzle of his pump clanged against the metal of one of her chair's handles.

"It's Jesus," he repeated.

And then they broke into laughter.

❁ ❁ ❁

The next day Carmen's coworker Brenda came to see Jesus. It had been a whispered, self-conscious invitation that Carmen had extended, feeling rather ridiculous. She wanted—*needed*—someone else to witness what she and Mossy Rivers had seen, because how long would it last? How long until the alley was just an alley again? How long would Jesus stay? Carmen didn't know Brenda very well, but she figured anyone who wore a tiny gold cross every day to work wouldn't mind being invited to see Jesus in an alleyway.

Brenda invited her entire Bible study group, all twelve of them.

"Too many people!" Mossy Rivers complained, leaning against the wall as he always did, only now he stayed put and ate his half sandwich in dainty little bites, as if eating it slowly would make it somehow be more filling, as if a loaves-and-fishes sort of miracle had taken place. The Bible study group milled around, murmuring and whispering and clutching Bibles, peering down the alleyway, watching one another for signs of holy visitations, stealing glances at Carmen, moving their heads from side to side and bobbing them up and down as they tried to bring Jesus into focus.

"They're trying so hard," Carmen whispered to Mossy.

"They look like chickens," he answered.

Carmen tried to swallow her laugh, but she must have done a poor job of it, because one of the Bible-holders glared at her and put her finger to her lips.

A moment later a shriek filled the alley: "I see him! Lord above, *I see him*!"

The group spontaneously broke into the Lord's Prayer.

Carmen watched them, feeling decidedly not in the mood to join in, wondering whether she had done the right thing after all by inviting Brenda to see Jesus. Who were these people? Would Jesus ever be *hers* again?

Mossy Rivers ate the last of his sandwich. He crumpled up the wrapper and put it into his pocket. "Hmph," he said, so softly Carmen barely heard it.

"What?" she asked.

Mossy pointed his chin toward the alley. "See that? There's new stuff."

Right where Jesus's body would be, if he had one, someone had dumped garbage: a burger wrapper, bits of torn cloth, cigarette butts. Carmen frowned. Would the extra things change the image? Which made her wonder, how long would the image remain? Would the wind take it away? Would a hard rain ruin it? What if the visitors started taking bits and pieces as souvenirs?

❊ ❊ ❊

The next day when Carmen arrived after work, she found a small crowd waiting. She also found a red circle painted on the pavement, at the best spot for Jesus viewing. Mossy was solemnly telling the crowd that Jesus viewing wasn't open until he and Carmen had greeted Him, said their prayers (Mossy winked at her), and collected a small "donation for charity" from each person, to be deposited in an old fishbowl with a single chip on the rim thoughtfully covered with duct tape so no Jesus viewer might cut him- or herself. "Please line up on the painted line," he went on, waiting a moment as the fifteen or so hopeful viewers compliantly arranged themselves. "Each person gets a full minute to see our Lord Jesus! *Two* minutes with an additional donation to the fishbowl!"

"Mossy!" Carmen rolled up to him and pulled on his hand, barely noticing that he wore an almost-new jacket, one without gaping pockets. "You can't do that. You can't charge people to see Him! It's probably against the law or something."

"They want to give us money."

She just looked at him.

"It's true," he insisted. "It makes their experience more…"

"Holy?"

"Meaningful, I was going to say. Meaningful. Having to spend money always makes things more meaningful." He leaned in close to Carmen, then lowered his voice: "Unfortunately, yes, it is illegal."

Carmen looked over the now-organized crowd, saw the fishbowl being passed from person to person. A white-haired woman with a youthful face (what a wonderful combination, Carmen thought) tucked a limp twenty-dollar bill into the collection bowl and then held the bowl out to Mossy. "May I stand in the circle now?" she asked hopefully. "Have you opened for business?"

Mossy executed a gallant bow. "One moment, please," he said to the white-haired woman in a voice loud enough to be heard by all. "Lady Carmen must have her daily visit with Our Lord. When she finishes her prayers, we will open for public viewing."

"You, my friend, are full of shit," Carmen hissed at him as she maneuvered her wheelchair inside the red circle.

"I know. What kind of sandwich did you bring for me?"

It was ham and cheese on a baguette. And an entire raisin-oatmeal cookie, a giant one.

Jesus almost took her breath away, he was so beautiful. The line of his jaw, the arch of his eyebrows, the curve of cheek and lip, even if made of street garbage—it was enough for her to want to force money on someone.

His robes were longer now, she decided, and his hair was too. She took in every detail, feeling as though He were someone she might know, or maybe someone she ought to know, or someone she might meet, say, at the grocery store or in line at the bank, if only she looked hard enough. She sighed. *Get a grip, girl*, she told herself. She gave up her place at the red circle and joined Mossy by the wall. She didn't ask what he planned to do with the money. She didn't want to know.

As she watched people taking their turns in the red circle, her fingers traced the cracked vinyl of her wheelchair's armrests over and over, fiddling with the wispy white fluff that escaped each hole, and she wondered for the millionth time where the Jesus picture came from, because there was no way it was divine, not in the world she knew.

So then, what was it? Where did it come from?

After a while Mossy took a mostly used-up roll of leopard-spot duct tape from his pocket. "Let me fix that." He pointed at the closer armrest. At her nod he went to work. He peeled a strip of duct tape from the roll and smoothed it over the tears and cracks. And then he taped the other armrest.

"Thanks," she said. Her fingers were already tracing the new landscape of duct tape ridges. She rather liked the leopard spots. They made her feel jaunty.

"Thank *you*, Lady Carmen."

Her laugh sounded suspiciously like a giggle.

❊ ❊ ❊

The next day more than a hundred people came to see Jesus, and they made the local news. The fishbowl overflowed. Carmen called in sick from work; her boss just laughed. "Honey," she said, shaking her head, "you've been chosen. Don't you come back until it's over. Hear?"

The news spread: *Jesus is here! Come see Him!*

Stand in God's Holy Red Circle! Touch Lady Carmen's wheelchair!

Don't forget to bring donation money.

❊ ❊ ❊

Two days later the crowd was so big the line of hopeful Jesus viewers snaked around the block. A police detail was assigned to the site. Porta Pottis were set up. Plastic barriers shut off the closest streets. A taco truck, a sandwich truck, and seven news vans with telescoping satellite units drove around the barriers and parked across the street.

And the people! So many people! How their voices rang with joy when spontaneous hymns broke out. Among the visitors that day: a woman with hair dyed the exact hue of Mossy's red viewing circle; seven male priests with clerical collars; two female priests, also with clerical collars, who threw unreadable glances at the other priests but kept their distance; a group of Catholic schoolgirls in matching scratchy-looking sweaters; Carmen's roommates, who seemed dubious but turned hushed and sober after they'd spent their thirty seconds in the red circle (Mossy had just that morning changed the rules so the line would move quicker); members of the press, complete with cameras with long, heavy lenses; and a blind man with his German shepherd guide dog.

"Why would someone who can't see…" Carmen whispered to Mossy.

Mossy was emptying cash from the fishbowl. It was full already. "Always leave a few bills to seed the pot," he said as he patted a handful of bills into a wad and slipped it into his pocket. He peered at the blind man. "Well. You never know what a holy apparition might do."

Carmen raised an eyebrow. "Do?"

Mossy knelt in front of her wheelchair. He extended his long-fingered hand and pretended to pluck a rose from the rim of the right wheel. She drew in her breath, almost seeing the flower that wasn't there, admiring his sure, graceful movements. "He might appear to a blind person as a choir of angels, right?" he suggested. "Or as a wonderful aroma."

"Ambrosia," she said, not taking her eyes from the invisible rose.

"Ambrosia. Sure." Smiling his gentle one-side-turned-up smile, he leaned in close and wove the invisible rose stem into

Carmen's hair. She breathed in deeply, not minding Mossy's overpowering scent, not really.

"Mossy." She cleared her throat. "Can I ask you a question?"

He knelt at her side, one eyebrow raised.

"At night. When it's cold, or rainy. Don't you have anywhere else to go...?" She faltered, realizing that she'd never talked to Mossy, not really, not about important things. She knew nothing about him. What was his real name, for instance? How old was he? How long had he been homeless? *Why* was he homeless?

He shook his head. Looked away. Shifted his weight, as if to rise to his feet.

She put a hand on his arm. "Do you have family somewhere?"

She didn't think he was going to answer, but he did. "A sister. She died."

"Oh. I'm sorry."

"It was seven years ago."

They watched the Jesus-viewing line; it moved a couple of steps closer to the red circle.

"Is there no one else, Mossy?"

"You," he said finally.

He wasn't looking at her, which was just as well, because she was blushing. No one had ever said such a thing to her, and no wonder, because what use could she be to anyone? What could a wheelchair-bound, mousy-looking woman with too-thin limbs, who tired too quickly, who would rather stay at home and read a good book than go out and party *do*?

Maybe she wasn't as useless as she'd thought.

"Thank you," she said.

❊ ❊ ❊

The next day there was so much cash Mossy replaced his bowl with a ten-gallon fish tank.

The day after that, it was apparent to everyone that Jesus was sitting on something. It was all people could talk about. A stool, some said. A bench at the Last Supper, said others. The banks of the River Jordan, was the consensus of a large group of nuns who were visiting that day. Not so, said a Native American mystic; it's clearly a thunderbird—can't you see the beginnings of its outstretched wings? Both the *Christian Science Monitor* and *Guideposts* websites had articles and artists' interpretations of it.

Carmen thought it was none of those things. Jesus clearly was riding a donkey. Or whatever people rode in those days. She could just barely make out the shape of its head, off to the side, and didn't that other side look an awful lot like a tail?

Maybe, allowed Mossy, maybe.

❁ ❁ ❁

The next day they shared an enormous double-chocolate-chip cookie that someone had left on the offering table, and settled down to watch the crowd, she in her wheelchair (which now sported zebra-print fabric neatly covering the threadbare back cushion), and Mossy perched on a stool that had so much of his leopard-spot duct tape on it that she couldn't see any wood. The crowd, unsurprisingly, was larger than ever.

The place was crawling with priests. Carmen watched two of them lift Mossy's table, move it far to the side, and set up their own table in the place Mossy's had been. The new table was twice as large and looked far grander and more official than theirs ever had: It had a red velvet altar cloth, three large posters of Alley Jesus in different stages of being, offering dishes that already had handfuls of cash in them, prayer cards featuring Alley Jesus, and gray-speckled candles for sale that were said to contain holy alley dirt.

"They moved our table. They can't do that!" Carmen gripped the arms of her wheelchair.

"It doesn't matter," said Mossy. "Look."

They watched the line shift so that it passed both tables. There was already a layer of offerings lining the bottom of the fish tank—the Jesus viewers were giving to both collection bowls. Why did people feel compelled to give away their money? Which reminded her: What *was* Mossy doing with the money, anyway?

Certainly he wasn't buying new clothes, or decent living accommodations, or food.

"It's a rocking horse," he said after a while.

"It is not a rocking horse."

"I'm pretty sure it is." He ate the last of the cookie.

"Why would Jesus ride a rocking horse?" she asked, trying not to laugh. "That's stupid."

"Jesus can do anything he wants."

She couldn't think of a good answer to that, so she said nothing, just shrugged. Her words would have been lost in any event, because the crowd had started singing a hymn to the tune of "Amazing Grace." The lyrics, helpfully printed on sheets of lime-colored paper, were passed out by the cohort of female priests, and were quite stirring:

Alleyway Jesus, how sweet the sight,

Revealed to a wretch like me.

I once was blind, but now I see,

The likeness, my Lord, of thee.

A sound crew with boom mikes and recording equipment flitted around the worshipers like damselflies in mating season—saying that the recording they made would be available for purchase in two days' time.

But it wasn't. Because it all came to an end.

That night a storm came through, wind, rain, lightning, thunder—the whole bit, as if the heavens were angry at their wayward son for choosing to appear in such a disgraceful way to people as unworthy as herself and Mossy Rivers. Carmen didn't sleep at all. She lay awake, imagining the destruction in the alley, knowing that the bits of effluvia that made up the image would never be able to withstand the storm. Jesus would be ruined. His soulful eyes would be taken by the wind. His hair would be pounded into mush, down to the last noodle. His graceful neck would be distorted and unrecognizable, his shoulders broken under the weight of the storm. She would never know whether Alley Jesus rode a rocking horse, or a donkey, or a thunderbird.

She would never again share the wonder of Alley Jesus with Mossy.

❁ ❁ ❁

Carmen rolled into the alley at first light the next morning, hours before her usual viewing time. She didn't bother going to Mossy's red viewing circle, but stopped in the shadows near the back entryway of her building, letting the rain wet her hair and run down her cheeks, wishing it hadn't ended so soon, so abruptly. The alley looked just as it always had. Dirty. Dank. Dark. Scattered garbage. Pizza crusts. Cigarette butts. Sludge over the sewer grate. There were even a few surviving noodles. She leaned over and picked up a dripping hymn lyric sheet from the day before, spread it out on her lap, flicked a flake of something green and rotted from the word *thee*.

It was over.

There was movement at the far end of the street. Mossy. He didn't see her. He stood for a long time, hands on hips, gazing at the destruction, the ratty hood of his velvet jacket pulled over his head. He seemed slumped, small, deformed even. She couldn't take her eyes off him—did he keep dry last night? Was his place under the stairwell flooded; were his few things ruined? She was about to call out to him when he leaned down and moved a pizza crust a few inches to the right.

He wiped his hands on his pant leg, then used the edge of—what? A broken flowerpot?—to slide a thick ridge of muck to a different position and then slick it down as if the goo were oil paint and the sliver of fired clay were a palette knife. Carmen sucked in her breath, transfixed, as he collected stray noodles, repositioned matchbook covers, sprinkled handfuls of dirt here and there, kicked away hymn papers, stared at the ground from many angles, nodding or shaking his head, looking like a crazy genius—van Gogh, maybe, or Einstein.

And then she understood.

At the same moment he saw her. "No!" he cried, stomping a foot, a dirty, streaked, naked foot—had his shoes been lost in the storm? She must find a new pair for him—and then he dropped the handful of garbage he'd been clutching, scattering torn candy wrappers and cigarette butts into the still-windy morning. "No, no, *no*! Go away, Carmen. You're not supposed to see this!" He turned, ran down the alley, disappeared into his stairwell.

"Mossy!" Her hands slipping and straining on her wheelchair wheel grips, she made her way down the alley, trying to avoid the areas where he'd been working but leaving tire marks anyway. "Mossy!"

She rolled up alongside the waist-high concrete barrier that formed part of his stairwell and pulled herself forward enough to peer into his cobbled-together home, which she had never done before; she had somehow known from the beginning that it was necessary to respect his privacy. A blue tarp patched with the same leopard-print duct tape he'd mended her armrests with flapped in the wind, one of its corners having come unmoored. Soggy piles of—what?—blankets? clothing? bedding?—littered the area under the stairs. The fishbowl they'd first used to collect money lay on its side on top of a dingy gray blanket, empty but for what looked like a half-eaten package of mini doughnuts. The stairwell reeked. The stench permeated everything, old urine and vomit and other unsavory things. Her breath caught in her throat, a sob that hurt in its intensity. It was *his* smell, only stronger. But Mossy wasn't there. He was gone. He must have slipped out the other side of the stairwell and climbed over the fencing.

He couldn't be gone. Where would he go?

Carmen waited, and waited, but he never returned.

A day passed, with priests and visitors milling around looking lost, with journalists taking pictures of the not-Jesus alley, with Carmen sitting in her wheelchair in her customary place bundled against the wind, waiting, hoping, still clutching his fishbowl.

A second day passed. Crews of volunteers cleaned the alley, wrangling shiny black garbage bags that billowed in the wind. They wore matching red sweatshirts that read *South Place*

Methodist Church. Carmen reached into the nearest bag and retrieved part of a poster: her and Mossy, posing beside the red circle, smiling at each other, not knowing that it was all about to end. She tucked the fragment under her coat, next to her heart, where it would be safe.

A week passed. She went back to work, hoping she still had a job. "Honey," said Brenda (who had exchanged her tiny gold cross for a larger one), "being the one Jesus appeared to is the best reason to miss work I ever heard." So that, anyway, was good.

Another week passed.

And then, seventeen days after the storm, a stranger knocked at Carmen's door. "Carmen Cruz?" he asked. "Delivery. Talk about bells and whistles." He had her sign a pale blue paper held on a clipboard, then reached behind him and carefully maneuvered a power wheelchair through the front door. It was beautiful, like a spaceship, sleek and shiny, and it was *hers*.

Carmen knew who'd sent it. She even knew where the money had come from.

Still, she missed him.

About a month later, something amazing appeared in a New York City alley. Garbage art, it was called, said the reporter from the nightly news, and it was created from "naturally occurring refuse" and "ambient detritus" by an anonymous, brilliantly innovative artist who was taking the country by storm. This first image—one of many, for these artworks would amaze and delight people for many years to come—was of a smiling young woman with kind eyes and long brown hair, someone people all over the country claimed they knew the identity of, but didn't.

But Carmen, she knew.

Thank God for Max

By Nancy Bonnington

(Based on the prompt, "But unfortunately, that's illegal.")

L*ife sucks, but thank God for Max.*

My mom's a bitch. We've been fighting since I recently turned twelve. She videoed me throwing a shit fit—for good reason, I might add, since she woke me up out of a sound sleep and kicked me out of bed—and threatened to send it to Dr. Phil. Whoever the hell he is!

I want my freedom. I deserve to be trusted. I'm twelve, for God's sake.

Dad doesn't do shit, but he's never home. I can't blame him.

When I want to go out, Mom says no. When I don't want to go out, she throws me out. She's a psycho like that. A psycho bitch!

I know what you're thinking. She feeds me and gives me a roof over my head. I'm just spoiled. Well, let's talk about that.

The food. To begin with, Mom doesn't cook. I doubt she even knows how. She feeds me packaged crap, like prison gruel, frankly, and when I ask for more, she says, "No, you're too fat, Fatso!"

How many moms behave like that?

Yes, I'm fat, because I'm not stupid. I can take care of myself. I go down the street to the Hawkins', who are always nice, cook fantastic meals, and never begrudge me seconds. I enjoy their company. I'll even in the same night cross over to the Bakers, because the Hawkins never do dessert. Mrs. Baker is just that, a baker. Pretty funny, huh? I don't mind baked goods now and then. Okay, more now than then. Ha!

And a roof over my head? Sure, I have that. But I expect a little better than the bare-minimum requirements. Like any American. You know what I mean?

Sometimes when I'm sad at night, I sneak into Mom's bedroom and try to climb into bed with her. I know I'm too old for that, but I still get scared when there's lightning and thunder, or windstorms that shake the roof. But Mom yells and shoves me out of the bedroom, almost throwing me like a rag doll. PMS? I doubt it. She treats me like some kind of unwanted vampire.

I love my mom, obviously, but I don't *like* her. We used to spend quality time together. I could curl up with her while she read a book to me. Or we'd play games.

What's changed? My little brother was born. That's what!

I love my little brother too, but I don't *like* him. He spends all of his time crying and shitting his diapers, and getting all of Mom's attention.

I don't have any friends, because of my prison-guard mother who never lets me do what I want. Everything is illegal. Everything is *verboten*! Everything is a punishment waiting to happen.

But last month I met Max. Oh, God, thank you for Max. He was down at the cul-de-sac; he just moved here. I was so fucking excited to meet him, I literally danced in circles. Maybe he thought I was nuts. I made sure to be seen a lot around the neighborhood after that, so I'd run into him again. And again and again. I admit it, I think I'm in total, massive *love.*

He's good-looking—hotter than shit, really—and he even *smells* good. Which made me know I'd have competition. So I had to be bold.

Sometimes I manage to sneak out a window—screw Mom if she doesn't like it, because she worries too much. I'll sneak out a window and go down the street and see if Max is around. I'll call for him when I'm out of earshot of Mom, and we'll meet up. Always in the woods at a grassy knoll. That's our place.

Max is the best. He's nice and treats me the way I'm meant to be treated. I would never, never, never invite Max home, because Mom wouldn't get it. She never gets anything. She'd probably kick his ass from here to kingdom come.

The first time we had sex, I didn't even know what was happening. He took me by surprise, and I let him. Max is not one for kissing or foreplay, but he gets down to business and he's good, and gentle enough. The truth is, I enjoyed it right from the start.

We started meeting up more and more often, and it always leads to sex. We don't talk about it. It just seems totally natural. To both of us.

Last Tuesday my mom was spying on me and I didn't know it. Max and I were in the woods at the end of the block, in the same cool, grassy knoll between shade trees where we like to do it. All of a sudden this big cow of a woman comes charging through the brush screaming, "Get off her! Get off of her. Get… off…of…her!"

It scared the shit out of Max. So much so that he kicked up

a dirt storm and beelined for a fence that my mom isn't spry enough to jump over. Otherwise I think she would have chased him over it and beat the crap out of him.

That night I was sent to the basement, where it's dark and damp. I was chilly and frightened and could only think of the Hawkins' warm kitchen. You can bet their kids were never sent to hell for having sex. Mom's such a prude.

I snuck upstairs.

She was doing the dishes. Lots of rattling and crashing of silverware on plates. My little brother was lying on a blanket in the middle of the living room floor. He was cooing like a dove. He looked all happy, fiddling with his toes and trying to pull his feet into his mouth and all.

All of a sudden I wanted to run away from home. I wanted to grab Max and head for the next county over. I wanted to ditch this life and start a new one.

And then a terrible, wicked thought crossed my mind. I could kill my baby brother. I could pounce on him and scratch his eyes out and gobble him up—blue blankey, white socks, fuzzy head and all.

I could devour his ass.

But unfortunately, as you might have guessed, it's illegal to touch the baby. In fact, Mom would have a conniption fit, I would end up back at the same vet clinic where they clipped my claws before the baby arrived. And more likely than not they'd give me a new pink collar with a shiny tag that says something lame, like, "Beware of Feral Cat."

Like I said, life sucks.

I think I'll go pee on my mom's bed.

The Diary of Lisa Contrallo

By Susan Whiting Kemp

(Based on the prompt, "But unfortunately, that's illegal.")

April 1

Today none of our electronics worked. My next-door neighbor Josh Hanmeyer told me he'd heard there was a coup. Against who? I said, and he said, you mean against whom, and I said nobody says whom anymore but that doesn't matter, answer the question. But he didn't, because these guys in lime-green polo shirts came and told to us gather for news at the new, one-story-tall screen they put up in the Thriftway parking lot.

I had better things to do than follow a bunch of dorky guys to a parking lot, but I went because I wanted to know what was going on and they seemed like they had some kind of intel. Little did I know. Anyway, there were about a hundred of us. Josh didn't go, and neither did Joe Malett, who had the flu, or Trudy Goodland, who had a broken leg. The men in green polo shirts told us that they were taking them away to a nice farm in the country where they could run and chase balls and get scratched behind their ears. We were all like WTF? They said it like it was a good thing, like they truly believed it. We're talking about people, not dogs. Sure, Josh was annoying—he always said things like, "That's spectaculous"—but it's spooky. I get the feeling I'm never going to see him again.

The screen had pink snowflake images and plunky piano music. Then the words, in Times New Roman font, said that the second day of the week was called Margery. It had always been called that, and would always be called that. To call it anything else would be illegal.

There was more plunky music, and some green snowflakes, and that was it.

Right away Pete Youngtown said the word that wasn't Margery, and the men in green polo shirts took him away. They said we have to gather at the screen every day at noon. And then they took off in their smart cars.

Couldn't get any more real information from anybody, just speculation. Somebody said the country of Bleckistan was taking us over, and I said there's no such place, and they said there is; we'd just never known about it until now. I said the hell with it and came home and now I'm going to bed and hoping that it will all make sense in the morning.

April 2

Today there were bouncy diamonds on the ginormous screen, the same plunky music, and the screen told us to gather all our paper clips and bring them to the parking lot immediately. Most people did, but Louise said she wasn't going to be treated like an idiot, so of course she was the next one to get taken away, apparently to a nice place with swings and all the bananas she could eat. And the people who tried to stop the men in green shirts from taking her got taken away by more men in green shirts. There seems to be an endless supply of those guys.

Those men in green polos, I can't overstate just how nice they were. Regular guys, like your best pals. You felt like they really cared about the people they were taking away. It confused the hell out of us. We would have understood where we were with men wearing black uniforms wielding batons and pepper spray and transparent shields. But guys wearing golf attire, treating us like their best friends? Weird, so weird.

April 3

Today Len Smith brought his rifle to the square. Len has a cleft in his chin so deep you could fold laundry in it. He's kind of a manly man, or thinks he is. But just like the electronics, guns don't work, and of course the men in green polos took Len away. There were bouncing balls on the screen and it told us we couldn't wear purple. My T-shirt had purple. Other people had purple on their shirts, glasses, hats. We took them off. Olive Sanders had on purple underwear and didn't take them off. She must have thought nobody would be able to tell, but somehow they knew. They said they were taking her to a water park where they would toss her some nice herring and she could cavort on fake icebergs. How did they know? If they know about her underwear, then what about this diary? I guess they would have already taken me away if it was a problem.

Some people are saying this is one of those TV shows where they punk you. A really elaborate punk. I'm not a fan of those shows, and I'm not pumped about being in one.

April 4

The screen told us we're supposed to wipe our faces with lace napkins at two p.m. every day. I can't go to work; I can't call my family; I don't know what's going on. One of the people here is a lawyer and he told the guys in the polo shirts that he was going to sue them and they just smiled at him and laughed like they were all having a grand time.

People were still saying this is a reality show, but I said, Then why don't the electronics work? Why don't guns work? So now the theory is that the polo-shirt people are benevolent aliens. And that when they take people away, they're eating them. Somebody said we should eat a lot of hot sauce so they won't like the way we taste and they'll go away, and somebody else said not to because they might like their humans spicy.

April 5

It's the Year One, according to the screen.

The green polos left some paperwork in one of their smart cars, and Rhonda found it, and it turned out to be waivers that we all signed to be in a show we gave our permission to give us a memory-wiping drug to forget we signed it. So we're thinking that whoever makes it to the end without being taken away will probably make a ton of money.

Rhonda said she was going to get more screen time and get really popular on the show so she could be on other shows too and be superfamous. She started cutting up and laughing so hard she sounded like a donkey. Then she peed on one of the smart cars, on purpose. They took her away, but didn't tell us where they were taking her.

I'm going to do everything right, and make it through this.

I'm going to win if it takes all year. There are ninety of us left. It might take a while.

April 6, Year One

We have to make paper airplanes and fly them for five minutes every day.

They told us Olivia Wallend tried to go away in a kayak last night. I was always kind of jealous of Olivia. She has natural eyelashes to die for, like the fronds on a Venus flytrap. But she's gone now. They took her to a place where she could use a running wheel all day long and eat pellets to her heart's content.

April 7, Year One

I was thinking about it, and those waivers we're supposed to have signed had to have been fakes. I'm not really the kind of person to seek the limelight, even for a lot of money, and my life has been kind of a controlled burn, so I wouldn't have wanted that kind of exposure. Besides, it was just too easy for Rhonda to find them; they had to have been planted there just for that. So now we're back to wondering what else could be going on. And somebody said, it's exactly the thing the government would do to get us used to being controlled. I don't know. I just know that the idea of being taken away weirds me out.

May 1, Year One

I haven't written in a while because I've been so discouraged. I never thought it would last a whole month. But I'm still determined to make it through, even though it's getting harder to remember all the things we're supposed to do every day. They've been taking people away like crazy. There are only four of us left. Today they added that we have to sing the plunky music from the screen when we walk past a stop sign. I'm lucky I have a good memory.

The polos brought us this bland stuff they called vitamin slurry and said we must eat it at seven fifteen a.m. every day. I wasn't sure what it was made of—some kind of grain. It wasn't horrible. I worried it was drugged but I felt the same after eating it.

May 3, Year One

John Neiman, my weirdy-beardy neighbor who calls himself a recovering technologist, wouldn't drink the vitamin slurry and is now gone. Three of us left now.

May 7, Year One

Lynn Abbey asked the polos to take her away. Of all my neighbors, I thought Lynn was the most intelligent. She always said smart things, pearls of wisdom. No, not little pearls, but big hulking chunks of wisdom. So when she said it sounded good to run in a field with all the kibble she could eat, for just a moment I wondered whether I should ask to be taken away too. But I will never give in.

Norman said those polo-shirt guys have to be aliens, because the whites of their eyes look kind of pearly, like slug slime. I tried to see it. I don't know. Maybe in the right light.

Norman and I are the only ones left. He's bald as a snowcone and so nervous that he'll forget a directive that he developed this tic of tapping his skull with his fingers. He's remembered everything up to this point; he needs to have confidence in himself. I wonder whether he would be better off with pellets and a running wheel. Yes. I'm sure of it. That's what he needs.

May 10, Year One

Tonight Norman used the word that is not Margery to name a day of the week. He slipped on one of our first-ever directives. I can't help but think that it was meant to be. They took him off to wherever it is they take people.

Then…they gave me a green polo shirt. They just handed it to me and left.

It felt so weird and wild. Like I'd just gone through a car wash without a car. I was crying; I was ecstatic; I was whooping. I, out of a hundred of my neighbors, made it through.

I finally calmed down and came home because I didn't know what else to do. I'm writing this thinking that soon I might know what the hell is going on.

But maybe I never will.

I'm not going to sleep tonight.

Somebody's at the door.…

Greg, We Need to Talk

By Evelyn Arvey

(Based on the snippet of overheard conversation: "Greg, we need to talk.")

The stench of gasoline would cling to her shoe for hours, Janet knew. Who would have thought it was so hard to get gas into a lawn mower? Filling the mower used to be Greg's job. He'd managed to do it all these years without fumigating himself. Why couldn't she?

She'd put this off too long. It was the middle of April and every lawn in the neighborhood was beaten into submission but theirs. *Their* lawn was overgrown, and—she soon discovered—damp. The lawn mower chopped unevenly at the grass, depositing masticated clumps of brilliant green. Greg never left turds of grass on the lawn. He didn't leave ragged uncut patches. He didn't accidentally cut down a swath of daffodils. He didn't wait too long to empty the bag. He didn't have to pull the cord seventeen times to get the dang thing started.

He'd made this look so easy.

Worst of all, he was watching.

He'd walked his wheelchair with little kicks of his slippered feet all the way from the kitchen, where she'd left him with his coffee half an hour ago, to the front room, where a patch of sunlight illuminated his cheek and right shoulder. How had he maneuvered the chair through that tight space by the refrigerator? Down the narrow hallway? She squinted up at him. He waved. If it weren't for the fact that he was wearing his bathrobe at eleven forty-five on a Tuesday morning, he might be the old Greg. If she ignored the wheelchair and the catheter bag.

She killed the lawn mower and waved, sweeping her arm in a wide circle to show off her work. *See? I did it.* He clapped, she bowed. He mimed a kiss, she mimed it smacking her in the chin, like she always did. He grinned.

Come in, he gestured.

I'm not finished, she indicated. *See? It looks like a tornado.*

Come in, he waved, both hands flapping. *It's fine. You've done enough.*

She wheeled the mower across the yard, down the driveway, and into its designated slot in the garage. She inched it close to the wall as Greg's fishing poles rattled and swayed and threatened to tumble. Sighing, she steadied them and shoved the smallest tackle box—the blue one, the one that used to go on short drives when Greg "probably wouldn't be fishing"—in with the others. Janet stared at the row of boxes. She was tired, so tired.

But he was waiting for her. She shut the garage and padlocked the door.

"Nice flowers," he said a few minutes later.

She headed to the kitchen; he kick-wheeled himself behind her. She leaned over the sink, snipping at the stems of a handful of daffodils she'd rescued from the lawn mower. She plucked a mangled bloom from the bundle and tossed it into the garbage. "Thanks. They're the ones under the flowering cherry. They're almost gone, and I didn't even notice. These are the last of them."

"They're still pretty."

"I messed up their stems. See?" She held the flowers out for his inspection, then stuck them in a vase and plunked the vase on the counter. "Greg. We need to talk."

He kicked at the floor, rotating his wheelchair a quarter turn to face her. The small front wheel dragged on a chair and shoved it out of position; he didn't notice. "What?"

"We can't go on like this."

He didn't answer. His fingers worried at the belt of his robe. One slippered foot tapped nervously atop the other. Pee accumulated in the tubing draped beside his legs, the same color as the daffodils. She looked away.

"*I* can't go on like this."

His eyebrows bunched in that way that made him look like a petulant five-year-old. "I'm the sick one here. What do you mean, you can't go on?"

"Look at us! We don't fit here anymore! Your chair doesn't fit. You can't even get into the house! Lou and Bradley have to hoist you up the stairs every time we come or go."

He looked out the window. "I'm getting out of this chair. It's not forever."

"That's what Dr. Morgan said, yeah." She pulled out a daffodil and held it to her chin. "Humor me. Look at my neck. Can you see yellow? They used to say if you could see a yellow reflection on your neck, butter wouldn't melt in your mouth."

"Whatever that means."

The flower trembled in her fingers. *I'm scared*, her eyes said.

"I'm getting better, Janet. I'm not sleeping all day."

"Right. But this house is old. The yard is huge. I can't do all the things you did."

He peered at her. "Yellow. I see yellow."

She replaced the flower. "Just don't ask me to churn butter." She leaned against the counter. "I never appreciated how much you did around here. I had no idea."

"And I never knew how much I could lean on you until this happened."

They fell silent, both of them staring at the vase of daffodils.

"We can hire people, Janet. Gardeners. Cleaners. You don't have to do it all."

"I don't know. Maybe."

"You're doing a *fine job*. Nursing me. Handling the family. Paying bills. Spending hours doing research on the internet—yes, I know you do that. You've been amazing. Really." His voice turned thick and soft. "And I love you for it."

Heat prickled Janet's neck. She was blushing. He'd told her on a long-ago date that she looked sweet as a cherry when she blushed and that he could just eat her right up, hard bits and all. Now her cheeks were prickling too. "I don't feel amazing," she murmured. "I feel like…like one of those bruised flowers I just tossed in the garbage." She stifled a laugh, throwing her still-damp, still-gasoline-smelling hand over her mouth.

He patted his lap. "C'mere. Have a seat. Remember when you used to sit on my lap? Before the kids?"

She took a step toward him. She smiled. "I'm afraid I'll hurt you. The catheter…"

"To hell with the catheter." He held out his arms.

His lap didn't feel any different than it had all those years ago. It was still warm and welcoming, still *Greg*. She rested her shoes next to his slippers. Together they wheeled away from the table, then stopped.

She giggled.

"Hold on. Tighten your seat belt. Here we go." He took hold of the hand grips and she put her hands on top of his. Inch by inch, they worked their way across the kitchen, avoiding the chairs but banging noisily into the cabinet next to the stove. "And there we have it, people—*pole position*!"

She laughed aloud.

His arms encircled her. "We're the same people we always were, Janet."

She nestled into him. "I'm scared."

"Me, too."

"Can we do this?"

"We can."

"We're not young anymore."

"No. But we're not dead yet."

He hugged her. He kissed the soft private place on the back of her neck. Then he backed the wheelchair away from the cabinet and they resumed their journey.

A Peaceful Solution

By Nancy Bonnington

(Based on the snippet of overheard conversation: "You never know what you'll find down there.")

I pick up my purse, sling it over my shoulder, and glance around the living room. Everything is in perfect order—the twin upholstered chairs in dark velvet fabric and paisley design, surrounding a bare teak table; the black leather couch with its white pillows neatly fluffed and set in place beside the armrests; the coffee table, its marble surface wiped clean; and on the walls the neatly framed pictures of his family—mother, father, son, daughter—a black-and-white portrait of a grandfather, and an oil-scape of a Greek harbor with plentiful sailing boats—many at dock, some moored in the ocean, and a few lucky ones under sail in sparkling blue waters.

And then there's the grand piano, probably his prize possession. There is a perfect rectangle of stacked music collections beside the music holder. I can see Mozart and Bach and Chopin on the spines. The wooden bench, dusted and polished, is tucked under the keyboard, which is shut. The lid of the piano is propped open at the angle of a seagull's wing in flight, and half of it is shining in the pale light of early dawn, the other half hidden beyond the light of the window. He would have closed the blinds so the sun wouldn't hurt the finish.

I move to do this small, near-forgotten task, twisting the pole that folds down the oak slats until the light disappears and the piano is completely covered in shadow.

Next, I look at the body. He is in a perfect state of rest, having been transported to another world without evidence of fright or pain. His legs are beneath the grand piano, crossed at the ankles above his well-clad feet; the leather Italian loafers show not a single scuff. His hands are folded over his rib cage, perhaps staged too much like a corpse at a funeral parlor, yet it works. The only other thing out of place in the room—the only thing that would draw your eye—is a still pool of liquid forming a perfect circle around his head and shoulders. Standing above him and looking down is like seeing a postcard of the man in front of a bloodred moon. It is ironically a thing of beauty.

I squat down to examine the scene of the body beneath the piano—you never know what you'll find down there. Up close, it is still a perfect job. No debris, no struggle, no evidence.

I'm not proud of much, but a well-executed execution... that is grounds for a hefty pat on the back. I do have limits. I won't kill a child, or a pregnant woman. I won't kill an animal. I won't work for any less than the last job. And I don't ask questions. I don't care whether the subject is good or bad, a politician, a bricklayer, a wife, a teacher, a poet.... I'm not the judge; I leave that to the one who hires me and his or her god.

When I was fifteen—some twenty-odd years ago—I stumbled on my way of life through serendipity. My addict dad and his third wife pitched me out the door on the less than fair grounds that I was a loser; my mom was a couple years dead by then, and I guess I felt older than my years. And bitter.

Maybe I was reincarnated from one or two steps beneath human, or I was just a minion from hell inhabiting the body of a teenage girl. My past was rotten, but no more so than those of good people who cope and have feelings. In any case, I had no intention of analyzing my spiritual collapse, or changing. Put it down to bad genes or a tangled cord around my neck before birth.

It all began with Keith Hanover, the kid who was picked on at school, who lusted after the girls way out of his league and put his foot in it all the time. I guess he deserved to be the school punching bag, the freak who showed up naked on the internet, clutching his shorts between his teeth on a dare, the laughingstock. But even then, I didn't judge.

Keith came to me with a deal that perhaps he didn't believe in, but which I took for a matter of fact. He said he'd give his whole bank account to wipe Jason Bower off the face of the planet. It didn't take me long to learn that his bank account amounted to eight hundred dollars and some odd change, which is a small fortune when you're sleeping in a two-door Volkswagen with a broken camshaft and showering in the high school locker room. It also didn't take long to learn Jason's address and routine.

I did it with a knife. Back then I didn't know how to get my hands on a gun. My fuckup of a father had never taught me anything—certainly not how to acquire and handle a piece.

I lifted a six-inch hunting knife from Jason Bower's own locker—perfect irony—and practiced lunging it into a sack of straw at the deserted archery range behind the high school gym. Then I drove to Jason Bower's house in the dead of night.

I knocked on the door, already knowing that his parents were out at a pickleball match and there was a three-hour window during which Jason—Keith's nemesis and nightmare—would be home, jacking off or studying, but either way, home alone.

Finally he came to the door in a bathrobe, looking scrawny and stoned and a bit shy. Not like a bully, but then bullies are usually cowards.

"Huh?" I playacted like I had the wrong house for a moment, squinted up at the dead porch light—dead because I'd moments earlier unscrewed the bulb; then I stepped in toward him. Jason automatically took a step backward.

"What do you want?" he said, his voice more nervous than irritated.

But at the same time he spoke, I plunged the six-inch blade into his gut around his midriff—below the solar plexus—and up to the hilt. And I twisted. I hadn't even planned on the twist, but it came naturally—or perhaps, I admit, as a result of a mild panic that I wouldn't kill him dead in one stab. However, having only mild panic the first time does, I think, foreshadow a certain fitness for this lifestyle.

Bower's mouth gaped like a fish, silently, like he wanted a breath and couldn't get one, and his eyes went big. He collapsed into my body, me shouldering his weight with my left arm, my right hand still on the grip of the fatal blade. Thick white spittle ran down his chin, and I felt the warmth of blood on my arm from his wound, a warmth that would become too familiar over the years during my knife phase.

As he toppled to his knees, I went down with him and

we landed in a pile, which today I would say was an amateur debacle.

I pulled the blade out and he rolled facedown in the entry of his home, blood overshadowing the blond area rug.

I got up, stepped backward, shut the front door with a gloved hand, leaving him just as he lay—a mess of carnage.

The deed was clumsy but quiet, and nobody stirred in the neighborhood, save Jason Bower's black cat that jumped up on the porch step to rub against my calves. The only guilt I felt was when the damn cat purred and arched its back, showing all the feline signs of happiness. How long, I wondered, until it would be fed again in the aftermath of its master's demise?

I was never caught. But the image of Bower's mangled pose stayed with me. There were so many mistakes. No prior stakeout of the neighborhood, no plan for disposal of the weapon, no regard for the repose of my victim and what images would be left in my head.

I have learned a lot since then, eventually graduating from the silent knife to the silencer on a nine-millimeter. And I do it cleanly, with one shot between the eyes, the subject always unsuspecting.

Also, I carefully arrange the body. If I do dream of my work, the images are largely those of a corpse in a comfortable configuration, or staged as if for a neatly composed photograph. At times I have touched up the countenance with concealer, be it man or woman, leaving a radiant finish and no evidence but a common brand of drugstore makeup. Once I even attached the artificial leg of my subject who had removed it before bed, because I did not want to dream of a dismembered victim.

I hug my purse tighter, pull a wool scarf completely around my neck. Outside, I'm greeted by a brisk, cold breeze. I climb into the stolen car about a half block from the condominium, knowing the on-site property manager will probably get a call from the man's employer…or mistress…by midafternoon. I'll ditch the car long before that.

I'm a bit stiff. I had waited all night in the man's front coat closet, just to do my job right and take him by surprise.

I have no one to boast to, but I do whisper praise to myself, because the police will remark on the restful look of this man—his surroundings untouched and his face as steady and calm as any angel. No sorrow, no pain. No extraneous bruises. Only a small hole in the bookcase where I dug out the casing. They will wonder who did it and why.

They won't understand that I gave this man all I have to offer, what I'm good at, and what I'm paid for—a deliberate, peaceful solution. The alternative, from some cheap hack hired in a smoky bar, would have brought the man to a panicked, overwrought, painful conclusion. I have seen the police photos.

I ditch the car and walk a half mile to a popular bus stop, where the late-night crowd gathers for one of three separate metro lines. Several of us ascend the steps of bus number eleven, each exhausted from our respective evenings—whether from drinking, lovemaking, or murder.

Before breakfast, I'm home. I toss my coat and purse in the closet, change my sweaty shirt, and scramble some eggs. I am shoving down the toaster lever when my husband comes up from behind and kisses me. He is used to me coming home early mornings…from the gym.

"I don't have time for breakfast," he complains. "There's been another night-stalker murder, this time up on Queen Anne Hill. Once again, staged all pretty and no clues."

As he straightens his tie, grabs his gun from the hall drawer, and holsters it, I blow him a kiss. Perhaps I don't love him in the same way others love. Perhaps my heart is only for pumping blood. Perhaps I am a psychological anomaly. But I like having him around—I like the way our marriage makes me feel *normal.*

"I'm sorry you have to rush off to work," I tell him, as he's headed to the foyer. "But good luck catching the killer."

"Later," he calls to me, before I hear the door latch click.

"Later," I say.

Your Dreams Will Take You Very Far

By Susan Whiting Kemp

(Based on the overheard snippet, "Your dreams will take you very far.")

Dreams float like clouds, thought Donna, looking out the number twenty-one bus window at the sky beyond the Aura apartment building. They shift and reshape themselves, billowing and dispersing. Sometimes one comes into your head. Once there it thickens, turns to sludge or hardens like cartilage. And sometimes it hides.

The man who sat next to Donna on the bus had a musty smell. Homeless, she thought, though there were other reasons for not washing clothes. She considered changing seats, but the smell was no worse than an old paperback left in the basement too long.

Donna had been looking out the window, so she didn't see what the man looked like before he sat, and a glance now would be awkward. Still, she could tell he was tall. The distress of his jeans could have been fashion design, or caused by hard living. Some of each, she decided.

She opened a news site on her phone. A burger ad filled the screen with its juicy lusciousness. Caramel-colored bun; vibrant orange cheese; moist, thick patty. Somebody in some marketing department somewhere had done an exceptional job, pushing out a photo so startling that Donna wasn't surprised when her seatmate said, "That looks really good."

"Doesn't it?" It became a shared moment, so now she could look at him. Stringy brown hair. Half her age. A kind expression on a weather-beaten face.

The bus rumbled past the Luna Park Café. Donna considered telling the man that they had good burgers, but he probably didn't have the money to eat there. The bus went under the overpass on the way to the West Seattle Freeway. The conversation was done.

After a while, the man sang, "Your dreams will take you very far." Just the one line, from Earth, Wind & Fire's "Shining Star," so quietly she almost didn't recognize it. And so Donna was back to thinking about dreams floating outside. When not in the body, she thought, dreams are chameleons, hiding anywhere and everywhere. Or Silly Putty, gathering images and stretching them unrecognizably. Dreams didn't always make sense. Donna wondered whether it was the same way calculus didn't make sense if you hadn't learned it. That she just hadn't learned dreams.

The man sang some more, but distractedly. Not actual songs, but notes, as if he were searching for a song he'd lost. He talked to himself, random phrases without sense. Maybe the poor man was mentally challenged.

In college—many years ago—Donna had written a paper on the medieval European's reaction to the insane. She didn't remember much of it, except that in those times some would have viewed the man sitting next to her as having a direct connection to God. Others would have tried to cure him through bleeding, ice-water dousing, or trepanning—drilling through his skull.

She'd chosen the subject for its novelty. She hadn't known any crazy people at the time, or so she thought. Now she knew better—that most people have a notch on the insanity gauge, lower or higher, though you couldn't always see it. And for those who didn't—wasn't complete sanity a form of insanity, if only because of its scarcity?

She herself was going through her own type of madness, where things that appeared in her dreams also appeared in her waking life. It used to be the other way around, and she avoided working right before bedtime so that she wouldn't have to work all night in her dreams.

But now most nights she dreamed but didn't remember until it happened the next day. She didn't want to. Because she knew she wasn't a fortune-teller. She understood it was a symptom, not a superpower.

What happened to the real dreams? The ones that were usurped? Why did they give up so easily? Dreams usually did surrender to the daytime, it was true, but why was her false sensation of having dreamed something crowding out the memory of her real dreams?

After descending from the bus onto Third Avenue and walking into a building lobby, Donna wasn't seduced into thinking she'd really dreamed about the furniture in front of her, even when her mind seemed sure of it. Even though she recognized the impossible chairs and impossible rug, designed within an inch of their lives, when she'd never been in this building before.

The chairs were impossible because only an alien could fit them. Butterfly chairs almost, the wings curved inward. She was early for her appointment, so she tested one to see whether it was as uncomfortable as it looked. It was, until she brought her knees up and leaned sideways, so that her spine curved like a cat's.

From there she gazed at the impossible rug, thick and white, flowing across the lobby like a pre-climate-change glacier. Just like in her dream.

No, she told herself. She hadn't really dreamed this.

Donna took the elevator to the twenty-first floor. She'd never met the psychiatrist, but her condition made her think she recognized her from a dream in which she wore the same blue blazer, asked the same questions, and nodded the same way, with her head tilted just slightly to the right.

After they talked for a while, there was a long pause while the doctor thought. Donna wondered what it was like to be her. To work in a profession where you had to repair something, but couldn't take it apart and put it back together. The best you could do was take an image of it, or make a model of it, like the plastic brain that sat on the psychiatrist's shelf. It looked like wadded-up chewing gum stuffed into bowl, then upended.

The doctor's head tilted left now as she gave a diagnosis that wasn't a diagnosis. Donna had aspects of several different disorders, but didn't fully fit any of them. Donna worried that the psychiatrist might say there was nothing they could do about her condition, so it was a relief when the doctor suggested medication, though she might need to try several until she found the right one for her.

When the doctor printed her prescription, Donna folded the paper until it fit in her pocket. She did that with important things, in case her purse was ever stolen. What went into her pocket rather than purse was based on the magnitude of trouble it would take to replace.

On the bus home, she settled in next to a man who was looking at his phone. The screen showed a picture of Croatia, or somewhere like it. White houses with red roofs. Striking. It made her want to visit. Somebody in some marketing department somewhere had done another exceptional job. "That's gorgeous," she said.

"Absolutely," the man said, turning to her. Probably getting his first real look at her. What did he see? Did he look at her with the type of pity with which she had viewed the homeless man? He himself was smartly dressed, a triangular blue handkerchief lurking in his suit pocket. From the perspective of his mid-thirties, perhaps he only saw her age, without knowing that she was happier than she'd ever been. Not knowing that she'd done what she'd wanted to in life, so far, at least.

She looked toward the front of the bus at the benches running lengthwise. There was the homeless man who had commented on the burger earlier that day. He was wearing different clothes, different hair, and a different face. Though he was twenty years older, she was sure it was the same man, and there was one way to prove it. Donna made her way over and sat next to him.

She pulled out her phone and called up the site she had viewed earlier in the day. There was that picture of a burger, the startling one. Those colors had to have been Photoshopped. Donna faced the phone toward the man.

"I don't believe in killing animals," he said.

So he wasn't her homeless man after all. But she'd known that. If he'd told her the burger looked good, she still would have known it. Lately it took effort to keep imagination and reality separate. Not everything was connected. At least, not in a way that could be seen.

Donna pressed her pocket and heard the prescription crinkle. It was still there along with her ID, bank card, and credit card. She looked up at the clouds, which spilled across the sky like quilt stuffing. She would take her first dose when she got home. Hopefully soon the dreams would no longer hold so much sway over her waking hours.

❁ ❁ ❁

Over the next three weeks Donna took the pills. She was less confused. Less distracted now that she didn't have the false feeling that she'd dreamed the day's events. But also she stopped dreaming altogether. No false dreams, but no real ones, either.

That wasn't dangerous, the psychiatrist assured her. She was still dreaming during REM sleep, even if she didn't remember it.

Some people never had dreams, Donna knew. Back in the eighties she'd worked with such a man. At the Rainbow Grocery, a health-food store. He was smart and personable, and had a good memory.

That was okay for him, but for Donna, something was missing. It wasn't the strangeness of dreams. There was plenty of strangeness in real life. For example, the homeless man who lay on a table downtown, a blanket drawn over his head, like an abandoned surgery patient.

Nor was beauty missing. It was everywhere. A prism casting

rainbows all around. A child's smile at a silly noise. A mural painted on a brick building.

And of course, real life had things that dreams never seemed to, like the smell of the bread as she passed the French bakery, which of course they pumped outside to make people like her come in; and of course she did, to buy a brioche.

No, something else was missing now that she no longer dreamed. A feeling of lightness, perhaps. That was the only way to describe it.

❁ ❁ ❁

Donna was on the bus again one day when it rattled over a short stretch of pavement that needed resurfacing, then stopped to wait for a train. This was what they called an industrial district, with manufacturing and wholesale businesses. Pot shops. Starbucks world headquarters. Seattle City Light.

And the School of Acrobatics and New Circus Arts. In an old warehouse-size building with a high window. While Donna watched, a woman's body rose into view, then fell away every few seconds. Trampoline, she guessed. At the apex of each leap, the woman unfolded her arms like angel wings, then dropped out of sight.

Donna closed her eyes. She imagined herself as the woman, the trampoline yielding to her weight, then propelling her upward. For just a moment Donna felt the lightness she'd been missing for weeks. The sensation was fleeting, but Donna understood now that it hadn't vanished for good. To her, that meant the good dreams might someday return. And that would do for now.

A Girl Named Toenail

By Evelyn Arvey

(Based on the prompt, "Passport.")

The Peruvian immigration agent was dressed in olive green. His matching cap was perched smartly on the crown of his head, his shirt was pressed so hard it looked like it would crack if folded, and his thin-lipped mouth was pursed as if he'd tasted the fruit of my grandmother's crabapple tree. He peered at my passport and then at me. "Toenail?" he demanded. "Your name is no possible! Your name, it is… *Toenail*?"

"*Sí.*" I might as well use my high school Spanish; maybe he'd like me for trying to speak his language. Maybe he'd take pity on me and wave me through his immigration cubicle instead of grilling me about my name. I took a wavering breath. "*Sí, señor. Mi nombre es Uña en español. Uña.* Toenail."

It was printed in my passport in black and white, just like it was on my birth certificate: Toenail Maria Chesney. It was the biggest secret of my life, and now the man was—oh, my God—showing my paperwork to the agent in the next lane, jabbing at my passport, pointing at me, laughing. Everyone was looking at me. "Toni," I said in a small, gasping voice. "I actually go by Toni."

That was how the first leg of my journey began. Inauspicious. Embarrassing. It might have sent a less determined person scurrying back onto the airplane.

Later, after a domestic LAN Airlines flight to the jungle city of Iquitos, I found my hotel, a tall, narrow place on the bank of the Amazon that leaned toward the river as if it wanted to leap in and follow the current to a better place. I checked in, dumped my backpack in my room, took a tepid shower, then made my way down a slippery, splintery staircase to the docks at the edge of the river. It was early evening, at that special time when it is neither light nor dark. I breathed in the fishy-muddy-gasoline smell; had this aroma greeted my parents when they'd first arrived twenty-five years before? I'd thought that Iquitos, this magical, mystical place, would smell of palm trees, of flowers, of living things—like a Hawaiian island, maybe, but no. It was nothing like that.

I peered upriver, trying to make out the buildings through the gloom. Where had my parents stayed? Before heading out into the jungle they'd spent four nights—or was it five?—in one of the older hotels along the Amazon. Would they have chosen the one I was staying in, or had they selected the one next to it, with the veranda overlooking the river? Or maybe they'd stayed in a hotel I'd passed on the way here, a place with mopeds lined up in front for guests to rent.

I tested my weight on the weathered dock in front of my hotel (which looked like it might have been old even in my parents' day), wondering whether I ought to wait until tomorrow to begin this quest of mine to find the village they had lived in—tomorrow morning when I would be rested and refreshed and my Spanish might be more functional. I watched riverboats go back and forth, including two blue-and-white-painted ones that said "Lineas Amazonas" on their flanks, and I thought they could only be water buses, considering that each was full of tired-looking people sitting in neat rows. I hesitated, was about to turn away and make my way up the stairs, when a man stood up in the smallest of the four boats tied to the dock, and spoke to me. "Señorita?"

I waved.

He clambered out of the boat and made his way toward me. I took in his faded blue jeans, his damp gray shirt with a frayed hem, his sun-ravaged skin, the fact that he was missing three fingers of his left hand. He looked to be about ninety years old, but his eyes were bright as he listened to my broken Spanish as I told him of my unusual quest, and his voice was strong and confident when he answered me. No, he told me, I could not rent a boat and a guide for two days to take me up the river to a place I didn't know the location or the name of. So sorry, but absolutely not possible. Absolutely not.

So imagine my surprise when, early the next morning, the old man came into the room that passed as my hotel's restaurant, his too-big flip-flops flapping and slapping, his hands propelling a younger man in front of him. "*Mi sobrino*," he said, "my nephew. Rubino. He will go up the river with you and help you with your search for your parents' village. He speaks English."

The catch—for of course there was a catch—was that I must pay for the boat, and for the nephew, in advance, in cash. I must also shop for food for both of us while the old man collected gasoline and other supplies, which I would pay for. Of course.

"And, oh! Señorita!" He held up his two-fingered hand and pointed at me with his pinkie. "You must leave within the hour."

It was simultaneously the longest and the shortest hour of my life, a fevered running around in which I stuffed the few things I'd taken out of my backpack back *into* my backpack; I pleaded with the front-desk lady (who reminded me very much of that horrible immigration agent, right down to her starched green blouse) to *please* refund the money I'd prepaid; the old man steered me to a nearby street corner to meet his amigo the moneychanger, where I changed most of my cash into Peruvian soles (how illegal was such a transaction? Would I be handcuffed and dumped into one of those infamous Peruvian prisons?); and took my life in my hands to cross the busiest little street I'd ever seen to an open-air market because I could find nothing even remotely resembling a grocery store, where I bought six family-size packages of wheat crackers (how much do two people on a boat eat, anyway?), a round of hard cheese, a bag of mangoes, a case of Spam, four chocolate bars, twelve cans of tuna fish, and a six-pack of Coke, each from a different vendor.

"Water?" growled the old man when I stumbled my way back to the hotel, down the stairs, and onto the dock with my haul. "Where is the water? How you live with no water?"

I thrust my damp wad of *soles* into the old man's palm, and he handed some to Rubino, who took the stairs two at a time and disappeared from view. I realized that Rubino was probably no older than I was. I dropped my bags and collapsed onto the dock, shaking, panting, glaring at the old man, wishing it weren't already ninety degrees out even though it was only eight fifty-two in the morning, annoyed with myself because

I shouldn't have just given this man whose name I didn't even know most of my money. A drop of sweat fell from my nose and onto the dock, where I swear it sizzled.

And then Rubino was back. He tossed my backpack and groceries into the rocking boat, and also four sloshing tins of gasoline his uncle handed to him. He held my hand as I stepped in and took a seat, then started up the outboard motor with a roar that had me covering my ears as he hollered back and forth with the old man in a Spanish so rapid I didn't understand a single word.

We motored out into the flow of the river. The next thing I knew I was craning around to look back as Iquitos receded from view, already feeling sick to my stomach from exhaust fumes. I'd imagined tranquil waters and dugout canoes, not this busy waterway that clearly served as a jungle freeway for the local population. We sped along the river for half an hour, Rubino looking ahead, me looking every which way and trying to see everything all at once as we left civilization and entered an enchanted land of ten thousand shades of green, glittering birds, and chittering animals.

No wonder my parents had talked about it all the time when I was little.

Rubino was trying to say something over the noise. "Señorita! Señorita!" He leaned toward me. "My uncle said you want to go into the jungle and told me to help you find the village you seek—but why are you going alone?"

His English, I decided, was pretty good. Certainly better than my Spanish. Where had he learned it? For the first time I took a good long look at my guide (who was also my captain, my river navigator, and my liaison with the local people), the person I'd placed myself in the care of in this foreign place. I could see echoes of his uncle in him, the same long, wiry body, the same beak of a nose, the same fluid movements and easy confidence. I wondered what it would be like to grow up in a backwater of the Amazon, in a city that no roads led to.

"Why?" he asked again.

"I am trying to find the village my parents lived in."

"But what village? Why don't you know the name?"

"All I know is that it was a day's boat journey away from Iquitos, to the south."

Rubino turned away from me. He fiddled with something on the motor. He rewound a bundle of rope that lay at his feet, then picked up, shook, and folded a large, fine net. A mosquito net? Every guidebook I'd read said that people in this area were fastidious about their mosquito nets. He set it on top of the rope, then dug into his faded green day pack (was every piece of fabric in this place faded and colorless?) and pulled out a baseball cap. "The sun is hot. Do you not have a hat, señorita?"

"Please call me Toni," I said. "No. I don't."

He motioned for me to take his hat. "But there are—how you say in English?—there are very many little rivers on the *Rio Amazonas*." He spread his hand, fingers like tributaries spreading from his palm. "What little river? What village? There are many, señorita."

"Toni," I said, frowning. I put on the hat. "Call me Toni. I don't know what river. All I know is that the village had grass-thatched huts on stilts arranged around a field, on the banks of the river."

"But, Toni, that is every village."

"Oh." I watched a large bird swoop overhead, then dive into the water. I sighed; what had I expected? It was all I had, and it wasn't enough. "My father used to say that he could paddle a dugout across the water in eleven strokes."

"Eleven strokes only? A small river, then." Rubino gazed into the trees at the edge of the Amazon, as if he could make the waterway appear if he tried hard enough.

"You know where it is?" I asked.

He didn't answer.

I took his silence as a maybe. A definite maybe.

The village took me by surprise, hidden as it was around a sharp curve in the river and by enormous trees that seemed to wave their branches and leaves toward the center of the water. My insides shivered with excitement because maybe this was it—maybe this was their river and maybe this was their village! There was a field, as promised, and there were huts on stilts, also as promised. There was also a long flight of wooden steps up the bank from the river.

"Come," said Rubino. He tied the boat to a narrow dock between a motorboat the same size as ours and an honest-to-god cutout canoe. I took a picture. Then I took a picture of Rubino holding his hand out to me. "Come," he said again.

Five or six children gathered around us at the top of the stairs, all hollering at us in rapid-fire Spanish that, again, I didn't understand a single word of. Rubino chattered away with them, flashing wide white teeth whenever he smiled. He turned to me. "Come," he said again.

I followed him and the children (one of whom, a little girl, took my hand and swung my arm with great energy) to a lodging across the field, an enchanting house surrounded by flowers the exact shade of the reddish-orange lipstick that my grandmother used to wear. The house was raised up on stilts. It had open sides and a palm-leaf roof and a half ladder, half staircase and two parrots on perches to the left of the entrance, and—oh, my, oh, my!—a real live honest-to-goodness baby monkey tied to a railing that was so cute I wanted to bring him back home to Seattle with me. I took picture after picture.

Rubino ushered me inside the hut and motioned for me to sit on a long bench built into the wall that faced the field. "Wait one minute," he whispered. "She will be here soon."

"Who will?" I whispered back. I took a picture of the parrots, and several pictures of the bundles of dried herbs that hung from the ceiling. I handed the camera to Rubino. "Here. Take one of me."

He complied.

"Whose house is this?" I asked.

"Someone old enough to maybe remember your parents," he said.

A wizened old lady who looked at least as old as Rubino's uncle hobbled in from the other side of a sheet hung from the ceiling, making me wonder how she could possibly manage the ladder-staircase to her own home. She stood leaning on a cane made of some lovely polished jungle wood, and talked at us in a thin, high voice. She had no teeth. I made a move to pick up my camera, but Rubino put his hand over mine and shook his head. One of the children popped up from the ladder and stood next to the old woman and took her hand.

"He is her grandson," Rubino whispered. "He will translate."

"Translate? Why?"

"She speaks an old language. The boy will translate to Spanish, and I will translate to English for you. This is how she does it." He paused. "But first you must give her a gift."

I rummaged around in the oversize pockets of my jungle cargo pants. Three Band-Aids. ChapStick. Two quarters. A tin of mints. A shortie pencil. A stick of roll-on mosquito repellent. Sunglasses. The stub of my last boarding pass. A travel-size roll of toilet paper in a nifty plastic container. I gave her the tin of mints; at least it was half-full. I felt bad for the boy, so I gave him the pencil. He didn't seem upset that most of the eraser was gone, just turned it over and over in delight, then tucked it behind his ear as if I'd given him a golden scepter.

Before I could ask her any questions about my parents, the old woman started speaking, her language soft and sibilant, full of "S" sounds and vowels. She augmented this with ample arm gestures, and occasionally a laugh or a snort or a quick shake of her head. The grandson watched attentively, and at each pause he would translate for Rubino—but I wondered how accurate his words were, since he transformed her monologue into a few sparse sentences, which Rubino then refined down to one solitary phrase: "She says welcome," or, "She says people come to her from far away for healing," or, "She distills the cures from her own herbs." He turned to me. "She is very famous around here."

"Rubino!" I whispered. "I want to ask her my questions!"

"She says do you want to try her medicine?"

"Medicine? What? No! I want to find out what she knows about my parents. What does she think I am, a tourist? I'm not here for medicine."

One of the parrots squawked. The old lady yelled at it. I pushed my sweaty hair behind my ears, patted the wetness at the back of my neck, wished I had brought one of the bottles of water with me. Rubino flicked a fly from his leg. He didn't look at me. "You will insult her if you refuse the medicine. She says it is good medicine."

The old woman rummaged around at the other side of the

hut. She came back cradling a clear plastic two-liter soda-pop bottle half filled with a pale green liquid and—alarmingly—twigs, leaves, and seeds. She held out a green cup that I was pretty sure had begun life as a Tupperware sippy cup; it was perhaps the only thing in this place that had retained its original color.

I accepted the cup and thanked her for the generous slosh she poured into it. I stared down at the black flecks floating in it.

"Drink it," Rubino said.

I could tell by the smell that the stuff had so much alcohol in it, it could strip paint off a wall. I sipped; I gagged; I picked flecks off my tongue.

"She says it can kill intestinal worms," Rubino said helpfully.

I made a face at him, hoping the drink didn't *give* me worms, even though I knew rationally that no worms would survive in that alcohol bath. I took a picture of the medicine bottle, of the cup (of which I'd drunk only half of), of Rubino's grin, of the old woman gesturing to her grandson.

I took a deep breath. I'd been waiting for this moment for years; I'd planned and saved and studied Spanish and pored over maps of the Amazon basin. I'd practiced what I would say, word for word, to a succession of bathroom mirrors. And now—right now—I was here, and it was time.

"My parents came here before I was born," I began. "They lived and worked in this area twenty-five years ago, teaching the local people farming methods and textile production, and modern hygiene and midwifery. Their names were Roger and Marilyn Chesney. They were here for four years, and then I was born. I was born here, in a hut, along the river." I sat up as straight as I could, and spoke slowly. "I am Peruvian. I am one of you." I searched her face for the answers I was looking for. "Do you remember them? Did they live here, in this village? Please help me."

I clasped my hands together and waited for Rubino to translate. Then the grandson turned to his grandmother and said a scant few words; he had disregarded the majority of my carefully prepared message, or maybe Rubino had; it was hard to tell because my Spanish seemed to be worse with every passing hour. I heard nothing from either of them that sounded remotely like the words Roger and Marilyn Chesney. The old woman made motions for me to scoot over on the bench; then she sat down next to me and began to jabber, but the boy was now sitting on the floor playing with the baby monkey, cooing to it in a falsetto voice, forgetting his translating duties.

Rubino said something. The boy ignored him, instead taking the pencil stub I'd given him and teasing the monkey with it, tossing it a few feet and waiting for the monkey to pick it up with delicate little fingers and bring it back to him.

The old woman picked up my left hand, kissed it, placed it gently back onto my lap, stood up, and wandered off behind the hanging sheet. We'd been dismissed. The most important two minutes of my life, and they were over. All I got for it was a gut full of paint stripper and no information at all about my parents. I still didn't know if this was the right village.

"Rubino!"

But Rubino was already at the ladder-staircase. "Toni. We need to leave now."

"Please! Go get her. I need to know what she said. I can't go yet."

"We are visitors in her home. We need to leave now."

Back in the field in the middle of the huts, in the shade of a lone tree at the edge of the riverbank, I plopped myself down cross-legged on the coarse grass and waited for Rubino to get the boat ready for the next part of our journey. The sun was already high in the sky, but I figured when he came back from the boat I'd ask him to help me find another old person to talk to before taking off. We still had hours left in which to visit the next village. Rubino had a place for us to spend the night, at his cousin's place in yet a third village near a different branch of the river. I glanced up from the stalk of grass I was methodically stripping apart to find the little girl who'd swung my arm earlier was standing next to me, looking like she also would like a pencil stub. She began talking to me in a solemn voice, having no idea that I didn't understand a word she was saying.

"She says she was on the stairs spying on you," said Rubino, coming up to me. He handed me a bottle of water. "She says you should not sit on the grass. She also says you are not Peruvian."

"Oh?" I took a long drag of the water. "She was listening?"

The little girl chattered away to Rubino. Finally he put up his hands to stop her. He turned to me, looking surprised. "She says Doña Fernandina—that is the medicine woman—said she remembers two Americans who came many years ago."

I sat up on my heels, scratching an itch on my thigh. "Oh! What did she say?"

"She said the Americans lived two villages away." He paused, then said to me, "Puesto del Sol. That is where my cousin lives. We were going there anyway."

"Puesto del Sol? That's what my mother named her cat! We called her Sol."

"It means sunset."

"I know." I picked up a stick and tried to get at a bothersome itch in the middle of my back. "I didn't know it was the name of the village! They never told me, or if they did I was too young to remember. What is she saying now?"

"She says you shouldn't sit in the grass."

"Okay, okay." I stood up, suddenly feeling itchy all over. "But what about the Americans?"

"She said they came to Doña Fernandina to cure a—what do you call it? an infection?—on the skin of the leg of the man."

"An infection," I said slowly. My father had had a scar the size of a silver dollar on his shin. "Yes, he had an infection. That's right. He came here? To see the medicine woman?"

"Yes. And one more thing," said Rubino. "She said the American woman was pregnant. Big pregnant."

Rubino and I glanced at each other. "That was me," I said unnecessarily.

"Then maybe you *are* Peruvian," he said, shaking his head.

I finished my bottle of water. "Let's go. Let's go to Puesto del Sol."

He gestured toward the little girl. "Give her something. And not your empty water bottle."

I made a face at him as I felt around in my pocket and plucked out the roll of ChapStick. "Here. Tell her it is medicine for her lips. To rub on them, not to lick or to eat. Let me show her." I took the cap off the ChapStick and motioned for the girl to come near. "Like this." I dabbed the tube gently at her smiling little lips, then showed her how to smack them together. She took the tube, flashed one last smile at me, then ran off.

"Let's go," I said again. I scratched my ankle.

Later, an hour or so after leaving Doña Fernandina's village, after Rubino and I had shared a surprisingly delicious lunch of cheese and crackers, and mangoes and Coke, Rubino turned off the motor. We were in the middle of nowhere, not a shred of civilization in sight. The river was narrower here, but the trees were larger, forming a lush ribbon of viridian reflected in great detail against water black with tannin (so said Rubino), an upside-down counterpoint to the real world. "Listen to the trees," he said. "Just sit and listen." He leaned back on his bench and closed his eyes.

The world was flooded with the loudest silence I'd ever heard—with air so thick, so rich it seemed my hand could make waves through it. "Rubino," I said after a while, "it's so beautiful here."

"It is." He didn't open his eyes.

A toucan flew from one side of the river to the other. I sighed; my parents had followed the flight of toucans over the river. They'd heard the calls of monkeys far off in the forest. They'd trailed their hands in the cool water and wet their foreheads in the heat of the day. They'd seen these very trees. They'd been here; for the first time I felt it as a truth rather than as an abstract concept. I *knew*.

"Why are you crying?" Rubino asked softly.

"My mother. My father."

"They're dead, aren't they?"

"A car crash." I caught my breath. I scratched an itch on my shoulder. "It happened when I was thirteen."

"I am sorry, Toni."

"I miss them. I miss them every day."

"Of course you do."

"They were good people. They wanted to help the people here."

"I know they did."

"My mother, she was a nurse and a midwife. My father was

a teacher. He wanted to improve sanitation here, and the water supply, and who knows what else."

"Noble intentions."

"They gave money to help people. They started a trust fund for the local Amazonian children. It is still going."

He didn't say anything.

A rustling in the trees made me look right, left, upward. A bird? An animal? Or the wind blowing through the trees? As much as I was falling in love with this place, I was still a stranger here. I waited for my eyes to stop watering, for my breathing to become even again. "May I ask you something, Rubino? How is it you speak such good English?"

He sat up, yawned, started the motor again. "I was selected as a child to receive a special education. I went to school six months of every year in Lima, each year with a different host family from America."

"This itching is driving me to distraction," I complained, scratching at my neck. I met his eye. "That must have been tough for you, Rubino."

He gave me a strange look. "It was." He looked away. "No one ever said that to me before." He steered the boat into the center of the river to avoid a low-hanging branch. "They all said, 'How wonderful for you, Rubino'…or, 'How lucky you are, Rubino'…or, 'Why you and not me, Rubino?'"

"But you didn't feel lucky?"

"Sometimes. Not all the time." He gazed, eyes squinting, into the water. "There are fish down there. Too bad we don't have lines." He looked up at me. "You have chiggers," he stated.

"What?"

"From the grass. Remember? The girl told you not to sit there."

"Chiggers?"

He took up his backpack, stuck his hand in it, and started to rummage around. "Little bugs. They live in grass around here. They burrow under your skin and lay eggs. Ah! Here it is."

I thought I might throw up. I was itching before, but at his words my entire body became one giant, glorious itch. I thought I could feel the little buggers wriggling around under my skin, taking bites of me, pooping inside of me, laying sticky, poisonous eggs. I contorted my body into a pretzel, trying to itch everywhere at once. "Get them out! Get them out!"

"I will. I brought some limes." He cut them into slices, then ordered me to take my shirt off, and my pants too. "They don't like lime juice. When they feel it and can't breathe, they'll back out of your skin and fly off."

Under different circumstances, I might have objected to undressing in front of him. But the horrific idea of bugs laying eggs under my skin convinced me to do as he said, and quickly. I huddled in my underwear with my back to him as he carefully squeezed lime juice—the sting of it was almost welcome—on each and every lesion, rubbing vigorously. "There," he said. "That'll do it. We'll put more on tonight, okay?"

"Yes," I said as I slipped my clothes on again. "Thanks, Rubino."

We continued down the river, the noise of the motor making our conversation awkward, coming in fits and starts. After a while we came around a bend and motored up to a village that might have been the twin of the one we'd visited earlier in the day, except the river was somewhat narrower and there were sapling trees and red-as-lipstick flowers growing at the top of the riverbank, and teenage boys were kicking a soccer ball around the grassy field. I wondered whether the grass made them itch too.

At the top of the ubiquitous stairway up from the river, I hesitated. Puesto del Sol was the place I was born. I was sure of it. In the lengthening shadows of late afternoon, the place looked soft, round-edged, sleepy. I wanted to explore, to peek into each hut and guess which one was my parents'; I wanted to check out each flower garden, to discover pet parrots and monkeys and sloths, to find the village children and join them in their play. Rubino came up behind me, carrying backpacks, bags, mosquito netting. He motioned with his head. "Over here, Toni. Come."

I followed him to a stilt hut halfway around the field. He hollered a greeting, and a middle-aged man looked over the railing. "*Primo!*" the man said, clearly delighted.

Cousin, I translated. *Male cousin*, to be exact.

"Primo!" Rubino clambered up the ladder-stairs, motioning me to follow. This hut, although smaller than that of Doña Fernandina, looked just like hers except that there were no bundles of herbs hanging from the rafters. We even sat down on a long bench along the open wall facing the field, like at Doña Fernandina's. Had I lived in such a place as an infant? As a toddler? Which made me wonder: How did people with wall-less homes perched on stilts keep their children from tumbling out? I'd never asked my parents these questions; the thirteen-year-old me hadn't been all that interested in their history.

Juan Carlos, Rubino's cousin, didn't remember my parents, but he'd lived in a different village until his marriage eighteen years ago. "But wait," he said in Spanish slow enough for me to understand. "I will ask my *suegra* if she remembers."

"His mother-in-law," said Rubino helpfully. "My *tía*. My aunt."

The *tía* insisted on feeding us first. She and her two daughters—Rubino's cousins—peeled and chopped and cooked and fried in an outdoor hearth on the ground in back of the hut, saying *no, no, no*, with wide smiles and feigned horror when I asked whether I could help. Family members and friends arrived one by one or in pairs to take a good look at me and maybe also to see what was on offer for the special meal being prepared for their American visitor, who just might be Peruvian, at least by birth. Who had ever heard of such a thing? Who in the village might remember?

After we'd eaten, Rubino stood up and thanked his relatives and friends on my behalf for the lovely meal. Then, nodding in my direction, he told them my story, embellishing and gesturing and making me wonder what he was telling them. "*Y su nombre es* Toni Chesney," he finished up.

This I understood: Her name is Toni Chesney.

"No," said a voice from behind the cooking pit, in Spanish. "It is not."

Every head, including mine, craned to see who had spoken. An old man—it was hard to say how old, but I didn't think he was as old as Rubino's uncle back in Iquitos—stood up and made his way to stand in front of me and Rubino.

"Señor," Rubino greeted him in a hushed voice.

"Señor," I echoed, hoping it was an adequate greeting, feeling my heart begin to pound, because this man must know something about my parents—he must.

The man sat down between us. He smelled of wood fire, of green growing things, of wild rivers and forest and earth. I liked him, but I couldn't say why—because Rubino seemed slightly afraid of him. "Señor," he said again.

The man turned to me and spoke in slow, careful Spanish, and I found I could understand him. "Your name is not Toni, is it?"

"No, sir," I said softly. I'd never called anyone *sir* in my life.

"Your name is Uña Maria, am I correct?"

"Yes, sir." I thought I might faint. I clenched my hands in my lap to keep them from trembling. Who was he? How did he know this, the secret I'd kept for most of my life? I stared at him, not blinking, not breathing, barely aware of the hushed circle of people watching the best entertainment they'd had in months, in years.

"*Uña?*" whispered Rubino, his eyebrows jumping into his hairline. He looked at his fingernails, then at me. "Really? *Uña?*"

I ignored him.

The man took his time. He patted his hair. He straightened his pant legs. He made a loud hawking sound, then spit in the dirt behind us. Then he turned to me. "It was I who gave you that name, although it wasn't quite my intent. My dear, I knew your parents."

"Tell me? Please?" I took a deep breath. "I want to know."

The crowd was settling in. Parents sat young children on the ground at their feet, where they fell quiet and attentive; people from nearby huts made their way into the circle; the boys who'd been playing soccer earlier came in a group and hung out together amid the stilts of Rubino's cousin's hut, lanky and sun-kissed, radiating youthful energy yet every bit as attentive as everyone else. No one made a sound. The jungle sounds rose and swelled in response, the whirs and clicks of insects, the shrieks and calls and whistles of birds, the rustling of tree branches, and underneath it all, the sound of moving water. I almost laughed aloud: In all the times I'd imagined hearing the story of my life, I'd never once imagined it being told to me in front of an audience.

"On a spring day not so different from this day," the man began, "two Americans came to our village. They were sent by the American Friendship Corps."

The Friendship Corps? What was that? It sounded made-up! Hadn't my parents been sent to the Peruvian Amazon by the Peace Corps?

"They said they were here to help us, but what help did we need?" The old man spread his hands wide, and wider, encompassing the entire audience, the entire village. "They brought books, but who here could read English?" He looked from person to person. "They came as if they owned the place. As if God had told them we needed them. But we didn't."

I shifted in my seat—where was this going? I didn't like him quite so much anymore.

"They talked to one man and said he was our chief. He was not our chief! They saw our meeting hut and thought it was empty. It was not! They thought it was for them." His voice raised a notch. "It was not! They told our men to put their heavy American things in it, and they moved in. We closed our hearts and did not say anything. We let them do as they wished. As we *ribereños* always do."

There were nods around the group. I glanced sideways at Rubino. He met my eyes, looking worried, and put the palm of his hand up, a *wait* sign.

"They were a couple. But they were not married. They lived in sin!"

A gasp went around the audience. Americans! Living in sin! How awful!

"The woman, she said to teach our women how to birth babies. Are we so stupid we do not know how to do this? Our people have birthed babies forever!" The man was gearing up; he was enjoying this as much as I was suffering it. "And the man… he thought we should poison the water to drink it! He thought we should stop burning our garden patches! But what did he know? The burning controls the biting insects; it enriches the soil! Our people have burned our gardens forever!"

Noble intentions, I thought, *what about their noble intentions? They wanted to help!*

"They took food. They took wood. They took canoes. They smiled and said Friendship Corps and took whatever they wanted. They took our children to talk to them each morning about their American ways." He paused. "What did they give? I ask you: What did they *give*?"

My eyes were wet. I swiped across them with my arm. These were my parents! My dead parents who were not here to defend themselves—who would probably be misunderstood if they tried to defend themselves. There was only me to defend them, and what good was I? A girl with a joke of a name who sat smack in the middle of skin-burrowing bugs even though she'd been warned not to? Rubino reached across the back of the man and squeezed my arm. I was so grateful for his small kindness that my tears began to fall in earnest.

The man was still in his element. "They stayed and they stayed. Peace Corps volunteers stay only two years; we knew this from experience—but these two of the Friendship Corps, they didn't leave. Harvests came and went, and still they stayed. Our people met in the field for our celebrations instead of the ceremonial hut, and still they stayed." He paused for effect, then went on: "And then the woman, she was pregnant."

Gasps. Again. What was so wrong with having a baby?

"Surely the Americans would leave! Never had Americans had a baby here. But still they stayed. And when the day came, the woman did not go to our women for help. Her man attended the birth!"

More gasps.

"A man! Where a man should never be!"

Mothers clutched their young children. The teenage boys snickered. I felt my chiggers come back to life.

"But listen! Listen!" The man waited for the audience to calm. "The baby, she was a sweet thing. She was pure. She was a gift from God, beautiful in spirit. I saw this. I saw this because they asked me to come and see her. You see, they thought I was the chief."

The audience chuckled. Many of them glanced at me knowingly.

"They thought I was the chief, and the spiritual guide of our people." He lowered his voice. "In that they were not so very wrong, am I correct?" Nods all around. "So I visited the baby and saw that she was pure. But the man and the woman—it was time for them to leave." More nods. He lowered his voice even more. "So I told them about a curse. On their baby. The Curse of the Jaguar, I called it. I told them their child would die if they did not leave. Oh, I was very persuasive! I sang; I took sips of what I told them was ayahuasca; I scared those Americans so much that they agreed to leave."

A child in the audience cried out, and was hushed by its mother.

"But there was one more thing they must do, I told them.

They must name their child Cuña. Cuña Maria. A strong name." He laughed then, a laugh so loud and harsh that I jumped, that I bit the inside of my cheek, that I almost wet myself. "Those Americans! They did not deserve this child! I told them to name her Cuña, which in our language, as you know, means 'cradle' for a baby, and also is the beautiful cradleflower." He pointed to a clump of the red-flowering plants I'd become so fond of. "Cuña is a lovely name among *ribereños*, as you know. In the old language, Cuña means 'pure of spirit.'" He looked at me, an unfathomable, deep, searching look. "Your parents gave you the wrong name: Uña, which means 'fingernail' or 'toenail.' They never were good with our language; they preferred to speak English. They did a great wrong to you. Do you know this?"

I shook my head, tears dripping from my face. "No," I said, hiccupping. "I loved them."

"You are pure of spirit still. I can feel this." He put a hand on each side of my head, on my forehead and just above my neck, and I let him. "I hereby rename you. You are again and forever Cuña Maria, she who is pure of spirit."

"I am?" I breathed, not knowing whether it was a question or a statement.

He bestowed upon me a gentle smile.

He stood up, twenty, thirty, forty people watching his every move, and wended his way among them, touching this one and that one on the top of the head, and then he was gone into the trees and I could see him no longer.

I sat there on the bench in front of the cooking fire, hunched over, eyes closed, long after everyone else had left. The picture he painted of my parents, it made me shudder. Had they been refused by the Peace Corps—and came anyway? Why had their sojourn in the village been such a failure? There must have been culture clashes between them and the local people, surely? What my parents had done was deceptive and ill-advised, maybe, but they were good people! With the best of intentions! I *knew* them. They gave money for the local children, for God's sake. I concentrated on my breathing. I knew without looking that Rubino was sitting nearby, waiting. He was a good person too.

Pure of spirit? Me?

I didn't feel like it, but...but. The man had such power to him, such weight to his words. A spiritual leader. Maybe he could see such things.

"Rubino," I said finally

"It was your parents," he said softly.

I nodded.

"Your parents who paid for my education."

"I think so. Yes."

We looked at each other then. And everything was all right. My parents had been who they were, I was who I was, and Rubino was who he was. And in very important, beautiful ways, we were all connected and always would be. And I had found the answers to my personal mystery.

"I need to put my education to good use," he said.

"And I need to change the name on my passport."

We grinned at each other, feeling like family lost and then found. After a while, we crawled under our mosquito nets and went to bed.

Passport

By Nancy Bonnington

(Based on the prompt, "Passport.")

I was not in a good mood, my mother having received a black eye from my father that morning before breakfast. I poured my own Trix and got myself off to school, pretending not to notice my mother sobbing in the bathroom. My father went to work as a milkman, back when everybody had theirs delivered. He never hit me, though I knew the day might come. He raised his fist once when I quipped about taking out the garbage, and said, "You should get what's coming!" He didn't wallop my mother in front of me, either. The truth is, he didn't know that I knew, but my mom knew I knew, even though she pretended not to know.

Outside it was gray and sprinkling, and I shivered and zipped my hoodless coat up. I refused to carry an umbrella or wear a dorky rain hat. I had been a wreck for at least six months, since turning eleven, guilt like a skyscraper weighing down on me. My mom had been receiving more bruises on her arms, and one day I walked in on a bloody nose. I was an only child, so it was my job to do something to help her. "Let's move somewhere without Dad," I told her, as she leaned her head back and dabbed her face with a Kleenex.

"Why on earth would we do that?" she said. "He's the breadwinner."

"I can get a job," I said.

❁ ❁ ❁

Mrs. Baldacre grabbed my arm as I strolled past the attendance office. The low buildings of classrooms were laid out in two rows of three, with the office and gymnasium taking up a prominent front position, like guard posts. "Dr. Burton wants to see you, Darcy. Your friend Allison has a very sore mouth and blisters on her lips."

I winced but tried to hide it. "Allison said so?" I asked.

"Nope. Janet Green told us all about it."

"Oh." I would have to have a talk with Janet.

I was in the sixth grade, at the top of the pecking order—finally—at Three Points Elementary School. I'd been going there since kindergarten. I knew everybody. On the one hand that meant school life was a bit predictable, but on the other hand I'd wheedled my way into the in-crowd, a feat that would have been impossible had I changed schools a lot, like Allison Dorcester, whose father was in the military—deployed all over the U.S., then finally sent to Vietnam.

I liked Allison—she was funny and softhearted. But Janet Green was my best friend. I didn't like Janet all that much—she was okay, though she had a big mouth—but we did everything together, largely because we lived next door to each other. Also,

Janet was stunningly beautiful, with powder-blue eyes and silky long hair the color of vanilla pudding. She helped me be popular in that proxy kind of way that a friend of a friend can be accepted. I was certainly not one of the prettier girls, but I was smart and willing to let others cheat off my quizzes—for a price. Given that, along with being Janet's best friend, how could I not have wielded a substantial amount of social power at Three Points?

I sat across from Dr. Burton, who was middle-aged, with a large, muscular frame and a penetrating gaze. He naturally dwarfed any child. I remembered when he arrived at the school three years earlier, when Miss Dick, the librarian, introduced me to him, and I said, "If you're a doctor, what are you doing running a school?"

Dr. Burton had chuckled, then explained to me what a PhD was. He always said hello to me in the hallway, and once, when I was sent to his office for talking in class, he said, "You might be bored, because you're so smart."

I loved him for that, but I was still wary of his power.

That morning in his office I squirmed in my seat across from him, as though the chair were connected to live electricity. Dr. Burton was just finishing up a phone call.

When he hung up, he looked at me over the dark rims of his eyeglasses and said in a deep voice, "I understand you've been selling cinnamon toothpicks on the playground, young lady."

"Um..."

He lifted a finger. "I want the truth. Where did you get them?"

"Um, I made them."

"Where did you get the cinnamon oil?"

"Um, from a store."

"Well, the children are getting blisters from sucking on them," he said. "Plus, it's rather dangerous to run around the playground with a toothpick in your mouth. And some parents are not happy at all. That was Allison Dorcester's mother—"

"I tell the kids not to run," I began, though it was a lie.

"The point is, you can't sell things here at school. In fact, it's *illegal.*" He leaned forward to drive that last word home.

"Oh." I felt myself turn red. "I didn't know."

"So. No more selling items to the other students, okay? And no more toothpicks."

"Okay."

"Understood?"

"Yes."

"You don't want me to have to call your parents, do you?"

"No, *sir,*" I said. My father would no doubt kill me.

"And there's no need for you to be fleecing your friends, is there?"

"What does *fleecing* mean?"

"Hm. Your assignment today is to go look it up. Come back to my office before you go home and tell me what *fleecing* means."

At morning recess, the sun broke through and the playground was ablaze with light and noise. At least five students came to me to refill their cinnamon toothpicks, which they all kept in tin Band-Aid cases. But I dutifully said no; the toothpick business was closed. A year earlier I'd sold cigarettes from the gas station machine. Mac the mechanic never noticed me or didn't care. The year before that I made macramé bracelets for the girls—custom-made to their three-color preferences. Both of those endeavors had fared okay, but the cigarettes went only to boys and the bracelets to girls. The cinnamon toothpicks had bridged the gender gap, and I'd been making gobs of money, compared to my fifty-cent-per-week allowance.

This year I had a very special purpose for the money. The entire sixth-grade class was going to go on an all-day field trip to the Woodland Park Zoo, including a barbecue lunch and a pony ride. But it would cost fifteen dollars per student. That would mean asking my parents for money, which was out of the question. My father controlled every penny, and his wallet was hopelessly clamped shut, like the jaws of an alligator.

"Why did you tell on me?" I cornered Janet by the baseball diamond.

"Because. I couldn't very well lie, since everybody in the world knows you're the one who sells the toothpicks."

"Oh." Her logic seemed solid, so my anger deflated a bit. "Well, don't do it again." I dropped my shoulders and said, "Let's go play tetherball. C'mon."

After the school day ended, and everyone including my teacher had headed home, I decided to look up *fleecing*—partly because I was curious, and partly because I figured I'd better do my assignment. I hoisted open the huge unabridged Merriam Webster's dictionary that sat on a podium in the back of the classroom, for the most part gathering dust. I thumbed through until I found this (after ignoring all references to shearing sheep):

Fleecing. a: to strip of money or property by fraud or extortion; b: to charge excessively for goods or services.

I pulled my eyebrows into a question mark and felt my dander rise. I did not see any way in which my activities could be considered *fleecing*. My buyers were always happy; I did not defraud them but gave them exactly what they paid for, and at a fair price. Surely, it was not immoral to make a profit in America!

I copied the definition onto a piece of paper and reviewed it several times, just to be certain I understood it. Finally I decided to march down to the principal's office with an appropriately righteous attitude, for surely Dr. Burton was a fair man and would see that I was, by definition, not *fleecing* my peers.

It was getting late—the yellow school buses had all left the parking lot—but the attendance-office door was still unlocked. I stepped inside the main foyer and found Dr. Burton's door open, though his office was empty. I strode down the hallway past the nurses' station—the dreaded place where we would line up for immunizations—and toward the faculty lounge. Of course, students were forbidden to go into the lounge, but I would just poke my head inside.

The door was slightly ajar; I could see the ceiling lights within dimly flickering, and a pale light fell across an empty, blond conference table. Then I leaned farther in and peeked around the corner, where I was struck by a warmer temperature and the strong odor of coffee grounds.

Then I saw them—Dr. Burton and Miss Dick. They were wrapped up in a lovers' embrace, lips locked and bodies entwined. I stumbled backward before they could notice me, and leaned against the outer wall. Perhaps it was shock that kept me from running away.

I looked at the piece of paper in my hand with the definition of *fleecing* on it, and I wondered how I would report my findings to Dr. Burton now.

I was just about to sneak away when Miss Dick exited the lounge, nearly tripping over me in the hallway. She was flushed with excitement and laughed when she saw me. Then, in a giddy manner, she held up the back of her hand as if to display a treasure. "Oh, sweetie, you'll be the first one to hear the good news—Roger and I are engaged to be *married*." Only later did I realize she was probably showing off a ring.

She twittered more giddy words as she spun on her heels and out the door.

I didn't wait for Dr. Burton but ran out of the building and all the way home.

When I arrived, my mother reminded me that Janet, Crystal, and Angela were coming over that night for a slumber party. My mother's face was drawn and blank. She shrugged when I asked if she was okay.

"When is Dad getting home?" I asked.

"Six or so," she said. She glanced at me and told me that she had an accident carrying boxes to the garbage today. "Stumbled and fell against the fence."

She had a black-and-blue circle around her left eye, like a colorful doughnut, though she had done a fair job of covering it with makeup.

"Sorry," I said. I ate some peanut butter on soda crackers and sipped a pop.

"I've been so clumsy," she said. "You know me."

"Maybe Dad will meet somebody on his milk route," I said.

My mother pulled her head back in surprise and gasped.

"You know, maybe he'll fall in love and we'll have to move," I continued. I looked down at the counter and swallowed my snack. I was ashamed I had to tiptoe around this topic.

Do something, my mind would always tell me, but my heart would stall. My father's temper was like an unpredictable furnace; it could flare up at any moment, and I knew I could get burned. Of course, I could tell somebody, but nobody would believe me. To all outward appearances he was jovial and well loved. A hard worker. A family man.

"Don't be ridiculous," my mother said. "Your father and I are *married*."

"People get divorced," I said, meeting her eyes. "John Harden's father took off with a woman he met in AA."

"Darcy! You shouldn't be in other's people's business like that."

"Like what? I heard it through the grapevine."

"Well, your grapevine has loose lips."

❁ ❁ ❁

The slumber party started out okay. There were four of us camped out in the rec room downstairs with sleeping bags drawn in a circle like a wagon train. We talked about making costumes for Halloween, a month away. We took turns swatting a Superball against the brick wall over the fireplace. We played Twister. Then I made up a ghost story—it started out with animals disappearing and ended with a bloody vampire attacking children on a playground.

Crystal and Angela were duly impressed, but Janet said, "Let's play something else. Let's tell our deepest, darkest secrets to each other."

"You mean like Truth or Dare?" I said. "I *hate* that game."

"Yeah, but without the dare," Janet continued. Her sly smile won the others over. "It'll be so fun!" she squealed. "And we'll be like a club of the closest friends at school, because nobody else will know our secrets. Swear?"

"I swear!" Angela said.

"Me too," Crystal said.

Then they all looked at me. I felt a small shiver run up my back, but I nodded.

The first two girls whispered, in turn, about their secret crushes, and we all giggled. Then it was Janet's turn. I expected more than we got. She had a big buildup—all about how we were never, ever to tell a soul, cross our hearts or hope to die! Then she told us she was in love with Tommy Bersdale, and she and Tommy had kissed behind the bowling alley. "With tongues," she added.

Then it was my turn.

"Your deepest, *darkest* secret," Janet said, like a warning.

I pictured my mother that morning—though I had not been present this time, I had spied it before. I pictured her begging my father not to punch her, and him shoving her against the refrigerator and insisting she deserved what she got. And then I pictured my father's shotgun, tucked in a corner of the storeroom, and I knew it was loaded. My fantasy of protecting my mother was sometimes as violent during the day as in my dreams. I would walk right up to him with the shotgun and demand he leave the house. And if he didn't? Well, if he didn't…

"I know a lot of secrets," I said. "A dead kid tells them to me!"

"What are you talking about?" Janet asked. She was hoarding the popcorn bowl, and finally stopped dipping her greasy fingers into it.

"There was a kid murdered in this neighborhood a long time ago. And he got stuck in limbo. It's in this place called… Etherland. And he watches everything and knows everything that goes on around here. With the *living.*"

"Really?" Crystal said.

"Oh, sure," Janet said. "A dead kid—"

"He *talks* to me!" I cut Janet off. "But you have to have an open mind to believe in things that you can't see. Unfortunately, some people aren't capable because they don't have an *open mind*."

I shot a look at Janet and she stuck her chin out. "I can believe in things," she said. "My grandmother says she can see angels."

"My brother said he saw a Sasquatch," Angela told us. "He was alone in the woods—"

"It's not like that," I said. "In this world you can only enter through a trance. And you…you have to have a passport to go there."

"Why?" Janet asked.

"It's a mystical place." I took my time to look each of the girls in the eyes and then lowered my voice: "I shouldn't be telling you this; I told our priest about it, Father Kendall, and he said he'd heard of it. He studied with the Jesuits in Romania and said that Etherland was a holy place 'cause people who were wronged get stuck there until…you know, they have to…wait until they can go to heaven."

I nodded until they all followed suit, though I cringed in my gut for lying about our priest, who I had never spoken to in my life.

"The thing is, the dead kid—his name is Kenny—he has to decide if you are trustworthy enough to hear his secrets. And I've been thinking of giving each one of you a passport."

"Yes!" they all screamed.

"Shh! Keep your voices down! You have to swear never to repeat what I tell you. Or your passport will be *revoked*. And there's no getting it back ever."

"We won't tell!" they agreed.

"Okay then." I reached for a handful of popcorn and nodded.

"Well?" Janet said. "Where's the passport?"

"I'll give it to you at school tomorrow. It only costs…twenty-five cents."

"Okay," Janet agreed. "But you gotta give us proof first."

The other girls, who were starting to pull their sleeping bags tight up around their necks, agreed.

"I'll give you one secret for free," I said. "If it's okay with Kenny. What time is it?"

Janet glanced at her watch. "It's almost midnight."

"Where'd you get that?" I asked.

"My daddy gave it to me," Janet said. "It's a Barbie watch with a sparkling bracelet."

I glanced at my own empty wrist and felt a surge of shameful hatred for Janet. "Well, you're lucky, because it's easiest to talk to Kenny at midnight. That's the exact hour when he died."

"How did he die?" Crystal asked quietly.

"He was murdered in his sleep. During a sleepover," I added. "His best friend stabbed him in the back. The police found him still trying to pull out the blade, but it was exactly in the middle of his back, where he couldn't reach it. Then he died."

I let that hang in the air for a while; then I crept out of my sleeping bag and plodded over to the light switch. "I'm going to contact Kenny, but it's easier when it's dark. And you guys have to be absolutely quiet. And concentrate."

When I snapped off the light, the room was lit through the curtains by a single porch light so that everything glowed an eerie yellow. Aside from the smell of popcorn, there was a distinct edge to the night, for the sliding window was cracked enough to let in the crisp air, and the occasional whir of crickets rose and fell.

"Okay," I whispered. "Close your eyes." I sat down on the floor and crossed my legs. "Just think of Kenny's name over and over. Concentrate. You might start feeling funny, because you'll cross over from this world into Etherland. But try not to get scared."

For a full minute I breathed in and out slowly, counting each breath silently to myself—*one Mississippi, two Mississippi*—until I reached sixty Mississippis. By then I almost believed in Kenny myself.

I cleared my throat.

"Well? Did he talk to you?" Janet asked.

I nodded.

"You have to tell us, because we all told secrets," Janet said. "And if you don't, we won't buy a passport."

"I don't know; my mom says, 'Loose lips sink ships.'" I said. "And I'm not so sure you can keep quiet."

"Hey, you guys, maybe we shouldn't do this," Crystal said. "Does anybody else think it's suddenly cold in here?"

"No, no, it's okay," I said quickly.

"Well, what is it?" Janet nearly shouted. "What did Kenny say?"

For a moment the silence was accompanied only by a dripping water tap in the downstairs bathroom—*plop, plop, plop*. Then we could hear the Thompsons' dog baying down the street, not unlike a wolf.

Crystal reached out and grabbed Angela's hand. "I don't think this is a good idea."

"You know Dr. Burton?" I began.

"Yeah…?" Janet sat up straight and leaned toward me.

"You know Miss Dick, the librarian?"

"Yeah, we all know Dr. Burton and Miss Dick—what about them?"

I felt Janet about to explode, so I blurted out the only secret I thought I could prove: "They're lovers and they're going to get married!"

"No way!" Janet said.

"I'm just telling you what the dead kid told me," I said.

"Oh, yeah?" Janet asked. "You mean like in a million years when we'll all be dust and you can't prove it right or wrong?"

"No," I said. I lowered my voice: "Soon. You'll see. Very soon."

"I don't believe it. Miss Dick is old and ugly." Janet flung her head so that her beautiful blond hair would lie perfectly over her left shoulder.

"Okay," I said. "You don't have to believe, Janet. If you don't have an *open mind* to mystical things, you can just wait and see if it's true. And if you don't want a passport, that's okay with me too."

I dropped back into my sleeping bag and fell silent, and soon enough the nighttime wrapped us all in slumber.

❁ ❁ ❁

By the following Monday the news was out—Dr. Burton and Miss Dick had announced their engagement and it was in the local newspaper. All three sleepover friends gave me a quarter and in turn I handed them a homemade passport, each affixed with a golden seal that I had purchased from the Hallmark store.

After that, I set up business in stall five of the girls' bathroom next to the gymnasium. It was the handicapped stall in the far back, so there was plenty of room for me and one client during afternoon recess. They stood in line outside stall five, the three girls who had slept over, and I traveled with them to Etherland—warning them to wear their warm jackets because the spirit world is chilly—then gave them each a gossipy secret, largely invented.

Soon other students heard about Etherland—I made sure of it—and about the dead boy and the way I mysteriously knew things. They wanted passports too. And I obliged.

At lunchtime, the girls' bathroom no longer belonged to the girls. Both boys and girls lined up against the wall across from the sinks to take their turn in stall five, where they would close their eyes with me and travel to the other world. Upon return they were rewarded with a secret.

For the first few days the coins poured in, largely because my secrets were about the students at Three Points Elementary School, and the things I invented did not disappoint. Also, I made it very clear that if anyone was caught repeating a secret, their passport would be revoked.

The ideas began simply enough, and I decided not to name names, because I had the foresight to know I could get caught in a lie:

There's a kid here who has two penises, believe it or not.

A girl, whose name starts with a J, stole a diamond necklace from Bellevue Square.

One of the mothers in the PTA practices witchcraft, but I can't say who.

One of the boys, who has curly hair—that's all I'm going to say—roasted his dog and ate it. For real.

There's this girl who has a steel plate in her skull from when she got hit by a hockey puck, and if you tap her head it'll hurt your knuckles.

One of the popular kids—you all know him—his older brother got a high school teacher pregnant. And the teacher had to get an abortion!

This was brilliant, in my opinion. But too soon the money and interest dwindled. My passport buyers wanted names to go along with the secrets. And to make it worse, the teacher announced that we would be collecting the money for the Woodland Park field trip the very next day.

I ran home and counted my coins—though they filled half a jelly jar, I was seven dollars short.

I agonized over my next business step. It would be one thing to get caught making up harmless tales, but to attach a student's name…what if Dr. Burton found out? What would he do to me? What if my parents found out?

That evening I asked if I could have Janet over to play. My mother agreed because it was all part of the we-have-a-normal-family facade. Janet arrived at four p.m., her homework supposedly done, and ate dinner with us. My father carved a roast and whistled the *Andy Griffith* tune. The kitchen smelled like a pleasant household. My mother made gravy from scratch, and I smiled and thanked both my parents for such a nice meal.

Then Janet and I went back to my bedroom to play Time Bomb. I wound up the black orb and tossed it to her. It ticked loudly as she tossed it back to me. Hardly fun to play with only two people, but I had other things on my mind.

"Business is slowing down," I told Janet.

"People are getting tired of you," Janet said as she caught the bomb again. She quickly threw it back to me, hard enough that it slapped my palms with a sting. "Why don't you just quit?"

"What do you mean, they're getting tired of me?"

"You know, they don't want to pay if you're not going to tell real secrets…about *real* people." She tossed the bomb.

"Maybe I should," I said. "Name names."

"Darcy, that would be horrible!"

I shrugged. "I need the money."

"Why?"

"For the field trip, you idiot." I threw the hard plastic bomb back at her.

I had been to Janet's house. Her parents always greeted me with a hug, and they showered each other and all their children with affection. I had fantasized that one day Janet's parents would adopt me.

"Why don't you just ask your parents for it?" she said.

"I can't."

"Why not? Why are you always trying to make money? Your family's not *poor.*" She spit out the last word with some distaste, and I couldn't help but blush a little.

This time when I caught the time bomb it went off with a loud metallic *clack* that startled me.

"You lose," Janet said. "And anyway, they said there's a fund to help if you don't have the money. So just go ask the teacher for the money if your parents won't give it to you."

"You don't understand anything," I told her. "And I never said we're poor."

While I began to wind up the time bomb again, my parents' voices rose in the kitchen—audible but unintelligible, like a couple of angry geese.

"Are they fighting?" Janet asked, as though she'd never been exposed to such a thing. She turned her head, like a cat might tune its ears in the right direction.

"No," I said, cringing. "Just ignore it."

The unmistakable crash of china smashing into shards made me out to be a liar.

My mother screamed, "Don't, don't!" Which was followed by loud banging noises, as though pieces of furniture were flying into the walls.

"Oh, my god," Janet said. She raced out of my bedroom and down the hallway.

"No, Janet!" I cried. I had no choice but to run after her.

In the doorway of the kitchen, Janet stood gaping at my parents. My father had my mother in a clutch-hold around her neck and was swinging an open hand at her face. Each slap was followed by a gasp from Janet.

My father looked up and saw my friend. "Get the *hell* out of here!" he yelled, his voice laced with uncontrollable fury. But he dropped his hands and my mother slumped to the floor.

Janet stammered, "Sorry, sorry," and I saw tears escape her wide eyes as she turned and dashed for the front door. I grabbed her shoulder but she pulled free.

"I hate you!" I screamed at my father.

I sped downstairs and paced the rec room, crying. I knew my mother would just endure it forever if I didn't help soon. And I wondered if Janet would tell everyone at school. Would she—or any of my friends—ever play with me again?

I unleashed so many tears, my vision was all blurry. I yanked open a cupboard door. My father's shotgun leaned against the back of the cabinet. From upstairs I heard nothing but the occasional footfall and low murmurs. But if my father was going to come after me, I'd be prepared.

I had never touched a firearm of any sort; my hands shook with fright just as fast as my lips quivered with rage.

I hefted the gun gingerly, alarmed by how heavy it was. The smooth wooden stock rested along my right arm as my hand felt the cold metal of the trigger area. I had no idea how to shoot it. Did I pump it, cock it, or just pull the trigger?

It was as though my bad dreams were turning real. The trick would be not to get too close to him, because he could snatch the gun away. And I'd have to aim carefully.

I closed my eyes and choked on my own sobs for a while, as the weight of the gun bore down on my arms. Then I heard footsteps coming down the stairs. My head jerked back and my eyes flew open.

I took a deep breath and held it. Then I lifted the shotgun and with great effort aimed at the door to the hallway.

Just pull the trigger, I told myself. *And if that doesn't work, crack the gun over his head.*

* * *

I was shaky, with snot running down my face, the gun barrel swaying a bit back and forth, when someone appeared.

I squeezed the trigger as hard as I could and screamed, "No!"

Nothing happened.

It was my mother who had turned the corner, and I nearly vomited with fright. I dropped the shotgun with a dull thud on the shag carpet and collapsed beside the weapon, sobbing through the last ounce of my energy.

"Darcy." My mother looked from me to the gun and threw her hands to her head. "Oh my God, what are you doing? No! No! You can't ever touch this thing again! Do you hear me?"

"Mom," I began.

"This is not a toy!" Her voice climbed to a high pitch as

she apparently grasped the full picture. Then her whole body seemed to shiver.

"No *shit*!" I yelled. "But why do you let him…?" I cried. "Why?"

She picked up the shotgun carefully and shook her head at me, and I could see that she had the muscles to wield the deadly weapon. But then she put it back in the storage cupboard and squatted beside me.

"Don't ever, ever touch this gun again," she said. "Ever. Ever. Promise me."

"I promise!"

"And anyway, I'm going to make sure your father locks it up."

I tried to apologize, but mostly what came out was foamy spit between my sobs.

"We've had a talk, honey. Your father's very sorry. And I'm so sorry you had to see what you saw. He's going to get help now. We've agreed. We all are. As a family. Wouldn't you like that?"

I wiped my eyes, though the tears kept coming.

"Really?" I whimpered.

"Really. It all stops now." She kissed me on the head and said, "I promise. It's going to be okay. No more of this."

She gave me a look that made me half believe her, and I let out a sigh.

❋ ❋ ❋

Back in bed I breathed lighter, as though the air were laced with helium—or a bit of hope. I was stunned that I'd nearly killed my mother, but perhaps my dangerous tantrum had at least opened a conversation with her.

But something had changed within me too. I felt older and I didn't like it. I realized I had just grown up a notch—as though the whole process of aging is not a smooth transition but one of suddenly being yanked up a whole step on the ladder of life, like it or not.

Well past midnight, my body finally relaxed into the mattress and I fell asleep.

❁ ❁ ❁

The following day the girls' bathroom smelled of ammonia. I stood in stall five and told Tommy Parker, "If you climb to the top of the water tower during a lightning storm and put your ear against the metal, you can hear God's voice. But only if you're not a sinner."

I sighed when he squinted at me. If Tommy didn't hear God's voice, it wasn't my fault.

As he was leaving the stall, I heard him say, "That's stupid." Then I looked beyond the stall door to see Janet collecting money from the lineup. There were at least a half dozen students from grades three through six handing quarters to her.

"What are you doing?" I yelled.

"I'm going to tell secrets too," Janet said.

"You can't," I said. "You don't hear Kenny's voice—"

"Yes, I do!" She shot me a look like a red-hot poker.

The kids shuffled their feet and watched us. I grew nearly mute with anger.

Janet paced up and down the line, paying particular attention to the third and fourth graders. "The dead boy talks to me too," she said. "And he tells me *everything*!"

The kids held out their coins, and I looked at Janet in disbelief.

"You can't prove it," I exploded. But my voice was shaky and I felt my heart flutter.

Janet spun around and grabbed my arm, while a growing audience waited for stall five to get back to business. She tugged on my blouse collar so that she could whisper into my ear; I could feel her hot breath and I couldn't escape it.

"I'm going to double your money," she whispered, low and airy, "and you're going on the field trip!"

She let go of my collar, then swung her head around to show a big smile to the crowd.

"Janet." I pulled her aside. "You know...this is *illegal*!" I whispered. "You can't—you could get in big trouble."

She shrugged and said, "No biggie."

For the remainder of recess, stall four was in business right next to stall five, and from what I could tell, Janet knew how to make up real whoppers, for her clients came out looking both stunned and satisfied.

When recess ended, Janet poured two whole handfuls of coins into my pocket.

"I hope it's enough," she said.

I nodded and thanked her and felt my eyes water. I didn't even try to speak.

"It's okay," Janet said. "And I'm really sorry about…you know…your parents."

"Yeah, I know." I gulped.

❋ ❋ ❋

The following morning my mother made me pancakes. I ate

them, sopping up the last bit of syrup, and told my mom that I was best friends with Janet, for real.

"I know you are." My mother gave me an odd look.

I flew off the counter stool before she could question me. I wasn't prepared to talk about the dead boy or the secrets or the money. Or how my heart had just flown open because of Janet.

My father was putting empty cartons in the back of his delivery truck, whistling, and he threw me a quick wave as I headed down the driveway. I hesitated, then waved back.

I kicked a plum-size rock all the way to school, then tucked it in the weeds beside the bus turnaround, where I knew I could find it again to kick it all the way home. It was almost like having a pet.

At morning recess I couldn't find Janet anywhere. I looked up and down the playground and decided she was probably in the bathroom telling lies, so I played tetherball with Christy Jackson, who basically did nothing else with her life, and so she creamed me.

That afternoon at recess, it was cold and wet and I huddled with Janet, who I found under the basketball shed playing jacks, until Mrs. Baldacre flagged us down. Dr. Burton wanted to see Janet.

Janet shot me a strange look then dropped her head. I was confused for only a second until I realized Dr. Burton must have caught wind of all our nasty lies.

I turned red. I didn't say a word as Janet, her whole body bowed like a weeping willow branch, followed Mrs. Baldacre off the playground.

After a few guilty minutes, I knew I couldn't let Janet suffer alone. I left the jacks scattered on the paved ground, like toys suddenly too young for me.

I took my time walking down the long, covered corridor through the row of low-lying buildings. A side breeze blew a light mist across my face, and I thought about how I would tell Dr. Burton we were not fleecing the students, and especially I would drive home that we were not naming names. Still, my stomach felt sour, for I didn't want him to call my parents.

A policeman stood in the office beside Dr. Burton's desk. He wore a stark blue uniform—his badge neatly on display—and my knees nearly buckled when I saw him. Behind him on a classroom seat, her feet twisted around the low metal support rods, Janet slumped and stared at the tips of her sneakers.

"Darcy." Dr. Burton looked at me, surprised. "I was just going to call for you."

I brushed the dampness from my cheeks. Fear crept all the way down each of my arms. I knew my face must have been emblazoned with scarlet splotches. I wasn't certain what was happening, but I plopped down into the 'electric' chair and slid one of my homemade passports across to Dr. Burton. "It's not Janet's fault!" I declared. "This can't be *illegal*! It can't be *illegal* to make a profit in America. This is *America*.... "

"Darcy," Dr. Burton interrupted; he picked up the passport but didn't look at it.

"I'm not *fleecing* them!"

"Sweetie..." He shook his head slowly, then drew his lips into a deep frown. "You're not in trouble. Neither is Janet. Your father's been arrested."

My mother came through the doorway on my left, limping. Her right cheek was stained crimson, her upper lip swollen, and her wispy hair all askew—as though she'd just blown in from a windstorm.

A female cop guided her by the elbow, then nodded at the male cop. "She's okay. And we got her statement."

"Darcy—" My mother's voice caught in her throat. Then she said, "It's all right, sweetheart."

I got up and threw myself into her arms and held her tight.

"I'm sorry," she whispered, rubbing my back. "I'm so sorry, honey. But it's okay now."

"Are you sure you feel well enough to go home with your daughter?" Dr. Burton asked my mother gently.

"Yes." She took a deep breath and raised my chin up to capture all of me in her beautiful eyes. "Listen, Darcy, your father…went too far this morning."

"Are you okay, Mom?"

"Yes." She let me go and nodded at Janet. "And don't be mad at her. You have a better friend there than you'll ever know."

I watched my friend bite her lip, then glance over at Dr. Burton, who nodded and said, "You did the right thing reporting this, Janet. It took a lot of courage to speak up. I wanted to tell you that in person. But you should go back to class now."

Dazed, I watched Janet get up, avoid my eyes, and wander out the door.

Shortly after, I found myself in the back of a patrol car. The police officers took us home to where my mother and I would begin our new lives together without a man in the house. It was sad and scary at the same time, and startling how quiet the place was. My mother and I avoided any heavy-duty conversation, mostly shooting worried glances at each other and bringing up dumb topics like the weather. Though once in a while my mother would suddenly cradle me in her arms and muss with my hair. Then brush it back in place and kiss my cheeks.

My father's seat at the head of the table was empty. I felt

that I might explode, but I figured things were as they had to be and that time would heal us. I waited for a fresh signal--like my mother buying a new dress, baking something special for desert, or folding my socks into a neat row in the top drawer. The time would come, I hoped, when the delicate ice would break and we would meld somehow, just the two of us, into a small but complete family.

It would be a week before I would talk to my best friend again or know what to say, the peculiar mixture of gratitude and shame rendering me mostly mute all the way up to the field trip.

Near the elephant enclosure, the walkway was sticky with spilled soda and scattered with peanut shells.

I broke my silence. "Thanks," I told Janet. "I guess I was too scared…but…I should have had the guts…you know...I should have helped my mom."

"Phew, I thought you were mad at me." She grabbed my hand at the same time I reached for hers and I felt a comforting squeeze. "You couldn't, it's that simple"

Then we both watched a baby elephant trot across the paddock and sidle up to its mother's belly. "Anyhow," she said, "you would've done the same for me." She glanced at me sideways and added, "I couldn't stand it if you blamed me."

I shook my head.

As the rest of the class started moving on, Janet tugged at my arm to hold me still. Her head was cocked and serious, her eyes a bit watery, when she finally burst out, "Oh Darcy, I'm so sorry. Do you miss him? This must be *really* hard on you."

I struggled to speak, a lump in my throat catching all my words. Then the air was too thin to breathe. If I were able to, I would have told her I missed the *idea* of a father. And then

Janet, who seemed a natural at this, was hugging me--my body shaking in silence like a dumb rag doll--until all the other students were long out of sight.

It felt right, and it was the closest I had ever come to having a sister.

Under the Passport Theater

By Susan Whiting Kemp

Rumor had it that a man lived amid the Passport Theater's underground machinery, but I never saw the Mechaniker. He supposedly spent his days oiling and polishing the gears that raised, lowered, and turned the stage. As I grew, the rumor grew, so that when I was seven it was said that the machinery stretched across the United States, and the Mechaniker rode conveyor belts from coast to coast. Being just a young boy, I believed it, but thought it to be an exaggeration. Surely the machine-works and its excavation could reach only so far before bumping up against the Columbia River, the gold mines, or roots of the Cascade Mountains.

I thought the extent of the machinery might be why certain parts of backstage were forbidden to me. I was bad with directions and would get lost, as I did in the town of Yakima whenever I was sent on an errand. I told myself that someday, when I was much older than seven, I would be just like Bold Boulder the Strongman, who could lift me while I stood on one of his hands (which I did to great applause). I vowed that someday I too would be a strongman; my sweating skin would reflect the footlights like a foundry worker's, and my shoes would have soles thick as bricks. With my strength I would break into the underground and see the Mechaniker for myself.

Or perhaps I would manage to sneak down there. My parents advertised our theater as having "First-class variety performances suitable for men, women, and children." The vaudeville acts that passed through the Northwest on their way to more lucrative venues often had need of the area below the stage. My parents' reputation for stinginess caused entertainers to be leery of our theater, but we were the only one for miles around, and the long distances required performers to play here on their way to other venues in order to make money to continue on. They complained about the stink, and the rafter sparrows that shit on their heads. But still they came.

And so I tried to slip through the below-stage door several times, when performers were storing their props there, but all my attempts were thwarted by Jem Sprightly, the stage manager.

Curiosity grew in me day by day until I thought I would burst. I had to meet the Mechaniker myself. But when I asked to go there, instead of answering, my parents said, "Zachariah, mend those wigs," or "Zachariah, sew those chemises," or "Zachariah, take care of Lavender Dashable's singing armadillo," which wasn't an armadillo and didn't sing. It was a short-legged mutt with a chain-metal costume, and it whined because it hated the costume, and rolled head over heels trying to gnaw at its straps, which convinced the audience that was how an armadillo traveled. It also soiled its cage, but couldn't be taken outside to do its business lest the audience see they'd been had.

My parents so far were quite disappointed in me. I had no

natural talent, but they hoped I would develop a viable skill: juggling, tumbling, yodeling, plate spinning, or oratory—or even better, some niche skill that could draw the crowds and make my parents rich. Shooting a bow and arrow with my toes, perhaps. But I was clumsy, lost all senses when upside down, and couldn't remember lyrics or lines.

I feared I would never acquire a talent, and that my lack of ability might ultimately mean banishment from the magic world of the stage to the mundane world outside, which to me was dull and repugnant. The people out there seemed bored, with faces straight as planks. They brightened once they arrived at the theater, as though a glass bell had been lowered over them and the atmosphere inside sparkled.

Or rather than banish me, my parents might lock me in the Passport Theater's underbelly for good. For they threatened it sometimes if I didn't apply myself to the learning of pratfalls or the playing of washboards. I wondered whether the Mechaniker was an older brother I'd never met whom they'd given up on. Though the mere thought of visiting the underbelly terrified me, I became sure that my fate depended on learning the truth.

One day I told Jem Sprightly, the stage manager, that I needed to get something from the underbelly. He didn't bother to take the cigar from his mouth. "Where's your passport, Zachariah?" he drawled. In spite of the theater's name, I didn't know what a passport was. I imagined it was a key, heavy and made of iron, perhaps as long as my forearm. But then Emma the Bearded Lady, one of the many acts that my parents booked for a week or a month, told me passports were made of parchment, stamped with a seal. You used them to go from country to country in times of war. So was the underbelly another country? I was even more intrigued.

Sometimes a traveling troupe folded during a run. The troupe would run out of money, or its performers would have too many differences among themselves, or a primary actor or actress would elope, melting away into everyday life. My parents would sell any abandoned props, but sometimes I squirreled away a treasure or two before that happened. A toupee here, a basket there. And so I had a parchment from a comedic play. During the play, a town crier unrolled the parchment, saying, "Hear ye, hear ye," and then turned it upside down to read "ye hear, ye hear."

Now I retrieved the parchment. Jem untied the ribbon, unrolled the paper, and squinted at it, taking much time examining it from top to bottom. Finally he said, "Such an elaborate seal could not be fakery. This script that leans like trees in a strong wind, and this signature—the loops above, the loops below, the flourishes—such veracity. There's no doubt as to this passport's authenticity, my young Zachariah."

Everybody who worked at the theater was at one time or another given to ornate monologues, even me. And Jem Sprightly was not immune. But in the end he let me through the thick wooden door, and that was what mattered.

I slowly descended the uneven pine stairs into the underbelly of the theater. Even with Jem right behind, my heart beat like a military drum. It was indeed a very large place. So large I could imagine that it extended at least to California after all, if not China.

At first I could do nothing but gawk at the machinery. The cranks that drove wheels that powered belts that pulled chains that lifted walls. The bars that tugged ropes that squeezed bellows that made sparks fly.

Not real sparks. Not in a theater made of wood, full of

fabrics, stuffed with tissues. No, the "sparks" were pieces of metal foil tacked to the ends of ribbons that fluttered upward through a trapdoor in the stage floor when the bellows wind blew. An imitation of fire that was more beautiful than real life, like everything onstage.

I often worried about fire. I knew that fire had burned London, Rome, and many a fair town, and if flames could lay a great city low, it could level our theater and burn me in my backstage bed. Father always said there was nothing to fear, that the narrow aisles kept the people from going out to piss, so they soaked the floorboards where they stood, and that while other theaters might go up in flames, ours would stand till the end of days, or until people no longer wanted entertainment, whichever came last.

Father's words calmed me, but only a bit. The Passport Theater did smell of piss, it was true, so perhaps the moisture would protect it. It also smelled of damp mold, which I decided might also guard against flames. These were comforting smells to me. I had grown up with them. But I couldn't be sure of their protection in a blaze.

I gathered my courage to move further into the underbelly, and was startled by a giant mechanical octopus. This week and the previous, every evening with three matinees and four midnight showings, the octopus had emerged, roaring, during the *Mutiny on the High Seas* show to devour a sailing ship, leaving only half a mast—and an ingenue and a gentleman to ride the mast away.

Though the octopus lay quiet now, its tentacles still, it seemed as if any moment it could awaken and pounce on me. Nearby were tubs of water in which mermaids would splash;

later tonight these would be cranked upward onto the stage through various trapdoors.

Above me was one of the trapdoors through which, in previous weeks, Lucky Lucifer rose up from Hades, wearing red long underwear, red face paint, and curving horns that he let intentionally slip from side to side for hilarity, while he spouted tried-and-true witticisms about life, love, and the pursuit of "sappiness." The trapdoor also allowed Baby Lucinda in her daisy costume to "grow" from the ground, singing the much beloved "Springtime in Sprig City."

Whenever I looked closely at Baby Lucinda, I could see the chin stubble of a forty-seven-year-old man named Richard. He'd played Baby Lucinda since the age of three. Most child performers lose their cuteness as they grow, and his act eventually metamorphosed into a profitable comedy. So audiences never allowed him to pursue another act, which made him mean as the dickens.

"Baby Lucinda, Baby Lucinda. That's all people want," snarled Richard.

"So do something else," I said. "Shakespeare goes over well."

"Spiteful child." Richard raised a hand to hit me, but I dodged it.

I was surprised that evening when, instead of a watering can, Richard carried a scepter and spouted King Lear, bellowing, "Blow, winds, and crack your cheeks! rage! blow!" We could all see that he was much better suited to be a tragic king than a silly baby. But my parents forced him to play out the month as Baby Lucinda, because that's what they were paying him for, and so that's what he would be.

And so they made an enemy. One of many, along the way.

Jem shooed me back upstairs before long. It was time to

assist Nimwit the Clown; his wife was busy preparing for her own performance, which involved hanging from her teeth. Nimwit required help to apply his makeup; of course the duty fell to me. I wiped the sleep from the corners of his eyes, taped back his sagging skin, smeared whiteface on the mounds and creases, drew quizzical, uneven eyebrows, and blended in rouge. Later my parents would charge Nimwit for my assistance. And he would not take it well. So he became another enemy.

Nimwit began his performance with a seditious smile so big it could be seen in the very back of the balcony. Such a cloying smile. Then he lifted his violin. When he played the footlights seemed to brighten on their own, highlighting the folds of his baggy sweater and the bottom of his round chin. The sound was so sweet and penetrating, I could have sworn I smelled cloves instead of piss.

I hadn't heard him rehearse. Other musicians warmed up before a show, but not Nimwit. So I was shocked that such a bumbling, sloppy man could coax such satisfying sounds from a violin. It boggled even my large imagination.

I truly believed our stage was magical, because on it Nimwit the Clown transformed everyday objects. The things he could do with a stool, for instance—balance it, climb it, twirl it, toss it. He could breathe life into anything he touched. That frightened me. I worried that if he could animate a thing, it could work in reverse. I did not want him to turn me into a chair.

Mischievous, they called him. But his wife had another word: *philanderer*. I had no idea what she meant, though it reminded me of the word *philodendron*, which I knew was a plant. Many words flew over my head like the sparrows in our rafters, especially during the burlesques. I always asked questions, and some performers found it entertaining to explain things a child shouldn't know. In this way, I came to understand the meaning of words such as *fellatio* and *arson*. Thus I feared that someday my Falstaff might be bitten off, or the theater burned to the ground to spite my parents.

After Nimwit's performance came the Great Pickerpath. He gave readings from the superior plays of great antiquity, plays that were only recently discovered stashed in vessels in hillside caves. These works were translated by a triple PhD linguist, copied onto sheepskin, loaded into a trunk, carried across stormy seas, and delivered to a dying duke, who bequeathed them to the Great Pickerpath, so that their words, after lying dormant after some thousand or two years, might live once more.

When the Great Pickerpath spoke the words from the superior plays of great antiquity, he stretched many of them longer than the Good Lord intended, as he admitted himself, so that they might cover more territory than any set of words before, and have a greater impact on the ears of the audience. I listened with astonishment as he emphasized one clump of words or the other, in order to leave the audience gasping and swooning.

At a certain time during the performance, Jem Sprightly hissed at me—for I could not remember the timing myself. I wiggled the great iron sheet that made such thunderous noise that I would frighten my own self each time, and then I turned the crank on the lightning machine to spew out great electric bolts that danced between two poles on the stage. But I did these things in the wrong order—thunder before lightning. No matter how many times Jem berated me for doing so, and no matter how often I resolved to get it right, I failed. I glanced at Jem, who scowled.

Earlier that day, the Great Pickerpath had whispered to me that he could stop time with a flick of his finger. I assured him that I was a worldly child and not as impressionable as he thought. He shrugged and left. And I began to fret. I knew he was not so capable on his own, but our stage was magical. Perhaps tonight he would do the impossible.

Clementine now stepped into the spotlight. Clementine was a male impersonator, or a female impersonator, whichever was required. I never saw a person with such a talent for transformation. When Clementine dressed as a woman, you were sure she was a man, and vice versa. Even among the backstage folks, nobody was really sure, so we called Clementine *he* or *she* interchangeably, and it seemed to make no difference to him. Or to her.

Clementine's voice was as high as the clouds—too short a range for opera and not nimble enough for comedy, so Clementine stuck to ballads and slow Irish folk songs. There was rarely a dry eye when she finished singing "The Bold Fenian Men."

Clementine filled the room. Not her size, but her presence. I imagined in the largest hall in all the world, you'd still feel jammed into a corner by her very being. When she sang, her voice stole your breath, as if she needed it herself to sing. And your emotions—those she didn't steal from you; she filled you so full of them you would drown in them. I could listen to her singing for the rest of my days.

As if to answer my wish, now on the stage one of Clementine's notes went on and on, as if floating on an endless River Shannon. The audience did not move. Not a turn of the head, not a motion of the arm, not a clearing of the throat.

Was it true then? Had the Great Pickerpath stopped time? Was Clementine caught up in his magic? Were we all?

I saw the Great Pickerpath watching me furtively and I grew deeply suspicious. I found it hard to move, as if my feet were glued to the backstage floorboards. So I knew he had stopped time. If I didn't act, we would all be frozen forever.

I fought through Pickerpath's spell and burst onto the stage while Clementine's note still hung in the air, crying to the crowded theater, "Time is askew and must be repaired!"

Later, though the audience had been entertained by my outburst, my parents docked the Great Pickerpath his pay for lying to me and causing me to interrupt the show.

And so they made yet another enemy.

Sometimes people would tell me that my parents were not nice people (which I already knew). My parents would charge a performer a fee for laying a mat in the hall to sleep, or for a broken pail that had already been cracked, or for my help with costume changes. Perhaps these victims thought I could influence my parents, but I knew better. I worried that someday one of them would exact revenge on my parents. And I still worried about fire.

I explored the underbelly a few more times. In several instances I thought I saw the Mechaniker, but I was never sure of it. One time I came to retrieve the four axes for the *Lumberjack Soup* show, and I thought I saw eyes—dimly lit but following me—though it could have been the glint from the mechanical octopus. Later I decided I had seen oil lamps set in places where they wouldn't ordinarily be, but who knows?

One evening I was serving as set dressing for *Mutiny on the High Seas* by wearing a starfish costume and sitting very still beside a pile of large seashells. My parents were offstage, perhaps ten paces away, watching me to make sure I did my starfish cartwheel at the right moment, this time without slipping on the shells.

I smelled something burning, then saw a tendril of smoke rising up from the floorboards.

Somebody yelled, "Fire!"

The theater erupted in chaos, but I could not move, except to look to my parents for help. They looked from me to the smoke. For a moment it seemed they were going to say something. Then they turned around. I saw them slipping into the narrow hallway toward the exit. My stomach felt suddenly empty as I watched the back of their heads retreat; it was like some small part of me had died.

I jumped through the opening in the stage beside me, down into the underbelly, to warn the Mechaniker. Whether or not he was my brother, I did not want him to perish.

Bold Boulder the Strongman followed me, calling to me to come back. I discovered a set of chairs burning intensely. Bold Boulder lifted a tub of mermaid water and doused them, but there were other fires—one spouting from a chest of costumes, another lapping at a scrim painted with Mount Fuji, and yet another engulfing the octopus, whose tentacles began curling and uncurling, flailing dangerously, nearly skewering us. The fires raged so fiercely we could not extinguish them.

Bold Boulder lifted me like a suitcase by the seat of my pants, hoisting me back up to the stage. There he stood indecisive. The crowd was crushed into a mass at the narrow hallway my parents had escaped through, and nobody seemed to be getting out. Five hundred people trapped in a room that was now rapidly filling with smoke. I could hear the audience members shouting for help, and youngsters crying, and performers shouting that the stage door was locked.

The unbearable din and the steam from the burning, piss-soaked wood made me dizzy. But the pounding of the trapped theatergoers on the wall gave me an idea.

"The axes," I shouted. "Over there!"

Bold Boulder, still carrying me like a suitcase, scooped two axes up in his other arm and headed with me for the nearest wall. We both swung with all our might, alternating strokes at the same spot. My arms reverberated with each swipe of the axe, my body nearing exhaustion. Before the smoke could overcome us, we managed to make a hole large enough for escape.

Everybody poured through the hole like cockroaches from a drainpipe—then stood outside in the warm night air and watched the orange flames consume the Passport Theater, along with its piss, mold, and magic.

My parents were nowhere to be seen.

I heard later that everybody survived. But the Mechaniker? The mysterious engineer of the theater bowels, who might even be my brother? I would never know.

I could still see my parents' faces as they judged the distance between themselves and the exit, between my life and theirs. Slowly I drew myself away from the crowd, the burning theater, and the only home I had ever known. My back, which had warmed from the fire's heat, gradually chilled as I walked down the road. And then trotted, and then ran as fast as my feet would carry me.

Made in the USA
Middletown, DE
05 June 2019